Silent as
the Grave

Silent as the Grave

Rhys Bowen
&
Clare Broyles

MINOTAUR BOOKS
NEW YORK

First published in the United States by Minotaur Books, an imprint of St. Martin's Publishing Group

www.minotaurbooks.com

Library of Congress Cataloging-in-Publication Data

Names: Bowen, Rhys, author. | Broyles, Clare, author.
Title: Silent as the grave / Rhys Bowen & Clare Broyles.
Description: First edition. | New York : Minotaur Books, 2025. |
     Series: Molly Murphy mysteries ; 21
Identifiers: LCCN 2024042595 | ISBN 9781250890818 (hardcover) |
     ISBN 9781250890825 (ebook)
Subjects: LCGFT: Detective and mystery fiction. | Novels.
Classification: LCC PR6052.O848 S55 2025 | DDC 823/.914—dc23/eng/20240917
LC record available at https://lccn.loc.gov/2024042595

Our books may be purchased in bulk for promotional, educational, or business use. Please contact your local bookseller or the Macmillan Corporate and Premium Sales Department at 1-800-221-7945, extension 5442, or by email at MacmillanSpecialMarkets@macmillan.com.

First Edition: 2025

10 9 8 7 6 5 4 3 2 1

To my improv troupe, The Outcasters,
who remind me to say yes to the story and to laugh.
—Clare

Silent as
the Grave

❧ Prologue ❧

Monday, April 19, 1909

"No," I said, moaning rather than screaming. Screaming would have been useless as the train thundering mere inches from me drowned out all sound. "Stay with me, my darling." I cradled Bridie's limp body in my arms, hoping to see a flicker of life, wanting to see those beloved blue eyes open one more time. My heart was beating crazily.

So many innocent decisions had led to this moment. Perhaps if Daniel had been home to forbid this, or if Sid and Gus had been less encouraging. But I had dared to think that life was for fun and adventure, and I'd forgotten that any moment could bring disaster. If only I could go back, I told myself as the train disappeared into the distance and I sat in the new silence with dread in the pit of my stomach. If only I could go back and warn myself.

❦ One ❦

Eight days earlier
Sunday, April 11, 1909

Y ou are the most infuriating man, Daniel Sullivan," I muttered angrily as I shoved the leg of lamb into the oven. "I can never count on you, not even on Easter Sunday."

"Who are you talking to, Mama?" My son, Liam, looked up, startled, from under the table where he had made a fort and was playing explorers. "Has Daddy been bad?"

I was instantly remorseful. "No, my sweetheart," I said with a softer tone. "I'm just a bit disappointed he will miss our special lunch. I was so pleased to be able to get a lovely leg of lamb as a treat and now he has to work on Easter Sunday of all days."

I was used to Daniel's job as a police captain meaning unpredictable hours, but the last few weeks he had barely come home. Though I loved my life as a wife and mother, I was beginning to feel trapped in the house and a bit lonely. I suppose I was still rather over-emotional after having given birth to Mary Kate in November. Facing the prospect of an Easter meal alone with the children when I had looked forward to a day together as a family seemed the last straw. When I paused to analyze my silly outburst I realized that my anger was really keeping at bay the nagging worry in the pit of my stomach: Daniel's "work" today was standing guard at the coffin of a fallen fellow officer.

We had planned to go uptown to watch the Easter Parade, then come back to a late lunch of roast lamb with all the trimmings. Watching the Easter Parade wasn't something I'd normally have chosen to do. I wasn't the kind of person who gazed in admiration and envy at the new hats and outfits of New York's rich elite as they either strolled or rode in their carriages up Fifth Avenue after church. But we had a reason to watch the parade this year: our adopted daughter, Bridie, was taking part. Bridie's best friend, Blanche, had invited her to ride with her family in their carriage. Bridie was now attending a fashionable institute for young ladies, thanks to the generosity of my neighbors, and mixing with the daughters of the Four Hundred. She had made a particular friend in Blanche McCormick and spent every spare moment with her at her mansion on the Upper East Side. I can't say I was keen on this—I felt it was only showing Bridie a taste of things she could never have—but I had to admit that Blanche was a true friend to Bridie and her mother was sweet and generous.

A cry from upstairs made Liam and me both start for the door quickly. Mary Kate, I'm afraid, took after me and had a healthy set of lungs on her. We both knew better than to let her get into her stride. Once she had started crying, she was too stubborn to stop.

I raced up the stairs and was met by our maid, Aileen, holding Mary Kate, who was mercifully not crying, in her arms.

"Here she is, Mrs. Sullivan," Aileen said in her soft Irish brogue. "All ready for her next meal."

The arrival of Mary Kathleen Sullivan on November 20, 1908, had upended our household. We had named her Mary after Daniel's mother and Kathleen after Bridie's dear sainted mother who was no longer with us. Liam had been a placid little baby who played hap-pily between naps. I had expected the same experience the second time. But Mary Kate, who already had a shock of fiery red hair, was a very different baby. She demanded to be fed or entertained, crying angrily if ignored. For the first time in my life, I had some sympathy for my mother. I could picture her looking down from the pearly gates and laughing. "Now you're reaping what you've sown, Mary Margaret," she would say. And I thought, on the whole, she would have a point. My mother had often been alone in the cottage managing the children with no help, but I had Aileen and sometimes Bridie. I knew that I should be thankful for their help and for the baby that Daniel and I had hoped and prayed would come for so long. She had finally arrived, healthy and strong. I told myself to count my blessings.

"Oh, there you are." Daniel poked his head into the room, eyeing me as I sat nursing the baby. He was wearing his smart dress uniform and looked unusually handsome. "What time do you want to leave?"

"Bridie said they'll be coming out of Mass at St. Patrick's at eleven," I replied. "I'll have to leave the baby with Aileen. I'm not pushing a pram alone through a crowd all the way up Fifth Avenue."

"Are your friends across the street not coming to watch the pa-rade as well?" Daniel said. "I should have thought they'd be walking in it themselves, although Lord knows what kind of costumes they'd choose to wear."

I chose to ignore this last remark. It was true that my friends Elena and Augusta, usually known by their nicknames, Sid and Gus, did have high-society connections, and it was true that they were rather bohemian in their style of dress, but they had been wonder-fully kind to me, and I treasured them.

"They have a guest for lunch," I said. "And you surely know that society events are not their cup of tea, even if their precious Bridie is going to be part of this one."

"If you can hurry to get ready, I'll ride with you on the El to St. Patrick's," he said. "I have to be there anyway to make sure everything is in place for the parade before I go down to the Old Cathedral on Mulberry for the Petrosino viewing."

He put a hand on my shoulder, but I shrugged him off. "Oh, come on, Molly. You know I'd rather be spending the day with my family. It wasn't my idea to have the funeral ceremonies for Lieutenant Petrosino on the same day as the Easter Parade."

"You're a captain," I said. "You're head of homicide. Surely you could have got out of simple crowd control."

"I can't ask my men to work and not be there," he said calmly. "Twenty thousand people are expected at the Petrosino viewing today, and more than that for the funeral tomorrow. All the police in the city will be paying their respects. Not only is it one of their own who was brutally killed, but it's the first time that Italian mob, the Black Hand, has dared to kill a policeman. I'm glad that the city will be showing solidarity with us, and what's more, I'm glad to be part of the tribute to him."

After that there wasn't much I could say without sounding childish. I knew that my husband's job came with its risks. And now one of their own had been killed. I could just as well be Mrs. Petrosino, whose husband would never come home for Easter dinner again. Daniel had had his own dealings with the secretive Sicilian mob that called themselves the Black Hand. I sent up a quick prayer of thanks that I had my husband safely at home, feeling ashamed of my annoyance.

"Aileen, we're ready to go," I called as I came downstairs with the baby. "She's been fed so she should be all right until we come back."

"Very good, Mrs. Sullivan." Aileen took the baby from me. "Now you're with me, you little tyke," she said with mock severity. "And you'd better behave yourself."

Mary Kate grinned at her and made happy noises. I regarded them both fondly.

"And don't worry. We'll be home in good time for you to visit your family this afternoon, Aileen," I said. I had promised her the rest of the day off.

She nodded, hitching the baby onto one hip as she carried her through to the kitchen.

I took off my apron, then reached for my hat hanging on its hook in the hall.

"I should have bought you an Easter bonnet," Daniel commented, coming up behind me as he took his own cap from the hall stand.

"Don't be so daft." I gave him a playful slap. "And why would I ever be needing a hat I'd only wear once? Especially not the sort of hats they'll be wearing with fruit and flowers and God knows what else."

"I'd like to buy you nice things," Daniel said. "You've been a bit down in the dumps lately."

"I know," I said. "I think having a baby has really tired me out. Especially this baby. Up at all hours and screaming her head off."

He nodded. "She's a feisty one, all right. I can't imagine who she takes after." He gave me a knowing look.

I affixed my hat with a couple of hat pins and wrapped my shawl around my shoulders. "Right," I said. "Come on, Liam, we're going to watch the parade."

"Are you sure it's wise to take him?" Daniel asked. "All those people."

"He wants to see Bridie," I said. "And he's a big boy now. He'll be fine. Besides, I could use the company."

Daniel said no more. We called out goodbye to Aileen and then we headed for the El station on Sixth Avenue. Daniel nodded as we passed several policemen already going in the other direction to the Old Cathedral, wearing their smartest uniforms. They were certainly giving their colleague a grand send-off. And this was just the visitation today. Tomorrow they'd be escorting the fallen officer's body all the way to Calvary Cemetery.

The train was crowded with people like ourselves from humbler neighborhoods going to gawk at the spectacle of fine folk strolling up Fifth Avenue. Liam was squashed into me, and I had a horrible flashback to the time we were in a train crash when he was a baby. Perhaps I should have left him with Aileen . . . but after a change in the very crowded Grand Central Station, we alighted safely at the Fifty-Third Street station and made our way over to Fifth Avenue. Daniel found us a place to stand where it was not too crowded, just up a little from the big new St. Patrick's Cathedral, then he gave me a peck on the cheek and ruffled Liam's hair. "Look after your mama for me, big man," he said.

"Okay, Daddy," Liam responded solemnly.

"I'll try to be back as soon as I can," he said with an apologetic nod. And then he was off, blending into the crowd as he headed for St. Patrick's. I watched him go, feeling a shiver of apprehension. Was I going to feel this worry every time he left us from now on?

"Mama!" Liam tugged at my skirt. "Mama, lift me up. I can't see. There are too many people."

I had been so lost in my thoughts that the crowd had moved in around us, blocking our view. I swept him up into my arms. "I'm sorry, my darling," I said. "Mama wasn't paying attention to you. We'll find you a perfect spot to see."

We moved down the street until we came to a big plane tree, and I sat Liam on the curb in front of that. Fortunately, we didn't have to wait long before we heard a murmur going through the crowd and the first cries of "Here they come now."

We leaned forward. Liam stepped out into the street as the first of the procession approached. Here came men in top hats and ladies in sumptuous gowns, some with parasols. They strolled, chatting easily, as if they were taking the air on any normal day, seeming unconscious of the crowd watching them. Liam was entranced. "Look, Mama. That lady has a bird in her hat!" he shouted. "Is it a real bird?"

"No, my darling, just a pretend one," I said. "It's a bit silly, isn't it?" Some of the hats were ridiculously high. The fashion this year seemed to be fruit. Some women looked like they had a whole orchard piled on top of their heads. I was glad I had not let Daniel buy me one. What use were these hats to man or beast?

"When is Bridie coming?"

"I'm not sure. We'll just have to wait and see," I said. The strollers were now followed by a double line of moving vehicles, long lines of carriages and hansoms, each filled with their complement of well-dressed people. We scanned each one, trying to spot Blanche and Bridie.

"She's not there," Liam said angrily. But then his eyes lit up. "Look, Mama. Autos," he said. Like his daddy, he was fascinated by the automobiles that were now appearing more regularly on our streets. They passed us, one after another until . . .

"There she is!" Liam jumped up and down, waving his arms excitedly. "Bridie!"

The chauffeur sat at the front of a big burgundy-colored automobile and in the back seat sat Mrs. McCormick, Blanche, and Bridie. Bridie had left our house wearing her white muslin dress and a straw bonnet, but she was now dressed in what looked like pale blue silk with a silk bonnet trimmed with flowers. I was glad to see it was appropriate for her age and no fruit was involved. Obviously, she had borrowed more of her friend's clothes. I had to admit she looked an absolute picture in them, but I wasn't quite comfortable with my daughter pretending to be something she wasn't.

Blanche spotted us, nudged Bridie, and they all waved. We waved back. And then they were gone. I took Liam's hand. "Right, boyo," I said. "Let's go home and eat that lamb, shall we?"

❧ TWO ❧

The El was crowded on the way home. I wondered if it was all spectators returning from the parade or if some were mourners making their way to the Old Cathedral on Mulberry Street. It was a grand thing that the whole city should turn out to honor one of its finest. The thought crept into my mind unbidden to wonder whether they'd do the same for Daniel if the worst should happen. Holy Mother of God—what a thing to think on Easter Sunday.

We arrived home to be greeted by the aroma of roasting lamb and the deafening cries of Mary Kate.

"She just woke up, Mrs. Sullivan," Aileen said, apologetically. "There's been no consoling her."

"Forever hungry, that child," I said, taking the red-faced baby from Aileen. "The sooner we start her on solid food the better."

I carried her upstairs to the rocking chair, fed her, and she was for once quiet and happy as we laid the table for our meal.

Aileen left to visit her own family, and as two o'clock drew near, the front door opened and Bridie came running in.

"The chauffeur drove me home in their automobile," she said, her eyes bright with excitement and her cheeks flushed. "You should have seen the faces when we stopped outside Patchin Place. I felt like a queen."

"You should consider yourself lucky to have more than one dress," I said. "When I was growing up it was one dress for everyday and one for Sundays. That was it."

Bridie rolled her eyes in the way that only a fourteen-year-old can do. "I'd just die if I only had one dress," she said. "I don't know how you could stand it."

"We had no choice," I said. "We were poor. Sometimes there wasn't even enough food to go around. So, count your blessings, young lady. And put an apron over that dress while you eat."

We ate our lunch, Bridie entertaining us with tales of life with the McCormicks and what the parade had been like. "And I saw people in the crowd pointing at me," she said, excitedly waving her fork, "and I heard someone say that Blanche and I must be this year's debutantes. Fancy that, Mama."

"Just don't let it go to your head," I said. "Blanche may well be a debutante one day, but you won't. You come from a nice, respectable family and be grateful for that."

We finished the meal with bread pudding and custard, one of Daniel's favorites. I felt a pang of guilt again that I had berated him for working today. Of course he'd rather be sitting here with us, eating his favorite foods, than standing guard for hours at St. Patrick's. And tomorrow he'd have to walk with the coffin to the Calvary Cemetery.

"So, what are we going to do now?" Bridie asked, as we washed the dishes. "If I'd known Papa wasn't going to be here, I could have stayed at Blanche's. Her brother was going to visit with friends he'd made in Paris. It would have been swell." She gave a dramatic sigh as she flourished the dishcloth.

"I know," I said, still trying to sound upbeat, "let's go and see if the Italian ice cream shop is open today."

"Ice cream! Swell!" Liam at least sounded cheerful. He had picked up Bridie's favorite word of the moment.

"I'll go and get Mary Kate. She hasn't had an outing yet."

I had scarcely gone up two steps when there was a knock at the front door.

"Who on earth . . ." I began, but Bridie reached the door first and I heard Liam's delighted, "It's Aunt Gus!"

"Happy Easter, children," came Gus's smooth Boston tones. I hurried to join them. She was holding a basket of colored eggs and candies. "To enjoy later," she said. "We thought we would not intrude on your holiday, but one of our guests is dying to meet you, so we wondered if you had time for a cup of tea and cake."

With "tea and cake," Liam was out of the door before I could grab him.

"Thank you, we'd be delighted," I said. "I'll have to bring the baby. Aileen has the rest of the day off."

"Of course, you have to bring our precious goddaughter," Gus said. "We wouldn't dream of it otherwise."

In spite of neither Sid nor Gus being Catholic and thus not official godparents, they had designated themselves godmothers and would no doubt spoil Mary Kate horribly until she grew up. Not that I objected to this. The Good Lord knows I'd have welcomed a bit of spoiling in my own harsh childhood.

"And the captain?" Gus asked as I took the basket from her with thanks.

"Is working," I said. "Supervising the big funeral rites for the slain policeman."

"Oh yes, of course. They expected record crowds, didn't they?" Gus nodded. "So did you put off your Easter feast until he got home?"

"We didn't," I said. "Who knows what time he'll be home. But there's plenty saved for him. He won't starve."

I tiptoed upstairs, managed to pick up Mary Kate, transfer her to the wicker bassinet she had used as a small baby, and carry her across the street without her waking up, which was indeed a feat. We placed her in the dining room and then followed Gus through to the parlor.

"Here they are," Gus announced. "Mr. Armitage, I'd like you to meet my dear friends and neighbors, Mrs. Sullivan and her children Liam and Bridie."

I spotted the man draped languidly in the armchair. He was slim, elegant, with light hair, light eyes, and a fair mustache. I noticed the lace on his cuffs. I was about to say something to him when Gus added, "And of course our other guest needs no introduction."

As I stepped into the room, flamboyant Irish playwright Ryan O'Hare rose from his seat on the couch and came toward us, arms open to embrace.

"Molly, my dearest. What a sight for sore eyes you are. How I've been pining for you these long months I've been in England." Ryan, as usual, looked as if he had stepped out of the pages of a romance novel. He pushed his dark wavy hair back from his eyes and revealed his own new, luxurious mustache. He was dressed in a light brown linen lounge suit with a straw boater, for all the world as if he were a Vanderbilt at the seaside.

"Full of blarney as always, Ryan," I said, but I was chuckling as he hugged me.

When he came to Bridie, he stopped short. "And who is this fashionable person?" he asked. "My, but you are moving up in the world, Molly, if you now entertain such fine ladies."

"It's Bridie," she said before I could answer. "You saw me last year, remember?"

"But no, last year I saw a little girl. Now I'm looking at an elegant young lady, wearing Thai silk if I'm not mistaken."

"And she's just been part of the Easter Parade," Sid said, taking Bridie's hand and leading her to sit down. "Definitely moving up in the world."

"But my dear, you are stunning looking," Ryan went on. "That lovely blond hair. Those blue eyes. Molly, you must take her to England right away and present her at court. She must snag at least a duke or an earl."

"She will do no such thing, Ryan," I said. "She is only fourteen and she's just been lent the outfit for the occasion. Tomorrow she'll be a dressed like a normal schoolgirl again."

Bridie began to say that she'd been given the outfit but a stern glance from me made her close her mouth again.

"And we are certainly not taking all this trouble with her education for her to be an adornment in a duke's palace," Sid said. "We expect her to follow us to Vassar and then do something brilliant with her life—a doctor or chemist or even an author."

Bridie gave a shy smile. "I don't think I could be a doctor, Aunt Sid. I don't like the sight of blood."

"I fell down and got blood on my knee," Liam said, wanting to show his scab to the newcomers. "And I didn't cry."

I remembered the other man now sitting primly in the armchair. "I'm sorry, we've completely neglected your other guest," I said. "How do you do, sir. I'm Molly Sullivan."

"Delighted to make your acquaintance, Mrs. Sullivan." He had a smooth English voice and held out a hand to me. I found myself wondering if I was expected to shake it or kiss it. I did neither but took a seat beside Ryan on the couch and pulled Liam onto my lap.

"Cecil Armitage is an actor," Sid went on. "He was in Ryan's play in London."

"A dazzling success as always," Ryan said. "I've brought the reviews. Everyone was stunned by the witty dialogue and the quality of the acting."

"He said modestly," Gus remarked with a grin to Sid.

"I was brought up to be truthful," Ryan said. "Can I help it if the world adores me?"

"So why have you left your dazzlingly successful play and returned to America, apart from missing your friends?" I asked.

"One gets bored with doing the same thing after a while, doesn't one, Cecil?"

Mr. Armitage nodded. "Especially when the world is so full of new opportunities and new people to meet." He smiled charmingly at me.

"You might have new opportunities here?" I asked.

Ryan put his finger to his lips. "One never knows," he said. "But tell me, will that brute of a husband of yours allow you to come out with me tomorrow afternoon?"

"My husband, who is in no way a brute, Ryan, will be fully occupied tomorrow," I said. "If you've only just arrived back in New York, you may not have heard that a fellow policeman, a lieutenant who worked under Daniel, was killed by the Black Hand. His body is lying in state in Old St. Patrick's Cathedral today and the burial is tomorrow. The whole of New York is expected to attend and pay their respects."

"Including you lovely ladies?" Ryan looked absurdly disappointed.

"I don't think we will brave the cathedral," Sid said. "But it does seem quite callous to go out and enjoy ourselves in the morning."

"I agree." Gus nodded. "But we should be free in the afternoon. We'd love to do something fun with you, even if you won't tell us what it is."

Now Ryan glanced at Mr. Armitage and gave an enigmatic smile. "I won't tell. It's a surprise, but I can say that you'll love it."

"Am I invited too?" Bridie asked. She glanced at me.

"Of course. Absolutely."

"Will it be suitable for a young girl, Ryan?" I asked. I had no idea what his surprise might be, but I knew he mixed with questionable people.

"I'll have you know that my surprise is perfect for Miss Bridie. In fact it's perfect for the whole world, to whom it will soon be offered," he said.

"Goodness," Gus said, "you make it sound like a new tonic."

"A tonic for the senses," Ryan said. "So, it's settled, then. I will give you directions on where and when to meet me and we'll take it from there."

And he refused to say any more.

❧ Three ❧

It was after dark when we crossed the cobbled alley back to our house. I had sprung up ready to take us all home the moment that Mary Kate had woken and sat up, expecting immediate disaster. But she proved to be as fascinated with Ryan as the rest of us and sat on his knee grabbing at the handlebar mustache he had grown. All the excitement of the day and the strong coffee that Gus had served kept me up until Daniel got home. One look at his tired face melted any lingering resentment over his absence.

"Come in, my love. I'll heat you up a plate of dinner," I said gently as he walked through the door. He gave a grateful smile.

"Thanks, Molly, I haven't eaten since breakfast. You wouldn't believe it. It seemed like all of the city came to the viewing. They kept coming long after dark. Between that and all the parades, every policeman in the city was working today." He took his cap and coat off and followed me into the kitchen as I served up the lamb, parsnips, and potatoes I had set aside for him. "And tomorrow will probably be worse." He took a large bite of the lamb with mint sauce and gave a groan of pleasure. "I'm sorry I missed dinner with the family."

He ate with the appetite of a starving man while I filled him in on our dinner together and Bridie's adventures of the day. I was suddenly filled with gratitude to be sitting here with my husband, knowing my children were safely upstairs. "I can't believe the Black Hand would blatantly kill a police lieutenant," I said, thinking again of Petrosino's poor widow.

"They have shown themselves to be quite ruthless," Daniel said. "The problem is that it's impossible to shut them down. As long as there is poverty there are going to be gangs."

I hardly dared to say the words. "Are you yourself in danger, Daniel? Are we in danger?"

He didn't meet my gaze. "I don't think so at the moment, as I am not in charge of the squads investigating racketeering or extortion. I only come into contact when there is a homicide among them and thankfully there haven't been too many of those. People usually pay up, and the gang doesn't kill because dead people can't pay."

I shivered. "All the same," I said. "I can't help remembering what happened to our house with that bomb."

"I know." He stood up, came over to me, and enveloped me in his arms. "I don't think we'll ever quite forget it. But I'm hopeful that the strength that we've shown and will show tomorrow will let this mob know that the whole city is against them."

I nodded, still thinking, still picturing the lieutenant's widow, trying to be brave. Did he have children? "Perhaps I should take the children to the funeral tomorrow out of respect."

"I don't think that's a good idea, Molly." Daniel shook his head. "All the seats inside the cathedral are spoken for. You would just be in the crowd outside. I'll be marching with the other police behind the coffin. That will show our family's respects."

"That's true," I said, somewhat relieved. A funeral for a policeman was too close to home, even one I had only read about and never met. "I suppose you'll be home late tomorrow as well. I hope you can have an easier day on Tuesday."

"That's something I need to talk to you about, Molly," Daniel said, pushing back from the table. "You remember Mr. Wilkie from the Secret Service?" I did. I had even done some work for him myself. "I heard from him a couple of days ago." My stomach dropped. I had hoped that Daniel's days of investigating for the Secret Service were over. "He is no longer allowed to hire investigators," Daniel went on, "but the government is putting together a different Bureau of Investigation that will look into federal crimes. He put my name forward."

"Forward for what?" I imagined the worst. "Not for investigating the Black Hand?" I thought of Petrosino again. People snooping into Italian gangs very often ended up dead.

"Not in the way you're thinking." Daniel put his hand over mine. "I suspect the first task of the new organization will be to investigate them, but at the moment they just want the opinions of some police captains on how to set up the bureau. Mr. Wilkie suggested me. It just means a trip to Washington."

"Washington? For how long?" I was tired and I had not been myself since the baby came. Fear flooded through me. "You're not suggesting we pack up and go to Washington then?"

"No, Molly, calm down." Daniel looked concerned. He was used to me being hotheaded but rarely fearful. "I'm going for a week for some meetings, right after the funeral. That's all. Then I'll be home."

"But will they ask you to join this new investigator group?" I asked, still fighting back the fear. I stood and cleared his plate, putting it in the sink to soak.

"They might, they probably will," he said. "But if that happens, I promise we will talk it over together and not in the middle of the night." He pulled out his pocket watch and groaned. "It's nearly eleven o'clock and I have to be at the precinct by six." He rose. "I'm sorry to talk about this so late but I have no idea when I will be home tomorrow, and I have to catch a train to Washington early Tuesday morning. Will you be all right here by yourself for a week?" He looked at me with real concern. Holy Mother, I thought. What am I doing? I had never been the weak and weepy woman and I wasn't going to start now. Pull yourself together, Molly, I told myself sternly.

"Don't you go worrying about me, I will be just fine," I said, using my most confident voice. "I have Aileen, and Bridie is a big help. She has her Easter holidays this week, so I'll have an extra pair of hands." I lowered my voice to a whisper as we started up the stairs. "Now for heaven's sake, don't wake the baby."

Liam was so happy to see Aileen when she returned that she might have been gone for months rather than one night away. I sent Daniel off with a hearty breakfast and a kiss. With Aileen's help we left for our daily walk to the park, Mary Kate in her carriage and Liam running ahead, full of energy. Aileen was a calm and confident eighteen-year-old now, different from the rather timid girl whom we had first met as a maid in our house on Fifth Avenue. Then she was sixteen and newly arrived from Ireland.

I was just thinking of a chance to let Liam play a bit. But groups of people, many dressed in black, or wearing black armbands, were walking through Washington Square in the direction of the Old Cathedral on Mulberry. They were going to watch Petrosino's coffin as it made its way from the Old Cathedral to the cemetery in Calvary. I decided that I just couldn't stay away. It seemed disrespectful to not honor the man in some way when my husband faced the same dangers. The four of us went down to Prince Street and then stood watching the solemn procession as Petrosino's coffin passed. The pavement was crowded with people from all walks of life speaking many different languages, Italian prominent among them. Even the shops emptied as everyone on the street came out to pay respects. The men removed their hats and the women crossed themselves. I did too and said a prayer for the safety of my Daniel and all the police. We saw Daniel pass with other police captains in dress uniform walking behind the coffin.

"There's my daddy!" Liam yelled out when he saw him, and the people around us smiled. It was hard to keep gloomy thoughts with Liam around. I did stop and let him play in the park before we returned home. As I sat and watched him my thoughts turned once again to my friends. What could Ryan's surprise be?

The afternoon was bright but cold as Bridie, Sid, Gus, and I set out for the address that Ryan had given us on Bleecker Street. It felt good to walk through Greenwich Village with my friends, laughing and chatting, to remember that I was more than just a mother. We each had a guess about what Ryan's surprise might be. With Ryan one never knew. The chances were even that he could be introducing us to royalty or a carnival worker, a millionaire or an anarchist—a new play, a new script, or a new lover.

When we came to the address, Ryan was waiting for us outside a box office window in a building that had a sign that read BLEECKER THEATER. Ryan was getting strange looks from passersby, as he was wearing a natty suit and top hat and his new mustache was waxed and glossy.

"Have you written a new play?" Gus asked brightly as she came up to him. "Is this the big surprise?"

"This is my work," Ryan said, flinging his arms wide with excitement he couldn't contain. "But the Bleecker Theater is showing moving pictures now. I've written a film script!"

"I didn't know moving pictures even used scripts," I said, surprised. Of course, I had seen films before but only brief views of moving trains or people walking in the city. I had been busy raising a family and had not had much time for moving pictures.

"They haven't up until now," Ryan said with animation. He paid a nickel for each of us at the box office and we entered the theater. It took a moment for my eyes to adjust coming in out of the bright day. "They wanted me to just tell them the story," Ryan's voice did not lower in volume, "but I insisted on writing a script. After all, I am a playwright."

"We've been regulars at a storefront theater near us," Sid said as we took our seats. "The films now have proper stories, and those stories are getting exciting. But I didn't know they were hiring real playwrights."

Once my eyes adjusted, I looked around curiously. The seats were arranged like those in a regular theater. The floor sloped down slightly toward the front of the theater where a crimson velvet curtain hung. A piano was off to the right of the screen and the piano player started to play a popular tune just as uniformed employees turned down the gas lamps that lined the sides of the room. The velvet curtain opened with a flourish and, instead of revealing a stage, showed a large white screen lit with brilliant light. *Ah*, I thought, *the silver screen!* That's what they called it these days. I could hear a mechanical sound and looked back to see a man in a booth at the back of the theater turning a crank. *That must be the projector*, I thought. The screen was filled with the picture of a child's teddy bear. As we watched, the bear moved on its own and danced around. Some people in the audience gasped. I confess I was one of them. Then other bears came in and danced along. It looked like magic. After the bears the screen briefly went dark and then letters came on and formed a kind of train that swirled across the screen, finally coming to rest to form the word "Biograph."

"That's the studio that makes these pictures," Ryan whispered.

"Shh." A man in front of us turned around and glared at Ryan's interruption. The screen went dark once more, and the whirr of the projector stopped.

"Is that it?" I softly asked Sid, who was sitting to my right.

"No, that was just the first reel. They'll put on the feature film now," she whispered back. The screen brightened again, this time with a magic lantern slide: a colorful still image of a mother and father with a baby in the cradle. The piano player started to play a popular song and the audience sang along.

Then the feature film began. It started with a view of a newspaper. GENTLEMAN BURGLAR GETS AWAY WITH JEWELS! the front page read. The piano trilled with excitement. Then the scene changed to a wealthy drawing room. The piano music became tranquil. A man read the same newspaper while his wife and daughter calmly did their needlepoint. When the man lowered the paper to speak to his wife, the three of us gasped and Ryan laughed loudly.

"Mr. Armitage!" Gus exclaimed.

"The same!" Ryan attempted to whisper but still received another stern "Shhh" from the man in front.

The dialogue was written on a black screen with white letters.

Perhaps we should take your diamonds to the bank until they catch this blaggard, dear.

On screen, the fashionable woman clutched her daughter.

Will we be safe?

The piano music heralded the approach of danger. A policeman was shown walking past the mansion. A man in a black suit and top hat evaded him and climbed up the ivy of the mansion. As his face appeared in the window, I couldn't believe my eyes.

"Gadzooks!" Sid exclaimed. "It's Ryan!"

❀ Four ❀

W e sat riveted as Ryan's character held the poor family hostage and was finally bested by the brave policemen who came to their aid at the last minute. I could tell that Ryan was dying to tell us how he had started his career as a moving picture actor, but the other patrons kept giving us dirty looks every time he tried to speak.

Ryan's film was about a quarter of an hour long and was followed by another sing-along and then a very funny film in which Italian bakers covered one another with flour. I laughed so hard that my side hurt. When the pictures ended, we spilled back out onto the street with the rest of the crowd. Ryan stood beaming as we peppered him with questions.

"Children, children, calm yourselves, all will be answered," he said. "But now my public awaits." I saw now why Ryan had worn his outlandish costume. Quite a few people exiting the theater recognized him as the gentleman burglar and pointed him out to one another. One young lady thrust a paper at him.

"Can I have your autograph, mister?" she asked.

"Why of course, young lady," Ryan said, signing the paper with a flourish. Bridie was standing by Ryan's side looking at him with adoration.

"Are you in pictures too, miss?" the young lady asked Bridie, who went pink and shook her head.

An older lady scowled at Ryan and shook her finger as she went past us. I thought at first it was because he had been speaking during the picture but then I overheard what she said to her companion.

"He didn't oughta have taken that poor lady hostage. She coulda died on account of being so afraid."

The five of us looked at one another and burst into laughter.

"Now tell us," Sid demanded, "how did this happen?"

"My dear, I'm weak with hunger," Ryan said. "And there is much too much to tell standing in the street."

"Let's go back to our house, then," Gus said. She convinced us to stop into Porto Rico's to buy coffee beans and an Italian bakery to get pastries she called cannolis. The afternoon had warmed up and we strolled through Washington Square trying the pastries on our way home. They were divine little pockets of sweet fried dough with a cream inside them. When we were comfortably in Sid and Gus's living room, each with coffee in hand, Ryan was confident that he now had our full attention.

"After my last play ended, Cecil convinced me to come back to New York for a while because he had a role in a moving picture. Lots of actors are doing them. Then his production shut down because of some sort of copyright issue. It seems that the filmmakers can't use a novel without paying the author."

"That seems fair," Sid put in. "Don't you agree, as a writer?"

"I do!" Ryan said. "But it put Cecil in a terrible mood. He had his heart set on playing Ben-Hur. So, I decided to step in. I offered to write them a script for a film if I could act in it. Mr. Griffith, he is the director, took one look at this face"—he accompanied the words with a gesture—"and jumped at the chance. And you saw the end result!"

"Absolutely brilliant, Ryan!" Gus said. "That was a clever twist. A gentleman burglar."

"Well, it's much more fun to play the villain, but I couldn't bring myself to play your typical riffraff. In my next film I play a villainous count."

"Your next film!" I exclaimed. "Is this your new career, then, Ryan?"

"I expect that I will get bored eventually, but I certainly am enjoying myself at the moment, even if it doesn't pay the way the theater does. Now if I can only get the studio—that's what they call the whole production—to add my name to the pictures. There's no program like in the theater. How are the public to know the playwrights or actors?" Ryan took a bite of his third cannoli. Cream squirted out onto his fingers, and he licked them with a wonderfully sensuous gesture. "This is delicious, Gus. I shall have to remember that bakery."

"I shall buy you some more after your next film if you promise to come and visit again," she said with a smile.

"I can do better than that!" he said. "We're rehearsing tomorrow. I can give you a tour."

"They're rehearsing a new one already?" I was surprised. "But this one just came out."

"My dear," Ryan turned his piercing gaze on me, "Biograph Studios films a moving picture each week. I finished the script yesterday. We're rehearsing tomorrow and Wednesday and shooting the whole film on Thursday and Friday."

Bridie's face was flushed with excitement. "Can I come too, Mr. O'Hare?"

"Why, of course you can, you charming creature." Ryan reached

over and took her hand. "I will be devastated if you don't." Bridie
giggled, then turned to me.

"Can I, Mama?" she said. Sid, Gus, and Ryan all looked at me with
such expressions of pleading that I had to laugh.

"Why not," I said.

Daniel was home by the time the shepherd's pie I made was bub-
bling in the oven.

He came over, kissed the top of Mary Kate's head, and then repeated the favor to me. "I'm so glad you could get away early today,"
I said. "Supper is almost ready."

He sank onto a chair, leaning back. "What a day, Molly. I am
quite whacked. You would not believe it. They say two hundred
thousand people were lining those streets. The service itself was
very moving and then the walk behind the coffin . . . everywhere
we went the sidewalks were packed, people were hanging out of
windows and standing on rooftops, all the way to the cemetery, over
the Brooklyn Bridge, and right up to Queens. And a good number
of people followed the coffin all the way to the grave site too. I must
say it did my heart good to know what New York thinks about its
policemen."

"You wouldn't get that love if you became an investigator for this
new bureau in Washington," I said, giving him one of my looks.

"We'll just have to see," he said. "You know I'll do what's right for
my family."

I let it go. We had a pleasant family dinner. Bridie recounted every detail of the films we had seen to Liam, who hung on her every
word, and Daniel, who listened indulgently.

"So we are going to watch them make a film tomorrow!" Bridie
finished.

"Should be interesting, I suppose." Daniel did not sound very interested. He did not approve of Ryan O'Hare or the sort of people he mixed with. There was too much of his mother in him!

I was up early next morning, making sure that Daniel had everything he needed for a week's trip to Washington. I packed his bag with clean shirts and underclothes and made him a good breakfast of sausage and biscuits.

"You're a good wife, Molly," he said, giving me a kiss as we stood at the door in that awkward pause before saying goodbye. "I'll miss you."

Bridie had also arisen remarkably early for one of her age on a non-school morning.

"Bye-bye, Papa," she said, coming forward to give him a hesitant kiss. She was still a little reticent with Daniel. "Come home to us soon, and don't say yes to that horrid man in Washington."

Daniel laughed and ruffled her hair. "You look very nice," he said. "Are you going somewhere special?"

"Only to the studio to watch them acting in a film," she said.

She had put on one of the new dresses Blanche had handed on to her. It made her look older than her years, in a dark green that highlighted her blond hair.

Daniel seemed reluctant to go and pulled me into a hug. "I won't be long, Molly. Stay safe, my darling."

"I will." I let my head rest against his chest briefly. He gave me another kiss and was just heading out of the door when I heard a wail from upstairs and I had to focus on feeding a now screaming child. Two hours later I, too, was dressed in one of my nicer outfits—a two-piece in navy taffeta, edged with white lace around the neck and cuffs—and topped it with my white straw hat with a navy-and-white polka-dot band. No flowers and birds for me, I'm glad to say. My hats were practical in the extreme.

Sid and Gus were waiting for us and it was a pleasant stroll up Sixth Avenue to Fourteenth and then across almost as far as Fifth Avenue. Some of the passersby stared openly at Sid. She was wearing a royal blue cape over black velvet culottes and what looked like riding boots. She also had a red bandanna around her neck. Gus, more demure, as usual, was wearing a gray silk dress, but topped it with a white fox fur—the whole fox, with his head eating his tail, around her neck—and a matador's three-cornered hat. We mounted stone steps into what looked like a regular large brownstone. A uniformed doorman stopped us in the foyer and checked for our names on a list. They must have been there, because he picked up a strange-looking telephone with buttons on the case, spoke into it, and in a few minutes Ryan appeared. He was dressed in a long morning coat. He had his hair slicked back and his mustache was curled at the ends.

"Perfect timing!" he said. "We've just been given a break." He ushered us through a door. I expected to see a living room but instead a vast space opened up before us with a wooden floor like that of a stage. As if he had read my mind Ryan said, "We call this room where we film 'the stage,' just like in a theater." Ryan gestured around as if he alone was responsible for having created the entire production. If this had been a house, the second story must have been entirely removed. The ceiling was high above us. Natural light flooded in through a large opening in the ceiling. A crew of men and women carried things in and out of the space. Several men were painting a large backdrop, while another carried in a realistic-looking tree.

Several scenes like those in a theater were set up on the far wall. There was a living room with a wallpapered back wall complete with fireplace and wingback chairs. The walls and door looked real from inside the room but on the outside it was clear they were wood and canvas, propped up from behind. A bright light was positioned to shine in through the window and other electric lights were hung on scaffolding over the scene.

Right next to it was an old-fashioned girl's bedroom, with a canopy bed and a dressing table. Pretty white dresses hung in an open wardrobe. This scene had the window on both sides of the more sturdily built wall, with a window box on what would be the outside of the house.

"We are in our final dress rehearsal," Ryan said, walking us over to the first scene. "And trying on different costumes to see which looks better on camera." A pretty young woman was sitting on the sofa reading a dime novel. She was dressed as a maid in a black dress with a white apron and cap.

"Daisy, these are some dear friends come to visit," Ryan said. "Dear friends, this is Daisy Vokes." Daisy got up and shook hands as we introduced ourselves.

"Pleased to meet you," she said with a smile. "Are youse theater friends of Ryan's as well?" Her voice was high and nasal with a Bronx accent that made the words come out sounding like "Pleased to meetcha."

"No, we're from his wicked bohemian days," Sid said with an answering smile, "before he was a respectable playwright."

"I'm highly insulted," Ryan said with mock indignation. "I am just as bohemian as I have ever been. Respectable indeed!" He turned to Daisy and asked, "Are we released to get some food, do you think? I'm famished."

"Not yet," she said. "Alice has one more change of outfit for the girl and she wants to see how it affects the 'composition of the shot,' whatever that means. These moving picture people are a strange lot."

"Is this your first film, then?" I asked. She shook her head.

"No, it's my second, but it's a little hard to get used to. I've been working in the theater where we have weeks to rehearse and a script and an audience."

I wondered what roles she might have played in the theater with that voice and accent. Maybe she was a singer or dancer. She stood up, smoothing out her skirt. "Here we have two days, and the director just shouts at you the whole time."

"I have written a script, as you well know," Ryan said. "And I shall thank you to keep to it."

"Alice says you are not to show it to DW under any circumstances. He never works with a script," Daisy said. "But don't worry, I have my lines memorized. I only have a few." She turned to me. "A lot of us theater folks are doing a film or two. It's hard work but you're done in a week, and it pays ten bucks, which isn't bad. The only thing I hate is the hours. I prefer the theater where I can sleep until noon." She sat back down on the sofa and picked up her novel again.

"As should any civilized person," Ryan said. "Now, who wants to hear my brilliant script?" We all looked suitably interested. "Let me get in character," he went on, picking up a black top hat from the table beside the chair and putting it on.

"I am the evil Count Rosokov," he began. "Daisy here is the maid and that pretty young thing," he gestured to a girl dressed in an ankle-length white frilly gown, who had just come into the room and was making her way toward us, "is my ward. I was her father's business partner before her parents died and it is up to me to raise her and take care of her large fortune."

"I think I read a novel just like that once," Daisy said, turning the page in her book.

"Nonsense," Ryan said, "it is entirely original."

The girl came up to us. She was wearing a blond wig and was

dressed like a young innocent girl, but I could see now that she was older, perhaps in her midtwenties, with a rather curvy figure, and wearing a corset.

"Let's get this over with," she said to Daisy and Ryan, completely ignoring us. "I'm ready for a break."

"Lily, these are my friends," Ryan said pointedly. "And I am explaining the plot of my brilliant film. Now," he went on, turning to us, "I have cleverly kept my ward," he gestured to Lily, "away from all society since my evil plan is to marry her as soon as she turns eighteen. But, alas, she has fallen in love with the young gardener who has spoken to her through her window."

"That's Johnny Bruce," Daisy said, looking up. "You probably saw him in that picture last year about the prizefighter."

"We saw that!" Gus exclaimed. "We are fans of the moving picture shows."

"I did too!" Bridie's voice was excited.

I turned to her, surprised. "You did?"

"Yes, Blanche and I went together. All the girls at school see the picture shows. We loved Johnny Bruce. He was so handsome."

It seemed I was very behind the times. I had no idea those storefront theaters had become so popular. I saw people queuing up to pay their nickels, but somehow I had pictured reels of images like the ones of people bathing at Coney Island.

"Where is Mr. Bruce?" Bridie asked, looking around.

"In the dressing room with Alice and the costume ladies, I guess," Daisy said. "I hope he hurries so we can get something to eat."

"Wait until the girls at school hear I met the actor from the prizefighting film!" Bridie said, her face alight with excitement.

"I've been in six pictures," Lily put in, deigning to notice Bridie for the first time. "People often stop me on the street and say they know me from somewhere." She paused, perhaps waiting for one of us to say we had seen her. "I keep telling DW," she went on angrily, "he needs to put our names on the pictures so the public will know who we are. Lily La Rosa should be a household name."

"Good luck," Daisy said. "DW says he'll have to pay us more if we get our own stage door Johnnies. I wouldn't mention your thoughts to him if you want to keep your part."

"I dare him to replace me!" Lily's eyes flashed. "He needs me for this picture."

❧ Five ❧

Just then a young man emerged from the door in the back of the stage. He was handsome with dark, curly hair but was strangely dressed in a bright red suit with a green shirt under it. A woman strode ahead of him toward us.

"There are Johnny and Alice," Daisy said. "She looks all business, Ryan. You had better introduce your friends to Johnny later." Alice did indeed march across the floor with great purpose. She looked a formidable woman though she could not have been much older than thirty. Her divided skirts showed she was a follower of the rational dress movement. Her hair was swept up into a bun that had a number of what looked like sticks stuck into it. She carried a large sheaf of papers that she glanced at as she came up to the set. Ryan made a shooing motion toward us, and we stepped out of the living room scene.

"On your marks for opening, please," Alice said with no preamble. "No, you're sitting in the chair stage left, Lily," she barked as Lily had been sitting in the right-hand chair and quickly moved. Ryan stood behind her. Daisy stood just inside the doorway. "Now hold your positions while I get the cameraman." She studied the scene for a minute in silence and then moved the open chair over an inch to the left.

"Where do you want me, Alice?" Johnny asked.

"What?" Alice said, still intently staring at the scene before her. She pulled a pencil out of her hair and scribbled a note on one of the papers in her hand. Johnny repeated his question.

"I need you in a minute outside the bedroom window," Alice said, coming out of her reverie and focusing on Johnny. She stepped back from the scene and started making notes furiously, glancing back and forth between the scene and her papers.

"Alice, why does Johnny look like a Christmas elf?" Lily asked nastily. "Isn't he supposed to be a gardener?"

"It's for the gray scale," Alice said without pausing in her work. "The red looks better than gray on camera." Still looking at the scene, she raised her voice. "Edward! Camera two over here please."

"Coming, Alice." A man came running across the floor to an enormous camera, which he wheeled into place. There were wheels on two of the legs and he opened the third leg out to form a tripod. Alice joined him at the camera, and they consulted for a number of minutes, moving the camera to different angles until finally Alice was satisfied.

"Let's try the opening sequence, please," Alice said, staring into the camera. "On my mark. Action."

"You need never leave this house, my dear," Ryan intoned, his face now displaying an evil grin. "Once you are of age, we will marry."

"Uncle, I care for you, but my heart belongs to another," Lily said, turning her face away from him, scrunching her small features and pouting her lips.

"Freeze there, that's enough." Alice was peering through the camera. "The dress is too white. Lily, we need to put you in the pink one. The rest of you can break for a moment."

"But Alice, I'm famished!" Lily complained. Alice went off toward the dressing room without a backward glance. Lily sighed and flounced after her.

The cameraman wandered over to us. "Newcomers, O'Hare? Are they actors?"

"No, just friends of mine, curious to see my latest venture," Ryan said. He introduced us to the cameraman.

"Edward Shepherd, pleased to meet any friends of Ryan," the man said, shaking hands with each of us in turn. He was a young man with light hair parted in the middle. Like most of the crew I could see, he was dressed in a rumpled and stained shirt and pants held up by suspenders. It reminded me of my days working in a theater. The front of the stage could look like a palace while behind the scenes everything was messy and half finished.

"To echo Lily, I'm famished," Ryan said. "The best part of this job, apart from the dubious fame and fortune, is the food. Alice insists on the best. She says it attracts a higher quality of performer."

"She ain't wrong," Daisy said as we went over to a long table piled high with food. "Ten bucks a week ain't much but I eat enough for the whole day here."

"And we are invited to partake as well?" Gus asked.

"Oh yeah, they won't care. Help yourself." Daisy was loading her plate with fresh bread, fruit, and cold cuts of meat. I followed her example. I felt constantly hungry while I was nursing Mary Kate. As I thought of my little one, I began to feel uncomfortable. I would need to get home to feed her soon.

The cameraman had not come over to the table with us. He was still back at his camera outside the living room scene making notes of his own in a little Juneau notebook. Edward looked up and saw me watching him. He gave a little nod and put the notebook away in his back pocket.

"Ryan, do you think I could be in one of your pictures?" Bridie asked, her face alight with excitement as she put sliced apples on her plate. "I do well in speech class at school."

"I told you, my darling, you could take the stage by storm." Ryan smiled back at her. He reached over and stroked her cheek. "You are a delight. I don't imagine this film business will ever be able to compare with the theater, but if you want to try your hand at it, I don't see why you couldn't."

I was about to intervene before Ryan promised her things we'd never allow her to do but Alice was already back out on the stage floor, posing Johnny Bruce in front of the window, and someone yelled, "Quiet on the set!"

"Edward!" Alice yelled and the cameraman swiftly took up position at his camera.

"Look out for his blarney, Bridie," I muttered, leaning close to her. "Ryan is a big flatterer, but I would take what he says with a grain of salt."

Ryan overheard, turning back to us. "I'm hurt to the quick," he said dramatically. "I am perfectly serious, Molly."

"She does have a nice figure for the stage, I would say," Daisy put in. "She's going to be quite a looker."

I stared at my daughter and realized again that she did look like a young lady now. She was only fourteen but her round, girlish face had thinned out and her big blue eyes and golden curls made her a beauty. I had never felt beautiful as a girl. If ever I had been paid a compliment my mother would have told me not to get above myself and let the devil put ideas in my head. American parents were much more ready to tell their children how beautiful and talented they were. *And what's wrong with that?* I thought.

"You are going to be quite pretty, my dear," I said, giving her a little hug, "but remember a woman is more than her looks."

"Hear, hear," Sid said. "Look at Alice." She pointed at the woman who was now looking intently through the camera at Johnny in front of the exterior scene. "She seems an expert at the film business."

Lily had come out of the changing room in a frilly pink dress and was wolfing down a pastry from the table. She heard Sid's last statement and snorted. "Much good it does her," Lily said. "She's DW's secretary, that's all. I heard she wants her name on the pictures as an assistant, but surely the actors should be more famous than secretaries."

Alice looked up and frowned across the room as if she had heard what Lily was saying, although she seemed too far away. She waved the actors back over and they made another tableau, this time in the girl's bedroom. Johnny stood outside the window and Lily just inside. Daisy looked on from the door.

"On my mark, action," Alice said loudly.

"He's coming," Daisy called with exaggerated alarm.

"My uncle will catch you," Lily said in a stage whisper.

"The count will catch you," Ryan corrected from outside the scene.

"Stop. Ryan, you're not in this scene," Alice said angrily.

"They must stick to the script," he protested. "The count is not her uncle, it's confusing."

"But no one will hear us anyway," Lily said.

"They'll read your lips. People can tell the difference between 'uncle' and 'count,' surely." Ryan's voice came again from behind the wall.

"Read our lips?" Lily was incredulous.

"No, he's right," Alice said, changing her mind. "The audience should be able to see what they are saying. Let's get this right before DW sees it. You know what he's like. He'll blow his top." She looked through the camera again and turned the crank. "The pink is much better, Lily, we'll stick with that. On my mark again. Action."

"The count will catch you," Lily said in her stage whisper.

"Come with me," Johnny said, holding his arms out to her through the window. "I'll protect you."

"Please don't tell my un— the count, Clara." Lily looked back at Daisy imploringly and sat on the windowsill, one leg raised, ready to climb out. "I'll die if I have to marry him."

"Hurry, my love," Johnny said, reaching up to her from outside.

"Stop," Alice called. "Johnny, we have to see your mouth as you say 'hurry.' Make sure you're looking at the camera."

"Got it, Alice," Johnny said.

"And Lily, learn your lines."

Lily looked at Alice and gave a nod to show she understood but didn't answer. Alice rehearsed the group in several scenes for another twenty minutes until she was satisfied.

"Okay, we're ahead of schedule." Alice sighed with relief. "I'll tell DW we can shoot the first scene this afternoon."

"Shoot?" Gus exclaimed. "There are firearms involved?" Alice looked up and saw our group watching the action. She frowned.

"Alice, these are my friends." Ryan stepped out from behind the false wall and began introducing each of us in turn. "Elena and Augusta, Molly and her daughter Bridie." Alice shook hands with a firm grip. I noticed there was little formality in the moving picture business. It was all first names.

"There are no firearms involved, Augusta," Alice said with a smile. "We have to crank this arm on the camera to make the film go through." She pointed to the handle that the cameraman had been turning. "It looks like a machine gun crank so we call it shooting a scene."

"Fascinating," Gus said. "You are a busy woman, I see. I also notice you are a follower of the rational dress movement, as is my friend Elena."

Alice looked at Sid's outfit as if wondering how rational or practical it was. "I'm up and down stairs and ladders all day," she said. "I'd wear britches if DW didn't insist on skirts. But divided skirts do the job. Are you interested in moving pictures?"

"Absolutely fascinated," Sid said. "I'm dying to learn more about how these cameras work."

"I am!" Bridie said eagerly. "My favorite is *The Great Train Robbery!*"

"Don't say that around here," Alice said with a laugh. "You'll be thrown out. That's an Edison film. He's our arch nemesis."

"He is?" Bridie asked uncertainly, unsure if she had done something wrong.

"I read in the paper that Biograph and Edison are in business together now," Gus said. Gus always seemed to know the current events. After becoming friends with a lady journalist last summer, she read *The New York Times* cover to cover each day and prided herself on being up on the news.

"Yes, that's true. We've gone from suing one another over our inventions to working together," Alice said. "But it doesn't mean that we're not trying to outdo each other. I suspect he has spies in the studio. I had just developed a way to make inanimate objects move, and the next week Edison films were doing it too."

"You made the teddy bears move?" Sid asked. "That was charming."

"It's done by splicing film together, you see. We have this machine and—" Alice broke off her explanation as a man came into the stage area.

"Cripes, there's DW. I have to go," she turned to us, "but if you want to see some picture magic, stick around. We make several moving pictures at once and we're about to film a water rescue in *The Shipwrecked Lovers.*"

"What, here in the studio?" I asked, surprised.

"Yes, Molly, is it?" She kept her head turned toward me as she began to walk away. "There's a tank under the floor." I was impressed that she had remembered everyone's name, including mine. She had seemed in control of every situation all morning. Holy Mother of God, I thought. A woman in control. There was hope for the world yet!

"Alice!" a man's voice bellowed from across the stage.

"Coming, DW," she called, gathering up her papers as she hurried over to a big and powerful man who had just entered.

❧ Six ❧

A s we watched, Alice crossed the stage floor to a tall man in a light brown suit and fedora. He towered over her. He had a firm jaw, a determined scowl on his face, and from his gestures he was the type who gave orders and expected to be obeyed. DW, she had called him. She listened to him for a moment and then nodded, then started directing crew members to attach a series of hooks and ropes to a section of the floor. They used pulleys to hoist a sixty-foot section of the floor twenty feet in the air, revealing a giant tank of water.

"Jesus, Mary, and Joseph!" I couldn't help exclaiming. What would they think of next? We went over to investigate, careful to stay out of the way of the crew. The water was clear and about four feet deep. Sid knelt down and tested it with her hand.

"My, but that's cold," she said. "I'm glad I don't have to get in there."

A crew member had gone over to a handle at one end of the tank and thrust it up and down several times causing the water in the tank to rise and fall. Sid jumped up before she got wet.

"It must be waves," Gus said excitedly. "To mimic the ocean. How clever!"

We moved back quickly as the crew began to position tall lights on stands all around the water. As they were turned on, one by one, bright light sparkled on the water and the corners of the stage were thrown into gloom.

"Watch out," someone yelled. There was a creaking, a whooshing noise as a backdrop descended behind the tank. It landed with a loud thud and two stagehands maneuvered it until the bottom touched the water in the tank. I had seen backdrops when I worked undercover in the theater. It was how they changed scenes quickly in plays. This one was a giant painted scene of a coastline with a lighthouse and green hills in the background, a stormy sky above, and whitecapped waves in the foreground. It looked remarkably realistic and made the pool suddenly appear to be much bigger than it really was.

Then two crew members carried out an enormous rock that must have been made out of something much lighter than stone, because they moved it easily across the room and set it in the tank. They then placed several lightweight folding canvas armchairs in front of the tank.

Crew members including, I noticed, another cameraman this time wheeled the cameras into position. The new cameraman was wearing an old shirt, sleeves rolled up, and red suspenders that contrasted with his dusty trousers. He adjusted his camera, nodded with satisfaction, then yelled, "Edward. Get over here. Take camera two. You focus on the rock. I'm getting the action shots of the guy diving in. Got it?"

"Right you are, Billy," Edward said, hurrying forward.

At that moment an actress and actor came out of the dressing room in costume. The actress was petite with glossy brown hair in a cascade of ringlets. She wore a tea dress that had a torn sleeve. The actor was handsome but with more delicate bone structure, unlike the man who had played the prizefighter. As he stepped from the deep shadows into the spotlight I recognized him: Cecil Armitage, the man we had met at Sid and Gus's house on Sunday. They both wore exaggerated stage makeup. The actress's eyes were lined with kohl and her lips were a bright red.

"Jeez, it's freezing," the actress exclaimed as she was assisted into the water. "I hope we're not going to be in here long, DW?"

"Not if you do it right the first time, honey," he replied.

She waded over to the rock and clung to it. The actor climbed in the other end of the tank with some cursing at the coldness.

"That's my friend Cecil," Ryan said softly, pride in his voice. "You met him on Sunday. Such a nice chap. Well-built, isn't he? Used to be a ballet dancer."

A crew member started pumping the handle we had seen before, making the surface of the water splash up the rock, which caused a shriek from the actress. Finally, DW himself sat in a chair and took up a giant megaphone.

"Clear the set," he yelled. Then, without warning, he leaped to his feet, staring into the gloom beyond the lights. "What damned fool just opened a door?" Then I saw his expression change to one of shock.

"We weren't expecting you today, boss," he said, going to meet a man and woman who had just entered.

"I have to keep you on your toes, DW," the man replied with a hearty laugh as he slapped the director on the shoulder. "Actually, we had to come into the city on business and I'd told Fanny about the new water tank. She was anxious to see it in action. I must say it looks pretty darned good. I bet Edison will be green with envy."

"What's the betting he'll rush to build one of his own?" The woman had her arm through the man's and was looking at the water tank intently. "Bigger and better." She was petite and stylishly dressed. Her words were delivered in a crisp upper-class English accent.

"Rome wasn't built in a day," the big man said. "It will take him a while to catch up with us this time." He was quite portly, with chubby cheeks, a ginger mustache, and red-blond hair. He was wearing a tweed suit, an impressive gold watch chain stretched across his yellow waistcoat.

"That's Harry Martin," Ryan whispered to us. "He owns the studio. He seems like a nice fellow. Not at all standoffish."

"And who's the woman with him, his wife?" Sid asked. I looked more closely at the woman who was looking up at Harry fondly.

"No, I believe that's the widow of Andrew Prince," he said. "Fanny Prince. Her husband was in the picture business too. She's one of the investors in my picture. I think she came on board when she heard that a playwright of my stature was involved." He said the last with his usual dramatic flair.

Alice glanced back at us and put her finger to her lips. We moved quickly to the back of the room, standing in the shadows. I hoped the bigwigs hadn't noticed us. I didn't want DW to turn around and yell at us to get out of the room. Luckily, he had been intent on making the studio owner welcome.

"Here, take my chair," he said, pulling up the canvas armchair for Mrs. Prince. "Alice, get over here. Bring them a coffee or whatever they want."

"I was just setting up the shot sequence," she said, annoyance showing on her face.

"Oh no, we're just fine," Mrs. Prince said hurriedly. "We can't wait to watch the filming."

"And we're freezing to death in here," the actress called.

"All the more realistic, honey." DW leaned down toward her.

"Good costume, my dear," Harry Martin said. "I like the way it clings to her figure now it's wet. Delightfully revealing. What's your name, girlie?"

"It's Mary, sir," she said. "Mary Pickford."

"Well, Mary, you're quite a looker," he said. "Let's see if you can act." He turned back to DW. "Come on, then, get on with it. Can't you see the poor girl is freezing?"

DW picked up the megaphone.

"Quiet on the set," his voice boomed out, unnaturally loud. A man with a slate stood in front of the cameras. Numbers were written on it in chalk: Scene 12, Take 1.

"Lights," DW yelled. The overhead lights went out and the lights that had been placed around the tank were turned on.

"Camera," he said, and the two cameramen began cranking the handles of the cameras. It was silent on the stage except for the whirring sound.

"Action!" DW shouted. The man with the slate stepped back as the cameras focused on the woman in the water, now clinging to the rock. The wave machine started to churn. Suddenly there was a shout of alarm. One of the big lights around the pool had started to topple. A stagehand leaped forward and grabbed it before it could hit the water.

"Boy, that was close," he commented as he righted it. His face was white with shock.

"What are you trying to do, kill your stars?" Cecil shouted. He also looked stunned.

"It's okay. I got it. No harm done," the stagehand called as he set the light back into place with the help of one of his fellows. "I don't know how that happened."

"Not again!" Alice stalked over to where two electricians were now checking the cables. "Can't we ever get this right the first time, people? No more crossed cables!" When everything was to her satisfaction, she moved back to DW. "We're good to go again now, sir."

"Let's get it right this time." DW picked up his megaphone. "No more accidents, okay? I've had enough of accidents in this studio. I'll fire the next person who doesn't do his job properly. Got that?"

"Accidents?" Fanny Prince turned to Harry Martin. "Have there been accidents?"

He patted her hand. "Only what you'd expect on a moving picture set, my dear. Nothing for you to worry about."

DW turned to give them a warning look.

"Action!" he shouted. The waves splashed. Mary clung to her rock.

"Stay out of the shot, Cecil. Now, Mary, look more desperate, slip down the rock. Now yell 'Help!' Let's see your lips say 'Help.'"

The actors followed his instructions. The young actress looked quite desperate. If I hadn't known that she could easily stand in the tank I would have believed she was slipping to her death.

"Now, Cecil, swim into the shot," DW said. The man swam to the rock, moving with easy and graceful strokes, then raised his head and looked around. "Say, 'Don't worry, I'll save you.'" Cecil repeated the words. "Now, Mary, you faint, and Cecil, pull her out." The young actress fainted and slipped into the water. "Cameras, slow the crank." The cameramen slowed their speed of turning. Cecil wrapped his arms around her and pulled her toward the side of the tank.

"Cut!" DW called. "Alice!"

"Yes, boss?" Alice was there by his side.

"I think we got it, take this back and take a look at it. Decide which camera angle to use."

"You got it, DW." She nodded and conferred with the cameramen. The two actors pulled themselves up out of the tank and toweled off, shivering as they chatted with one another.

"Right, let's get back to rehearsals," DW said. "We're doing O'Hare's story about the evil count in studio two. Do you want to come and watch, Mr. Martin?"

"No, I think we've seen enough for one day," Harry Martin said. "I'm more concerned that this delectable creature doesn't catch pneumonia." He went over to Mary and put an arm around her shoulder. "Let's walk you to your dressing room, my dear."

"If walking's all he's going to do," a voice muttered behind us.

"He's got Mrs. Prince with him. He'll have to behave himself," another voice answered.

But Fanny Prince didn't follow him immediately. She went over to the camera that Billy was using and examined it closely. "I like this lens modification," she said, careful not to touch the glass as she peered at it. "And it looks like the shutter speed can be increased and decreased?"

"Yes." Billy gave a genuine smile. "It's affected by the rate of the crank. When we want a scene to play back more quickly, we just crank more slowly and it will appear that the action is faster when the film is played back."

"Fascinating." She looked up at him and smiled. "I've been really impressed with your work, Billy. Each picture seems to get better."

Billy now smiled warmly. "I didn't realize you were so interested in the behind-the-scenes work. You know a lot about film cameras, Mrs. Prince," he said.

"Well, my father-in-law invented the first one. The first film ever is of my husband as a little boy playing in his garden in Kent. That's in England."

"Really?" Billy seemed both astonished and doubtful. "I thought Biograph and Edison were fighting it out over whose camera was the first one."

"Well, Biograph's was based on my father-in-law's camera. Harry and I are trying to prove that in court."

"I think I heard of your husband. He and the Martins were going to run the studio together, weren't they?" Billy said, focusing on Mrs. Prince, oblivious of the crew walking by with props and dragging ropes and cables across the stage floor.

"Yes." A wistful look came over her face. "A long time ago now. We had such dreams for the pictures we would make."

Billy grinned. "I hope we're doing Mr. Prince proud."

She put a delicate hand on his shoulder. "You are. I just wish Mr. Prince was here to see it."

Alice called to Billy, "Can you move over to studio two so I can get some light levels?"

"Sure, Alice," Billy said to her and turned back to Fanny Prince. "Nice talking to you, Mrs. Prince." As he turned away Alice clapped her hands.

"Okay, everyone, back to studio two. Let's run through the scene where the count comes in and catches them."

Lily jumped up from where she had been sitting watching the action from the other side of the room. She came toward us and almost collided with Harry Martin, who was heading toward Mrs. Prince. "Excuse me, Mr. Martin," she said loudly as she brushed past him. He turned his head to look at her. She smiled and he winked.

We followed Alice across the room. I would have loved to stay and see Ryan act out his scene, but I was becoming too aware of my need to get back to Mary Kate. I turned to Bridie. "Darling, we will have to go soon. I need to get home to feed the baby."

"Mama, can't I stay?" she asked. "I want to see Mr. O'Hare 'shoot' his scene." She paused over the word "shoot," carefully using the correct terminology.

"Molly, we'll bring Bridie home if you need to leave." Sid had overheard, and she jumped in to support Bridie, as usual. "We simply can't tear ourselves away. It's so fascinating that we absolutely must stay. And we can get you a taxi home, so you won't have to walk by yourself. But why don't you stay? I'm sure your maid can feed the little one."

I tried not to let my feelings show on my face. She and Gus were my greatest confidants but neither of them had ever had a child.

They had no idea what it was like to have to keep to a child's schedule, and the uncomfortable feeling in my own breasts if I left it too long. Their whole lives had been about pleasing themselves. I loved them dearly but there were times like this when I wanted to give them a good shaking. Of course, I didn't.

"The baby needs me." I gave them a sweet smile. "I don't like to have Aileen give her a bottle unless it is absolutely necessary."

"If you must, dear Molly." Gus put a comforting hand on my shoulder. "You are such a good mother to those children. I hope they'll grow up to appreciate it. And don't worry about Bridie. We'll see she comes to no harm."

Thus reassured, I turned down their offer of a taxicab and walked the few blocks back to Patchin Place. I still felt rather uneasy about leaving Bridie. I knew Sid and Gus would keep an eye on her, but that toppling lamp had shown me that studios could be dangerous places.

It might have been the funeral or Daniel's absence but the feeling of danger still lingered. A prickling in my shoulder blades made me turn. Had someone just ducked into the shadow of that building? I paused as I turned into Patchin Place. There were pedestrians on the street but none of them were looking my way. Still, I couldn't shake the feeling that I had been followed on my way home.

I arrived home just in time.

Mary Kate took one look at me and let out a big yell.

"All right, all right," I said, hurriedly unbuttoning the top of my two-piece and laying it over the back of a chair. "I get the message, you impatient child. We'll eat right away."

I took the baby and settled her on my lap, where she started nursing as if she hadn't been fed in months, then fell asleep in my arms. I sat there, not wanting to disturb her, enjoying watching my son, his face a picture of concentration as he put one block on top of another.

"It's going to be the biggest skyscraper in the world," he said. "Bigger than all the skyscrapers in New York."

"Good for you," I said. "Only be careful, you're about to defy gravity . . ." As I finished speaking the tower tottered then crashed to the ground, scattering blocks over the floor.

"Oh oh," he said. "Now I have to start all over again."

I carried the baby up to her crib and laid her down, humming one of the old Irish songs that Aileen always sang to her and Liam. I was actually feeling sleepy myself after being up so early. So I went through to the parlor and put my feet up on the sofa.

I don't know how long I drifted off, but I was awoken by a loud shout. I sat up hurriedly, my heart thumping in my chest.

"Mama? Where are you?" The voice was Bridie's, not Liam's.

"In the front parlor," I called back. "What's wrong?"

She burst in through the door, her eyes positively sparkling with excitement. "You'll never guess in a million years what's just happened to me!"

❧ Seven ❧

W hat is it?" I asked, my fear giving way to amusement at
Bridie's manner. "What's the good news?"
"I'm going to be an actress in Ryan's picture. I'm tak-
ing Lily's part."

This is what comes of leaving her with Sid and Gus, was my first thought.
What I said was, "The devil you are, Bridie Sullivan."

Her face fell. "I thought you'd be as excited as I am. I'm going to
be an actress in a picture show. What's wrong with that?"

"How can you be an actress?" I stood up but before I could go on,
there was a knock on the door.

"That will be the ladies." Bridie darted toward the door, obviously feeling that reinforcements had arrived. "They were just going
to take their coats off and come over."

"Did you hear the news?" Gus said before she was even fully into
the parlor. "Bridie's going to be a star."

Sid was right behind her. "You have to hear all about it, Molly!"

Three faces looked at me eagerly. I sighed. It was clear that I
was raising Bridie to be more like my adventurous friends than the
proper young lady my mother-in-law Sullivan would hope for. That
thought gave me pause. I liked my friends much better than Daniel's

mother. I was sure that she would say that acting was not a proper career, but I had been on the stage myself and I liked a lot of the people in the theater.

"Tell me about it." I sat and motioned for the three of them to do the same. "I'm not making any promises," I continued as Bridie let out an exclamation of glee, "but I want to hear."

"Well," Sid began, "they were acting out—"

"You mean *shooting*," Bridie interrupted.

"Yes, *shooting* the scene that we watched earlier," Sid said. "And that actress—"

"Lily something," Gus put in, and Sid frowned at her.

"Am I telling it or you?"

"Sorry, my dear, go on."

"Lily couldn't remember her lines. She kept talking about her uncle instead of the count. And she didn't like being told what to do."

"DW was furious. Alice said that every time we stop a scene we waste two cents a foot on the film," Bridie said as soon as Sid stopped for breath.

"And that silly girl argued with the director instead of concentrating on her lines," Gus said. "She said the scene made no sense, which made Ryan angry. He stopped feeding her the lines from offstage—he had been trying to be helpful—and she got even worse."

"Then DW said that any girl off the street could do it better than Lily." Bridie's eyes were shining at the memory. "He turned around and pointed right at me. I jumped out of my skin!" She gave a little jump to illustrate the memory. "He said, 'You, girl, do you know the lines?' And of course I did. I had heard them about twenty times already, so I said, 'Yes, sir.' And he said, 'Come and show me.' So, I went up and said them and . . ." At that point Bridie blushed, not wanting to be boastful.

"And she was brilliant," Sid finished for her. "DW said, 'You do it, girl,' and they shot the scene right there."

"So, you see, I have to do the picture," Bridie pleaded, "because I'm already in that scene and film costs two cents a foot and that's an awful lot of waste according to Alice." She was so serious I had to stifle a laugh.

"But Bridie," I said, "lots of girls of your age are out earning but you've chosen to go to school. Your education is important."

"I know," she said. "And I've been thinking about it all the way home. The picture will be finished in a few days, so I won't miss any school. And I'll make ten whole dollars so I can help you and Papa. You're always saying that with bread at eight cents a loaf, how can a body afford to eat. Think of how much bread we can eat for ten dollars!"

I had been known to mutter that to myself as I saw the ridiculous price of bread these days. "Your papa makes a good wage and we've plenty to eat," I reassured her, "without you going out to earn. So, if that is the only reason . . ."

"It's not," she put in hurriedly. "There are so many reasons. Think what the girls at school will say! And this could be a whole career for me. You're always saying that women should have careers and not just wait to start their lives until they get married."

"I was thinking more of a respectable career like a journalist or a scientist."

"But you like Ryan. Is he not respectable?"

That was a hard one to answer truthfully, especially to an innocent girl.

"And," Bridie went on, "you keep reminding me that I'm not a debutant like Blanche. I'm going to have to make a living. Why shouldn't I try to see if I like acting?"

I was used to a Bridie who cried or pouted when she couldn't get her own way, but this Bridie was making logical sense. There was one more objection.

"You'll need to be chaperoned," I said, "and I can't be there the whole time. Your brother and sister need me."

"We'll do it," Gus spoke up immediately. "It would give us an excuse to watch the making of a picture. I have to say we are fascinated!"

"We are thinking of investing in a moving picture camera ourselves," Sid said. "Perhaps we could capture life as it is in Greenwich Village."

"So, can I, Mama? Please?" All three of them looked at me pleadingly.

"It will only be in your holidays?" I asked.

"Yes."

"And you will be chaperoned the whole time?"

"Yes." Sid and Gus nodded.

"And you'll put half the money in a savings account."

"And the other half can go toward school outings that we can't really afford. You know how I wanted to go with the school to Boston, but you said it cost too much."

I gave a cautious nod. She was gazing at me, her eyes pleading with me.

I gave a short sigh. "Well, I don't suppose it can do any harm if we keep an eye on you and you don't miss your schooling."

I held out my hand and she took it. I gave a firm shake.

"Deal."

The next morning Bridie and I left the house by 7:30 A.M. The same man was at his post in the foyer of the brownstone.

"Are you guests of Mr. O'Hare again?" he said, checking the list for our names.

"I'm going to be acting today in one of the films," Bridie said proudly before I could answer. "DW said so. I'm Bridie."

"Oh yes, your name is here, Bridie Sullivan. And this is?" He searched for my name.

"I'm her mother, Molly Sullivan," I said. "I'll be her chaperone, and I'd like you to also put Miss Elena Goldfarb and Miss Augusta Walcott on the list. They will be trading places with me later." Although Sid and Gus had promised to chaperone, I knew that asking them to accompany Bridie to a rehearsal that started at 8:00 A.M. was stretching their generosity. The man carefully wrote out their names on the list.

"I'll double-check this with Alice but I'm sure it's okay. Go on in, miss," he said to Bridie. As she went through the door, he touched my arm to detain me.

"A word, Mrs. Sullivan." I turned to him. His tone was low and confidential. "I'm glad to see you come with your daughter. I have a daughter myself and I think you are wise to come as a chaperone."

"Bridie is just fourteen," I said. "I wouldn't let her go anywhere unchaperoned."

"I've seen younger girls in here by themselves," he said in a low voice, "and you'll never hear me say anything against DW or the studio, but make sure someone keeps an eye on your daughter."

"Thank you, I will," I said, now feeling slightly uneasy, "and you'll make sure Miss Elena and Miss Augusta can be admitted later today."

"Don't worry about it," he said. I went through the door into the stage. There was no one on the stage floor and no electric lighting was on yet. It felt eerie to hear our footsteps echo in the large space. As we made our way across it, I hoped very much we didn't stumble into an unseen water tank!

"Did someone tell you where to come to this morning?" I asked Bridie.

"No, just the studio." She sounded a little scared.

"Well, we have seen actors coming out of this back room," I started to make my way over to a half-open door, "so I am guessing it may be the dressing room."

"That's right! I wonder if I can wear that pretty dress that Lily had on yesterday?" Bridie was right behind me. "She seemed ever so angry. I hope she didn't tear it or anything."

"She didn't, thank goodness." A voice from out of the darkness made me jump. I turned quickly to see Alice coming toward us.

"Lily knew it would come out of her paycheck if she did anything to that costume." Alice looked at Bridie appraisingly. "But let's get you into the dressing room. I think your figure is a little trimmer than hers. I might have one I like better on you. Just follow me."

We followed through the door in the back of the studio and into a confusing warren of rooms. We passed a costume shop where one lady was sewing and another pinning flowers onto a hat. We entered a prop room. The rock from the ocean rescue scene was sitting to one side. There were shelves lined with plates and cups that ranged from golden goblets to a simple wooden cup. There were playing cards, pairs of glasses, baskets, several telephones, pipes, books, candles, and lamps. There were neatly hung table-cloths, wall hangings. There was a stand of different walking canes. Firearms of various types were hung on one wall. A chest was open to reveal glittering pirate gold. There was enough in the room to decorate a castle or a hovel, all organized by item. It was all quite fascinating, and I'd have liked to linger, but Alice strode out ahead of us, a lady on a mission.

As we came out of the prop room, we crossed a hall and into a narrow room with racks of dresses and suits. The word WARDROBE was printed on the door. Alice examined the racks, shuffling the dresses until she found one she liked.

"Here, try this one on." She handed the dress to Bridie and motioned her to the side of the room that had privacy screens set up for changing. "And we'll go over that scene you did yesterday."

"I thought we already shot that?" Bridie was surprised. She disappeared behind the first screen.

"In your street clothes?" Alice laughed. "That was DW being dramatic, and I presume he wanted to teach Lily a lesson. But we did get you on film. He had me check and see that you look good on camera. Not everyone does."

"Do I?" Bridie's face poked out from around the screen.

"No, you're terrible, that's why I'm getting you dressed for a part in the picture," Alice said sarcastically.

"I want to meet DW before Bridie begins work on the film," I put in, feeling that this morning was getting away from me. "We're only allowing her to do it on the condition that she is chaperoned and that the picture is finished by the time she starts school again on Monday."

"We should be done by Friday, so no problem there," Alice said. She looked up from a clipboard she was carrying. "DW won't care two figs if she is chaperoned or not as long as you don't get in the way of the picture." She saw the anxiety on my face and her expression softened slightly. "But I'll make sure she's taken care of."

"I've been on the stage myself," I said, trying to find a point of connection.

"So you know what the business can be like." She put her hand on my arm briefly. "I'll keep an eye on her."

Then Bridie emerged from behind the screen. I gave a little gasp. She really did look beautiful in the light taffeta dress. Bows accentuated the sleeves and drew in her waist.

"Look, Mama!" She twirled around.

"Okay, no time for chitchat." Alice was all business. "Bridie, we'll have Daisy show you how to put on your pancake makeup and do your eyes and lips. And Mrs. Sullivan, if you want to catch DW, he's in his office at the very end of the hall." Bridie followed her obediently. I watched them hurry off, wondering exactly how I could keep an eye on my daughter if she was constantly being whisked away like this. I took note of the room they entered, then stepped out into the hall. It stretched back past a door with CUTTING ROOM on it, then another that was unmarked. A bronze plate with DAVID W. GRIFFITH engraved on it was mounted on the last door before the hall opened into a small but grand foyer. *This must be the business entrance on Fifth Avenue*, I thought, looking at the decorative oak door to the outside and ascending spiral staircase. At the foot of the staircase was a small desk with an appointment book lying open on it. A man was sitting behind it.

"Can I help you?" He looked up, frowning, as I came into the foyer.

"I need to speak to DW," I said.

"Have you signed in?" He motioned to the fountain pen beside the book. "Are you on the list?"

I was getting annoyed now. He had just seen me walk in from the hallway. How did he think I had entered the studio?

But all I said was, "Yes, at the other entrance."

"Very well, that's his office there." He gestured to the first office on the right.

I went back to it and knocked.

"Come." DW was sitting at a large mahogany desk covered with papers. "Yes?" he said, frowning as well, as he saw me.

"Mr. Griffith, I'm Molly Sullivan, Bridie Sullivan's mother." He looked none the wiser. "The young girl you hired to work on Ryan O'Hare's picture," I went on.

"Oh, yes." He looked back at his papers, dismissing me. "My

secretary handles hiring matters. She can tell you the terms of the engagement."

"Alice said I might find you in here," I said, standing my ground.

"Did she," he said, his heavy eyebrows lowered in a frown. "I'll have to talk to her about that. Okay, well, you're talking to me. Out with it."

"I'm not sure you are aware that my daughter is only fourteen years old. Her father and I have agreed to allow her to act in a picture, but I wanted you to know that she is from a respectable home, and she will be chaperoned while she is working."

"I let Alice handle all of that." DW turned back to his papers. "Goodbye, Mrs. Sullivan, I'm a busy man." He dismissed me with a wave of the hand.

I refused to be dismissed. "Miss Augusta Walcott of the Boston Walcotts will be one of the chaperones," I said smoothly. "And my husband, Captain Sullivan of the New York Police Department, will expect to hear from me that she is being treated well." DW finally looked up then. Did I see a flicker of alarm in his eyes? "He is currently in Washington consulting with the Secret Service, or he would be here himself."

"Very well, Mrs. Sullivan." DW's manner had changed. He stood up. "We love our boys in blue," he said heartily, "big contributors to the benevolence fund, you know." He came around the desk and shook my hand, taking my hand in both of his. "I'll take care of little Birdie—"

"Bridie," I corrected.

"Bridie, like my own daughter." He patted my hand. "Not to worry, mother." I heard steps clattering down the metal staircase. A chubby face with a ginger mustache poked around the door. "Are you in, DW?" DW dropped my hand and looked around. Harry Martin entered. He had on a bow tie and a bowler hat. His silk waistcoat was considerably strained by his large stomach.

"Absolutely, Harry, come on in." DW's geniality was in complete contrast to his earlier rudeness. "This is Mrs. Sullivan. Her young daughter, Bridie, is going to be in the picture we were rehearsing yesterday. Mrs. Sullivan, this is Mr. Martin, the head of the studio." I held out my hand.

"I saw you yesterday in the studio, but we weren't introduced," I said. Instead of shaking my hand he took it, brought it to his lips, and kissed it.

"A pleasure to meet such a beautiful woman. Mr. Sullivan is a lucky man." His boyish smile made his words seem charming rather than boorish.

"It's Captain Sullivan of the NYPD," DW put in. "Mrs. Sullivan is here to make sure we take good care of her daughter." He gave Harry a meaningful look.

"Of course we will." Harry let go of my hand. "I thought we had that film cast?"

"I had to let Lily go." DW's eyes slid away from Harry and looked fixedly at a paper on his desk.

"Oh dear, why was that?" Harry pulled a wry face. "I liked Lily. Spunky, quite a looker, and uh, fun-loving. I thought she'd go places."

"Well, that's as may be, but I won't have actresses arguing with me. I must have creative control." DW did look at Harry now, a frown on his face. His temper seemed to simmer just under the surface.

"Might not have been a wise move, DW." Harry put a big, meaty hand on the director's shoulder. "Lily is Italian, you know. They have strange ideas on revenge."

"In that case they also take good care of their young women," DW countered. For a long moment the two men glared at each other. I felt awkward now, standing between them.

"I'll go back to my daughter, then." I nodded to DW. "Nice to meet you, Mr. Martin. Mr. Griffith."

"At your service, Mrs. Sullivan." Harry Martin raised his bowler hat to me, almost a caricature of an old-fashioned gentleman, even though he couldn't have been more than thirty-five. As I went back down the hall toward Bridie, I heard DW's voice.

"Let's stay away from the Sullivans, mother and daughter, Harry. The last thing we need is the police coming down here."

❧ Eight ❧

As I looked for the makeup room, I thought, *Good*. I had made sure they would not take me lightly. I felt a little guilty that I had used Daniel's rank when he was not even yet aware that Bridie was in a moving picture. We had decided to surprise him since he wouldn't be home until she was back at school anyway. *Would he really approve?* an annoying small voice in the back of my head wondered. I had often gone off on my own harebrained adventures and Daniel had sometimes been at his wit's end with me. *It will be a happy surprise*, I convinced myself, *and an adventure for Bridie. Besides, what could go wrong if we are there to keep an eye on her?*

I found Bridie sitting on a stool at a long oilcloth-covered table in a dressing room facing mirrors that covered the back wall. Her hair had been curled in neat ringlets. Her lovely costume was covered around the shoulders in a white cloth, and she was concentrating hard as she applied bright red lipstick, not too successfully. Daisy was beside her doing the same. There were bright electric lights in this room and their glare made me blink. Bridie's face was covered with chalky white pancake makeup highlighted with green contours.

"Is it just this lighting or do you have green makeup on your face?" I wondered if she had misunderstood Alice's instructions somehow. But then Daisy turned, and I could see that her face was similarly highlighted.

"Good morning, Mrs. Sullivan." She smacked her lips together to set the lipstick and checked her teeth for red marks. "We're meant to look like ghouls," she said, grinning. "Alice says that green shows up much better than red on camera."

"Alice seems to be a remarkably capable woman," I remarked.

"My ears are burning," Alice said as she came into the room. "That's very nice of you, Mrs. Sullivan." She pulled open a drawer and started looking through neatly lined-up tubes and sticks of makeup.

"Please call me Molly." I smiled at her. "I must say it's grand to see women succeeding at their profession. It does my heart good."

"Are you a professional woman, Molly?" Alice grabbed a tube out, opened it, and squirted some darker green on a metal palette sitting on the table. She dabbed experimentally at it with a nearby makeup brush.

"She was a detective," Bridie piped up proudly. "She solved murder cases."

"Really?" Alice stopped what she was doing and looked at me as if truly seeing me for the first time.

"I did have my own detective agency," I said, somehow feeling that I wanted to impress this woman. "Generally I was hired to find missing people or prove someone's innocence. But unfortunately, I have come across some murders."

"Which you solved." Bridie had not put on her lipstick as expertly, having never worn makeup before.

"That's very impressive, Molly," Alice said, still looking at me intently. "I have found we women have to work twice as hard to be accepted into a profession. I come up with the creative ideas and I'm down on the studio list as a secretary. But I put up with it because I love this new medium so much."

"Actresses certainly don't get the same respect that actors do," Daisy put in. "And we have to put up with directors and executives. And not only yelling at us, if you know what I mean."

"It certainly was true that no one took me very seriously," I said, remembering what I had gone through in those early days. "But there are advantages as well. A woman can sometimes go places that a man can't." I turned Bridie round to face me. "Here, I think you better let me help." I took a cloth and wiped off the lipstick where Bridie had smudged it above her lip. Then I dabbed some makeup on to make a new base and reapplied the lipstick. "For instance, the time I went undercover in the theater. It's where I learned to do makeup." I smiled in satisfaction. "There, that's better."

"Here, Molly, a new idea of mine." Alice handed me the palette with the darker green. "Can you do the brow and down the nose in this?" I took it and applied it as Alice directed.

"Thanks, Mama." Bridie studied herself in the mirror. "I look like Frankenstein's monster."

Alice laughed. "We'll see what that does on camera today. I think it will bring out your pretty features." She turned to me. "You're quite good at that. I'm going to talk to DW about hiring someone to do makeup full time. If you're interested, let me know."

Now I was the one who laughed. "I have a little baby at home and a five-year-old. I won't be working anytime soon. But I'm happy to help with Bridie's makeup when I bring her in the mornings."

"That is one reason I have never wanted to marry or have children," Alice said, already gathering up her papers again. "What if my husband forbade me from working? I wake up every day excited about what we can accomplish here. I'd die if I couldn't do it anymore."

"I do miss my detective work," I said. "But I love having my little darlings at home." An alarm sounded somewhere in the studio.

"Time we were on the set." Alice jumped into action. "Daisy, see if Ryan and Johnny are ready, will you?"

I spent a very pleasant hour watching the four of them rehearse a scene in the girl's bedroom. Bridie confided in the maid that she would never marry the count. Johnny appeared at the window. Bridie climbed out to be with him. Alice yelled, "Cut!" and stopped the action.

"At this point we will have you appear in the top window of the house," Alice was saying as I felt a tap on my shoulder.

"How is our darling girl doing?" Gus whispered as she came to stand beside me. "Taking the stage by storm?" I was amused to see that she was wearing her divided skirt and a cotton blouse that looked suspiciously like a man's shirt. She obviously had been impressed with Alice and was dressing the part of the woman film director today. She even had a pencil stuck into her hair and a small notebook with her.

"She seems to be taking to it well." I gave her an affectionate hug. "Thank you so much for agreeing to chaperone. There is no way I could be here the whole time." I looked around to make sure no one could hear us. "And no way I would leave her unchaperoned. I've already heard things that make me think the men here take liberties."

"Have no fears," she said breezily. "I shall watch over her like a mother hawk." I raised my eyebrows in query. "That's like a mother hen but much fiercer."

I laughed, looking around. "Where's Sid?"

"You'll never guess." Gus chuckled. "Sid, my dear, is scouring the city to see where we might find a film camera." She went on, "She's absolutely enraptured with it and says we won't have a better opportunity to learn how to use it."

"Is that something anyone can just buy?" I was surprised.

"As you can imagine, it is a bit of a specialty item," she said. "But Sid is determined to find one. We have seen one advertised called a Kinora. She asked me to get a peek at what the cameramen here are using."

"Shall I wait with you until she arrives?" I asked, mostly out of politeness. I was beginning to feel that I should be getting home.

"Not at all, I'm perfectly happy to be here." Her gaze drifted over to Alice, who was consulting with Billy the cameraman in low tones. "I am dying to see how they put the whole film together. I wonder if Alice will let me back into the editing room. I understand that they cut the film up and glue it back together in the sequence they want. It's fascinating!" She opened her notebook and pulled the pencil out of her hair, ready to take notes.

It was a sunny but chilly walk home. Really the April weather was so changeable. The temperature must have dropped all of twenty degrees in a couple of hours. The wind coming off the Hudson was now bitter, and I did up the top button of my costume. I shivered as a cloud passed over the sun. I couldn't help thinking of my recent feeling that someone was following me. Coming from the busy cheerful studio, my fears seemed ridiculous. But Daniel and I had both lived in a dangerous world. Were his investigations somehow putting our family in danger? I told myself not to be overly dramatic. I couldn't suspect danger every time I walked the streets of my own city.

As I fed the baby, with Liam playing nearby, I found myself worrying a bit more about Bridie. Had I been reckless to let her do this? I had left her in a place where lights toppled over and where gentlemen clearly saw young actresses as their playthings. *Gus is with her,* I thought, then remembered that my friends, however much I adored them, could be easily distracted. If someone was demonstrating to Gus how to use the camera or took her off to show her the cutting room, would she realize that Bridie was then alone? I couldn't seem to settle to a peaceful afternoon and found myself rushing back an hour before I had intended, walking so quickly that I arrived somewhat out of breath.

The doorman recognized me this time and waved me through, but when I entered the large stage room, I found it deserted. The panels in the roof were closed and the room looked dark and eerie. Strange thudding came from above my head.

"Excuse me," I asked a man who was walking through with a basket, "but where have the actors gone?"

"They're up there." He indicated the ceiling with a jerk of his head.

"Where?" I remembered the staircase I had seen in the fancy entrance.

"The roof," he said, then seeing I didn't understand he elaborated. "They shoot outdoor scenes up there for the light. There's a stairway just through that door."

"Thank you," I said and went through the door he had indicated. A somewhat rickety set of wooden stairs led up. There were no gas lamps or electric lights in the stairwell, and I groped my way up to a hallway on the second floor. I easily found my way from there because light streamed in from an open door above. A steep metal stair wound up to the door.

At first, I couldn't see anything as I came out into the bright light of afternoon. As my eyes adjusted I made out a flat roof with people on it. DW was seated in his director's chair not far from me and in front of him were Billy and Edward, both with their cameras. Luckily, they were looking the other way and I had not interrupted anything. They were facing a wall that looked like the outside of a two-story house with stairs up to the front door. But behind it was nothing but a few feet of roof and the open air. I recognized it as the outside of the mansion in Ryan's previous picture. The top window was identical to the window in the girl's bedroom downstairs.

Bridie's face appeared high in the window. Johnny was clinging to the vines just below her. I couldn't quite catch the lines she was saying but I could hear DW through the megaphone. "Okay Johnny, climb down now. Lean out more, sweetheart, we have to see your whole face. Look scared. You're saying it's too high. You can't climb down. Camera one, focus on Johnny. Johnny, tell her to climb down. Camera two, on the girl. Climb out, girl." Bridie put one leg out of the window. "Okay. Pause here to reset the cameras. Everyone freeze."

I spotted Sid and Gus standing together a little to one side and slipped over to them.

"She's absolutely wonderful, Molly," Gus said. "A born actress. Did you see how scared she looked when he wanted her to climb out of the window? Hearts will melt across the country."

"And I've had a fantastic day," Sid said. "I've found a shop where they can order a moving picture camera for me. It will cost the earth, apparently, but it's for a good cause, isn't it? We can make suffrage propaganda pictures and show them to every women's club in America. We can—"

"Quiet on the set!" DW spun around and glared in our direction.

"It's not as if they record the sound," Sid said, giving him a cold stare.

"We don't want to get thrown out or nobody will be watching Bridie," I reminded her.

"Action." The sound of DW's magnified voice made me turn back to look up at the scene. I caught the swirl of pink taffeta from Bridie's dress as I saw her fall out of the high window and land on the roof with a great thud. I screamed.

"Holy Mother of God!" I rushed over to the set.

"Stop, stop." DW's voice sounded annoyed rather than concerned.

My heart was thumping crazily. I was sure I would find Bridie terribly wounded at the base of the wall. I gazed down at the figure in the taffeta dress. It took me a moment to realize I was looking at a dummy, a mannequin with hair and clothes identical to Bridie's.

"Mama, what's wrong?" Bridie crawled out from behind the false house front.

"Get that woman out of the scene," DW barked. His voice had gone from annoyance to rage. "Keep rolling, Billy, we'll cut it later." I let Alice pull me back out of the shot. Johnny scooped Bridie up into his arms. That didn't look entirely appropriate to me. I almost rushed back into the scene, but Sid was beside me now.

"It's okay," she said, pulling me back even farther behind the cameras. "They've rehearsed this a hundred times, no harm comes to Bridie. Just watch."

"Quiet!" DW glared round at us. "Action."

Johnny suddenly staggered under Bridie's weight, almost collapsing but just retaining his balance. He set her on her feet.

"And now the count." Ryan's face appeared in the window at DW's words. He shook his fist at Johnny.

"You won't get away with this," he said in the ringing tones of a theater lead.

"Great, O'Hare. Now, kids, run off." Johnny and Bridie held hands and ran from the house front.

"And stop camera, that's good." There was a general sigh of relief from all those assembled.

Bridie came over to me. "What's wrong, Mama? Why did you run into the shot?"

"I thought that was you falling from the window." My heart was still beating rapidly.

"No, silly!" She giggled. "They film me in the window and then the dummy falling, and then me in Johnny's arms." The way she blushed when she said Johnny's name made me decide to remind Sid and Gus about being vigilant at all times.

✤ Nine ✤

"How was I supposed to know that it was a mannequin?" I asked in annoyance as I sat with Bridie and Ryan on the way home. Ryan had insisted that he was coming down Sixth Avenue and passing Patchin Place on his way and would have the cab drop us home.

"My dear, your face." He laughed at me. "It was all I could do to keep in character so that DW didn't eat me alive. That man is a terror."

"Yes, but his pictures are out-of-sight!" Bridie was still animated after what must have been a long day for her. "He uses all sorts of tricks like that in the films. There was one we saw last year where a man got thrown off a train by a robber."

"That's right," Ryan chimed in. "I heard that the police were called by a dozen bystanders who thought the dummy thrown off the train was a real person. They actually arrested the actor dressed as a burglar and brought him to the police station before it was all sorted out."

"I'll have to warn Daniel of that, I suppose. He would feel very foolish to arrest someone for assaulting a dummy. But how did you learn of it? Haven't you been in England?" I asked, surprised.

"So many theater folk are doing pictures these days, my dear," Ryan said as the cab pulled up at the entrance to Patchin Place. Cabs couldn't enter our small dead-end street. There was no room for the horses to turn around. "It's such a small community and we love to gossip, of course." He leaned closer, putting a hand on my shoulder. "I'll have to tell you what I've heard about Lily La Rosa and a certain studio boss," he said meaningfully.

"The Lily that I got the part from?" Bridie was suddenly alert.

"Later, Ryan," I said as the cabbie came around and helped Bridie down. "Little pitchers have big ears. Thank you so much for the ride home."

"Adieu, darlings." He leaned out the window of the cab to blow a kiss to Bridie, who blushed happily.

"See you tomorrow, Ryan," she called with a little wave as we turned onto Patchin Place.

I frowned as I glanced at her. She was becoming all too familiar with grown-ups. I hoped this acting wasn't going to go to her head.

"You'd better bathe right away," I said as we arrived home. "That makeup can't be good for your skin."

Luckily Aileen had thought to turn the boiler on. We brought the hot water up and sent Bridie to have a bath while I cooked the liver and onions.

"Bridie. Dinner," I called when it was ready. There was no answer. "You serve up, Aileen, I'll go and get her." I ran up the stairs and into Bridie's room. She was in her robe on her bed, fast asleep.

"Come and get some dinner, my love." I shook her gently, but she didn't stir. I pulled the blanket up over her and went back downstairs. I would let her sleep.

I sat up that night after the children were in bed and started a letter to Daniel. *My dearest Daniel,* I began. *I hope this letter finds you well.*

We are all in good health and spirits, although we miss you. I stopped there. It was hard to know how much more to explain. So much had happened in the last day. I hesitated to tell him about the film studio at all. I had no idea where to send the letter until one arrived from him. He had not known exactly where he would be staying. And by the time his letter arrived, and I wrote back, he might already be on his way home. Sighing, I put the letter away. The house felt empty without him there.

The next morning was a repeat of the day before. I helped Bridie with her makeup at the studio, then left to walk home once Sid and Gus arrived to chaperone. They assured me that they were happy to bring Bridie home in a taxi. Sid was dying to get tips from the cameramen so she could be prepared when her own camera arrived.

"The older one, Billy, is quite helpful," she said, "and he knows his stuff. The younger one, Edward, can't give me the time of day. I don't know why. Most people are happy to share their skills, but he seems a grumpy sort."

I left them with Sid taking notes and Gus with her eyes glued to Bridie. At home I caught up on the chores I had neglected. With two small children, the house is never clean for long. I also took time to play with my small ones. I took them both out shopping. We stocked up on vegetables at the market and I bought pork chops for dinner as a treat. Then I took them to Washington Square, where they had fun feeding the sparrows and pigeons. Mary Kate was delighted with this and actually clapped her hands. Both children came back tired and happy. An ordinary but satisfying day, I thought. I could get pleasure out of the simple things with my family. I should be grateful.

"Who was the man?" Liam asked as I began preparing dinner.

"What man?" I asked distractedly.

"The man who was watching us when I ran after the birdies." I wracked my brain. Surely I had kept Liam in sight at all times? I remembered him running back and forth behind a big oak while I sat and looked around.

"He called me 'little man' and asked me where my daddy was. He said it's my job to keep you safe while Daddy's gone," Liam said proudly but my heart skipped a beat.

"What did he look like?" I asked.

"Blue," Liam said.

"Blue?"

"Yes, and tall like Daddy."

I thought of the impression I had that someone was following me. But blue? Had Liam imagined something? Or was someone watching my family? Someone who knew that my husband was gone.

Bridie was delivered home by Sid and Gus just as I was preparing the dinner.

"Thank you so much for taking good care of her," I said. "It's a load off my mind when I can't be two places at once."

"Don't mention it," Gus said. "Sid has been in her element all day. She's so impressed that the picture has a female director. Well, actually DW is the director, but Alice has the bright ideas, and she was trying to convince Sid that she could be employed as a cameraman."

"Wouldn't that be something?" Sid's eyes sparkled amusement. "Maybe a whole female team making moving pictures. Although I'm not sure we'd be strong enough to raise that floor for the tank or to lower and raise those backdrops. So, I suppose men do have their uses."

"Would you like to come in for some tea?" I asked.

"Oh no, Molly, thank you," Sid said. "I must type up my notes from the day."

"Type?" I looked at her in confusion.

"Didn't I tell you that I had ordered a typewriting machine? Since my handwriting is so disorderly, I plan to learn how to use it for when I write books."

So off they went to their own house across the street.

"A typewriting machine? Whatever next?" I said to Bridie as we shut the door.

Bridie giggled.

"We should take off the last traces of your makeup before dinner." I was about to steer her toward the stairs.

"I was shown how to take my own makeup off with the cold cream," she said. "You put big goops of it all over. It was fun."

Bridie went up to change as I put the dinner on the table and cut up Liam's meat for him. Aileen drained the cabbage and potatoes, and we settled down as Bridie came to join us.

"You're turning into a star of the motion pictures, so your mother tells me, Miss Bridie," Aileen said.

Bridie went pink. "Daisy says I'm already like a real professional actress and she thinks I'll go far. She says this business is only just beginning but it's going to be as popular as theater once it catches on and people are going to recognize me in the street. Isn't that amazing?"

"Just don't let it go to your head, sweetheart," I said. "Most theater people are like that. Probably not very sincere in what they say."

Bridie ate as if she hadn't had a meal for weeks, but then she paused between bites. "I forgot to tell you," she said. "We had something scary happen today."

"Scary? Miss Walcott didn't tell me." A vision of a blue man popped into my head, followed by a vision of Bridie falling out of a window or into a tank.

"These men showed up at the studio," Bridie said. "I don't know who let them in, but they came into the scene where I was acting with Ryan. And they started shouting at DW. They were yelling in Italian and English all mixed together, but I think they were angry that Lily had been fired and I've been given her part. One of them started to come over to me but Billy stepped between us, and then Mr. Martin came and talked to them and calmed them down and they went away again."

"How very alarming," I said. "Didn't Sid and Gus step in to save you?"

"Oh, they were chatting with Mrs. Prince at that moment and had gone to have a cup of tea with her," Bridie said. "Her husband's family invented the film camera, and you know how excited Aunt Sid is about that. The ladies were keen to hear all about the earliest days."

So, my chaperones could not be trusted to watch over Bridie every single moment, I thought. I should probably be there myself tomorrow for what would likely be the last day of shooting. "I think I'll come with you tomorrow," I said.

"Oh yes, you must come. It's going to be exciting," Bridie said. "We're doing the big scene with a train."

"A real train?"

Bridie nodded. "Yes, we're being taken to some train tracks near Grand Central Station and going to shoot a scene there."

Train tracks? And that a day after my daughter had been threatened by Italian gangsters? Then I was definitely coming to keep an eye on her.

"And speaking of shooting," Bridie went on, animated now, "do you know how Mrs. Prince's husband died? He was shot when he was out duck hunting. Daisy told me. Isn't that sad? But now Mr. Martin and Mrs. Prince are sweet on each other so that's all right, isn't it?"

How simple the young find things.

The next morning, extra early, I popped across to Sid and Gus before we left to tell them that I'd supervise Bridie as I didn't want to impose on them too much.

"Oh, that's good." Sid looked relieved. "Because I think my camera may come in to the store today and you know I'll want to start learning to operate it immediately."

Gus gave me a knowing grin. She knew that Sid would now be obsessed for days.

"Luckily it's the last day of shooting for this picture," I said. "Bridie goes back to school on Monday and life will return to normal. But Bridie tells me that today's shoot is on location, which means outdoors. They are filming a scene on train tracks, with a real train."

"Mercy me," Gus said. "I'd quite like to see that, but Sid would never forgive me if I wasn't there to witness the opening of the moving picture camera."

"We'll watch the picture when it is shown," Sid said. "I am so glad we went to the studio yesterday. Mrs. Prince is quite remarkable."

"Bridie told me her husband's family were the inventors of the first moving picture camera," I said.

"Yes, and tragedy has followed the family," Gus said mysteriously. "I wish you were still detecting. Maybe she could hire you to find out what happened to them."

"What do you mean?"

"Well, apparently, before she was married, her father-in-law, Lewis Prince, had planned a trip to America to show his film camera—"

"And beat Edison to the punch," Sid put in.

"Yes, this was before the Chicago exhibition." Gus picked up the coffee pot and a cup to offer me some, but I shook my head.

"He got on a train, and he never got off," Sid said.

"Her father-in-law? He was murdered?" I asked.

"That's just it, no one knows. There was no body. He just vanished into thin air, and then Mr. Edison showed his camera, and it was a big hit. So Mrs. Prince said that, as soon as he could, her husband came over to America himself to try to prove that his father was really the inventor of film."

"And he died duck hunting." I remembered what Bridie had told me the night before.

"So, you see there is a mystery there," Gus said thoughtfully. "I'm taking notes when I talk to Mrs. Prince. I feel that there is the making of an article there. Perhaps for *Ladies' Home Journal*, highlighting the struggles that Mrs. Prince has overcome." She smiled. "And I could use my new typewriter to write it."

I left, smiling at my friends and their gadgets. For the next month they would both be obsessed and then they'd move on to something else. But they were correct that poor Mrs. Prince's story was very mysterious. The man who held the patents for a whole new technology was killed while out duck hunting. And before that his father disappeared. Was his father perhaps running away from debtors or his family? Or was the moving picture industry really so dangerous that someone would murder for a patent? Was it worth that much money? I determined to keep a close eye on Bridie.

Liam had heard the word "train," which made him very excited. When I came back to collect Bridie he had apparently been told about today's adventure and was dancing up and down.

"Bridie says it's a real train," he said. "Can I come to see it too? Please, Mama?"

He loved anything that moved and the faster the better, so I decided to take him with me. He'd been such a good little boy all week. He skipped and bounced beside us all the way up Sixth Avenue to the studio, tugging at my hand as if we were not walking fast enough. There he watched in fascination as I helped Bridie with her makeup.

"Mama, she's all green. Is she going to be a frog?" he asked.

We were laughing when Alice came in to see that we were ready, and we were led down to a couple of wagons waiting on Fifth

Avenue to take everyone to the train tracks just north of Grand Central.

The crew was already at work when we pulled up outside a train yard on a service road that ran beside the tracks. To the left of where we stood, up a small embankment, five tracks interconnected with points. A boxcar sat on a dead-end track that ended in buffers, then a wooden fence. Two of the tracks went off to the east and three ran parallel past us.

"Look, Mama, a train!" Liam said as soon as we were assisted down from the wagons.

"Yes, sweetheart, let's keep out of the way." I grabbed hold of him, just in case he got too enthusiastic. "Make sure you stay very close to Mama all the time." I led us back to a spot where we could watch safely. Men were clearing grass from between the nearest tracks. Other crew members were setting up an enormously long backdrop painted with a vista of rolling hills behind the nearest track. About ten feet back from the embankment, a canvas canopy had been erected below the other chairs and equipment, and I spotted DW under the canopy speaking with two policemen.

As we climbed down, we heard a shout from down the line, "Train!" It was repeated by a closer voice. "Train." A bell clanged somewhere in the distance. The crew cleared the line and leapt to hold the backdrop. I held Liam's hand more tightly. A train came slowly through the yard and went by on the third line. Curious faces peered out of the windows.

"Hello, train people!" Liam called, waving to the passengers as they passed, and a few people smiled and waved back.

"Okay, folks, we have twenty minutes to get set up," Alice called. A police wagon pulled up. I was just wondering if we were breaking some sort of law being here and DW was trying to talk them out of citing us, when a crew member jumped down from the wagon, took the reins, and guided the horses toward the canopy.

"DW, where do you want the police wagon?"

DW came out with the two policemen and pointed them a hundred yards down the track.

"Start toward this spot when we raise the red flag," DW said. "Come full gallop." I noticed for the first time that the policemen were wearing pancake makeup and realized they were actors in the scene. "Edward, you get them racing this way while Billy focuses on the tracks. Stay on them so you follow the train as it goes by."

The area in front of the backdrop was a hive of activity as props were placed and the actors and cameramen given instructions. Alice kept pulling a watch out of her pocket and calling out the time. I found an empty chair under the awning and settled Liam on my lap.

A crew member came out with the slate with *Scene 26* on it. Billy started the camera rolling.

Ryan and Bridie acted out a scene in front of the backdrop. Bridie ran away and Ryan followed. As he grabbed her arm she fainted, and he dragged her across the tracks and tied her down tightly, looping the rope under the track and over her legs and arms. She woke up and cried out in horror.

"Make sure you get her face, Billy. Sweetheart, you have to look more scared. O'Hare, tighten those ropes." DW kept up a running commentary.

"If I can't have you, no one will." Ryan twirled his mustache as he gazed down at Bridie. "But I will inherit all you own." He threw back his head with an evil laugh.

"Train!" I heard the far-off cry. Ryan looked up and laughed again. My heart started to thump loudly. "Train!" I heard the cry nearer this time. The train was coming, and Bridie was tied to the tracks!

❧ Ten ❧

Bridie!" I screamed. I set Liam down and leaped up, ready to run and untie her, but before I could take a step Bridie slipped her legs out from under the loops of rope and raised both arms. Two crew members came from behind the backdrop; each took a hand and pulled her clear. The ropes that looked so tightly bound around her chest had been just draped around her body and released her instantly. I scooped up Liam and sat back down, my heart beating out of my chest. As soon as Bridie had cleared the track, one crew member helped her down the embankment while the other was putting the identically dressed mannequin onto the tracks. He ducked back under the canvas backdrop.

A Pacific engine came around a bend, puffing out steam. This train was not coming slowly like the one before it. It thundered down the track. The engineer must not have been told that a dummy would be on the tracks because suddenly the train whistle sounded again and again. The shrieking sound of brakes filled the air. What's more, Billy was now lying on the track itself behind the mannequin with the camera pointing at the oncoming train. Was he mad? I wanted to stand up again and shout for them to stop this right now.

"Flag," DW called, and the red flag went up. The police wagon now came thundering toward the train at full speed. The train slowed but it seemed impossible that it would not run over the mannequin or Billy. At the last moment Johnny darted up to the track and grabbed the mannequin by the arms. He dove out of the way of the train, pulling the mannequin with him. Billy rolled off the track, holding his camera, as the train missed him by inches. It took about twenty more yards for the train to stop. Passengers in the front car were screaming. The engineer peered out amid the smoke. He flung open the door of the cab just behind the engine and jumped out, white-faced, running back to where he expected to find a body.

"What the hell are you playing at?" he yelled at Billy, who was checking his camera for damage.

"Just getting the shot." Billy was distracted as he checked the crank to make sure it turned smoothly.

"I'm calling the police. You just watched that girl get killed. You and that fancy man in black." He caught sight of the police wagon.

"Help, murder!" He ran toward the startled actors who were dressed as police.

"Jesus, Alice, do something," I heard DW say. "Subdue the locals."

"I thought you let the railroad company know." Alice's voice sounded strained as she started toward the panicked man.

"It looked more realistic this way." DW seemed amused as he went up to Billy and clapped him on the back. "I bet no one has ever gotten that shot before."

I stood and took Liam's hand to guide him over to Bridie, who was also excited. "Did you see that, Mama? We practiced that so many times yesterday. I wanted to surprise you."

"I was scared out of my wits," I said, putting my arms around her. "I'm so glad you're safe."

"It was just pretend." She seemed surprised by my reaction. "Nothing could have happened."

"That train missed Johnny and Billy by inches and frightened the engineer to death."

"Oh dear." Bridie's eyes widened. "He looks mad."

Alice had joined the engineer and the police actors with Ryan, who was carrying the mannequin under one arm. They were all talking at once and it took some minutes until the driver was convinced that no one had been hurt. "You are all crazy," the engineer said, throwing up his hands as he stalked angrily back to the engine. "My boss is going to hear about this."

He climbed up behind the engine and moments later the train whistle sounded. He hung his head out of the window and yelled back as the train started to move slowly. "You'll be hearing about this from the company. You owe this whole train an apology." As the train moved past us, passengers stared out the windows, some curiously and some angrily. The train picked up speed, and then it was gone.

"That's it, folks!" DW said in a loud voice. "We've got the picture. Let's go back to the studio to wrap up and Alice will make sure you get your pay and some grub."

Everyone walked back to the wagons, laughing and talking. My heart was still beating wildly. I had to remind myself that no one had been hurt. I hadn't realized how serious the film people were about making an exciting picture.

"That was wonderful," Bridie said, leaning her head on my shoulder as we bumped back to the studio in the back of a wagon with Johnny and Ryan. "Can I do another one soon?"

"It's back to school on Monday for you," I said firmly. "That was enough excitement for me."

"I think Liam liked it," she giggled, nodding at Liam, who was standing and pointing out everything we passed.

"That an automobile. And that's a taximeter. And there's a mail man and a worker man and a lady . . ." I kept a firm hold on him by the back of his jacket.

"I think I'm done with the moving picture acting business," Ryan said, taking the hat from his head and wiping his brow. "It was oodles of fun, of course, and completely fascinating. But I prefer to make other people do all the hard work."

"I thought you wrote this character just for yourself," I said.

"I did, my dear, but it was exhausting." A bump made him wince. "If I write another character for myself, it will be a wealthy invalid who is pushed around in a chair and drinks whiskey." I had to laugh.

Ryan put an arm around Bridie's shoulder. "But you, my darling, were brilliant. An absolute natural. I predict a great future for you."

"Ryan, please don't put ideas into her head," I said. "She may have a great future but not as an actress. And certainly not in moving pictures. From what I've seen in the few days this week it's far too dangerous. Did you see how close that train came to your cameraman?"

"An artiste must take risks for the perfect work of art," Ryan said, waving his arms dramatically. I studied him, with his ridiculous black mustache, and realized that to him life was one big game, much as it was for Sid and Gus. I couldn't feel that way. I was all too aware that life was precarious. Sometimes one decision made the difference between life and death, and it was my job to keep my family safe.

We arrived back on Fourteenth Street. The doorman nodded as we all entered the building. Everyone was in good spirits, and the foyer echoed to the loud chatter and laughter.

"Let's hurry and remove your makeup, my darling," I said to Bridie, "and then we must be getting home. I don't like to leave the baby too long with Aileen."

"Oh, but you can't go home now," Ryan said, coming up beside us and putting his arm around Bridie. "It's a party. We have one when we've finished shooting every film. There's food and drink—sometimes DW even buys champagne."

"Champagne, Mama!" Bridie gave me a nervously excited look, half sure that I'd say no.

"And at the end Alice hands out the pay packets for the week. You won't want Bridie to miss that, will you?"

"Oh no," Bridie said. "I can't miss that, Mama. Ten whole dollars!"

I sighed. "Very well. I suppose we must stay until you've received your pay packet."

We followed the noisy crowd onto the stage floor. Inside that vast space the three sets had already been taken down. At the far end in complete darkness, the water tank still appeared to be open, but a barrier now partially blocked it off. In the rest of the space a number of benches and trestle tables had been brought in and a magnificent spread of food was set out on a long table. The room with no sets in it seemed enormous.

Champagne was poured for everyone. Glasses were handed around. When one was passed to Bridie, she gave me a pleading glance.

"Oh, why not," I said. "You've certainly earned it. And you don't have anything else you have to do today. But just a sip, understand?"

She took a sip. "It's fizzy," she said in delight. "And the bubbles go up my nose."

At that moment DW clapped his hands, gave a speech about how this moving picture had been groundbreaking, and said that the scene with the train would be the talk of the town. Then he proposed a toast to the actors and crew.

"And to Alice," Johnny shouted.

"Alice!" Everyone raised their glasses with a cheer. DW scowled and then, seeing everyone watching him, gave a halfhearted smile and raised his glass. There was only one glass of champagne each, but behind the food table were tubs filled with beer bottles, and the men on the crew grabbed them happily—not only the actors from Ryan's film but all the actors and crew who had been involved in the other films during the week. Ryan's face lit up in a smile when he saw Cecil.

"There you are, Cecil, old chap." He went over to him and for a moment I thought Ryan was going to embrace him. "I gather you were spectacular. You swam like a Greek god. I'll have to write a script for you in which you are Poseidon. And, my dear, you'll never believe it, but we had a close encounter with a train. Yes, a real fire-breathing train locomotive. I must tell you all about it." He took Cecil's arm and off they went, clutching their champagne glasses.

Mary Pickford, the actress whom I had last seen dripping wet and clinging to a rock, was helping herself to a plate at the long food table. Daisy ran up to Bridie and gave her an affectionate greeting.

"I didn't think you would be here today!" Bridie said, surprised.

"Every Friday," Daisy said with a grin. "They finish the pictures and take them to editing, then feed and pay the actors and crew. I wouldn't miss it for the world."

"The pay might not be much, but they feed us well," Johnny said as he helped himself. "Better than in the theater."

"Did you start as a stage actor?" I asked as I made a plate of cold cuts and apple slices for Liam.

"I did. Just small-time stuff, barely scraping by. Then I got a part in one of Mr. Edison's films." He piled his plate high as he spoke. "I did a few for him but then he moved his studio out to the Bronx, and I didn't want to leave Manhattan, so I tried my luck here at Biograph."

"I thought Alice said never to mention Thomas Edison in this studio." Bridie had been following our conversation closely. "I thought they were deadly enemies."

"They were when I first started," Johnny said. "I didn't let anyone know where I was working in case Edison was mad that I had changed studios. But eventually they stopped suing each other, and it seems that now they've gone into business together, so I figure I'm all right."

"If they're in business together, then why doesn't Alice want to mention his name?" Bridie said in a low voice.

"They're still competitors, they just decided they could make more money if they competed with their pictures and stopped suing each other." He lowered his voice as well. "I think they made some agreements so they wouldn't have to raise the actors' pay."

"What are you talking about?" a man's voice snarled behind us. "I won't have my staff gossiping in my own studio." I turned and saw a chubby man with red hair, silk waistcoat, and bow tie.

Isn't that Harry Martin? I thought, confused. It was the man who had taken my hand to kiss it earlier in the week, same red face and mustache, a bow tie and a fancy suit. But instead of the overly charming manner he had shown previously, he was scowling, his face contorted in anger.

"Sorry, Mr. Martin," Johnny muttered and made a hasty retreat. Mr. Martin turned his gaze on me.

"Who are you?" he barked.

"I'm Molly Sullivan, Bridie Sullivan's mother," I said, startled. "We met in DW's office on Wednesday."

"Never seen you before in my life." He stared at me. "Who let you in? What are you doing here? Helping yourself to my free food?"

"I'm sorry, but my daughter was in your picture and since she's only a child I'm chaperoning her," I said coldly.

He was still glaring at me. "Well, whoever you are, there's no need to be gossiping about that man we don't mention in this studio, young woman. He may think he has won because his name is on the trust, but he won't be able to match the pictures we're making here."

Luckily, Liam tugged at my arm at that moment. "Excuse me, my son needs me." I crossed the room and settled Liam to eat on one of the benches, giving frequent glances back at Mr. Martin. Either he was given to abrupt mood swings or Thomas Edison was a real sore spot. I couldn't reconcile this snarling man with the womanizer I had seen on Wednesday.

Apart from Mr. Martin, the rest of the actors and crew members were jubilant. Billy and Johnny were gently teasing each other about who had come closer to the moving train. Then Alice appeared out of the office. "All right, everyone. Who wants their wages?"

Nobody needed to be asked twice. A line formed. Bridie rushed over to join it. I stayed beside Liam, making sure he didn't spill his food. He was valiantly tackling a huge pastrami sandwich. I took a bite of a ham roll, but I couldn't take my eyes off Mr. Martin. What on earth had made him so angry today when he had been all charm when I last saw him?

Bridie came running up to me. "Look," she said, holding out ten one-dollar banknotes. "This is an awful lot of money, isn't it."

"It is indeed," I said. "When I was fourteen, I don't think I had ever seen that much money together. Although we had very different money. Pounds, shillings, and pence."

"I remember," she said, a wistful look coming over her face. "When I was in Ireland with my first mother she gave me a penny once to get a lollipop. Do you remember pennies in Ireland? They were big and heavy, like this." And she made a circle with her thumb and finger.

I nodded, smiling at her. "It's good that you remember your dear mother," I said.

She shook her head sadly. "I don't remember much, just her face when she used to kiss me goodnight. But it's all blurry now."

"Can I have a dollar, please, Bridie?" Liam said, tugging at her skirt and interrupting this nostalgic moment. He reached out to take one, but Bridie pulled them back.

"Your hands are sticky."

"Papa said one dollar is one hundred pennies. So I could buy one hundred candy bags at the store."

"That's excellent calculation," I said, "but Bridie's money is not for candy. Let me keep those safe now." Bridie handed me the notes and I put them in my pocket. "And we will open a savings account for you as soon as Papa returns." Whenever that was. I wished that I had a date to look forward to. It was hard not knowing how long it would be until I saw Daniel again.

"Can I use some of it go to the seaside with my school this summer?"

"We'll have to see what's involved."

As I watched her excited face, I was glad I had not kept Bridie from acting in the film. Ten dollars was a good wage for a working man, let alone a girl dressing up and acting. But then the memory of Bridie tied to the track with the train coming came back to me. Perhaps ten dollars a picture was too little for such dangerous work.

There was an enormous splash and loud laughter. I looked up to see the tank at the far end of the stage floor. One of the crewmen was spluttering in the water while his friends laughed at him.

"Hey, I can't swim!" he shouted.

"It's only four feet deep, you ninny. Put your feet down," one of them shouted back.

"What's going on here?" Harry Martin was walking toward the crew with Fanny Prince on his arm. I waited for the explosion of anger, but his face was creased in a smile. "Help the guy out, and that's enough beer for you all," he said, but he was laughing while he said it. "See, Fanny, I told you we had better check on what they were getting up to."

"That tank is a menace," Fanny said. "I'm afraid I'll fall into it every time I'm down here."

"Don't worry, Mrs. Prince." DW had hurried forward to intercept them. "The crew will lower the floor in place now that we're done using it."

"And my bride-to-be will stay safely on my arm while she is here so no harm can come to her," Harry said, patting her arm affectionally.

"What's this about a bride-to-be?" Another man was striding over to them. "What the hell are you talking about?"

"Congratulate us, Arthur. I've asked Fanny to marry me, and she has accepted." Harry beamed at the man.

"Holy Mother of God!" I exclaimed involuntarily. I wondered if I had drunk too much champagne. The man beside Harry Martin was identical to him in every way.

❧ Eleven ❧

"Am I seeing double?" I turned to Mary Pickford, who was sitting beside me.

She laughed. "I had the same problem when I first came to work here," she said. "They really are identical, aren't they?"

Alice was walking by and heard my outburst as well. "First time you realized they're twins?" She grinned and stopped to talk. "There's an unspoken rule around here that everyone has to discover that for themselves. It's their big joke." She slid onto the bench across from us, a glass of champagne in her hand.

"One of them is Harry Martin and the other is his twin?" I still couldn't take my eyes off them.

She nodded. "That's right. Mr. Arthur Martin. He's the junior partner. Harry Martin is the president. They run the company between them."

"Do they always wear the same outfits?" I asked. "Even their ties are the same. If I looked just like someone else, I would want to distinguish myself."

"Well, they're not very good looking," Bridie said, "so maybe they think it makes them more interesting."

I hastily shushed her, hoping that neither of them had heard.

Mary started giggling. She was not much older than Bridie, probably sixteen or seventeen. She was much smaller, daintier, under five feet. I guessed that DW liked casting a girl who would make the leading men look big and strong.

"That must have been Arthur who was so angry earlier," I said. "I thought Harry was a Dr. Jekyll and Mr. Hyde."

"The other actresses warned me to watch out for both of them." Mary leaned closer to me and spoke softly, glancing across at Alice to see if she was saying the wrong thing. "Arthur will yell and find fault with everything, and Harry has wandering hands. Anyway," she finished, "I have to keep on their good side if I want to do another picture."

"Have you done other pictures?" I asked.

"I've been acting up and down the country since I was little," she said, "even on Broadway. But this is my first film."

"This was your first?" Bridie said, impressed. "You were so good. I really thought you fainted in that scene."

"Thanks." Mary smiled. "DW already asked me to do another picture. Harry just has to approve the funding. Hopefully now that he's getting married, he'll keep his hands to himself."

"Highly doubtful," Alice said darkly.

"I doubt it too," Mary echoed, looking over at Mrs. Prince. "She doesn't really look like his type. It might be more a merger than a love match."

I looked at Mary with surprise. She might look almost as young as Bridie but her time in the theater must have caused her to grow up quickly.

"Well, you stay away from him," Alice said. "You *are* good, Mary, and DW likes you. He'll cast you based on your talent, so don't go upstairs with Harry and don't pay any attention to any promises he makes you. You saw where that got Lily."

"What happened to Lily?" Bridie asked.

"Well, she got above herself and forgot to learn her lines and gave you a wonderful opportunity to do the part." I stood up and gave Alice and Mary a look that said, *Don't say any more.* "And, now that we are full and you have your pay, I think we should go home."

"Do we have to?" Bridie said, forgetting about Lily and suddenly seeming very young. "This has been the best week of my whole life."

"You did a good job, kid," Alice said, patting her on the arm. "If your mother lets you act this summer, come and ask for me and I'll see if I can get you in another picture."

Bridie's face lit up. "That would be wonderful."

"I don't promise a leading role," Alice warned. "Everyone has to do their part. A countess one day, a serving girl the next, but it's good fun."

"Thank you, Alice, I won't forget." Bridie shook hands with her solemnly.

"I must make sure that the scenes we shot today get to the editing room. We have a lot of editing and splicing ahead of us this weekend. I'm really dying to see how those shots of the train turned out. Talk about groundbreaking. Edison will be green with envy."

She hurried off, efficient as ever. We went around the room, saying our goodbyes. As we exited into the sunlight Bridie had tears in her eyes.

"I liked that place; can we go there again?" Liam asked as we started home.

"I'll never do anything that exciting again!" Bridie exclaimed with a stifled sob. I didn't reply and a few minutes later she said in a happier voice, "But wait till the girls at school hear about it!"

"We must stop and buy some food for dinner on the way home," I said to Bridie. "And we should celebrate your success. What would you like to eat?"

"Roast beef and champagne," Bridie said.

"St. Michael and all the angels," I exclaimed. "You've started to think big very quickly." I laughed. "It will be a while before you have any more champagne, my girl. And as for roast beef, have you forgotten it's Friday?"

Her face fell. "Oh yes. So it has to be fish." She gave a dramatic sigh. I could see that any reactions from Bridie from now on would be of the exaggerated and dramatic kind suitable for the silver screen. Then her expression changed to a look of horror. "We already ate ham sandwiches. Will we have to go to confession?"

"It's not a sin if we genuinely forgot," I said. "But we will be having fish tonight. You choose. What sort of fish do you like best?"

It was clear that no fish was going to delight her. I had another thought. "It doesn't have to be fish," I said. "You like macaroni and cheese, don't you?"

Her face was instantly happy again. "Oh yes. Macaroni and cheese. I do like it."

"Then we're settled. But I'll think of a nice pudding for afters. You like my bread pudding, don't you? And custard."

We went home happy. Contrary to my worst fears, Mary Kate was asleep in her crib.

"She was as good as gold, Mrs. Sullivan," Aileen said. "I gave her the bottle and she still seemed hungry, so I cooked her up a little bit of semolina and sugar in some warm milk and she took to it instantly. It's what my mother used to give the babies."

Mercy me. Wonders would never cease. Aileen had found a way to quiet a fussy child.

The next morning was dark and rainy. I woke up late, made us a nice breakfast, then didn't feel inclined to do my normal Saturday chores. Instead I lit the fire in the parlor and we played cards. Mary Kate was clingy, perhaps because I had left her so much during the week. She was only happy in my arms, where she slept for most of the afternoon. I knew I should wake her, but I didn't have the heart. I had no desire to venture out into the rain, so I opened a can of pork and beans and we had it on toast. We were in the middle of our dinner when the telephone rang. I rushed into the front hall. We were one of the few families in the city who had a private telephone installed and this only so that the police department could reach Daniel in the middle of the night. So I knew something had to be wrong.

I took the receiver off the wall, holding it cautiously. I had hardly ever used the contraption and it still scared me. "Hello? Greenwich 625," I said.

"This is the Washington operator with a long-distance call, ma'am. Can I connect you?"

"Uh, yes. Go ahead." My heart was racing now.

"Molly, it's me." Daniel's voice came on the line sounding hollow and faraway.

"What's wrong?"

"Nothing at all. Just took the opportunity of using the telephone here at headquarters to call home and make sure you are all well."

"We're all fine and dandy, thank you, dear," I said. "Aren't you coming home tomorrow?"

"Uh, no—that's another thing I called you about," Daniel said. "They've asked me to stay on a little longer. We've a meeting with President Taft next week."

"The president?"

"Yes, and with Mr. Bonaparte, the outgoing attorney general, and a Mr. Finch."

"Daniel?" Should I tell Daniel about the man I suspected was following us? What could he do from so far away?

There was a long pause. The line hissed and crackled.

"Daniel?" I said, speaking loudly into the handset. "Are you still there?"

"I'm here." His voice sounded like it was coming from miles away, which I suppose it was.

"You won't say yes to moving to Washington, will you?" I asked. "Not without discussing it with us first?"

"Moving to Washington?" Bridie heard the words and came flying out of the kitchen. "Tell Papa we can't possibly, that it would ruin my chances—"

I held up a finger to quiet her. "Sorry, that was Bridie. She's had an exciting week that she'll tell you all about when you get home," I said.

"I must go," Daniel said. "I can't keep the line busy for too long. But I wanted to send my love to my family. I'll be with you soon."

"What is your address?" I started. "I'll have some news for you."

But there was a click at the other end of the line. I stood staring at the wall.

"Daniel Sullivan, you are a very annoying man," I said to the empty hallway.

I was still upset at midnight as I paced around the parlor. I suppose at the back of my mind was the worry that Daniel would be persuaded to take a job with the Secret Service in Washington and we'd have to move away from everything I knew and loved. Also, Mary Kate had been fussing and crying continually for two hours, maybe picking up my own tension, and I was tired of trying to comfort her.

So, I must confess that I was not in the best of tempers the next morning as I went about my chores, berating myself for my laziness the day before. Now I had twice as much to do. Liam was underfoot, playing wherever I needed to clean, so I sent him and the baby off for a walk with Aileen before she went home to her family until tomorrow. Bridie had neglected the schoolwork she had been assigned over the holiday week and was deep in a book of mathematics.

About eleven o'clock I decided that I might reward myself with a visit to Sid and Gus. They would be sure to have some strong coffee, which, while I didn't appreciate the taste, would at least wake me up. I had a fleeting thought that I was counting on my friends too much. For the first months after Mary Kate was born I had barely left the house, let alone spent time with my friends. This week I had presumed on our friendship quite a lot. Perhaps they wanted some time alone on a Sunday. But Gus's welcoming smile put those fears to rest. "Molly, wonderful," she said. "Come in and have some coffee."

"I would love some," I said, coming in gratefully. The living room had undergone a strange transformation. The sofa and chair were arranged in the corner opposite the new camera that was set on a tripod. Beside it was a large hooded lamp on a metal stand.

"It's my studio," Sid said. "Isn't it fun?" She flipped a switch on the lamp and the room was filled with a dazzling light.

"I'm afraid we don't have anything to eat with the coffee," Gus said apologetically, crossing the room and turning off the switch. "We haven't gone out yet. We were so busy yesterday. Sid got it in her head that we had to have lighting for her studio. The man who sold us the camera told us where we might purchase the arc lamp."

"You did all this yesterday?"

"Yes, we—" Sid was interrupted by a knock on the door. "Hold on, Molly." She went to answer it.

"I must speak to Molly immediately. She's here, isn't she? Bridie said she was." Ryan pushed past Sid and into the house. "Molly, it's an utter disaster. I set my sights too high like Icarus and the gods have struck me down."

"And good morning to you, Ryan." Sid's tone was dripping with sarcasm. "Oh, hello, my sweet," she said to Bridie, who had come in right behind Ryan.

"Good morning, Aunt Sid." Bridie stopped to give Sid an affectionate hug. "Ryan came to the door and said we had to find Mama immediately."

"I didn't like to tell the sweet girl anything while we were alone in case she fainted dead away." Ryan's tone was desperate, but I noticed that he was not too upset to pour himself a cup of coffee and look around hopefully for the croissants that Sid and Gus often had on Sunday mornings before continuing his story. "You won't believe it."

"For the love of Mike, Ryan, you're worrying me now. What on earth has happened?" I felt strangely nervous.

He gave a dramatic gesture. "There was a fire at the studio last night."

"Is everyone okay?" Bridie's face was creased with worry.

"Yes." Ryan waved away that concern. "It was contained to the editing room, but our film, everything we had shot. It's all gone!"

"What?" Bridie's word was a shriek. "What does that mean, gone?"

"The film is made of cellulose, which is highly flammable. Alice thinks someone left the lamp on in the editing machine."

"So they can't make the picture?" I was struggling to understand the scope of the disaster.

"My dear, there is no picture left. Luckily Arthur Martin had stayed late to do some work in his office. If he hadn't been there the whole place might have burned down." Ryan was pacing in agitation now, flapping his hands with each step.

"No film?" Tears sprang into Bridie's eyes. "All that work for nothing."

"There is going to be a film, my dear." Ryan took Bridie's hand and patted it. "Don't worry your pretty head. We'll just have to re-shoot it. That's what I came to say. And between us, I don't think it was an accident." He paused in his pacing, coming closer to me and lowering his voice. "I suspect it was sabotage."

I was used to taking Ryan's dramatic pronouncements with a

grain of salt but this time he might have a point. My investigator's mind started to spin. Everyone in the building had been an actor or a member of the crew. Security had been tight at the studio, with the doorman making everyone sign in.

"Were the police called in?" I asked. "They would normally investigate a suspicious fire." I pictured the faces of the people I had watched enjoying themselves on Friday afternoon. Could one of them have started a fire that could have burned down the whole studio?

Ryan said, "I don't believe they have. The Martin brothers are not enthusiastic about involving the police. But they are suspicious. Apparently, it's not the first thing that's gone wrong at the studio."

I remembered that huge light nearly toppling into the pool.

"Any ideas who might be behind it?" Again I did a mental count of everyone who was there for the party. Surely it was impossible for an outsider to get in. There was always a man at the door.

Ryan spread his arms wide. "Who can say? Perhaps it is a dastardly attempt to stop my next venture. They were all jealous enough of my successes in the theater, but now, if I'm going to be seen on screens across the country—nay, across the world—well, I can think of several people who'd want to stop me before I get started." Although the situation was grave, I tried not to smile at this. As usual for Ryan, it was all about him. It did occur to me to mention that if they wanted to stop him it would be easy enough to push him in front of an approaching trolley in the street, but that sounded cruel, so I merely nodded.

"But we will not be daunted!" Ryan's voice thundered dramatically. "I come bearing a missive from Alice. It's important that the show must go on. So we are going to reshoot it this week."

"We are?" Bridie looked up hopefully. "So I could do my part again?"

Ryan said, "Of course," at the same time I said, "Absolutely not." We looked at each other.

"Bridie has to be back at school on Monday." I kept my voice calm. "I let her do this during the holidays but she needs to go back to her studies."

"Come now—a few days more wouldn't matter." Ryan turned all of his charm on me, adding with a handsome pout, "So that my career as a film writer doesn't go down in flames, literally."

"I'm sorry, no," I said firmly. "If this was sabotage, I'm not sure it's safe for Bridie to return even if she could miss school. Plus I can't be there to chaperone her for another week."

"But I have to go back to the studio," Bridie wailed. "They need me. My school won't mind. Julia Cooper took a whole month off last year to go to Paris."

"Julia Cooper is not my daughter." I fought to keep my voice even. I understood that Bridie was upset, but I was not going to give in to this, especially as it now seemed that even more danger was involved than I had witnessed last week. "Do you remember that we had an agreement? I agreed to let you act in the film as long as it was finished by the time the holidays were over."

"But how could I know that the film would get burned up?" Bridie's voice was on the verge of hysteria. "You have to understand, Mama. It might be my whole future at stake. Aunt Sid, tell her." She turned to Sid for help.

"Well," Sid began sympathetically but caught the look on my face. "You need to listen to your mother, dear. When I have learned how to use my camera, I'll make you the star of my first film."

"But that won't be the same." Bridie was sobbing now. "Mama, please. It's just a few days."

She looked so devastated that I almost gave in. I hated to see her so sad. But I was the parent. I had to do what was best for her no matter how difficult it was.

"I'm sorry, my darling one," I said, and went over to Bridie and put my arms around her. "If you have the chance in the summer and I think it is safe, then you can make a film."

She wrenched herself away from me. "What if I never have the chance again? This was the only special thing that has ever happened to me. You're ruining my life!" And she ran out of the house and slammed the door behind her. There was an awkward silence.

"Girls are so passionate at that age," Gus said kindly.

I turned to Ryan. "I'm sorry I have to say no, Ryan. You're a good friend and I will do anything else to help, but I can't put Bridie in any danger."

"And moi?" Ryan said, his eyebrows raising. "What if I am in danger? Have you thought of that?"

I gave him a withering look. "If anyone in this world can take care of themselves, Ryan O'Hare, it is you."

The look that Ryan gave me was one of real hurt and I instantly felt sorry. I put my hand on his arm. "I'm so sorry this happened. You didn't deserve this." I suddenly felt like I might cry myself. With Daniel gone, all of the responsibility for the family was mine. Had I made the wrong decision letting Bridie act in the film at all? "Perhaps you should stay away from the studio until they catch the culprit."

"Oh no." He shook his head and winked at me, accepting my apology. "The show must go on."

"That's that," I said to myself as I walked back across the street. As much as Bridie protested, I would remain firm. But now I had another reason to wish that Daniel was home. He could investigate the fire at the studio. Perhaps film was so combustible that it had ignited by itself. But if the fire had been deliberately set, there was someone with access to the studio that might be willing to kill to stop this film from being made.

❧ Twelve ❧

That's the last of that," I said to myself as poured the oats from the tin to make porridge. My pantry was almost empty and so was my purse. Daniel must have two pay packets waiting for him at the station, but if he didn't hurry home I would have to go and ask for them or borrow money from my daughter. When Bridie appeared I looked up from the porridge I was stirring to see her dressed in lime-green silk—one of Blanche's cast-offs, I presumed.

"Why are you dressed like that, may I ask?" I demanded, my annoyance showing in my voice. "Since when do you wear silk to school? And what's wrong with your normal school dresses?"

"Oh, I wanted to look special today." Bridie actually blushed. "I'll be telling them how I was an actress in a moving picture opposite a famous London star. They'll be so impressed. Finally, I have something to shout about."

I supposed I couldn't begrudge her this moment in the sun. "Very well," I said. "But don't spill anything on it. It's a devil to get stains out of silk."

"Oh, I won't, I promise," she said. She slid onto the kitchen chair and attacked her dish of porridge, not looking up at me again. I sensed she knew in her heart that she was being silly, but all girls her age are known to be silly from time to time. If I'd had more clothes when I was fourteen, I'd definitely have worn them to show off occasionally. Instead I had to go to have lessons with the young ladies at the big house in my pitiful cotton skirt and apron while they looked down at me in their silks.

Bridie ate a few bites of porridge then pushed the plate away. "I should be going," she said. "I don't want to be late."

"Late? You're actually early for once." Bridie wasn't exactly speedy in the mornings and usually dawdled so that I had to shove her out of the front door. She got up, grabbed her book bag, and headed for the front door.

"Hey, young lady, don't I even get a kiss today?" I called after her.

"Sorry, Mama." She darted back, pecked me on the cheek, and raced for the door again.

"And what about your coat?"

"It's not cold today," she said. "I'll be fine."

And she was gone. She must be eager to get back to school, I thought. I supposed she had to put up with other girls bragging about trips to the opera, or their country estates, or even to Paris, since her classmates were mostly from the best families. Her best friend, Blanche, certainly was. And this was her one chance to shine. I smiled to myself as I got down to my morning chores.

"Washing day, Aileen," I called. "Are you heating the copper?"

"Already going, missus," Aileen said. "I'll go and strip the beds, shall I?"

She hurried up the stairs. We did a couple of loads, both red-faced and sweating by the time the sheets had been through the mangle. Luckily it was a fine, blustery spring day for once, so Aileen helped me hang them out on the line. They'd be dry in no time and not too much ironing needed. I was just running the carpet sweeper over the front parlor when I looked up to see a woman approaching my house. She was looking around as if she wasn't sure where she should be going. As she made up her mind and headed for my front door, I was surprised to see it was Lucy McCormick, Blanche's mother.

I hastily removed my apron and went to the door.

"Lucy, what a surprise," I said. "I'm afraid the house is not in the best shape to receive callers. We've all been rather busy in the past week."

"Oh Molly dear, I won't stay." Lucy came into the front hall. "I promised Blanche I'd check up on dear Bridie. Blanche was worried in case she had been taken sick."

"What?" I asked.

"Well, I happened to stop by the school this morning," Lucy said. "Blanche wanted me to deliver some items they were going to use as props in the upcoming play. And she came to me quite upset because Bridie wasn't at school. So she begged me to go and visit her."

"It's most kind of you," I said mechanically while my brain tried to catch up with my words, "but Bridie's not here. She set off for school like normal."

"Oh no." Lucy put a hand to her mouth. "What can have happened to her?"

"I've no . . ." I began, but then I had a flash of inspiration. The confrontation and tears over the weekend. The choice of a rather flamboyant silk gown, the way she avoided looking me in the eye and rushed off this morning, all added up to one thing. "Actually I do have a good idea where she's gone, Lucy. I think she is being most disobedient and I'm going after her right now." I peered down the street. "Do you have your automobile with you?"

"I do indeed," Lucy said. "May I take you somewhere?"

"If you don't mind dropping me off at Fourteenth Street on your way home, I'll explain as we go exactly where I expect to find Miss Bridie!"

I darted into the kitchen to ask Aileen to hold the fort until I got back. "I shouldn't be long," I said. It was going to be a painful scene and presumably embarrassing for Bridie, but she was going to learn a lesson. She should never defy and deceive her parents, however much she longed to be in the picture.

We drove up Sixth Avenue and the chauffeur pulled up outside the studio.

"Would you like me to wait and we can make sure Bridie gets safely to school this time?" Lucy said.

"If you really wouldn't mind," I replied. "I don't want to keep you from your commitments."

"Oh rubbish. I had nothing important to do today, other than a dress fitting, and that can certainly wait." She gave a little sigh. "Since my widowhood there seems little joy in acquiring new clothes. I hardly entertain anymore. It's only because Blanche will be coming out in the future that I keep myself motivated."

Without thinking I put my hand onto hers. "You'll marry again, I'm sure of it. You're still a handsome woman in your prime."

She gave a sad little chuckle. "I don't feel in my prime after what we went through these last two years. I lost my husband. I nearly lost my son. It feels as if life will never be the same."

"You should go to England this summer," I said playfully. "I hear there are plenty of dukes and earls just looking for a rich American wife."

"That may not be such a bad idea." She smiled now. "I rather fancy myself as Lady Lucy."

The chauffeur came around to open my door.

"I'll be right out again," I said.

The doorman stopped me as I stepped inside. "Who did you want to see, ma'am?"

"My daughter, Bridie Sullivan. I take it she's here?"

"Oh no, ma'am," he said.

My heart did a flip. If Bridie hadn't come to the studio, then where on earth could she be? I started to panic.

Then the doorman added, as if an afterthought, "None of them are here right now. They've gone off to shoot that train scene again, seeing as how it's supposed to rain for the rest of the week. So if you want your daughter I guess you'll find her by the train tracks somewhere. Don't ask me where though."

"I know where they were last time," I said. "I presume they'll want to duplicate the scene." I nodded a thanks to him and returned to Blanche's automobile.

"Was Bridie not there?" Lucy asked.

"The doorman says they've all gone off to shoot the scene with the train." I hesitated. I didn't want to ask her to go farther out of her way, but I was now anxious to get to Bridie as quickly as possible.

"I'll take you," Lucy said, sensing my conflict. "As I said, I have nothing pressing. This is the most exciting thing that has happened in weeks. Oh, I'm sorry." She made a face. "I don't mean to make light of your worry. I'm sure we'll find Bridie safe and sound."

I gave the driver directions to the train yard near Grand Central. As we headed uptown I alternated between worry and anger. Just let her be all right, I thought, and then, How could she be so irresponsible!

As we drove into the alley behind the train yard I could see the same police wagon and canvas awning. I tried to make Bridie out in the group of crew members and actors, but I didn't see her. A wooden barrier blocked us from driving any farther so we both got out and walked, picking our way over puddles and uneven ground toward the set, leaving the chauffeur with the automobile. Then the crew were given some sort of direction. They moved aside and I saw Ryan and Bridie standing up the embankment by the tracks. I gave a sigh of relief.

"There she is." I put my hand on my heart that was still pounding loudly. "Thank God." Just then I heard a train whistle. Ryan grabbed Bridie, she fainted, as they had rehearsed before, and he carried her down the embankment, laid her on the tracks, and tied her there with an impressive rope. The police wagon on our right sprang into action.

"That man just grabbed her," Lucy said, shocked. "She's on the track. Can we get the police?"

"It's part of the film," I said, putting a reassuring hand on her arm although I could feel my own heart start to race again. I could hear DW's instructions being shouted from his giant megaphone. "They are just acting. The crew will get her to her feet long before the train comes." I tried to sound more confident than I felt.

"Train!" I heard the cry in the distance. A train whistle sounded again. We were now standing right behind the canvas awning. Billy was in front of Bridie getting a close-up of her panicked face as she struggled against her bonds. I had to remind myself that it wasn't real.

"Train!" The cry was nearer.

"Okay, girl up, dummy down," DW said. I watched for the crewmen to come and lift her off the tracks. Where were they? I was vaguely aware that something was different. The sound of the train—what was it? Then it came to me. There was no sound of braking. No screeches of brakes or screams from the front car. This train must have been warned about the filming.

"Girl up, dummy down!" DW roared. "Now!" But the crewmen did not appear. Billy started up the embankment toward the track, but the rain had made it slippery, and he stumbled. The train was in plain view now, bearing down on us.

"Bridie!" I screamed. "Get up!" She sat up at the sound of my voice. The first look on her face was one of guilt and surprise. She did not expect me to be here. Then she realized how close the train was and cried out in fear. As she tried to pull her legs out of the rope around them, the buckle of her shoe caught. She pulled hard and the buckle must have broken. Her leg jerked out of one strand of rope but as she tried to get to her feet the other coil held her fast and she fell back down across the rails. Her panic made her movements jerky, nothing like the smooth ballet I had seen on Friday. I raced toward the embankment, cursing my boots and skirts and slipping on the mud.

"Ryan, help her, get her up!" I yelled. I knew he was in reach behind the track. He must have just realized what was happening because he reached her at the same time as I did. Bridie's face was white with fear and her hands were tugging at the rope that was anchoring her to the track.

"Mama!" she wailed as she desperately scrabbled with the ropes. The giant steam engine was close now, close enough that the engineer had realized what was happening too. He could see this was no dummy on the tracks. The train whistle sounded and the brakes screeched but I knew it was much too close to stop in time.

I reached her, grabbed her shoulders, and pulled as hard as I could, but her leg was still tangled in the rope. "Take her shoe off! Free her foot!" I screamed, as Ryan grabbed the loops. The rope still held her. I was aware of Johnny coming up beside him and together they fumbled with the rope until it came free. Johnny grabbed Ryan, pulling him backward, and Bridie, her legs suddenly free, fell backward onto me as the train thundered past. "Mama?" I saw her lips move but couldn't hear a sound. Then her eyes rolled up in her head and she collapsed onto the ground.

⚜ Thirteen ⚜

Bridie!" I cradled her in my arms, calling her name, knowing she couldn't hear me over the noise of the train. I checked for a wound, for blood or bruising. I felt her wrist and her pulse fluttered there like a little bird. She was alive. Thank God. Finally, the train was gone and there was silence.

Johnny and Ryan were standing on the other side of the track, their faces white. Ryan rushed across the track toward us.

"Why isn't she moving?" He stood above her, immobile for the moment himself. "Is she hurt? You got her off the tracks in time, didn't you?"

I believe it was the first time I had seen him being genuine and not acting. He knelt beside her, took her hand and gently patted her wrist. "Bridie. Come back to us, please."

Her blue eyes opened. She looked around her, confused at first, then realized where she was.

"Oh Mama, I'm so sorry. The train came and I couldn't get up . . ."

"Hush now, my darling." I held her close and stroked her hair. "You're quite safe now."

"But why," she looked up in bewilderment at Ryan and Johnny standing above her, "did I fall?"

"I think you fainted," I said, thankful it was no more than that. "You had quite a scare."

The thought flashed through my mind to thank God that Liam had not come with me today and seen his beloved sister almost killed.

DW's face was red with rage. He stomped up the embankment, grasped the canvas backdrop and with one giant yank pulled it backward. Behind it two crewmen looked up guiltily.

"What the hell are you playing at!" DW roared. "A girl was almost run over by a train because you missed your cue."

I saw then that their faces looked as white as Bridie's had.

"We called 'hold,'" the first one said. "We couldn't get the mannequin out in time."

"How can she 'hold' on the track when there is a train coming?" DW thundered. Really, his voice was so loud he didn't need that megaphone.

"She held on the track?" The first crewman looked scared and confused. "Why didn't she just get up?"

"Yes, or why didn't Billy help her up?" Edward had just reached us. He was panting from running and looked angry. "Or Ryan? I was filming the police wagon and looked up to see her almost run over!"

"I tried," Billy spat out angrily, "but the slope is slippery here. And apparently her legs got caught."

"And I was done with my part, so I had stepped back," Ryan said. "I hate being so close to a train. If it hadn't been for Molly's scream I would have had no idea what was going on until it was too late."

"It was your job to get the girl up. What were you doing?" DW asked the crewmen again. In response one of them held up the mannequin's head.

"The mannequin broke. The head's been detached from the body," he said. "Someone took the screw out."

"But we didn't even notice that at first," the second crewman said.

"The jacket was hooked onto the canvas backdrop. By the time we yanked it free, the mannequin's head fell off."

"I yelled 'hold' to see if we could save the shot if we had just another minute to get the head on." They were looking fearfully at DW.

"You are all crazy!" I yelled. "Caring more about the shot than my daughter's life." The two crewmen recoiled at my outburst. I had more to say but Bridie was shaking in my arms.

Alice came up with a shawl that she put around Bridie's shoulders. "Let's get her something to drink. Come and sit down." I let her lead us to the canvas awning and sit Bridie down on a chair. She pulled a bottle of Coca-Cola out of a basket. "I find these soothing." She handed it to Bridie. "Sip that, dear."

Bridie took a sip and then burst into tears. "I'm sorry, Mama, I lied and told you I was going to school."

"You what?" Alice looked at Bridie, surprised.

"I sent Bridie off to school this morning," I said, "but got word that she never arrived."

"I'm sorry," Bridie said again. "You saved me. I almost got run over by that train."

I crouched down and put my arms around her. "Hush now, I'll be angry at you later. Right now I am just so glad you are safe."

DW was still yelling at the crew. "Get this all packed up and get back to the studio." He went back to Alice and said in a lower voice, "Go ahead and fire those two imbeciles right away. Tell them they can collect their pay packets and get lost."

I stood up.

"I wouldn't do that," I said.

DW was clearly not used to being contradicted. He glared at me now.

"Why on earth not? You're the mother, aren't you? You like that they almost got your kid killed?"

"Of course not," I said, "but someone is obviously sabotaging your picture. If you fire those men, you won't have a chance to question them and find out who it is."

"How do you know about the sabotage?" DW looked at Alice. "Have you been blabbing?"

"I am using my own eyes and intelligence," I said hotly. "I heard people talking about accidents at the studio. And then there was a fire that ruined your picture. And now the mannequin? I assume her head was on when the crew brought her from the studio."

"Yes, it was. I checked it," Alice answered.

"That means someone here is sabotaging the film. And now they almost killed my daughter. So I want you to catch them."

"That shows some intelligence," DW said grudgingly. "Don't fire them for now, Alice, but for God's sake keep an eye on them."

"I will, DW," Alice said. As he left, she turned to me.

"You really think like a detective," she said. "Did you actually solve cases professionally?"

"Yes, I did," I answered, "before I was married." I didn't add that I had solved a few murders since my marriage.

"Molly, I could use your help." Alice's face was creased with worry. "This sabotage is getting out of hand. We really need to catch the person behind it."

Lucy McCormick came up to us. "That looked very real, Molly. I was quite alarmed for the child's life. Are all pictures this dangerous?"

I looked up in disbelief. "It *was* real, Lucy. That wasn't how the scene was supposed to go at all. They were supposed to substitute a dummy for Bridie, but they missed their cue. It was awful . . . we almost lost her." I put my hand up to my mouth, to stop the sob that had risen in my throat.

"Oh goodness gracious." Lucy put her hand onto my shoulder. "What a terrible shock. You must both come back to my house to recover. I'll have Cook make you a good broth with brandy in it."

"That's very kind of you," I said, "but right now I just want to get Bridie home. And I need to return to my baby . . ."

Alice had been standing to one side of us as the crew took down the set and started loading things onto wagons. Now she moved closer. "Do you have a carriage waiting?" she asked Lucy.

"An automobile," Lucy said. "My chauffeur is with it, just beyond the barrier."

"Oh, wonderful." Alice nodded. "We have to take Bridie back to the studio to change out of the costume," she said. "Maybe this lady could take us, and I could ride along with you. I want to make sure that Bridie comes to no more harm."

"With pleasure," Lucy said.

We followed Lucy to the waiting automobile. Bridie allowed herself to be moved like a rag doll, and once on the back seat she leaned her head against me as if she wanted the reassurance that I was there. Poor little thing. It was impossible to be angry now. If anyone had ever learned their lesson it was today. I didn't think she'd be deceiving me again in a hurry! We came to a halt outside the studio. I thanked Lucy. She hugged Bridie. "I won't tell Blanche about this," she said. "I'll leave it to you to tell her as much as you want to."

Bridie nodded. I could tell she was still finding it hard not to cry.

"Shall we go to a doctor, sweetheart?" I whispered. "Are you hurt?"

"No, please," she whispered back. "I was just scared and embarrassed."

"We'll see." I looked at her appraisingly. If she wasn't back to herself by tonight I wanted a doctor to look at her. We followed Alice inside, past the doorman, who regarded us with a curious look. He wanted to know why we had returned alone and so quickly but as Alice didn't bother to explain, I didn't either. Up the stairs we went and into the dressing room.

"Here, let me undo the buttons," Alice said. "Turn around, dear."

Bridie stood there, as stiff as a statue, as Alice started to undress her. When the dress came off Alice hung it up, then put an arm around Bridie's shoulders. "Now why don't you take your makeup off the way we showed you so that I can have a talk with your mother."

Bridie looked up at her and nodded, still too stunned to speak. When she saw Alice leading me off, she cried out in alarm, "Don't leave me alone. I'm frightened."

"You're perfectly safe here, dear," Alice said. "There's nobody else in the building apart from the doorman. Everyone else is still at the shoot. And besides, I don't think anyone actually meant you harm. It was a horrible accident, but it's all over now."

Bridie nodded as if she didn't quite believe her. "We won't go far," Alice said. "Just over here where your mother and I can have a little chat." Alice took my arm and led me down the length of the wardrobe room into the closet at the end. It contained two racks of clothing, one down either side, and the smells of perfume and sweat lingered unpleasantly in the air. There was one lone electric lightbulb hanging from the ceiling. Alice closed the door behind us.

"This is strictly between ourselves, Mrs. Sullivan," she said. "You must have guessed that I suggested coming back here so that we could talk in private without being overheard."

I met her gaze. "You think that was not an accident today, I gather?"

She nodded. "I'm sure it was more sabotage."

"So tell me about this sabotage. How long has it been going on, and who do you suspect?"

Alice gave a frustrated sigh. "It started a few months ago, just when we were getting into our stride with these new pictures that actually told a story rather than just showing the audience what a camera could do," she said. "It was little things at first . . . a can of paint knocked over and spilled on a set, a backdrop that fell un-expectedly. Such things happen when you are shooting a moving picture. We thought nothing about it. But then it turned to bigger things. You saw that lamp the other day. If it had fallen into the pool, it might have electrocuted poor Mary. It's made everyone really jumpy, I can tell you. People have started whispering about the studio being cursed or haunted."

"Haunted?" I smiled. Alice wasn't smiling. "You, being more practical, started to suspect sabotage."

She nodded.

"You have some ideas, obviously."

"I do have my suspicions," she said, "but it's tricky. We can't put a foot wrong at this stage."

My mind went back to the grand funeral a week ago. "You don't suspect the Black Hand, do you? Because I know they have been extorting businesses, scaring them into paying protection money."

Alice smiled grimly at this. "They'd find it hard to protect us, I would think. We shoot on location all over the city. They'd need so many men as bodyguards that it wouldn't be worth their while."

I think I let out a small sigh of relief. If she didn't suspect the Black Hand, then it couldn't be too bad. Although Sid and Gus had reported on a group of Italians making a fuss after Lily was sacked. Perhaps, after all, it had just been her family complaining about the way she was treated. But Alice went on, "If I had to say, I'd put my money on Edison."

"Edison?" I looked surprised. "I know you were great rivals once, but haven't you just signed a contract to enter into partnership?"

"Of a sort," Alice said. "Our studios have entered a trust. It means that our films will be shown at the same picture houses and advertised together. It also means that we will drop all the lawsuits over who invented the film camera."

"Didn't Mr. Edison invent his own film camera? He certainly is celebrated for it," I asked, surprised. "Why can't each studio just use their own?"

"That has been the subject of many lawsuits," Alice said. "They were each claiming that one had stolen the design from the other to try to stop its use. That's actually how Harry met Mrs. Prince. He and Arthur were in business with her husband, Andrew Prince. Andrew's father claimed he had taken the first moving pictures ever. But before he could prove it, he disappeared. He just stepped onto a train one day and never got off."

"I heard that story," I said. "And they never found a body?"

"Nothing, and if he was still alive, he never contacted his family again."

"What sort of proof did he have of his invention?" I asked.

"He had the film of his children taken in his back garden. So Andrew Prince himself was the proof. He was ten in the film, so you can date the age of the invention by Andrew."

"Did the film disappear with the father?" Once again, I felt the tug of this mystery.

"No, Andrew had a reel, and the original design for the camera in his father's writing. He wanted to keep his father's legacy going, so he and Harry and Arthur went into business to start making films. But Edison sued them, saying they were infringing on his patent. Harry and Arthur and Mr. and Mrs. Prince were all in a pretty bad spot. The lawsuit almost bankrupted them, but it made the four of them quite close friends."

"And then Mr. Prince died?" I remembered hearing this part.

"Yes, in a duck hunting accident, just before he was due to testify at the trial." Alice's expression was serious. "They never found the hunter that shot him." She leaned closer to me. "Some of the crew are saying it's his ghost that is haunting these studios. Utter nonsense, of course."

My mind was spinning. "And Mrs. Prince is now the only one who has this proof that her father-in-law invented the film camera? I think she should be very careful."

"Well, Harry and Arthur have it locked up in a safe somewhere," Alice said. "But the lawsuits have all been dropped, so it may not matter anymore. What matters now is getting the best pictures out there. Both studios want to be the first to do something really exciting."

"Like filming a girl getting run over by a train," I said sourly.

"*Almost* getting run over," Alice emphasized, "but saved at the last minute. Your daughter wasn't supposed to be in any real danger. That is what makes this so concerning. In truth, none of the studio heads have been saints. They've all behaved like bully boys in the past—roughing people up when they get in the way. So I suspect Edison is going to rush a film out with the same story before we can film this one. He's done that before."

"Oh, I see. So in fact your film would have no impact if the audience had seen a similar story right before it."

"The theaters wouldn't even bother to buy it," she said. "You know how it is with the moving picture business—they want new and sensational all the time. The drama on the train tracks would be a showstopper. The audience would be terrified. It would be amazing."

"I'm sure they would be terrified if you showed them what we shot today," I said dryly.

"That was the final straw, wasn't it? That was what made me decide that it has to stop now and to bring you into my confidence." She stepped closer to me even though we were alone in a closet. "You must realize that our studio is closed to outsiders. Our doorman makes sure of that."

"So it has to be someone from your cast and crew," I said.

"Exactly. An Edison plant, or maybe more than one, since some of the so-called accidents were complicated. Like today, for instance. Who would have had the time and opportunity to unscrew the head of a mannequin and hook the jacket to scenery?"

"Only someone on the crew." I tried to recall the scene. Just the thought of the train thundering down toward Bridie made my heart beat faster but I closed my eyes and tried to see it dispassionately. "He must have ducked behind the canvas backdrop and hooked the mannequin's clothing to it, then for good measure taken the screw out of the head. It was someone who knew that the scene took exact precision and any delay would ruin it."

"Only the crew would have known about the mannequin at all," Alice agreed.

"It also shows that this person has little regard for human life," I said. "He must have known that Bridie would be on the train tracks."

"He couldn't have expected her shoe to become caught in the rope," she said. "We have to give him that much. But he knew it would ruin the scene for the day, that DW had already paid off the driver of that particular train. Again it would slow us down, maybe alarm us so much that we abandoned the thought of using the train."

"Do you have any suspicions?" I asked.

She shook her head.

My own thoughts had been whirling around and I didn't like the conclusion I was coming to. "You really believe that this was an act of sabotage and not something worse?"

"Worse?" She stared at me. "What do you mean?"

"That someone was trying to commit murder? Maybe they hoped that the delay and confusion would cause an accident with the train. And that lamp that fell. If it had gone into the tank it would have electrocuted the actors in there, wouldn't it? I don't know much about electricity, but I do believe that an electric current in water can be fatal."

"I think you're right," she said. "We all took it to be an accident, but perhaps there is an evil force at work here." She ran her hand through her short hair. "I'm always so busy concentrating on what needs to be done that I don't have time to observe," she said. "I need an observer, Mrs. Sullivan. Preferably a trained observer."

And she was looking directly at me.

"You want me to come and spy for you?" For that moment I found the idea exciting. Back to my old job. Until I realized, of course, that I was a mother and my duties were in my home. "I'm sorry," I said. "But I can't just abandon my children."

She grabbed my arm now, squeezing it uncomfortably. "Your child was nearly killed, Mrs. Sullivan. You owe it to her to find the culprit, surely. And it can be at your convenience. I wouldn't expect you to be here full time."

"How would you explain my presence?" I was already weakening.

"We'd have to make you something official . . ." She paused. "Didn't you say you'd worked in the theater?"

"I did have to go undercover once in a theater production," I admitted.

"I watched you helping with makeup," she said. "You seemed quite adept. You could fill in as our makeup artist. We've been meaning to hire one, rather than letting the actors put on their own makeup. And that way you could chat with cast members and maybe learn things from them."

"I suppose I could," I said, still hesitant.

"We would pay you for your services, of course," Alice said. "We can start at fifty dollars for your time and I'm sure Mr. Martin would give you a nice bonus if you found the culprit and he could face Edison with proof. He'd enjoy that."

"Which Mr. Martin are we talking about?" I asked.

She laughed then. "Why, Mr. Arthur. His brother, as you've seen, is too easygoing."

"But I was told that Harry Martin is the boss, isn't he?"

"Harry's the one with the money," Alice said. "Money talks in this business as in every other. Harry set up the studio and brought Arthur in to handle the financial side. Arthur, as you might have seen, does not have his brother's charm. But he is a whiz with numbers."

"I see," I said. "So Harry will marry Mrs. Prince, and presumably she'll bring with her all the information on her father-in-law and husband's research and patents."

Alice nodded. "I'd say he'd got himself a nice deal. She's a pretty woman too. One more thing." She looked at me appraisingly. "I can take the money out of my budget. You might not want to mention your investigation to the Martin brothers until you have some results." She looked at me coolly. Did she suspect the brothers might sabotage their own picture? Or did she just think they would dismiss a woman detective? There was a silence as she looked at me, waiting to see if I would accept her offer.

Fifty dollars would keep me going for a month even with Daniel away. I must confess I had missed being a professional detective. And though now hardly seemed the time to reopen my detective agency, I knew I wouldn't rest until I found out who had endangered Bridie's life. I made up my mind. "I'll do it," I said, holding out my hand. We shook.

"We shouldn't leave Bridie alone," I said. We opened the door to find her sitting facing the mirror with cold cream all over her face.

"Well done, dear," Alice said. "Now wipe that off and you'll be as good as new."

"We have to remember there was a fire too," I said. "If anyone was in the building at the time they also might have been killed."

"Another murder attempt? Is that what you are suggesting? And Mr. Arthur was in the building as it happened, or the entire place could have burned down."

"I was wondering," I began as Alice grabbed a cloth and started to help Bridie, "if I might see the place where the fire started. Presumably it hasn't been put to rights yet."

"It has not. We've a claim with the insurance company that the fire started with a malfunctioning lightbulb, but I don't buy that myself. I was pretty sure that the machine was not on when we left the place. Someone slipped in there and turned it on, knowing that over a night and day it would become too hot, melt the celluloid, and start a fire."

She waited until Bridie's face was clean and glowing pink. "Well, come on, then. Let's hurry if you want to see it before anyone returns."

She led us along the hall, up a flight of stairs. I could smell the acrid odor of burning still lingering as Alice pushed open the door.

"This is where you make the films?" The room was a minor disaster: A central table held what must have been the editing machine. It was charred and blackened; the walls, ceiling, and a remnant of what might have been a fabric screen were smudged and blackened too. The chair that had been at the table was burned, as was the back of the door. A shelf on the far wall held metal canisters. A door beyond bore the hand-lettered sign DARKROOM.

"If that door hadn't been shut, it might well have spread," I said.

Alice nodded in agreement. "Thank God it didn't reach that shelf of film or the whole place would have gone up. And it was most fortuitous that Mr. Arthur came into the building to retrieve some papers and smelled smoke."

"This isn't just a malicious or spiteful act," I said. "This would have ruined you, put you out of business for years."

"How true," said a voice behind us. I spun around to see Mr. Arthur himself standing there.

❧ Fourteen ❧

W ho are these ladies, Alice, and why are they snooping around?" Arthur barked. I took a breath to tell him that we had met before, but Alice was quicker. She gestured to Bridie.

"This young lady is an actress. She was in last week's picture—you know, *Marriage or Death?* The one that was destroyed in the fire. I'm choosing a costume for her, and I wanted to see if all the film we shot last week was gone. I—" she hesitated, "I mean DW, tried some new color techniques and we wanted to see how they worked."

Arthur shook his head. "Nothing left from last week. At two pennies a foot we lost a lot of money on the film, not to mention the salaries we paid out that we will have to pay again."

"It's a blessing you were there, Mr. Martin." I put on a gracious smile. "Alice says that the whole studio might have burnt down if you hadn't discovered it."

"True." Arthur's scowl deepened as he looked at me. It seemed to offend him that I had dared to address him. I decided he was one of those men that need to feel superior to women.

"Was it burglars, do you think?" I cocked my head to one side and made my eyes wide. "Or criminals? How terrifying!"

"You've been watching too many of our pictures, little lady." His voice was less harsh. "It was pure carelessness. Someone left the electric light on in the editing machine. It overheated and celluloid is highly flammable. When I find out who did it, they will be out on their ear." He turned to Alice, waving a menacing finger in her direction. "And don't you try to protect them!"

"I wouldn't dream of it, Mr. Martin." She turned to me. "Shall we go, Mrs. Sullivan?" But I didn't know when I would get another chance to question Arthur Martin, so I didn't want to waste it.

"You must be a very important man, Mr. Martin," I simpered. "What were you doing here so late at night?"

This seemed to strike a chord. Arthur flushed and for a moment was at a loss for words. Then he recovered himself. "None of your business!" He studied me carefully. "Who are you, anyway? I've seen you before, haven't I? And you're certainly not an actress."

"I am . . ." I was about to say I was Bridie's mother and chaperone, but Alice got there before me.

"She's going to be our makeup artist. I've been showing her around."

I gave him a winning smile, then decided that my charm had gotten me as far as it could and bade him farewell. As we descended the stairs I couldn't help wondering about two things. The first was how long Arthur had been listening to us and how much he had heard. The second thing that struck me was that Alice was a very good liar.

We reached the ground floor, my skirt somewhat worse for wear from being dragged up and down the dusty stairs. Alice glanced back up them to see if anyone was in sight before she spoke.

"Thank you, Mrs. Sullivan," she said. "It will be a relief to know that someone is keeping an eye on us. Come when you can, preferably early mornings, as that's when actors need help with makeup."

"I will try," I said. "I have a small baby who requires a lot of attention and regular feedings, so it won't be easy."

"You'll do your best for us." She gave an encouraging smile.

"And perhaps you can help me out by giving me a list of all those employed here and how long they have worked for you."

She gave an annoyed little sigh. "That won't be easy. We've used different actors for each production, and stagehands tend to come and go as there is work."

"Well, you could start with the two crewmen who almost killed my daughter," I said with some heat. "I want to talk to them first."

"Yes, Willie Smith and Gino Scarpelli. They'll be at the top. And I can include the regulars. We keep our cameramen and electricians. I'll have a list written up for you and—" She broke off suddenly. "Oh, here's the first of the wagons arriving now. You should go."

She almost bundled us out of the door. Once outside I took Bridie's arm and led her around the corner to Fifth Avenue, where I hailed a cab. For once I thought the expense was justified. We'd both had too much of a shock to walk, and my head was already buzzing with suspicions. Why hadn't Alice shared with Mr. Arthur what had happened on the set and what she suspected? And why had he looked so uneasy when I had questioned him about the night of the fire? He was the junior partner, I thought, toying with this fact. His brother put him in charge of finances. Was all the money Harry's? Had Arthur been cooking the books? Or even worse than that—did he secretly want his brother's company to fail?

We were both silent for most of the cab ride home, lost in our own thoughts. I half expected Bridie to chide me for involving myself with the studio at all when I had forbidden her to continue. But either she was too contrite over her own behavior to bring it up or so shaken by the morning that she was lost in her own thoughts. My plan had been to send Bridie off to school in time for the afternoon classes but seeing her pale, serious face, I relented.

"Would you like to stay home today and start back at school tomorrow?" I asked as we walked up to the house.

"No thank you, Mama." Bridie looked near to tears. "I'll just eat something and go. If I sit around the house all afternoon, I think I will feel worse."

"That's a very sensible attitude." I put my arm around her. "And after all, you are not injured in the least. Don't dwell on what might have happened."

"I'll try not to." She looked at me. "I expected you to be angrier."

"I am furious that you disobeyed me, and there will be consequences for that later," I said steadily, "but I am so glad that you are not hurt that I can only feel grateful right now." I smiled.

After Bridie was off to school, the baby fed, and dinner bought and in the oven, I got out a small notebook and pencil to write down what Alice had told me while it was still clear in my mind.

Could it be accident and coincidence?
Lamp falling, yes. Fire, yes. Mannequin—no. That was deliberate.
Who had opportunity?
Alice and DW (unlikely)
Cameramen
Crew—especially the two on scene today
Actors
Who had motive?
Arthur—junior partner. Jealousy? But no opportunity this
morning if he was at the studio.
Lily or her family—revenge for being fired or to avenge bad
behavior
Edison or someone being paid by him—to stop the film from
being made

Was I missing something? It gave me a thrill to put down my thoughts in a notebook after so many years and reminded me of Paddy Riley, the surly investigator who had told me that women

134

couldn't be detectives when I first decided to try my hand. I had not given up in the face of his criticism, and, on the whole, I was grateful to him. Not only had he given me the chance to learn the trade, even though he had hired me originally as a cleaner, but without him I would not have my house at Patchin Place or my skills as a detective. And without my investigation skills, Daniel would not be a free man and our family would not exist.

Paddy Riley had been a good investigator, I mused, remembering how often he had fooled me with his disguises. But on the other hand, he had not had to solves crimes while running a household and taking care of three children. I gave myself high marks for that. And, as I opened the notebook and began to write again, the thought that I was going to challenge my wits with a new case gave me a little thrill of excitement.

That afternoon it was a different Bridie who bounded into the house, slamming the front door behind her out of exuberance rather than temper.

"I take it you had a good afternoon at school?" I raised an eyebrow. I took my hands out of the soapy water I had been using to wash dishes and dried them on my apron.

"Guess what, Mama." Bridie pulled out a chair and plopped down on it. It was unusual for her to come straight home after school. She normally went by Sid and Gus's house to report on the day's activities and have a snack.

"What?" I played along.

"Mrs. McCormick went back to school because Blanche had been so worried about me, and she told Blanche about what happened this morning and Blanche told everyone, and now I'm the talk of the school." It all came out in a big rush of words.

"Well, mercy me," was all I could think of to say.

"They all asked me when I was going to be in a picture they could go and see. I told them this summer. I can, can't I?" She looked at me anxiously. "I'm not lying. Only, Helen said I was making it all up and I told her she could see for herself this summer."

"Alice did say she would try to get you a part in the summer holidays," I said. "But I wouldn't set your heart on it. I don't know how trustworthy film people are."

"Well, *Alice* is trustworthy, I'm sure of that," she said happily. "Can I go and tell the ladies? They haven't heard about anything that happened today yet." It occurred to me that the lesson Bridie was learning from sneaking out this morning was not the one I had wished.

"You can tell them tomorrow," I said sternly. "Right now you need to go upstairs and write Mrs. McCormick a letter of apology. She spent her morning driving around the city looking for you."

"I wouldn't worry about that. She told Blanche it was the most fun she's had in ages," Bridie said breezily. Then she saw my face. "Oh all right, I'm going."

"And then start on your homework. After dinner you can help me with the chores that I didn't do this morning because I was running across the city after you."

"It sounds like you will be missing your chores every morning if you are going to help Alice solve the mystery of who has been sabotaging the studio." Bridie feigned an innocent look. "But don't worry, I won't mention it to Papa." Before I could answer she disappeared up the stairs.

It struck me that teenage girls were annoyingly perceptive. She had focused in on the main point. I was eager to be out investigating again but what was I going to tell Daniel?

Fifteen

I did not sleep well that night. What had I got myself into? I thought as I tossed and turned. Alice thought someone was sabotaging their pictures to make sure they were held up, so another movie could make it to the theater ahead of them. Catching the saboteurs should not be too challenging a task for me. However, two of the occasions that I had witnessed could have led to a death. Mary and Cecil would have been electrocuted if the lamp had fallen into the tank, and yesterday, Bridie . . . I cut off the thought abruptly. In my mind I saw that train hurtling toward us, I heard the noise of steam, the rumble of wheels. Was there something more evil at work at the studio—someone who was trying to kill the actors? And did I really want to get mixed up again in a murder investigation? One thing was sure—I was going to keep my precious Bridie well away until I had got to the bottom of this!

I had to get Bridie off to school and Liam and Mary Kate settled before I set off toward the studio the next morning. The doorman gave me a nod as I entered. "They told me you'd be coming," he said. "So you got yourself a job with the makeup, I hear."

"Just helping out until you find yourselves a full-time makeup artist," I said. "I'm afraid I don't know your name." I glanced at the list he held. "You know all of ours."

He grunted then gave a grudging smile. "Ted Johnson. Nice of you to ask."

"So how long have you been working here?"

"Since Mr. Martin started the studio," he said. "That would be twelve years now. I was a theater doorman before that, so I'm used to keeping out undesirable folks."

"Have you had any try to get in here?" I asked, keeping a smile on my face. "Any stage door Johnnies? I don't imagine so, since the actors are so anonymous. Nobody even knows their names."

"No, I can't say we've had that problem yet," he said. "But I expect you heard we had those crazy men last week. After they gave that girl the boot. Oh, her family didn't like that. They were waving their arms and yelling threats. Well, I'm assuming they were threats. Couldn't barely understand a word they said, sounded like they were fresh off the boat. But they made a lot of gestures. Going to cut me to pieces, apparently."

"So not gangsters, then," I said, thinking of the Black Hand. "If they were new immigrants."

"No, these guys didn't look too well connected," he said. "I did see a guy like that come by and ask for Mr. Arthur recently though. Well-dressed but kind of shifty looking. I don't know what for or whether he was one of those gangsters, but Mr. Arthur looked quite worried."

"You must see a lot from here," I said. "All the comings and goings. You haven't had anyone else from the outside try to sneak in?"

He looked at me suspiciously now, his head cocked to one side, like a bird. "You're a very inquisitive young woman. If I were you, I'd watch my step. Do the job you're paid for and don't poke your nose where it's not wanted. That's how you get by in this business." He paused, still looking at me. "Too many accidents in our line of work, if you get my meaning."

"Sorry, you're right," I said. "Thanks for the advice." I went on into the building. Had he just given me a general warning or was there something specific he knew about how the studio was run and what went on here?

"Ah, Molly. Good, you're here." Alice greeted me as I crossed the giant stage room already busy with crew members rushing around. "We've actors needed on set as soon as possible. We're trying to squeeze in the films that we lost as well as what was already on this week's schedule. It's so important to get the product into the picture houses on time, otherwise we lose our slot."

"I'll do my best," I said. We separated with a nod of understanding.

I rolled up my sleeves and put on the apron I had brought with me before going through to the makeup room. Ryan was there, almost done with his makeup. Cecil sat beside him, and the two were engaged in animated conversation. Farther down the bench was the young actress Mary Pickford, while Daisy sat at the far end.

"Molly!" Ryan looked up, surprised. "So you've let Bridie come back after all?"

"Because Alice said that I would be playing that part now," Mary added, frowning at me.

"Don't worry, Miss Pickford," I said, "Bridie will not be returning. She's gone back to being a schoolgirl. The role is all yours." I noticed that Mary relaxed. "But Alice said you needed help with makeup, especially this week when you're trying to catch up with the shooting, so I volunteered."

"I didn't know you knew anything about makeup?" Ryan gave me an inquiring stare.

"I did work once in the theater, Ryan, so I know a bit about stage makeup. Alice was demonstrating some of the film techniques last week. So I suggest you finish yours and let Cecil get on with his."

"I hope you're not going to be a tyrant," Ryan said. "My delicate constitution can't handle being yelled at."

I had to laugh and gave him a playful slap as I went past him. Cecil was now focused on his face and daubing generous amounts of green over his cheeks.

"Here, let me smooth that out," I said, reaching for a cloth.

"Make sure you highlight his cheekbones," Ryan instructed. "He has such fine cheekbones."

I tried not to smile.

"So Bridie is recovered from her ordeal yesterday?" Ryan asked.

"She is, thank you. I'm not sure that I am, however."

"I agree. It was a moment of pure terror, wasn't it? It was like one of those nightmares where you try to run but your legs won't work," Ryan said.

"What exactly happened?" Daisy asked. "I heard something about the train?"

"Bridie was supposed to be tied to the tracks, then replaced with the dummy as the train approached," I said. "Only, the crew members in charge of the dummy missed the cue and then the rope got caught around her legs as we tried to pull her up."

"Holy smokes," Daisy said. "I told my mom that this business is getting more dangerous by the minute. These directors will do anything to get a sensational shot. It's like a competition to them, especially now with Edison having moved closer to us in the Bronx."

"So why did the nincompoops miss their cue?" Cecil asked. "Were they fired instantly?"

"They missed it because apparently someone had tampered with the dummy," I said. "The head came off."

"See, what did I tell you?" Daisy said. "There is a curse on this studio. I reckon we're being haunted by the ghost of Mrs. Prince's husband, like they say."

"I don't think ghosts follow people around," I said. "I could understand the studio itself being haunted, but it would be a clever ghost that followed everyone to the train yard. There you are." I finished with Cecil's makeup and turned to help Mary. She was applying her foundation with a very practiced hand.

"Then how do you explain all the strange things that have happened?" she asked. She looked at me with big, frightened eyes. "When Cecil and I were in the tank, that lamp nearly fell. We could have been electrocuted." I picked up the kohl and started outlining her eyes.

"And we have to shoot that scene again this week, my sweet," Cecil said. "Let's hope no lights decide to topple."

I didn't wonder that Mary was worried. Not only would she have to go back in the water, but now she was going to be shooting the train scene as well.

"So you have to reshoot your picture too?" I asked as I worked, focusing on not smudging the black lines. "Look up, please."

"Two indoor scenes and the water tank scene." Cecil sighed dramatically. "Luckily the film we shot on location was safely stored in another room. I don't fancy another dip in the ocean."

"I think it's more likely to be someone with a grudge against the studio than a ghost," I said, throwing out this suggestion casually as I moved on to apply foundation to Daisy's face. "The fire in the editing room on Saturday . . . that sounds to me as if someone didn't want the pictures to be finished."

"Ye gods, it must be one of my rivals," Ryan said. "I knew the theater crowd would not want me to succeed in pictures. My rivals must hate seeing my face on screens around the country."

"But I take it you didn't notice any of your rivals here last week?" I said sweetly. "And anyway, how would an outsider get in past the doorman?"

"They could have found a way in at night."

"There was no sign of forced entry, and the doors were locked,"

I said. "In fact we could put the fire down as an accident if the other things hadn't happened. The head becoming detached from the dummy—that had to be deliberate, didn't it?"

They digested this in silence for a moment.

"Then it had to be one of us," Daisy said in a small voice. "Someone working in the studio."

"I was here when that light fell," I said. "I don't remember seeing anyone touch it, did you?"

"Anyone could have toppled it," she said, "except Mary and Cecil, of course. Even if someone wasn't near, there are cords and wires all over the place. They only had to tangle one around it and pull."

"And no one checked at the time," I mused. "Everyone has been assuming these are accidents."

"Or ghosts," Daisy put in.

"Yes, well the next time a 'ghost' causes an accident around here I think we should all check to see who was around when the accident happened," I said dryly.

"I can't believe this." Alice came in shaking her head, a letter in her hand. "This is too bad."

"Another accident?" Mary shot her a frightened look.

"No, but I am supposed to be shooting two pictures in the time it should take to shoot one, and now my cameraman Edward has handed in his notice and Johnny has gone missing. Am I to reshoot a film with an entirely new cast and crew?"

✂ Sixteen ✂

A new cast except for moi," Ryan said. "You still have your star, remember."

Alice gave him a look that shut him up.

"Well, I suppose Johnny was pretty shaken up yesterday," Ryan said. "Perhaps he just went on a bit of a drinking spree last night and has yet to wake up." That did sound like a logical explanation to me, but I couldn't help remembering that Johnny had told me himself that he started as an actor in Edison's studio. Could he have been the cause of the accidents? His disappearance at this point would certainly put the film even more behind schedule. On the other hand, what if something had happened to him?

"You're probably right, Ryan," Alice said. "I just have to assume that he will show up this morning sometime. I'm not looking forward to telling DW. Molly, will you be ready to do Johnny's makeup and rush him out to the set when he gets here?"

I nodded.

"Then let's shoot the interior scenes that he is not in this morning." Alice was all business now. "And go up to the roof for the outdoor scene once Johnny decides to show up. Mary, can you handle going back and forth between the characters in the two pictures?"

"No problem," Mary said confidently. "I grew up acting in melo-drama and taking different characters. I had to change costumes in under a minute backstage."

"Wonderful," Alice said. "Now I just have to tell Billy that he's lost his assistant cameraman. Edward at least did me the courtesy of letting me know he won't be coming in. Says he has a sick relative." I thought of Edward's worried face as he ran up to the train tracks yesterday, and he had watched Billy lying on the tracks to get the perfect shot. Perhaps he had decided that the job was no longer worth the risk.

The actors followed Alice out of the dressing room, still talking loudly. I hung back, putting the makeup away, taking the time alone to think. What did I need to know? Were the so-called accidents caused by a member of the cast or crew, or could an outsider possibly be involved? The latter did not seem too likely, given the way I was scrutinized every time I arrived. The first thing I wanted to find out was how easy it would be to get into the building. There were two en-trances, the one that actors used on Fourteenth Street and the fancier one that led out to Fifth Avenue. Ted Johnson at the Fourteenth Street entrance screened everyone carefully. I decided to check on the Fifth Avenue entrance. Could someone from the outside have come in and climbed to the upper floor from there? I headed down the hall toward the foyer, into the room, and was immediately addressed.

"Can I help you?" It was the same clerk I had encountered on my first day at the studio, sitting at his desk. I thought quickly.

"I'm just going up to see Harry." I gave what I hoped was a win-ning smile. He consulted a book in front of him.

"I don't seem to have an appointment for you, Miss . . ."

"Oh, but Harry will want to see me." I strode confidently toward the stairs. Before I reached them the man was up and blocking the way.

"You need an appointment to go upstairs," he said sternly. "No exceptions." He leered at me. "Don't worry, honey, if Harry wants to see you, he'll make an appointment." I flushed.

"I'll have you know it is about a business matter," I retorted.

"Yeah, sure it is." He was still grinning.

Just then the metal staircase shook with the steps of someone walking down it. We both looked up and Harry was coming down the stairs.

"Mrs. Sullivan," he said genially, "were you coming to see me?" He gave me a cheerful smile.

"I was trying to," I said, "on a business matter," I glared at the clerk, "but it seems I don't have an appointment."

"Nonsense, I think I know what this is about, and I would like to talk to you about it." He waved me up the stairs. "Come on up."

The clerk still had his arm out blocking my way. He dropped it at Harry's words.

"Thank you," I said, giving a triumphant smile, "I will." I climbed the stairs, thinking quickly. I had only tried to get upstairs to see how easily it could be done. What could Harry think I wanted to talk to him about? As I followed him up the stairs and down the hall toward his office, I had a sudden fear that the clerk had been correct in his supposition and Harry thought I was here for romance. If I had to fight him off, it would ruin everything.

"Come in, come in." He paused outside a door and motioned me inside. I entered hesitantly. There was a large mahogany desk and behind it a wall of books. Papers were strewn over the desk and onto several chairs. "Let me make some room for you," Harry said.

"Mrs. Sullivan, isn't it?" Fanny Prince rose from a chair in the corner. I relaxed. Surely Harry couldn't mean to have a romantic tryst with his fiancée in the room.

"Yes." I shook hands with her, feeling a little foolish and tongue-tied. I wracked my brain for a reason that I would need to meet with Harry. To my surprise he spoke first.

"I think I know why you're here," Harry said, moving papers off the nearest chair and motioning for me to sit. "I heard about the incident at the train yard yesterday."

I paused, waiting to see where he was going with this.

"That must have been terrifying for your daughter. I understand she has left the picture."

"Yes, though not just because of the danger," I said. "She is a schoolgirl. She needs to return to her studies now that her vacation has ended."

"Yes, I completely understand. And Alice has mentioned that she might want to do a picture in the summer. Great idea." He opened a leather portfolio and took out a large twenty-dollar gold certificate. He held it out to me. "I want to make sure your girl's okay."

I stared at it but did not take it. "That's not necessary," I said.

His expression hardened. "Mrs. Sullivan, I think you should take this. A court would not want to be bothered with this matter. And bad publicity would just spoil your daughter's chances of making a film later."

"Unless Edison has already promised her a part and paid off her mother," Fanny said dryly. "Maybe he is going to bankroll a lawsuit."

"The railroad is already threatening to drag me into court to stop us filming their trains," Harry said. He looked down at me and I felt the threat. "I think it would be better if you took the money." Now it made sense. Harry's world seemed to be one where people needed to be paid off.

"You're misunderstanding me," I said, continuing to ignore the bill he held out. "We're not planning to go to the papers, and I wouldn't have the first idea of how to sue someone in a court. It was an accident, and my daughter is just fine." His face relaxed. The friendly smile returned so immediately that it seemed like a mask.

"You have to forgive Harry," Fanny said. "He's spent so much time fighting in court that he thinks everyone is out to get him."

"Well, someone *is* out to get me." Harry gave her a look I couldn't interpret.

"Do you mean the sabotage, Mr. Martin?" I asked.

"What do you know about that?" he shot back.

"Well, I know my daughter was almost killed because of sabotage yesterday. And I have heard from the crew that there have been a series of accidents. Who do you think is behind it?"

A bell shrilled and I jumped. It rang twice before a young woman dressed in a professional linen suit came into the office.

"Mr. Martin, there is a telephone call for you."

Harry rose. "Thank you, Sarah." His eyes followed her figure as she exited. He nodded at me. "Excuse me," he said, walking out into the hallway.

I heard him yell into the apparatus before his secretary must have closed the door and the sound was cut off.

"That was surprising," Fanny said in her smooth upper-class English tones, looking at me appraisingly. "Not many people refuse money when it is offered."

I bristled. "I would hardly have been bought off for twenty dollars if my daughter really had been hurt."

"But you didn't come up here for money, and I don't think you came up here to try to seduce Harry. So why are you here, Mrs. Sullivan?"

In a split second I decided to take her into my confidence. I didn't see any possible connection between Fanny and the sabotage. Surely someone would have noticed if she had been hanging around the studio without Harry.

"I've been hired to investigate the sabotage," I said, "and I wanted to see how easy it would be to get upstairs without being noticed."

Her eyebrows raised. "You've been hired? That raises so many questions. Who hired you? I know Harry didn't."

"Alice asked me to look into it."

"Alice?" She laughed. "Isn't she DW's secretary?"

At first, I was surprised. How could Fanny have been around the studio and not realize what a big role Alice played. Then I realized that I had only seen Fanny at Harry's side, and DW made sure to be in charge every time Harry was around. "Alice does a lot of work behind the scenes," I said. "From what I've seen there might not be a production without everything she does."

"Harry has always said that women should stay out of the moving picture business," she said, staring at the door through which he had left. "I was hoping to have that chance when I invested in them. But apparently, I should have had more luck as a secretary." She gave a brittle laugh.

"Well, now you'll have that chance, won't you, if you and Mr. Martin are to be married?"

"You know our husbands don't want us working after we get married, Mrs. Sullivan." She played absentmindedly with the papers on her desk. "Or perhaps yours does, since apparently you are undertaking detective work."

"He doesn't know anything about it," I confessed.

She laughed, more sincerely this time. "I will need to take advice from you on managing husbands."

"But he does know I was an investigator before we were married," I added. "And he is a police captain himself, so we are well matched, like Mr. Martin and yourself."

"I want to get to the bottom of this sabotage myself, Mrs. Sullivan." Fanny moved some papers and sat down in the chair next to me. "My money is invested in this picture, and it is important to me that it be made."

"I also have a personal connection," I confessed. "Ryan O'Hare is an old friend of mine, and I don't want him to be hurt."

"The famous playwright? Mrs. Sullivan, you continue to surprise me." She looked at me appraisingly. "So what have you learned and where will your investigation go next?"

I wondered how much I should share. "Most of the crew would have had the chance to sabotage the film, although it is not in their interest to do so."

"Unless they were being paid to do so by someone else," she put in.

"Exactly," I said. "I have heard a number of people mention Mr. Edison in connection with sabotage. I would like to get into his studio to question some of his staff, but I confess I have no idea how to accomplish that feat." I remembered that Johnny had said that Edison's new studio was in the Bronx, but it seemed so far away I wasn't even sure which train to take.

"I may be able to help you with that," Fanny said in her smooth, posh tones. That was the last thing I expected to hear. "There is a document that Mr. Edison has asked me to sign about the patent I hold. I've been putting it off, but I could arrange a meeting at his studio to sign it."

"And how would I come into it?" I asked, intrigued but still not clear.

"I'll bring you with me as my social secretary. I can get you into the studio. What you do from there will be up to you." She smiled. "You are the investigator, not I."

"It's a grand idea," I said, impressed with her quick thinking. "Do you have a way to get us there?"

"I have an automobile, and I drive," she said, "an advantage of living without a husband for a time. One learns to fend for oneself. There is only one problem."

"What's that?" I raised my eyebrows in query.

"Edison is not often at his studio. I'll speak with his secretary, but I can't guarantee how long it will take to get an interview there, and meeting him at his other offices wouldn't do us any good if you want a chance to investigate at the studio."

"Well, it's a start." A door closed down the hallway and footsteps started back.

"Don't say anything to Harry," Fanny said quickly in a whisper. In a louder voice she said, "Let me show you out, Mrs. Sullivan." I followed her out of the office. "Mrs. Sullivan is going now, Harry," she said as we came up to Harry in the hall. "She has been charming about the whole incident."

"Thank you, lovely lady." He took my hand and held it a little too long. I followed Fanny down the hall.

"How can I find you?" she asked softly.

"I am doing makeup every morning before shooting," I answered in the same soft tones.

She gave my hand a squeeze and went back down the hallway toward Harry's office. I had been rather turned around but realized I was at the top of the wooden stairway that led to the stage. I was developing a picture of the building in my mind. This wooden staircase came out behind the large stage area. That stage was two stories high and its ceiling was the roof on which we had filmed the outdoor scene. On the Fifth Avenue side were the dressing rooms and a hallway leading to DW's office. Also there was the fancy foyer with the spiral staircase going up to this hallway with the editing room and the Martins' offices. Anyone coming in from the outside would be noticed, but from the stage area, anyone could have climbed the stairs to the editing room unnoticed. Then I remembered the narrow stairs from this hallway up to the roof. If the door on the roof was open, someone could have come down from there.

I tested my theory by clattering down the stairs in front of me. The stairs came out to the stage floor just as I had thought. I was behind the set walls. I heard conversation and decided they were not shooting yet, and it would be safe to walk around.

"Well, look who decided to show up!" Daisy's words rang out as I went around the set to the front of studio two. I stopped guiltily, wondering if they were directed at me. But all heads were turned in the opposite direction and Johnny was walking in with clothes so rumpled they looked as if they had been worn all night. He took his cap off his head revealing equally messy hair and stood looking at the actors, his boyish face sheepish.

"I told you." Ryan's voice was triumphant. He went over to Johnny and clapped him on the back, causing Johnny to wince. "Had a wee bit of the spirits, did we, boyo?"

"Sorry, Alice. I overslept," Johnny said. He fixed her with his large, sorrowful eyes.

"Think you're hard to resist, do you, Johnny?" Alice's sharp tone made him wince again. "You're lucky DW hasn't been on set yet. Go get into costume and makeup and we'll talk about this later."

That was my cue and I followed Johnny back into the makeup room. He was quiet while I was putting on the pancake makeup and lining his eyes. Then he appeared to come out of a fog. "You're Bridie's mother, aren't you?"

"Yes, but she's not coming back to the picture. She has to go to school." I dabbed some stray makeup off his ear. "Mary Pickford's taking the part. Bridie's just a young girl and she was quite distressed by what happened at the train yard."

"I was too," Johnny said. "I almost didn't come back myself." Johnny smelled of spirits and his eyes were troubled.

"Do you think there is a ghost, then?" I asked. "Behind the sabotage?"

"No." He sounded grim. "I think it's a real person."

His tone made me look at him sharply. "Do you know who it is?"

He shook his head. "It's not fair to say until I'm sure. I saw something at the train yard . . ." He trailed off. "But maybe the person has an explanation for it. I just don't know." The last words were muttered to himself.

"Johnny, if you know something you should tell me," I said, then realizing he had no reason to trust me, "or Alice or DW," I added.

"I don't know." He shook his head again as if trying to clear it of an idea. "I was probably mistaken." He smiled but it didn't reach his eyes. "Off to dress up as the hero and save the day. Thank you, ma'am." He clapped his hat back onto his head as he went into the men's dressing room. I stared after him.

I cleaned up, said my goodbyes, and headed home. But as I made my way through the blustery April day I couldn't stop thinking What had Johnny seen?

❧ Seventeen ❧

When I opened my eyes on Wednesday I lay in bed, enjoying the stillness of the early morning, hearing the distant noises of the city—the commerce at the Jefferson Street market, the clang of a trolley bell, the twitter of birds on the rooftop—and felt a moment of peace, until I reminded myself that I had work to do. I had snooped. I had asked questions, and I was none the wiser. There was the prospect of a trip to Edison's studio, but I had no idea when that would be.

The only things I had learned were vague. Arthur had been seen to have an encounter with a man who could easily have been an Italian gang member, and I had heard him warn his brother to stay away from the police. Harry seemed accustomed to paying people off, behavior that was suspicious at best. Also, the actors were jittery with the rumor about the ghost going around the studio. Edward had resigned abruptly, and Johnny had seen something he didn't want to talk about. That brought my mind back to gangs again. Not many people would want to go up against them.

I sat up in bed and reached again for the list that Alice had given me. The names of the two crewmen I wanted to talk to first were at the top: Willie Smith and Gino Scarpelli. Gino was an Italian name, wasn't it? I scanned down quickly. There was an Antonio Sereno as well. It wasn't surprising that there were Italian crew members, but I wondered about any connection to Lily La Rosa or Italian gangs. The recent funeral had me jumpy. Had someone been hired to do some sabotage when protection money was not paid?

I didn't see how I could find out more about that. During my days as a working detective I had taken stupid risks to get information from gangs, including finding myself facing Monk Eastman, one of the most ruthless of the gang leaders. I had come through unscathed and certainly wasn't about to take that sort of risk again. If Daniel had been here I could have asked him to uncover information. If only Daniel were here, I thought, and not just for my investigation. My heart gave a little pang as I wondered what he was doing today.

I arrived early at the studio and it was a good thing. They were planning to reshoot the train scene and wanted to do so while the light was good. The sun was threatening to come out soon and harsh shadows did not look well on film; they also gave away the time of day. Mary and Ryan were both pros and had their own makeup done in no time at all. Daisy and Cecil were not filming today. Johnny seemed preoccupied and apprehensive. That could just be nerves about the day's shooting. After all, he did have to jump in front of a moving train.

Gino Scarpelli and Willie Smith were putting ropes and canvas into a large box. I wasn't sure how to approach them, what reason I should give for talking to them. But as soon as Willie saw me, he let go of the rope and touched his cap. "Hey, you're the mom, ain't you?" He nudged Gino, who finished coiling the rope he was holding and turned around. "Gino, it's the mom of the girl. Remember, from the train yard?"

"How could I forget?" Gino gave me a sheepish look. "A pretty lady with bright red hair, looking like she was going to kill me." I hadn't realized before how young they both were, not more than twenty. Their accents told me they had grown up in this part of the city. They both had the same nasal sound that Daisy did, pronouncing forget as "fohgit" and yard as "yahd." Our part of the city was such a mix of accents. Immigrants like me had kept the accents of our home country. Bridie imitated the posh tones of Sid and Gus and the girls at her school. Young working people like those at the studio were making their own accent that was a mix of all the cultures.

"I'm really sorry, ma'am," he went on. "We were trying to make the shot and that damn—excuse me—that darn head came right off the dummy."

"Could it have been accidentally detached?" I asked.

"I don't see how." Willie looked just as concerned as Gino. "We checked it at the studio, and it must have been in place when we carried it from the wagon."

"Yeah," Gino agreed, "someone must have removed the screw after we got all set up."

"But who could have done that without you seeing?"

"Almost anyone," Willie said. "There was a problem with the axle of the police wagon because of the mud and we went over to fix it."

"And then Mr. Martin came by and wanted to talk to DW about something, so everyone grabbed a cup of coffee from the tureen and took a bit of a break."

"Which Mr. Martin?" I asked sharply. Either Harry or Arthur had been there at the train yard.

Wille shrugged and looked at Gino who shrugged as well. "Who can tell? I was just glad for a bit of a break. DW was mad though. See, the engineer of the train before had been paid off to go a bit slower but we lost that train because of the delay. I was surprised he decided to take his chances with the next one."

"That was a big chance to take," I said hotly, "and it almost cost my daughter her life."

"Not for nothing, ma'am, but your daughter is better out of it," Willie said softly, looking around to see if anyone could overhear him. "Things keep breaking around here, and the higher-ups are just pushing for the best, most exciting shots. Someone is gonna get hurt sooner or later."

"That'll be us, if we don't get this scenery up," Gino said with a false laugh, obviously wanting to end the conversation. "'Scuse me, ma'am." He touched his cap and walked past me without looking back. Willie shrugged again, gave me an apologetic look, and followed.

I was not invited to accompany the crew to the train yard and couldn't come up with a good reason to join them. I waited until they had departed, wondering what I could find by snooping around. The dummy, its head now firmly attached to its shoulders, had gone with them. Besides, how would one ever find fingerprints on a cloth dummy?

I heard Mr. Arthur's voice bellowing into a telephone somewhere upstairs. I couldn't hear what was being said but he sounded very angry. Home then, I suppose, I thought. I felt a bit lost in this investigation, no closer to knowing who was behind the sabotage.

I turned down Sixth Avenue and had to walk around a food cart that was sticking out into the road. I turned sideways and lifted my skirt to avoid dragging it in the dirty gutter. As I did, a flash of blue caught my eye. There! I was sure that someone had ducked back under an awning just as I looked. I was certain now. Someone was following me.

Don't turn around, I told myself, regaining my place on the pavement and strolling as if I had no care in the world. My shoulders were stiff and braced as if at any moment I might feel a gloved hand clasp me from behind. The street, which had felt crowded a moment before, now felt empty. I wanted to confront the person following me. This had gone on long enough. But I needed to do it with others around. Surely no one could attack me in a crowded street, could they?

But this stretch of street was empty; I could hear footsteps behind me and quickened my pace. There ahead, a group of women were waiting outside a bakery. Just beyond them I ducked into a small alley and waited, my heart pounding. Then, gathering my courage, I stepped out of the alley. And ran right into the chest of a tall man in a blue uniform.

"Oh, I do beg your pardon, ma'am," the man said, looking a little embarrassed.

Of course I recognized him right away. "Lieutenant Corelli," I said. "I'm glad to see you. I think someone is following me."

He had the grace to blush. "I'm afraid that I have been following you, Mrs. Sullivan. But please don't tell Captain Sullivan you spotted me."

I struggled to take this in. "You have been following me?"

"Well, not just me, but a few of the boys. Captain Sullivan didn't want to feel you were unprotected while he was away, especially with all the tension going on at the moment." He took off his hat and ran his hand through his hair. "This is embarrassing."

"Why not just tell me?" An angry blush spread to my cheeks. I had been feeling uneasy for days and all along it was police who were following me.

"He didn't want to worry you," he said sheepishly. I wanted to retort that it had worried me greatly to be followed around the streets of Manhattan. But it suddenly occurred to me that this was an opportunity I had been looking for. I could be angry at Daniel later.

I smiled at the lieutenant. "How very good to see you. Congratulations on your promotion."

He beamed then. "Thanks to your husband."

"You were most helpful to him when he was trying to solve the murder of Mr. McCormick and had no authority to do so."

He moved closer to me. "Between ourselves, I saw that we'd be getting nowhere if it was left to the other guy."

I realized as we spoke that he was, of course, Italian. One of the first Italian officers to be taken into the police department.

"It must have been so upsetting for you to lose a fellow Italian officer," I said. "Daniel was quite moved by the outpouring of love and respect at his funeral last week. I took the children to watch the procession myself."

He nodded solemnly. "It was a splendid send-off," he said. "And a sharp reminder to us all of the brutality we're dealing with. My wife worries about me every day. These guys in the Black Hand don't take kindly to fellow Italians going against them. In Sicily the police are paid to look the other way. They can't understand that we won't play along here."

"It seems they are getting more powerful by the minute," I said. "Are we in danger, Lieutenant? Does Daniel know of a threat to my family?"

"I'm afraid that everyone on the force is a little on edge right now. We aren't sure who will be next," he said solemnly. "I don't want to worry you. But we will be keeping an eye on you and make sure you don't come to any harm. You've been out and about a lot this week, if you don't mind me saying."

"I've been with our daughter Bridie at one of those new moving picture studios this week. She had a part in a film. And I got the feeling they were nervous about Italian gangs there too. Would you know if they are branching out into bigger and better things than small business protection?"

"I wouldn't put it past them," he said. "They move in wherever they see opportunity."

"Daniel was most interested when I told him," I went on, untruthfully.

"Especially when I mentioned a Scarpelli and a Sereno working on the set. Do either of those names ring a bell?"

He shrugged. "Half the Sicilians are called Sereno," he said. "And there are plenty of Scarpellis too. But as for the Black Hand getting mixed up in moving pictures, that's not something I've heard. Although I gather Mr. Edison is not above using thugs to prove a point. But I'll keep my ears open and let you know."

I fished the list that Alice had given me out of my pocket, glad that I had thought to bring it. "These are the men working there right now. They all seemed like fine people but . . ." I let my words trail off.

"But he would like me to check them out." Corelli smiled. "Anything to help Captain Sullivan."

Of course, Captain Sullivan had no idea I was even investigating, but I decided not to mention that.

"I do have my contacts in the Italian underworld," he went on. "I'd keep a close watch on your daughter, if you're worried."

I gave him my sweetest smile. "That's not necessary. She's back in school where she belongs now. And when she was there, I watched her like a hawk." Another thought occurred to me. "Did you speak to my son the other day?"

He grinned. "Yes, that was me. He's a cute little guy."

"Well, now that I know you are my protection, please walk with me, not after me," I said. "You scared me to death."

"I will," he promised, "if you don't let the captain know you spotted me."

"The captain is aware of my ability to tell when someone is following me," I said with a small smile, but relented when I saw his worried look, "but I won't say a thing."

He touched his cap. "I'm sorry again for having scared you. May I escort you to your house?" I agreed and he deposited me there with a small salute.

"I feel much better knowing you are looking out for me." I smiled.

The house was strangely quiet. Liam usually made his presence felt by singing to himself or providing his own commentary to his play. Mary Kate was not known for her prolonged silence.

"Aileen?" I called.

No answer.

I went from room to room. Had she taken them to the park? Usually she was good about asking permission before taking the children out. A feeling of dread crept over me. If Lieutenant Corelli had been protecting me, was no one watching the children? What if they were in danger? As I stood in our narrow hallway the memory of that bomb flooded into my brain: the flash, the boom, the wave of heat that threw me backward, Daniel lying unconscious in the hall as the fire overtook our house, and Liam rescued from upstairs at the last moment. It had all been too horrible to contemplate and had shown me that gangs would stop at nothing. Was Daniel involved in hunting them down right now? Had they decided to pay him back by kidnapping my children?

I didn't wait a second longer. I rushed across the street and banged on Sid and Gus's front door.

Gus opened it, putting her finger to her lips. "Come in quietly," she whispered. "Don't disturb Sid when she is being her creative best."

"But you don't understand," I said. "My children—"

"Are behaving wonderfully. Come and see for yourself. Sid is shooting some enchanting scenes." She ushered me into what used to be their dining room. Now it contained lights almost as powerful as those I'd seen at the studio, sheets draped from the walls, and on the bearskin rug on the floor lay my daughter, cooing with delight as Sid dangled a rattle above her. Liam sat to one side, watching with interest.

"And . . . cut," Sid said. She looked up to see me standing there.

So did Liam. "We can't go home yet, Mama. I haven't done my scene," Liam said, frowning at me.

"What exactly is going on?" I tried to keep my voice even.

"Why, I'm trying out my new camera," Sid said. "We finally got the room set up to be my moving picture studio, and who better to star in my first film than your adorable children?"

Aileen rose up from a chair behind the sheets. "I didn't think you'd mind, Mrs. Sullivan. Seeing as how the ladies are practically family and we didn't think you'd be back for a while."

"You're not angry, are you?" Sid studied my face. "Our goddaughter has been so good, laughing and cooing. I can't wait to develop the film and let you see it. And Liam has promised to build one of his amazing structures for us, haven't you, darling boy?"

"A skyscraper," Liam agreed.

"I was just alarmed when I got home and nobody was there," I said. "I couldn't think where you'd all gone."

"I should have left a note," Aileen said, "but I thought you wouldn't be back for ages."

"It's all right," I said, now trying to smile. "Of course I don't mind you experimenting with your camera on my children. And if something can keep Mary Kate happy and interested then it must be some kind of miracle."

Sid's focus was already back on the camera. "I'm worried it will be a little dark," she said, frowning. "Electric light just isn't the same as natural. I suppose that is why they have the large skylight at the studio." She studied the ceiling with interest.

"I'm sure this will turn out splendidly, dearest!" Gus said hurriedly. "But you are not cutting a hole in our roof!"

❧ Eighteen ❧

The next morning, as I walked back to the studio, I wondered what more I had to learn. I would have to wait for Lieutenant Corelli to get more information about possible gang involvement. I should have been apprehensive, going to a place where I knew sabotage was happening. But instead I was looking forward to my time there. Being around other adults, especially witty adults like Ryan and Alice, felt like waking up after five months of sleeping. I had to admit to myself that, although it was perhaps not logical or practical, I thrived on adventure and even on danger.

The mood there was also cheerful. The train scene had gone perfectly to script the day before and Alice thought it might be the most exciting film they had ever shot.

"I admit, it was a bit terrifying," Mary said as I lined her eyes with kohl, "especially knowing what happened to your daughter. But it was thrilling as well." Her eyes sparkled. Another woman who enjoyed life more when there was a spark of danger. So I was not alone in that.

"DW hired security guards to watch the studio until we finish the picture," Mary said. "He's not taking any chances."

"I don't blame him," I said. I was just cleaning up my makeup pots when I heard light footsteps coming into the makeup room. Fanny Prince was standing in the doorway.

"It's awfully good luck," she said as soon as I looked up. "If you're free, Mrs. Sullivan, we could go to Edison's studio today." She handed me a leather-bound notebook and a fountain pen. "You'll need this if you are to be my social secretary." I looked at the sensible but in no way fashionable skirt and shirtwaist I had on.

"I'm not sure I am dressed for the part," I said, wondering what exactly a social secretary should wear. Fanny was dressed in a neat dark blue silk two-piece over a white high-necked blouse with spills of white lace. Her matching dark blue hat was at a fashionable angle. She looked at me appraisingly.

"I think there is something in the wardrobe," she said and disappeared back into the dressing room, coming out with a dark lace shawl and felt hat. "Try this." I put on the shawl. Looking in the mirror I let down my hair and repinned it in a tighter bun, setting the hat on my head.

"Thank you." I gave her a smile. That obstacle solved, the next occurred to me. "Isn't it quite far?" I wondered if we could go there and back in time to feed the baby.

"It's in the Bronx," Fanny said with a confident smile, "but my runabout can get there in about an hour."

I followed her out of the studio, waving a goodbye to Ryan as we passed through the stage area. He raised his eyebrows in a question at my appearance, but I just gave another wave. Hopefully I would have some information to give him after my trip to the studio. It was such a stroke of luck that Fanny was going today and that she had a runabout. I had thought about trying to talk my way into the studio on my own, but the difficulty of getting to the Bronx and back on the train had given me pause. What would it be like to have an automobile in the city? I planned my trips to places that were on the El or the IRT lines.

Her jaunty little auto was parked on Fifth Avenue. It was a two-seater curved-dash Oldsmobile with the top on. She cranked the engine and then expertly maneuvered us past a waiting horse and cart, pulling the tiller steering rod far to the right. It struck me that women could drive just as well as men if their range of motion wasn't hampered by tight corsets and stiff material.

"Have you been to his studio before?" I asked as we turned right onto Seventeenth Street.

"No, I've only met Edison at attorneys' offices," she said, her face twisting in disgust as she said Edison's name. "I must confess I am a bit excited to see the studio. I've heard he has some amazing innovations."

"I wonder if he will let us see any of it, if he is as secretive as I have heard," I said.

"We will ask him to show us around first. There is a document that he really wants me to sign, so we are assured he will be nice to us until I have signed it."

"I was amazed to see you so soon," I said. "I thought it might take weeks."

"It's quite a stroke of luck," she said. "Apparently they are installing a water tank in the studio, and he wants to be there to oversee the installation."

"DW won't be pleased about that," I said. "Everything new that DW does, Edison is right behind."

"It's been that way for longer than you think," she said grimly. "Back at the beginning he insisted that my husband's father was copying his camera even though my father-in-law had all the evidence that he had invented it himself."

"I've heard your father-in-law mentioned." I wondered what it would be polite to say. "About his disappearance."

"Yes, it is a great mystery," she said. "The family and the police looked for him for weeks, but they never found him."

"What do you think could have happened to him?" I stared at her, wondering. "The police found no trace? No evidence?"

"Nothing." She shook her head. "Of course, our suspicion has always been that Mr. Edison must have had something to do with it. We do know he's used bully boy tactics to intimidate his rivals before—like with Tesla, you know. But making someone vanish? That's different altogether, isn't it?"

"It's horrible," I agreed. "And then you said your husband was shot while duck hunting?"

She nodded. "Again I have my suspicions, but I can prove nothing. Hunting accidents do happen, don't they? It might just have been a horrible coincidence."

I shivered. "I'm surprised you aren't afraid to do business with Mr. Edison."

"Mrs. Sullivan, when both your husband and your father-in-law have died in suspicious accidents, you move beyond fear. Andrew and I were not blessed with children. That camera was his child. And my sole purpose is to make his life's work mean something special."

"What is this paper that you are signing?" I asked, then continued, "If you don't mind my asking."

"It's a legal agreement that says we will stop suing each other. We're agreeing to honor each other's patents." Her face was blank as she spoke. I could not tell whether she was pleased about this settlement or not. The latter, I concluded.

There was a cluster of pedestrians and carriages as we turned left onto Park Avenue, and we were both silent as she navigated the traffic. "I wanted to keep fighting," she went on as the traffic eased and we sped up Park Avenue at a speedy fifteen miles an hour, "but Harry asked me to sign. Biograph's camera uses the patent I own, and he says we can't get tied up in another lawsuit."

"I heard that Biograph and Edison are in business together now," I said. "It was in the newspaper. Of course, when I first heard it, I didn't understand anything about the studios. I'm still very confused. It seems you are at war with one another and in business together at the same time."

She gave a sharp laugh. "I agree it is confusing, even to me. I only know that I want to make pictures. Those lawsuits blocked my husband and me at every turn. We were so certain we were going to win. The truth was on our side. And then Harry and Arthur were on our side and there seemed no way we could lose." She braked quickly as another automobile came out from Fifty-First Street without stopping.

"Woman driver!" the man shouted as he sped off. We looked at each other for a moment.

"How rude." I frowned. "It was clear you were in the right."

"I've heard worse," she said. She put her foot down on the accelerator pedal, and we lurched forward. We turned right and joined a road along the edge of the East River. Here there were no automobiles and we had to slow for horse-drawn wagons carrying freight.

"So you lost the lawsuits?" I was fascinated by her story.

"No, we won," she said. "But it never seemed to matter. There was always an appeal or a countersuit. It seemed that it would never end. But enough about me. Tell me about yourself, Mrs. Sullivan. I can hear that you are Irish. How do you come to be in New York? I ask as a fellow immigrant." She smiled.

"I suppose you had better call me Molly if I am going to pose as your social secretary," I said, returning her smile. "As for where I'm from, I'm from Ballykillin in Ireland, which I'm sure you've never heard of." I told her a version of my flight to America, leaving out the most harrowing parts. I didn't like to think about some of the things I had lived through. I did share some of my advenures, though. It was enjoyable to recount some of my detective triumphs to Fanny. She had a scientific and curious mind, asking about police procedures and the relatively new science of fingerprints. She was most interested to hear of the famous people that I had met.

"You really met Harry Houdini?" She was incredulous.

"And was on stage with him," I said. As I explained how this came about, we had left the East River behind and now drove beside the narrow Harlem River, spanned by several bridges. Fanny turned from the highway, and we drove over one of the bridges. Then we needed all our attention on the road. The Bronx was an area of recent development, since the two elevated lines and now the subway had made it more accessible to Manhattan. Row houses stood between scrubland and marshy areas and children played in streets that were not yet paved. There were some impressive mansions too, and plenty of factories. Clearly an area that was up-and-coming. Fanny had mentioned that the Edison studio was near the botanical garden and Fordham University, so I was expecting a more elegant neighborhood, but in fact it was on a street with motley brick-and-wooden buildings. One would have driven past not noticing except that the building itself was so extraordinary.

The studio was on the corner of Decatur Avenue and Oliver. It took up much of the block. A modern-looking, two-story, smooth-gray-brick building stood across a small courtyard from another building whose two facing walls were completely made of glass like a giant greenhouse. The roof was also of glass, rising diagonally to a peak and in stark contrast to the ordinary houses around it. They wouldn't have to shoot many scenes on the roof of the other building, as Biograph did, to get their natural light.

Fanny brought the automobile to a halt and we got out. A man in uniform stood just inside the metal gate to the courtyard.

"Can I help you?"

"Mrs. Fanny Prince to see Mr. Edison," Fanny said smoothly.

"Yes, ma'am." He picked up a book from a nearby table and consulted it. "You're on the list for eleven A.M. today." He made no move to open the gate. Fanny took a fine gold watch out of the watch pocket of her dress; it was just a quarter past ten.

"We've come all the way from Manhattan," she said. "Where can we wait for Mr. Edison? I do not intend to sit in my automobile when I am here on important business." The doorman hesitated. I could tell he was trying to decide how important we were, debating whether he would get in more trouble for letting us in early or for turning us away at the gate.

"Do those important papers have to be signed today, Mrs. Prince?" I said, improvising. "Or shall we just go to your dress fitting and tell Mr. Edison he will have to wait until we are in the neighborhood again?"

"I doubt I'll come this far for another month. That would make him quite angry, I imagine," she said with a laugh. "But if his studio wants to treat me as a peasant instead of a film investor, I think a dress fitting is an excellent idea. Shall we?" She turned to walk back to the car.

"Just a moment," the doorman said. Fanny kept walking toward the car. "Excuse me, ma'am," he called more loudly. She turned and gave him a questioning look. He looked anxious. "I'm sure I can find a place for you to wait, Mrs. Prince, if you'll follow me."

Fanny hesitated as if unconvinced, then relented. "I suppose we can wait, can't we, Molly?" The doorman turned away to open the gate and she winked at me.

"Yes, Mrs. Prince," I said meekly.

"Where is Mr. Edison now?" Fanny asked as we followed the doorman toward the large glass building.

"He's up on the roof." He turned and pointed up to the roof of the gray-brick building on the other side of the courtyard. There seemed to be men working up there and I saw hoses going up the side of the building.

"Is that where they are installing the water tank?" I asked. It was a complete shot in the dark, but I saw I had scored with it.

"Yes." The doorman visibly relaxed. "You heard about that, then? Damned fool idea, if you ask me." Evidently, we did both know Mr. Edison if we were aware of the new tank being put in.

"What a fascinating idea to put it on the roof," Fanny said. "Then they can take advantage of the natural light while filming."

"And knowing the boss, he'll be up there when there's a storm, waiting to film what will happen when the tank gets struck by lightning with people in it," the doorman said with a chuckle. "Anything new and different. That's what it's all about these days."

"Oh, surely not." Fanny Prince looked horrified. "Even Mr. Edison wouldn't risk the lives of his actors."

"I imagine it will be hard to keep free of debris," I ventured, realizing I was thinking of more practical things. "And freezing cold for the actors."

"I hear it will have a cover when not in use," the doorman said as he held the door open for us, "but I bet you are correct about the temperature of the water."

"Well, I know that directors seldom worry about the comfort of their actors." Fanny gave a tinkling laugh. We entered into a large open stage area much like the one at Biograph. The difference in this space was the light. I looked up and saw blue sky through the glass ceiling above. The glass walls were perfectly clear, and it was as bright inside as outside. "What an advantage it is to have glass walls," Fanny exclaimed. "It must make the picture clearer. And less in need of electric light."

"Are you interested in the technical details of film production, Mrs. Prince?" the doorman asked curiously.

"I imagine she is," a voice behind us said. "You're talking to the enemy, George." We turned around and in the doorway was Thomas Edison.

☙ Nineteen ❧

I recognized him from the many pictures I had seen in the newspaper. Sandy brown hair parted on one side and slicked down. A broad forehead and piercing blue-green eyes. A rumpled light brown suit with stains on the sleeves, presumably from his work installing the new water tank.

"Mr. Edison." Fanny held out her hand. He took it and pressed it to his lips in an old-fashioned gesture.

"Mrs. Prince, lovely to see you." His smile made his face seem boyish. "So kind of you to come all the way here. We could have met in the attorney's office."

"I confess I was eager to see your new studio," she said, looking around. "You have an amazing stage here, so much light."

"And you will run back to Biograph to tell the Messrs. Martin all about it," he said wryly. "I hear you are still involved in pictures, even after the death of your husband?"

"I am," she said. "I am marrying into the film business again." She whipped off her glove and held up her finger to show a large emerald ring. "Mr. Harry Martin and I are engaged."

"Congratulations," Mr. Edison said jovially but I caught an undercurrent of unease in his voice. This reminded me what I had come for. I had been so fascinated to meet the man responsible for so many modern inventions that I had momentarily forgotten I was here to investigate.

"What films are you working on right now, Mr. Edison?" I asked.

He gave Fanny a questioning look.

"This is my social secretary, Mrs. Molly Sullivan," she responded. "She is also interested in pictures."

"Good heavens. Don't tell me that women intend to take over the moving picture business," he said, again jovially. He held out his hand. "I'm pleased to meet you."

"In fact, my daughter has just been acting in a Biograph picture." I studied his face as I spoke. "Until an unfortunate occurrence. She was almost killed by a train this Monday when they were shooting a scene and she became trapped on the tracks." I watched for a sign of recognition. Was that a flicker of his eyes to the stage area?

"I'm so sorry," he said but without warmth. "Pictures these days are a dangerous business. I'm not sure I would want my daughter involved in them."

I looked over to the stage in the direction he had glanced. "I am as fascinated as Mrs. Prince. Might we have a tour of the studio?"

His cheerful demeanor was now completely gone. "I'm afraid I'm a tad busy, Mrs. Sullivan. Mrs. Prince, if you would follow me up to the office, I have those papers for you to sign. George," he called to the doorman, who came over, "Mrs. Prince's secretary will wait in the courtyard for her. Make sure she has a chair." And with that I was dismissed.

Fanny took a breath to argue but I gave a slight shake of my head and she smiled at Edison instead. I decided I would rather not follow them up to the offices but use my time downstairs to find out what I could about the sabotage. As they walked away together, I looked around the studio. Much like at Biograph, the enormous room was divided into stage sets. I was interested to see that several scenes were being shot at once. The room echoed to the sound of competing directions to the actors. Of course, the films being silent, this had no impact on the final product. The one closest to me was clearly a Gothic piece. The backdrop created an old castle or dungeon. A stone table was hooked up to a giant machine. *Frankenstein!* It came to me in a flash of inspiration. They were making a moving picture of *Frankenstein*. I had read that novel and had nightmares for a week. When an actor came onto the set with his face painted stark white, putting on a monstrous wig of frizzled hair, I decided that my guess had been correct.

"With or without the hands, Mr. Dawley?" he said as he held up a pair of hairy gloves.

"With," the man he had called Mr. Dawley said as he looked up from a conversation with a woman who was showing him different bolts of material. "The gray one," he said to her, and she nodded and walked off.

"Excuse me, ma'am," George touched my arm, "but Mr. Edison asked for you to wait outside."

"I'm such a fan of the pictures," I said, smiling at him. "Couldn't I just watch? Are they going to film a scene now?"

But he was having none of it.

"No, ma'am." He took my arm more firmly. "You have to wait outside." His voice was loud enough that a few people in the stage area looked up. I scanned the room for any more clues before I allowed him to lead me out.

"Please wait here," he said, gesturing to a bench in the courtyard, and I took a seat, thinking hard. I had not seen anyone that I recognized in the room. And would anyone stop and talk to me if I were able to approach them? Then I had an idea. The doorman's book. It must show everyone who had visited the studio. I needed to get a look at the book. As soon as the thought occurred to me, I acted. I gave a small cough.

"Excuse me, George," I said. "I'm quite parched from the ride." As I said it, I realized that I was not lying. My voice was dry from the long ride in the open air with the dust from the unmade roads. "Do you think you could fetch me a glass of water?" He hesitated and looked around as if he thought I had accomplices waiting to sneak in once his back was turned. But the street was empty, and it was a reasonable request.

"Yes, ma'am, wait here," he said and went back into the studio. I heard the door lock behind him. I sprang at the book, looking back through the appointments. I didn't recognize any names on the first page. The writing was cramped and hard to make out. I wasn't sure how long I had so I flipped back through the pages, hoping that something would catch my eye. And then I saw a name I recognized, from over a week ago, Edward Shepherd. Wasn't he the cameraman who had quit on Monday? I thought back to the dreadful scene on that day. I could picture his face, white as chalk, as he had run up to the train tracks. Was he the person behind the sabotage? Was he being paid to do it? And if not, what was he doing visiting Edison's studios?

I flipped back through more pages. Yes, his name was here again, several weeks earlier, and again a few pages earlier. This was indeed suspicious. If he had come here once I could under-stand that maybe he was seeking a better-paid job with Edison. But someone who visited on more than one occasion? Before I could look further, I heard the sound of the door opening and knew I had just seconds more. As I went to close the book another name jumped out at me: *A. Martin*, and beside it, *H. Martin*. But before I could read the date, the door opened. The doorman looked at me suspiciously. "Is there something I can help you with there, ma'am?" He had clearly seen me.

"A friend of mine said he works here," I said breezily, "and I ac-cused him of giving himself airs. I said I didn't believe for a second that he worked for the great Thomas Edison. Do you know him? Edward Shepherd?"

But in return he merely scowled, went over to the book, and snapped it shut. He handed me a glass of water and stalked back to the door where he stood stiffly, as if fearing I would break it down. I sipped the water and sighed. I would not get any more out of him. But perhaps I had solved my mystery. Edward Shepherd had visited Edison's studios more than once. Could he be working for Edison as a spy? Or even as the saboteur? I sat on the bench thinking. I needed to get inside that building again.

"Excuse me, George," I ventured, "where is the ladies' washroom?"

He scowled even more. I tried to look as if I was in distress. "We have a long ride home and I'll need to use it before we leave."

"Just in here." He unlocked the door. "Stay close to me and don't wander off. Please be careful, they're shooting. It will be more than my job's worth if I let you interfere with Mr. Edison's shooting schedule." He led me past the various sets to a small hallway that contained an indoor WC. I looked hard at the cameraman and the actors while I crossed as slowly as I could, but I didn't see anyone I knew. Once inside the washroom, I waited. How long would he wait for me before he went back to his duties?

When I finally pulled the chain and emerged from the washroom I was in luck. George was nowhere to be seen. I remembered the direction that Mr. Edison and Fanny had disappeared in and found a door that led upstairs. They must have the offices upstairs like they did at Biograph. I took the notebook and fountain pen that Fanny had given me out of my bag and headed up the stairs.

"Excuse me, who are you?" A man's voice rang out as I reached the top of the stairs. I didn't stop but held up the notebook.

"Mrs. Prince forgot something she needs for her meeting with Mr. Edison," I said. "I seem to remember it is this way?" I turned to the right and he nodded.

"End of the hall." He went back in the other direction. I continued to the end of the hall. The door was slightly open, and I paused outside. I heard Edison's voice within.

"I admired him, Mrs. Prince. He was like me, passionate and stubborn. I knew he would never surrender his patent. I offered them all a fortune to settle that lawsuit. Harry and Arthur were willing to negotiate. But not your husband."

"No," Fanny was speaking now in her smooth tones, "it was his life's passion."

"As I told the Martin twins at the time," Edison went on, "as long as Andrew Prince is alive, Edison and Biograph are going to be at odds with one another."

"My husband never told me you had met with the Martins. I wonder if he knew." Fanny's voice was strained. "But I think you will find I am just as passionate as he was."

"Ladies are much more sensible." Edison's voice was upbeat. "As you have proved by signing our agreement."

"Harry said you would bankrupt us if we didn't." Her voice was cold.

"My dear woman, you make me sound like an ogre." His voice was still full of cheer, but it sounded false to me. "It only says that both Biograph and Edison can use each other's camera patents. We both win and your husband's legacy is assured."

A chair scraped across the floor. Were they standing to leave? I pushed the door open and walked in.

Edison was standing behind a desk on which there were two identical documents. He picked up one of the documents and held it out to Fanny. "For your records," he said. Fanny took it and they both looked up at me.

"Excuse me, Mrs. Prince, I was afraid you would need your notebook or social calendar," I improvised.

"Thank you, Molly." She handed me the document. "Can you

take care of this?" I took the papers, glad that neither of them had asked me what I was doing upstairs. She stood and Edison came around the desk to take her hand.

"Let's put the past behind us now," he said in his deep voice. "We are partners after all."

He motioned for us to exit the office. We both turned to go. As I walked out first, I heard him say to Fanny, "I think you will find, as Harry and Arthur did, that it is better to be my friend than my enemy." I felt a ghost walk over my grave. What had he meant by that?

Edison followed us out to the end of the hall and shook hands with Fanny at the top of the stairs.

"There you are." The doorman pounced as I stepped into the studio. "Where have you been?" Fanny turned around and looked at the doorman in surprise at his tone.

"Mrs. Prince needed me," I said, brandishing her papers. "I am her secretary after all." I turned to her. "I'm sure George will show us the way out, Mrs. Prince."

He took a breath as if to speak and then let it out with a sigh. "This way, ladies." His shoulders were stiff as he turned to lead us across the studio stage, and I admit I felt a small thrill of triumph.

As soon as we were back in the auto and motoring through the Bronx, I shared what I had discovered with Fanny.

"One of the cameramen at your studio, Edward Shepherd, has been to Edison's studio at least three times," I said.

"I wonder if he is at the studio today?" she said. "I know if we tell Harry he will want to confront him immediately. When I think of what almost happened to your daughter, I imagine you will want to confront him as well!"

"He hasn't been at the studio all week," I said, "he resigned on Monday."

"Even more suspicious," she said. The ride back felt very long. We discussed the sabotage and Edward's possible role in it from every angle. Fanny thought that he had been present every time that an incident had occurred. "Although that is true of most of the crew," she admitted.

One thing did puzzle me. "I'm surprised you didn't come with your fiancé to sign the papers," I said. She looked at me quizzically.

"The Martin brothers were in the log," I said. "I assume they were signing the agreement as well."

"I don't like going anywhere with Arthur." She shuddered. "He is such an unpleasant man. But Harry is devoted to his brother. And I'm glad now that I didn't, because it gave me a chance to help your investigation."

How strange that she was marrying one and couldn't stand the other when to me the brothers looked identical!

We ran out of things to say by the time we reached the bridge and drove in silence down Park Avenue past the park. I sensed that she was tense and wondered what else had been said in Edison's office. It was well past noon, and I was anxious to get home to Mary Kate and quite uncomfortable from needing to feed her. When we pulled up in front of the studio, I climbed down from the passenger seat preparing to say my goodbyes and hurry home as quickly as possible. I pulled the papers and notebook out of my bag to return them and said as much to Fanny. She immediately offered to drive me home.

"Let me just run these papers up to Harry and I will be right down to take you home." She smiled at me. I accepted and sat back in the car waiting. The sun was bright, but a stiff breeze made it quite chilly. I pulled my shawl around me and realized that I should return it and the hat to the costume room since I was here.

I got out of the car and went up to the Fifth Avenue entrance, opening the fancy wooden doors into the marble foyer. The receptionist was sitting at his little desk as always. He did not look pleased to see me.

"Can I help you?" he said, his tone frosty.

"I just want to take these costumes back to the room. I won't be a minute," I said, pointing in the direction of the hallways that led past DW's office to the dressing rooms. Seeing that I did not want to go upstairs to the hallowed offices of the owners, he nodded. I rushed back to the costume room, not wanting Fanny to come out and think I had gone. I hung up the shawl and unpinned the hat, grabbing my hat from where it still sat on the counter. I was just returning to the foyer when I heard footsteps rattling the metal staircase. Fanny was coming downstairs.

"All set?" I said with a smile. She did not respond. I noticed that the papers were still in her hand.

"Was Mr. Martin not there?" I asked.

"He was there," she said.

"You still have the papers," I pointed out.

"I do?" She looked down at her hand as if it belonged to someone else. "Oh yes, how silly of me. Trevor, can you take these up to Mr. Martin?"

"Of course, Mrs. Prince." The clerk was all politeness to her.

"Did you tell Mr. Martin about Edward Shepherd?" I asked though I thought she had scarcely had time.

"No, not yet." Fanny seemed distracted as we made our way to her runabout. As I started to climb in, she stopped me. "I'm sorry, Molly, but I've just thought of something I need to do right now. Would you mind finding your own way home?"

"Of course not," I said, wondering why she had changed her mind. Or had Harry asked her to do something immediately? Had he asked her to do something that she didn't want to share with me?

I need to stop involving myself in other people's problems, I thought to myself as I walked home briskly. My connection to my children felt like a physical rope that I had stretched too far and was now pulling me home. This ache would not recede until I had them both in my arms. All my restlessness and boredom had gone. I just wanted my husband back with us and a quiet life with my three children.

That night I held Liam so close that he protested.

"I'm a big boy now, I'm ready for school!" he said.

"Not quite yet, my boyo," I said. "You're a little young."

"I want to go to school like Bridie." His voice rose and threatened to wake the baby who had fallen asleep beside me.

"I'll be your teacher." Bridie came to the rescue. "Let me get some paper and I'll teach you to write your name." Liam was not mollified.

"I want to learn Latin like you." He crossed his arms.

"All right," she said, "I'll teach you to write your name in Latin." She winked at me.

"Okay." Liam smiled happily. Bridie brought down a schoolbook and they passed a whole hour playing school. I sent up a prayer of thanks for my family with a pang of guilt for the few times I had gone to church this year. I decided to take the family this Sunday. The more I saw other people's lives, the more I felt I was a lucky woman.

❧ Twenty ❧

It was a dark day on Friday as I went to the studio for what I hoped was the last time. I would be able to tell Alice that I had found Edward's name in the book at Edison's studio. Perhaps he had a reasonable explanation for visiting with Mr. Edison so many times. I would let the higher-ups at Biograph find that out. And if the sabotage stopped now that he was gone, that would be a sign that he was behind it. It was a good guess that Edison had paid him to sabotage the picture or offered him a good job in return for his loyalty. Either way, I was now finished with my investigation and ready to return to caring for my family. Liam had barely glanced at me as I left this morning and I feared he was getting used to my absence.

The dark, rainy weather was proving a problem for the day's shooting.

"Use the lightest pancake makeup," Alice instructed as I entered the makeup room. Ryan was already in there, fully costumed and with his mustache waxed and gleaming. "We are going to be shooting with mostly electric lights since it is so gloomy outside."

"Shouldn't we just wait until next week?" Ryan asked. "There is sure to be better weather."

"DW says we will get these pictures finished this week or die trying," Alice said grimly.

"Well, Cecil is none too happy about getting into that tank this morning," Ryan said. "I told him the cold will bring out his manly figure."

"I wouldn't want to go for a swim in this weather," I said, and shivered. "But I am in agreement about finishing the pictures." I noted that only Alice and Ryan were in the room. "Alice, today will be my last day."

"Have you ended your investigation, then?" she asked.

"Yes, I found something at Edison's studio."

"You went to Edison's studio?" Ryan's voice rang out loudly. "You must tell me what it was like!"

"Lower your voice, Ryan. I don't want everyone to know," I said. "I found something there. They keep a log of all visitors and I found Edward Shepherd's name in the log."

"Did it say when he visited?" Alice asked. I nodded.

"Many times; the most recent one was just last week," I said. "I saw his name in the book at least three times, and there may have been more that I didn't have time to see. I think it is a good guess that he is the saboteur. After all, has there been any more sabotage this week?"

"No, there hasn't." Alice was thoughtful. "I hate to believe it of him, but it is a likely explanation. Perhaps they offered him a head cameraman position. He knows that Billy will always be in charge here."

"Whatever the reason, I'm going to leave it in your hands now," I said. "I'm returning home as soon as I have finished with the makeup today."

"Oh, but you must stay to see my final scenes today, Molly." Ryan waved his arms, almost causing me to spread makeup across his hair. "I'm brilliant in them. And it may be my last bit of acting before I return to life as an acclaimed playwright."

"I would appreciate it if you stayed a bit longer," Alice put in before I could answer. "After the filming I would like you to tell the Martins and DW what you found. Could you stay for the party?"

My first inclination was to say no. Alice could pass on my information. But the investigator in me felt that some ends were left to be tied up. What if Edward was not working alone? I decided to stay and watch the actors at least receive their pay packets.

"All right, I will," I said. "But after that . . ."

"Yes, I know," Ryan said, "it's back to a life of drudgery."

I laughed. "I'll have you know I enjoy my life very much, even though it is not all parties and there is hard work involved."

"Come to think of it, there has been much too much hard work involved in my life recently," Ryan said with an arch look. "I should not have let Cecil talk me into this business in the first place."

"Well, I must get back to my own hard work, if you'll excuse me," Alice said and went back into the stage room.

The morning's shooting was enjoyable. Arthur and Harry came down to the set stage midmorning to watch the filming. They were once again identically dressed. Really, film people are much like theater people in their outlandish dress, I thought. This morning they had chosen peacock blue seersucker suits with matching dark blue bow ties. I could only tell which brother was which because Fanny was on Harry's arm. She excused herself and came over when she saw me.

"What does Alice think?" she asked. "Does she think the cameraman did it?"

"I'm afraid she does," I said. "If it *was* him then we can hope that there will be no more accidents."

"Unless he had an accomplice," she said.

"I had thought of that," I said, surprised that it had occurred to her as well. "I think that is something that should be investigated."

"Will you inform Harry and Arthur of what you found after the filming?" she asked.

"You haven't told Harry already?" I raised my eyebrows. "I thought the two of you would have discussed it thoroughly by now."

"We haven't had an opportunity to speak yet," she said with a look at the two brothers that I couldn't interpret. Was she not able to speak to Harry in front of Arthur? If so, why did she want me to tell both of them the details? I realized that she was waiting for an answer.

"I'd be happy to meet with whoever you want and tell them what I found," I said. "But I won't be investigating any more after that. You know I have a baby at home. I've been away too long."

"But then you must stay for the party," she said. "I have asked Harry to put tables up on the roof as long as the rain stops."

Her attention was taken by Alice and Billy, who were trying out something new with the camera. "That's interesting, what are they doing?" she said. "Excuse me, Molly."

"It's an idea Billy and I had," Alice explained. "The scene will start with black and then fade in."

"That's good, Billy," DW said. "Can we reverse it at the end of the scene and gradually fade to black?"

"Yes, we can, DW," Billy said. Harry and Arthur had come over as well.

"That seems ridiculous," Arthur said. "Won't we just see a giant box?"

Alice shook her head. "No, the camera can't focus on the box. I'm sure it will work."

Harry clapped Billy on the shoulders. "Always innovating, aren't you, Billy—good man."

"To be fair, Alice came up with it." But DW was already raising his giant megaphone.

"Places, everyone," he called. "Lights." I saw Alice stalk off, her shoulders stiff.

"Alice, get back over here," DW yelled through the megaphone. "We need you to work the box."

Mary, Johnny, and Ryan filmed the last scene. Ryan was both funny and frightening in his role as the count. His rant as he was led off by the police in handcuffs was delivered in such ringing tones that it was a great pity that no one would hear it, only read the caption on-screen. The cast gave a great cheer as DW yelled "Cut!" on the final scene of the picture. But DW was determined to finish both pictures, so Mary rushed back to change for her role as Cecil's leading lady in the other picture.

The water scene was filmed last, and everyone gathered round to watch and commiserate with Mary and Cecil about the temperature of the water. The rain had stopped so DW ordered the roof skylight open to get a bit more light. I was very aware of the lamps clustered around the tank and kept a good eye on them, hoping that we had caught our saboteur and there was nothing more to fear.

Indeed the water rescue went off without a hitch. After DW called "Cut," Harry and Fanny themselves stepped forward to help the freezing actors out of the tank. Fanny was quick to run to Mary to pull her out and put a towel around her shoulders. Perhaps she had noticed Harry being overly solicitous the last time. When Mary and Cecil had taken bows to thunderous applause from all those gathered, they made their way quickly toward the dressing rooms to get changed.

"Can I have everyone's attention?" Harry raised his voice and the room quieted. "Well done, everyone. Those pictures are going to be the talk of the country. You'll all be stars."

"Will our names be on the pictures then?" Daisy asked excitedly. Harry looked at DW, who shook his head. "We'll talk about that later," Harry went on hurriedly. "We've decided to have today's party up on the roof as it looks like we've a break in the weather."

"I'll have your pay packets up there," Alice said.

"And Harry and I have put a little extra in them for all your hard work," Fanny added. The largest cheer yet went up.

"We'll get things started up there in about thirty minutes," Harry said. "Let's see how much of the set we can strike before that."

The crew went to work immediately, rushing furniture and props off the sets and hauling food and drink up to the roof.

"It seems a strange day to have a party on the roof," Ryan said, coming up to me and putting an arm across my shoulders. "My dear, tell me truthfully, was I magnificent or merely extraordinary?" I laughed.

"You know very well you were magnificent, Ryan," I said. "If you want to have a new career in pictures you certainly can."

"My darling, it is too exhausting," he said dramatically. "When I am writing I can stay up for days finishing a script and then sleep as long as I want for weeks after. Whereas Alice . . ." she was walking by and stopped when she heard her name, "is an absolute brute who drags me out of bed at an ungodly hour day after day."

"You really are good, Ryan," Alice said warmly. "I know that DW would love you to do more pictures. If I could only get that voice of yours into the picture, though."

"Do you think that will happen?" I asked. "Will they have pictures that you can hear the actors talk in?"

"I am working on it," Alice said. "I have been recording a few scenes of my own for the phonograph and Billy and I have been talking about how to get the sound onto the picture."

"We recorded my voice for posterity," Ryan said, quite pleased with himself.

"Mrs. Prince is a champion of the idea as well. The problem is getting the phonographs into every picture show and having them play at the same speed as the film," Alice said. "But I think we'll get there someday."

"Think of all those piano players out of work," Ryan said with a smile.

Something across the room caught Alice's eye and I followed her gaze. Edward Shepherd had just entered. Ryan saw him too. "Isn't that the traitor?" he said loudly.

"Shh, Ryan." I put my finger to my lips. "Don't scare him off. We want to find out what he was doing with Edison."

"Have you said anything to DW or Harry yet?" Alice asked me quickly.

"I haven't had the chance," I replied. "If he is the saboteur, why would he come back here?" We didn't have to wait long. Edward came straight toward us.

"Alice," he said, seeming a little sheepish but not guilty. "I am hoping that I still have a pay packet for the work I did on Monday, even though I left you in the lurch."

I could feel Ryan stir beside me and gave him a stern look.

"I do owe you for the Monday work," Alice said coolly. "It will only be a day's worth though." Her manner was completely natural— brisk and annoyed but not suspicious. "We're giving them out at the party in about thirty minutes, so you'll need to stay while I get yours together."

"Of course." He looked around the room. Billy was glaring in his direction. "I'll make myself scarce until then. I don't think I'm the most popular person here right now." He walked off. I wasn't sure where he thought he would hide for half an hour.

Alice put her hand on my arm. "We have to tell the bosses right away before he leaves." Her voice was shaking now. "Meet me in DW's office in about five minutes." She hurried off and I was left looking after her. It occurred to me that Alice was a cool customer. She had given no hint to Edward that we suspected him.

DW's office was crowded when I entered. Harry, Arthur, DW, and Alice were all there. I couldn't tell which of the men sitting side by side was Arthur and which was Harry. They had clearly been waiting for me and they stared at me in a way that made me quite uncomfortable.

"So," DW began, "I hear that Alice has been asking you to investigate our saboteur."

"She hired me to do so and I have given her valuable information," I responded, standing up for myself.

"What business a secretary has asking you to do anything is beyond me," one of the twins put in. So that was Arthur. "We should have hired a proper detective if we wanted this taken care of."

"Perhaps you should have," I said, flaring up. "If that is so, you will have no need of the information that Alice and I are bringing you today." I turned to leave, willing Alice to do the same.

"I'll get back to my secretarial work, then, shall I," she said frostily as she began to follow me out of the room.

"Wait a minute," Harry put in, his voice pleading. "Ladies, please." His tone changed to anger as he spoke to his brother. "Arthur, you are impossible, you have made everyone at this studio your enemy. Why, Fanny just told me how rude you have been to her this morning."

"Nonsense," Arthur spluttered, "I haven't said a word to Mrs. Prince all morning."

"And now you are driving away two women who just tried to do us a service." His voice was warm as he spoke to me. "Mrs. Sullivan, won't you tell us what you found, please?"

"Very well." I turned back and addressed him. "Alice knew that I had done some detective work in the past and she asked me to look into the saboteur." Arthur spluttered again but Harry silenced him with a look. "Of course, I was naturally inclined to want to find the man, since my daughter had almost been killed by him." I had everyone's attention now. "Mrs. Prince and I went to Edison's studio yesterday to sign some papers."

"Oh good, I was hoping she had taken care of that," Harry interrupted and then apologized as he saw my pointed stare. "Go on, please, what did you find?"

"They keep a log of visitors just as you do here at Biograph," I said. "I found your names in the log, Mr. Martin." I looked at Harry as I said it and he looked at his brother. They shared a glance.

"Well," Arthur roared, "we knew that we had visited. That's not your big news, is it?"

"No," I said calmly, "I just wanted to give you proof that I was not making up my information. I also found the name of a cameraman who worked on the last picture. Edward Shepherd."

"He quit on Monday," Alice put in.

"Are you sure he wasn't just asking for work?" DW said. "That would be disloyal but not criminal, surely."

"His name was in the log at least three times that I saw," I said, "weeks before he quit. Of course it is possible that he was just getting ready to make a move, but he is the best lead I have had so far."

"Excellent," Harry said. "Well done. And it explains why things have gone so smoothly this week while he has been gone." He turned to Alice. "But why all the rush, Alice? You could have told us after the party."

"Because," I put in, "he's in the building right now." Their faces registered surprise, except for Alice, who nodded.

"Let's have him in here right now," Arthur said with a growl in his voice. "I'll teach him what we do to those who are disloyal to us."

I held up a hand. "I think it might be better to wait until after the party."

"Why, so he can break more things while he's here?" Arthur asked sarcastically.

"No, so we can see who he talks to," I said, keeping my temper in check. "We need to find out if he has any accomplices at the studio."

"Good thinking." DW looked at me approvingly. "Alice, that will be your job. Don't let him out of your sight."

"DW, I'm a little busy," she said. "I have all the pay packets to give out. It will be hard to pay attention to one man."

"I'll do it," I volunteered. "He has no reason to suspect anything from me. I'll notice anyone who is particularly friendly toward him."

"Good girl." Harry smiled. "And then when everyone is upstairs on the roof, we can bring him down and confront him."

As we left the office, I wasn't relishing my assignment, even though it had been my suggestion. If Edward was the man behind the sabotage, he had nearly killed Bridie and I wanted him caught. But I worried that Arthur might carry out his threat with no new evidence. Had I just been a party to getting an innocent man beaten or even killed? I was following Alice and DW up the stairs when my conscience told me I should make it clear that my evidence wasn't proof, and that Edward deserved the chance to prove himself innocent. I turned back toward the office. The door was open, and as I approached I could hear Arthur's voice.

"You think you're in charge of me just because your position here is higher, brother?" I stopped. I couldn't bring myself to walk in and perhaps bring that anger on myself. "I know what you have done to get to this position," Arthur snarled, "and don't you forget it." I heard his steps coming toward me. I didn't want to be caught outside the office, so I fled.

"Who's there?" I heard his voice behind me. As I ran up the stairs I wondered if he had seen me.

❧ Twenty-One ❧

Is Harry coming up?" Alice looked past me down the stairs. "I need him to open the safe to start making the pay packets."

"I'm not sure." I didn't want to tell her what I had just heard. "I think he might be right behind me." I followed Alice along the hall toward Harry's office. The door was open, and Fanny was rearranging some of the papers that were strewn about the office. She looked up as we came in.

"Does he ever tidy up this place?" Fanny asked, shaking her head with a disparaging smile.

"Not that I have seen," Alice replied. "Perhaps you can reform him."

"At least the papers are off the chairs now." The office did look tidier, although the desk and bookshelves still had stacks of papers piled on them. Alice went behind the big wooden desk.

"The safe is still locked," she said, looking up as Harry came in.

"Am I being robbed?" His voice was light.

"I need the money to make up the pay packets," Alice said, indicating the safe. Harry moved around the desk to open the safe. She took out a bundle of bank notes. "You'll have the fifty dollars I promised you, Molly," she said as she counted them. Harry raised his eyebrows.

"It's coming out of the makeup budget, and she's earned it," Alice said firmly. He shrugged and made no further objection.

"I should make sure the furniture is set out on the roof." Fanny pushed past him toward the door. "Molly, would you help me? You are staying for the party, aren't you?"

I followed her up to the roof. Attractive little tables covered in checked cloths were set out along with a trestle table full of food and metal tubs of beer. I was glad the crew had closed the large wooden doors in the roof that opened to let light down into the studio. Even though cast and crew marched across them without a second thought, I went out of my way to walk around them, imagining what would happen if they gave way and I plummeted two or three stories down.

"They're perfectly safe," Alice laughed as she saw me step around them. "There's a reinforced steel grate below the doors."

"I'll take your word for it," I said and continued to avoid them. As it was decorated, the roof was a darling place to have a party. The false front of the house rising on one side made a pretty backdrop with its garden and ivy climbing up the brick. There was a brick parapet around the outside of the roof. I went over to it and looked out down Fourteenth Street, noting the busy traffic far below me. Then I realized I was not comfortable looking over a low wall with a long drop on the other side. I stepped back and made my way to the food tables. It was still cloudy but not raining and the breeze was warm.

The crew and actors began to arrive. The mood was light. DW gave a brief speech, thanking the cast and crew for their hard work.

"Even better the second time," he said. "Well done, everyone."

"Well done," Harry echoed. He took a beer and opened it, motioning for the other men to do the same. "Cheers."

"Don't let Billy get too close to the edge when he's had a beer," a crew member laughed, clapping his friend on the back as he handed him a drink.

Ryan and Cecil stood apart at the parapet, looking elegant and somehow out of place, smoking long, thin cigarettes and staring at the view across the city. Daisy and Mary emerged from the staircase and headed straight for the food table.

"I'm famished!" I heard Daisy say to Mary. "I splurged on a pair of shoes this week and I've been living on buttered toast for the last two days."

"You're a slave to fashion, my dear," Mary said and they both giggled. They had both removed their wigs but not their makeup. They looked like evil pixies with black-ringed eyes, bright red lips, and green-streaked cheeks.

Billy came up and Edward was right behind him. *I must remember to watch who he talks to,* I thought. But he seemed very alone, not catching anyone's eye or walking up to any group. Was he guilty of sabotaging the picture, or was he just uncomfortable for quitting and leaving his fellow workers in the lurch? Clearly Billy wanted nothing to do with him. He did not look back at Edward as he walked away. Perhaps they had had words. Alice and Fanny were up and down the stairs multiple times, directing crew members who were bringing more plates of food.

By the time Alice came up with the pay packets and began to hand them out, Edward just looked relieved to receive it and go. But as he headed toward the exit, DW and one of the Martin twins blocked his path. Which one was it? I looked around to see Fanny, assuming that she and Harry would be together, but didn't see her or the other twin. So, probably Arthur, then.

"We have some questions for you, Edward," DW said. His voice was low but menacing and several people stopped to watch what was going on.

"I'm sorry to have left Biograph, DW." Edward's voice was strained. "But I don't think it's a crime, so I'll just take my pay packet and be going."

"This lady here," DW pointed, and Edward turned to look at me, "saw your name in the visitor logs at Edison's studio."

"What business is it of hers?" Edward stared at me defiantly. "I barely know her."

I watched him closely. "I'm the mother of a girl who was almost killed on Monday." He flinched.

"What are you doing visiting with Edison while you are working for us?" Arthur Martin's face had flushed an angry red above his blue bow tie and his voice was a roar. Everyone was looking now.

"DW, Mr. Martin, maybe you should take this downstairs?" Alice came hurrying up. "Maybe in DW's office?"

"I don't have to go anywhere with you gentlemen," Edward said. "I've gotten my pay. I'll leave now." He started down the steep stairs and the men followed close behind him. I wanted to follow them down as well, but Alice put her hand on my shoulder.

"Come and get your pay as well before you go, Mrs. Sullivan," she said.

I hesitated, looking at the backs of the men as they descended the steep steps to the second floor. I really should follow them.

"You earned it," she continued, misunderstanding my hesitation. "You've given us the information we needed, and you did a marvelous job on the makeup."

I followed her a few steps across the roof to the wooden box holding paper envelopes, each with a name on it. "If you decide you want to work in pictures, I'll hire you to do makeup any day." She handed me the envelope with SULLIVAN on it. Inside were five crisp new silver certificates.

"Thank you," I said, taking it, my mind on the three men heading downstairs. I was surprised that Alice didn't want to hear what Edward had to say as much as I did. After all, she had hired me to investigate. "I'll come back up to say my goodbyes. I want to hear what Edward has to say." I tucked the envelope into my skirt pocket and hurried toward the stairs.

"Well, what have you found out?" Ryan was blocking my path, speaking in low tones. "I saw you watching our miscreant. Do tell!"

"I haven't seen any evidence that he was working with someone else. DW and Mr. Martin are questioning him right now."

"I'd not enjoy being grilled by Mr. Arthur," Ryan said. "A bad-tempered brute, wouldn't you say? And not above calling in his bully boys, so they say."

I couldn't wait a second longer to chat. I pushed past Ryan and started down the stairs. They were steep and I had to carefully pull up my skirts so that I didn't tumble down them. My shoes clattered as I stepped down onto the smooth wooden floor of the second level. I tried to walk quietly as I made my way down the hall, listening. Were they in Harry's office? But that door was closed, and I didn't hear a thing. Where was Harry? I hadn't seen him go down with Arthur and DW, but I also hadn't seen him on the roof. Had he gone to arrange for an *accident* to happen to Edward? I could feel tension building inside me.

I hurried down the spiral stairs toward DW's office. The reception-ist was not at his post, and the foyer was empty. So was DW's office. I heard muffled voices from somewhere in the building. Was that a cry? I froze, trying to locate where it came from. I hurried through the warren of rooms toward the stage area. I had just entered the props room when I heard a loud crash. There was a sound like an explosion and all the electric lights went out.

I froze in the pitch darkness, groping in front of me, trying to feel the closed door. My hand hit something long and wooden that fell on the concrete floor with a loud crash. I moved slowly forward with my hands in front of me, feeling every second that I was going to trip or run into something. I did not remember ever being in such darkness before, trapped in a building that had rooms with electric bulbs as their only light source. With that source suddenly gone I could hear my heart pounding and I felt I could no longer breathe. *Pull yourself together, Molly,* I told myself sternly. *Darkness can't hurt you.* I forced my way forward until my outstretched hands touched the door. I found the knob and opened it. To my relief I could see the faint outline of the long counter and chairs in the makeup room. The far door leading to the sets was open and a small amount of natural light was coming in. I hurried to the door and into the big open space.

"Hello?" I called. My voice echoed around, bouncing from the high ceiling. Some light was coming in from cracks around the wooden skylight door in the roof and a window on the far side of the vast space. No one seemed to be there.

"What happened? What's going on?" I heard a man's voice from the far side, coming from the other set of stairs. "Hold on. Let's get some light in here."

Footsteps crossed to the far wall and a few seconds later a curtain was pulled back, and enough light streamed into the room so that I could see. I breathed a sigh of relief.

"Did we lose electricity?" DW appeared, Alice right behind him.

"It sounds like we blew a fuse, DW," Alice said, efficient as usual. "I'll get one of the crew to fix it." She beckoned one of the crew, giving him an order before he hurried off.

Other members of the cast and crew were now coming into the room to see what was going on.

"It sounded like a cannon shot," Ryan said as he and Cecil came down. "Is it quite safe? The building is not on fire, is it?"

"I don't smell anything." Fanny's voice came from the other side of the room. "Harry? Where are you? Did you come down here?"

"Don't panic, it's just an electrical issue," DW said. "We'll sort it out."

I decided it was time for me to go as soon as the lights came back on. I didn't know how to find out what had happened to Edward. I would say my goodbyes to Alice and go home. I took a step toward her and slipped, almost losing my balance. The floor was wet. I realized I was standing not far from the tank. Natural light was coming into the room on the far side, but this area blocked by the giant pieces of scenery of the set was still in gloom. The tank lay like a long, dark shadow across the floor. Thank goodness I hadn't fallen in. Where had the water come from? I peered to see whether the tank was overflowing. As my eyes adjusted and focused above the dark water I gasped. There was something floating in the tank. A body, I thought immediately, and then scolded myself. It was the mannequin again. Really, how many times would I be fooled by that strange doll? But something else was in the tank, a long metal rod of some sort. I came closer.

And then I saw. "Alice," I shouted to her. "I think I know why the lights went out."

She hurried over. I pointed at the tank. A large lamp had fallen, and one end was in the water. Just what Alice had feared would happen.

"Not again!" Alice's voice was tight with anger. "Damn. I've just sent someone down to mend the fuse. We need to get this out before the lights come on again or we'll blow the whole thing or electrocute somebody. Fred. Robert. Help me with this. Quickly."

I stepped back as two burly stagehands dragged the lamp out of the water. But what was the mannequin doing in the tank? Was Edward trying to do one last bit of mischief? I glanced around but couldn't see him. As they laid the lamp down on the floor, I moved even closer and bent down to pull the mannequin out. It was floating at a strange angle, its skirts billowing out in the water, looking horribly lifelike. I reached into the water and jerked my hand back as it touched something cold and clammy.

I peered closer, willing the electricity to come back on so I could see better. And then I saw. Just under the water, emerging from the wooden form of the mannequin were two legs in bright blue seersucker. My movement sloshed water against the side of the tank and rolled the mannequin to one side. The thing below it bobbed to the surface, and I found myself inches from the open eyes of a dead white face.

I couldn't help it. I screamed and almost fell into the water.

"What is it?" Alice grabbed at me, pulling me back from the water, helping me up.

"Are you hurt?" Ryan was just behind her. I couldn't catch my breath to speak. I just pointed to the tank.

"Good God!" Ryan's exclamation echoed in the large space.

"What is it?" DW came up just after Ryan. "Holy hell!" He stared down into the tank without words.

"What's wrong?" Fanny ran across the room. "What is it? What have you seen?" She stopped when she saw the man in the tank. "Harry!" she screamed. "Harry, no!"

"Fanny, my dear," a voice from the doorway called. He hurried toward her, holding out his arms. "Fanny, I'm right here."

She looked at him and back down at the tank. "Harry?" She held one arm out to him and the other up to her temple. "Harry?" Before he could reach her, she staggered, almost falling into the tank. DW caught her as she collapsed in a dead faint.

"What the devil is going on?" Harry reached Fanny just as DW laid her down gently.

"Harry, it's Arthur," Alice said.

"What?" He was still focused on Fanny, patting her wrists. "Fanny? My love. Speak to me."

She stirred and opened her eyes, her face a mask of confusion and horror.

"I thought it was you," she whispered as Harry bent down to hear. Alice grabbed Harry's arm firmly enough that he looked up.

"It's Arthur." Her voice was louder. "Harry, Arthur is in the tank. He's dead."

❧ Twenty-Two ❧

This time Harry reacted. "Arthur?"

"He's in the tank." Alice's voice was shaking, her composure for once shattered. "He must have fallen in."

Harry stood up and looked into the tank.

"Oh my God! Get him out." Harry jumped into the tank and put his arms under his brother. "Help me."

Several other men jumped in with him and together they lifted the body out of the tank. All of them could easily stand in the tank, I noticed. The water was only up to their chests. So how could Arthur have drowned? I could see how he might have fallen into the tank in the dark, but why had he not just stood up?

The men struggled to lift Arthur's body onto the floor, then climbed out themselves.

"Where's the damned light? Where's a doctor? Somebody do something." Harry sounded frantic.

"Dino should have the electric lights on any moment now, Harry," Alice said as Harry pulled himself out and bent over his brother.

"Come on, Arthur, come back to me," he muttered as he turned him on his side and pounded him on his back, perhaps hoping to pump the water out of his brother's lungs.

I had seen those dead eyes and held no hope. The people gathered around were blocking the light from falling onto Arthur's face. As soon as the electricity came on, he would see that his brother was far beyond his help. I looked over at the lamp lying on the ground and I suddenly wondered, *What will happen when the electricity comes back on?*

The lamp was over on its side, the cracked light bulb in a puddle of water. I ran over and hastily stood it upright, dragging it far away from the water on the floor. Just as I took my hand away from it the lights in the building came back on. A giant spark arced inside the bulb; it let off a loud popping noise and turned black. No one in the building seemed to notice or care. Some were standing in the shadows in corners of the room, staring in horror, while others were gathered around the body. Harry had given up his attempt to revive his brother. Fanny was still on the ground, her face in her hands.

I confess I was feeling quite shaky myself. Arthur Martin had been an unpleasant man, but I had not wanted to see him dead. Another thought occurred to me: I knew someone who might have wanted Arthur dead. Where was Edward Shepherd?

Alice was the first to snap back into full efficiency. "Somebody should go to the office and telephone the police," she said.

Harry looked up from where he still knelt beside his brother's body. He reached up to grab at Alice's skirt. "Wait. Don't do that. We don't want the police involved in this, do we? It was a horrible accident, obviously. Arthur saw the mannequin floating in the tank and thought it was a person. He bent to pull it out, lost his balance, and grabbed for the lamp, pulling it in with him and thus electrocuting himself."

"There have been too many horrible accidents," Alice said.

"And the man who probably caused them was last seen going downstairs with Harry," I said, pushing myself into this conversation. "We must stop him before he gets away."

Harry stood up, suddenly determined. "You heard her. Don't let Edward Shepherd leave the building."

There was the sound of feet pounding down iron stairs. A little later several men returned. "No sign of him, boss. The doorman said he left. He's already well away."

"Now will you let me call the police?" Alice said. "There can't be any clearer proof of his guilt than running off like this."

"If you must, I suppose," Harry said. "You know how I hate getting involved with the police. They always start asking awkward questions."

"If you've done nothing wrong, then you've nothing to hide, my dear." Fanny now put a hand on his arm. "Best to bring the culprit to justice so these so-called accidents can stop, and we can get back to making wonderful pictures."

Harry took her face in his hands. "You're so right as always. Such a clever little girl."

I stepped back from this tender scene, feeling awkward and still shocked. If only Daniel were here, I thought. He'd know how to handle a homicide—because that was what it had to be. A grown man does not tumble into a tank and pull a large electric lamp in with him. Besides, I'd seen a trial run for this when the lamp almost collapsed into the tank while the actors were in it. Someone had wanted to see whether this would work, or, even worse, had wanted to kill people at this studio, not caring who they were. My thoughts immediately went to Edward, of course. Had he some secret grudge against Biograph? Was it just that he was being paid to sabotage by Edison, or was there something deeper—a family member killed in one of their dangerous stunts, maybe?

Towels were brought to dry off Harry and his fellow rescuers. A chair was brought for Fanny, and someone went for a glass of brandy, as she was still on the verge of hysteria. I couldn't see why she would be so upset about Arthur's death. Surely, she'd be overcome with relief that it wasn't her intended who died? But some women are delicate creatures and I had to remind myself that she'd just had to deal with the death of her husband. No wonder she got upset so easily.

I stood apart from the others, wondering if I could slip away and go home. But if this was now a crime scene then nobody should be allowed to leave. I went over to Alice.

"You should make sure nobody leaves until the police get here. It's a crime scene, after all."

She looked at me, long and hard. "You don't think this was an accident, do you?"

I glanced around to see who was within hearing distance. "I can't see how a fully able man, sober, would fall into the tank and pull a light in with him. If he had toppled in, he knew he could stand up." I paused, thinking. "I did hear raised voices somewhere in the building right before the explosion when the lights went out."

"You think there was an argument, and somebody pushed him?"

"They would have had to knock the lamp in pretty quickly if they wanted to kill him."

"Edward Shepherd," she said. "I hope they find him."

We didn't have to wait long before the police arrived in the form of Constable O'Malley—almost a caricature of the old-fashioned Irish cop. When he was shown the waterlogged body he looked horrified and crossed himself, muttering, "Jesus, Mary, and Joseph!" He then stared at the tank in disbelief. "You've got yourself a swimming pool in the middle of a building. What will they think of next?"

"We use it to shoot water scenes in our pictures," Harry said.

Constable O'Malley stared open-mouthed at Harry, just realizing that he was dressed exactly the same as the dead man and resembled him uncannily too. Harry saw what he was thinking.

"My twin brother. Arthur Martin," he said. "We've always dressed alike and done everything together. We own this studio. Or rather, we owned."

"I'm most sorry for your loss, sir," O'Malley said. "But if you ask me, I'm not surprised that a tragedy happened if you put a great tank of water in the middle of a room. I suppose the poor man slipped in and drowned."

"That's what we're thinking," Harry said. "Although it was worse than that, I'm afraid. He grabbed one of the large lamps we use to light up the sets and it fell in with him, probably electrocuting him instantly."

"Holy Mother." O'Malley went to cross himself again but then thought better of it. He looked around the room. "You seem to have a lot of people here, sir. Did none of them witness the poor fellow falling to his death?"

"There was a party on the roof," Harry said. "Almost everyone was up there. We always have a little celebration on the last day of filming."

"Up on the roof, huh? You people sure like to live dangerously." O'Malley shook his head.

I stood there, squirming impatiently, wondering when I should say something. Were they going to let this be written off as an accident, rather than finding the true murderer? If only Daniel were back, I thought. I could make sure he put a good man on the case or investigated it himself.

"Well, sir, there doesn't seem like much I can do for you right now, other than to summon the ambulance to take the poor fellow to the morgue. And of course the coroner will have to be notified."

I glared in Alice's direction. She saw me and interpreted my expression.

"Mr. Martin?" She stepped forward. "Are we definitely letting this go as an accident then? After what we know?"

"What's this?" O'Malley was instantly alert.

"Oh, it's just that we had some trouble with a cameraman earlier today. The dead man and he got into a bit of a spat."

"And you think the other fellow could have pushed him in and thrown the lamp after him?" O'Malley now sounded quite professional, and I began to feel less agitated.

"I suppose it could have been possible," Harry admitted. "Although . . ."

"Then I'll have to call in a detective and get statements from everybody here," O'Malley said. "Where they were and all that."

"Constable, I can assure you that we were all upstairs," Harry said impatiently.

I knew, of course, that this wasn't true. I had gone downstairs after Edward, Arthur, and DW. When I got to the lower level I had seen nobody. And met nobody on the stairs.

DW cleared his throat. "Officer, I went down with Mr. Arthur Martin to speak to Edward, but he was too quick for us and ran out of the building before we could apprehend him. I then came back up to join the others."

"And Mr. Arthur?" O'Malley asked.

"He said he had something he wanted to attend to first. I left him down there," DW said.

"So who else was down there that Mr. Martin might have wanted to see?"

DW looked around the room. "I really couldn't tell you. The receptionist usually, and the doorman. That's about it."

"So was it possible this Edward fellow, the cameraman who ran off, might just have been lurking until you were out of the way, then came back?"

"Hardly," DW said curtly. "Our doorman knows his job. He wouldn't have let him back in."

"We'll need to question the doorman," O'Malley said. "I think

I'd better hand this over to my superiors. I'm just a constable on the beat. This is not my job."

"I quite understand, Constable." Harry put a hand on his shoulder. "But I think we're all reading too much into this. If Edward ran off then I think we can say he's not responsible for this. Let's face the facts. Arthur was left alone. He needed to pick up something from the studio floor. He didn't bother to turn lights on, wandered in in the dark, and saw what he thought was someone floating in the water."

"What?" O'Malley started at this. "Who was in the water?"

"Nobody. It was one of our mannequins we use for stunts. I expect one of the crew threw it in for a joke."

O'Malley looked up. "Did any of you throw this . . ." he searched for the word, ". . . thing into the water?"

The crewmen looked around for a spokesman. "No, sir," Gino Scarpelli finally answered. "We were all up on the roof, drinking beer. And why would we do a thing like that?"

"Edward might have." As soon as I spoke the words I realized I should have kept quiet. All eyes were now on me.

"What do you mean, young lady?" O'Malley asked.

"The reason Edward Shepherd was in trouble was because he had been sabotaging our pictures," Alice said, coming to back me up. "He may have thrown in the mannequin as a last cruel joke, hoping that someone would think it was a drowning person."

O'Malley scratched his head. "So it seems to me that the one person we have to have a word with is this Edward fellow."

"Absolutely," Harry said. "Alice, can you give the policeman his address, and then let the rest of us get back to mourning my dead brother."

"Very good, sir." O'Malley nodded gratitude. "I'll have to write a report on this of course. And I'll go ahead and summon the ambulance to take the body to the morgue."

"That won't be necessary," Harry snapped. "I want my brother's body handled properly and with reverence. We'll arrange for his funeral."

"Oh no, sir," O'Malley said. "The body must go to the morgue for the coroner to do his autopsy. Required in all suspicious deaths."

"I'm not having my brother cut open!" Harry was bellowing now.

Fanny came over to him. "Don't get so upset, my darling. I'm sure it's just a formality. After all, what can an autopsy show except the poor man was electrocuted and drowned? They won't need to cut anybody."

Harry patted her hand. "You're right, as usual, my dear. Very well then, Constable. Alice will help you get your statements from everybody and then you can summon your ambulance."

"If you'll come to the office," Alice said, "I'll have everyone lined up for you."

"Much obliged, ma'am." O'Malley gave a little nod.

As she went to leave Harry grabbed her arm. "Why couldn't you have kept quiet," he muttered.

She looked surprised. "You don't want Edward apprehended?"

"We could have taken care of him in our own way," Harry said. That sounded ominous. As I waited my turn to be interviewed I walked around the tank. How could Arthur have fallen in? There was no jumble of wires or maze of props and costumes just off camera as there had been when we were shooting. There was just a bare floor. The only thing near the tank was the single lamp. I tried to imagine the scene. Arthur bending over to retrieve the mannequin, losing his balance and grabbing the lamp for support, the lamp toppling in. It could have happened that way, I supposed. But why would a grown man fall into the tank, and who would grab onto a flimsy lamp for support?

My uneasy feeling grew as I was called into the office to give my statement to Constable O'Malley. He seemed eager to declare the death an accident and didn't write down much more than my name and address. I repeated the argument I had seen between Edward and Arthur, but he merely said, "Now don't worry your pretty head about it, missus. We'll check it out."

"Constable O'Malley," I went on, "I think this needs more investigation. How could a grown man fall into a tank and pull a light on top of him?"

"Dangerous thing, electricity," he said solemnly. "I've seen my fair share of deaths. And as for him falling in, didn't his brother say there was drinking going on upstairs?"

Perhaps he was correct, I thought as I made my way out of the building across the large sound stage. An ambulance had arrived, and Arthur's body was being carried out on a stretcher. I had a sudden picture of the stage as it had been when I went upstairs for the party. *A clean stage*, I remembered thinking, *all evidence of the week's work neatly put away*. And suddenly, I was sure. The lamp had not been there when I went upstairs. And Harry? Why was he so eager to have this declared an accident? I went over the statements in my mind. DW and Arthur had said they came downstairs with Edward. But where was Harry at the time? I was sure he had not been on the roof. I almost turned around to tell Constable O'Malley, but I doubted he would believe my story after the reception I had already received. It was time to go home.

I had only walked a block toward home when it began to rain. In typical April fashion a cold breeze sprang up, making the raindrops blow sideways and sting my skin as the wind funneled down Fourteenth Street from the Hudson. The weather matched my mood. I have always been good at jumping into action and keeping my head in an emergency, but now that the shock had worn off my spirits sank. The rain ran in drips from my hat down the back of my collar making me shiver uncontrollably. A man had been alive this morning—shaving, dressing, making plans for dinner—and now he was dead. However unpleasant he was, he did not deserve that fate.

The rain made the sidewalk slick, and my skirt was sodden and muddy as I trudged through puddles, crossing Sixth Avenue and turning toward home. I was desperate to get out of my wet things and sit in my cheerful warm kitchen with my children. I'm sad to say that my gloomy thoughts touched them as well. What kind of world were they growing up in? Bridie had almost been killed in an accident. She was exploring a world that was dangerous, even deadly. Liam, and even Mary Kate, wouldn't be at home under my protection forever. They, too, could someday be full of plans, getting ready for the day, unaware that it would be their last.

My frustration built. How could Harry say it was an accident? Every instinct I had told me that Arthur had been murdered. What could I do to make the police listen to me?

I quickened my pace, looking for Lieutenant Corelli or another policeman, but didn't see them. Of course, now that I needed them, they were nowhere to be seen! The rain must have driven them inside. I hurried through Patchin Place, up my steps, and fumbled with the doorknob. It didn't open. The rain coming off the eaves in a shower drenched me as I stood on the top step. I turned it again and realized the door was locked. I banged on it, knowing Aileen must be inside to open it, and stood there, thoroughly miserable. I was just about to knock again when I heard the lock turn, and the door flew open. Daniel was standing there. In a second, I took in his blue traveling suit, somewhat the worse for wear, the stubble on his chin, and his eyes, tired but welcoming.

"Daniel!" I threw myself at him. He wrapped his strong arms around me, and I felt truly safe for the first time in weeks.

"My Molly," he whispered into my hair. Then he pulled back, still holding my arms gently as if not wanting to let go. "You're soaked.

Come in and get dry." I pulled my hat off in the hall and my wet coat before walking into the kitchen.

"Mama." Liam ran up to me. "Papa's home."

"I can see." I smiled. Daniel scooped him up and tickled him. Liam screamed with laughter and Daniel sat down with Liam on his lap.

"You look as tired as I feel," I said. "Let me get you some tea and then I'll sort out something for your dinner." I went over to the stove to put the kettle on.

"So, Molly?" The tone in Daniel's voice made me freeze with my hand on the kettle. I didn't turn around. He went on, "What is Biograph Studios and why I am investigating them?"

❄️ Twenty-Three ❄️

I wasn't sure whether to laugh or cry. But I didn't want Liam to hear what I was about to say.

"Up to your room, little man, while I talk with your papa." Liam started to argue but Daniel ruffled his hair.

"Go on, boyo," he said in his deep voice and set Liam down on the floor. He clomped obediently up the stairs.

"Oh Daniel," I said, turning to him, feeling too exhausted to even begin. "I'm so glad you're home. I need you to investigate a murder."

"What?" Daniel was instantly alert. "Are you hurt? Where were you?"

"I was at the studio," I said, "and I'm not hurt. But Arthur Martin is dead. The police said it was an accident, but I know they're wrong."

"Slow down, Molly," Daniel said. "Is this Biograph Studios? What is it? Who is Arthur Martin?"

I tried to collect my thoughts, sure I was not making much sense. "It is a moving picture studio. He was one of the owners."

"What on earth were you doing there?"

"I suppose I saw this coming," I said, thinking of what had led up to this moment. "With all the accidents that have been happening at the studio. I was sure they were sabotage."

"But Molly," Daniel said, his voice rising with the stress, "what on earth were you doing putting yourself in danger investigating sabotage at a moving picture studio?"

"Well, I had to, didn't I," my voice also rose, "after Bridie was nearly killed."

Now he stood up. "Bridie was nearly killed? What does Bridie have to do with this? Is *she* hurt?"

"She was in the picture, and they were filming at the train yard," I said as if it were obvious. "But she is fine. Would I be sitting here talking to you if Bridie were hurt?"

"Bridie was in a picture?" Daniel shook his head, an incredulous look on his face. "Please start again, Molly, and tell me what my family has been getting up to while I've been away."

It was hard to know where to start. So much had happened since Daniel had been gone. I thought back.

"Well, you remember that Ryan invited us to watch him make a film?" I started.

"Oh, of course. O'Hare." Daniel's voice held a note of distaste. "Is he mixed up in this? I'm afraid I was so caught up with the funeral and my trip I wasn't paying much attention."

"Well, we went to the studio to watch Ryan act," I started, and then told Daniel how Bridie had been invited to act in the film, then about the sabotage and the dangerous scene at the train yard.

"And you, a mother with a small baby at home, thought it would be a good idea to investigate sabotage in case it turned deadly?" Daniel sounded more bemused than angry.

"And I was right, Daniel," I said, "it has turned into murder, but the police aren't going to investigate it. You have to do something before it is too late and all the evidence has disappeared." At that Daniel seemed ready to listen to me. I told him that Edward had been arguing with Arthur right before his death. Daniel agreed that Edward, at least, should be interviewed, although he seemed skeptical of my assertion that Edward was in the pocket of Thomas Edison. I decided to wait until later to tell him about my trip across town to Edison's studio. For now it was enough that Arthur and Harry had believed Edward guilty of sabotage. I described the party on the roof.

"Daniel, I am sure that the lamp was not set up when everyone went up to the roof," I said. "Someone set it up on purpose."

"I will go to the coroner's and look over the police report in the morning," Daniel said. I started to speak again and he held up his hand. "And interview Edward Shepherd. Now, can I have a moment of peace and reacquaint myself with my wayward wife?" And who was I to say no to that? But before I set myself to making a good dinner and playing the dutiful wife I tucked the five bank notes into a drawer with my unmentionables. Daniel would be able to give me money for groceries and a woman should always have an emergency fund.

I felt guilty as Daniel left early the next morning. He had just come home and now he was rushing down to the precinct at my urging instead of taking a day to recover and spend with his family. But, I told myself, if he didn't begin an investigation all the evidence would disappear. A man had been killed and someone had to find out who had done it and why.

I couldn't settle to anything. I had suggested to Daniel that I come with him to the precinct but he had given me a withering look. A man did not include his wife in his investigations. In fact, he made me promise that I would stay home and "not go traipsing off across the city chasing a harebrained idea," as he so nicely put it. So I spent the morning pacing back and forth, wondering what he had discovered. In the afternoon I saw Ryan at Sid and Gus's door and decided that Daniel could hardly prohibit me from walking across the street to visit my friends. I waited until Aileen left to take the children for a walk and then hurried across the street.

Sid answered the door and ushered me into the parlor. Ryan stood as I entered. "My dear," he said, reminding me of a character in a play, "I have had the most distressing morning. I have been interrogated by a brute of a policeman."

"A policeman came to interview you?" I asked.

"Yes." He sighed and flopped back down on the sofa. "I am exhausted and had to come to my friends for some consolation. He practically accused me of causing Arthur's accident. I told him I have nothing to do with electricity, but he kept asking me where I had been all of Friday."

"I'm glad," I said, causing all three of them to look at me with surprise. I was normally a sympathetic ear to Ryan. "It means they are taking the investigation seriously." I took a deep breath. "I think Arthur was murdered."

"What?" they all three said in unison, their heads swiveling toward me so perfectly they might have rehearsed it.

"Ryan said that a lamp fell into a tank of water," Gus said. "Why do you think it was deliberate, Molly?"

"The lamp wasn't there when we went up to the roof for the party," I said, perching on a tufted ottoman. "Someone had to move the lamp close to the tank and plug it in for it to be in place for the accident."

"Is it more of the sabotage?" Sid asked. "Was it Edward?" I looked at her curiously. I hadn't told Sid or Gus that Edward was the saboteur yet.

Ryan solved that mystery. "I've told them all about it," he said. "Was it Edward? I saw him arguing with Arthur on the roof."

"He certainly is the first person that I have asked Daniel to interview," I said grimly.

"Oh, the gallant Captain Sullivan has returned?" Sid asked. "How was Washington, DC?"

"She'll tell us later, dearest." Gus was impatient. "Does he believe this was a murder too? He is investigating?"

"He is investigating because I asked him to," I said. "Even if there is an innocent reason that the lamp was placed beside the tank, I can't imagine why Arthur should fall in and drag the lamp with him."

"Perhaps the lamp had already fallen, Arthur tried to pick it up, and then he fell in," Ryan said, looking pleased at his theory.

"That's not how electricity works, Ryan," I said. "When the lamp hit the water it electrified everything in it and knocked out the power to the whole building. Arthur must have been in the tank when it fell. I think someone must have lured him with the mannequin and pushed him in."

"The mannequin?" Sid asked. "The mannequin that fell apart and almost killed our Bridie?"

"Yes," I explained. "It was found floating in the water of the tank."

"Does the studio have a ghost?" Gus asked seriously. "Has anyone else died there?"

"Ooh, that's an idea." Ryan was intrigued. "There was that crew member who fell off the roof last year."

"I've heard he was showing off after drinking too much," I said. "I doubt his ghost has come back for revenge on Arthur Martin." Then another idea occurred to me. "I wonder how often they have the end-of-week gathering up on the roof. Who would have known that the stage area would be empty?"

"And what was Arthur doing wandering around the stage if everyone was having a party upstairs?" Sid asked.

"He was seeing Edward out," I said.

"Well, there you go," Ryan said triumphantly. "Case closed. Edward killed him."

"Edward lured him onto an empty stage, got him to stand by

a tank while he connected a lamp, pushed him in, and then electrocuted him?" I queried. "I can't see how that could happen. But I
agree, Edward is my prime suspect."

"Your prime suspect?" Gus's face lit up. "So our intrepid detective
is going to investigate again?"

I hesitated. "Now that Daniel is back I should leave it to him,
but . . ."

"But you already know all the people involved," Sid added. "You
have a great advantage."

"And you couldn't let someone get away with murder," Gus said,
echoing my own thoughts.

"And think of the innocent people like moi that may be suspected
and questioned by brutish police," Ryan said, thinking of himself
first as usual. Then another thought occurred to him. "I wonder if
they will close the studio while they investigate. Our film is still being processed. It feels like my picture is cursed!"

That opened a whole new line of thinking. Was there something
about this picture? Did someone want to stop it being made strongly
enough that they would commit murder?

"I have an idea." Gus snatched up *The New York Times* from a pile
of newspapers on a side table. She turned the pages until she came
to the one she wanted. "There's an obituary in here for Mr. Martin.
It doesn't say how he died. Just *Arthur Martin, aged 43, lately deceased.
Funeral service to be held at 241 W. 23rd St. at 4:00 P.M. Sunday.*" She looked
up from the paper. "Molly, you should go!"

"I shall certainly go," Ryan said. "It would be rude not to pay my
respects and I would imagine that all the actors will go." He thought
about it some more. "Yes, Cecil and I will certainly come. Shall we
get a cab and go together, sweet Molly?"

I thought about it. It would be a perfect way to interview everyone about the murder. A part of me was fervently hoping that Daniel
was interviewing Edward Shepherd as we spoke and that he would

confess to murder or to accidentally killing Arthur. Then I could put this whole investigation behind me. Another part of me was already lining up suspects in my head. I was not ready to give up until I had solved this mystery.

"That is so kind, Ryan, but I will ask Daniel to take me." I was thinking of a plan as I spoke. "That way he will be able to meet everyone from the studio as my husband and speak with them more informally."

"I wish that we could go as well, but I don't think I can spare the time," Sid said, looking at the corner of the room where her film camera was sitting amid various pieces of equipment I did not recognize. "I was filming last night at the Women's University Club. Mrs. Pearce Bailey had some excellent points about women's suffrage. I'm going to develop it so that a professor friend of mine can show it in a class at Vassar."

"And I'm working on an article about it," Gus said. "There was already an article in the *Times* but it gave more room to the anti-suffragist arguments." She threw the paper she was holding back down on the table. "Yellow journalism."

"Speaking of yellow journalism," Sid said, picking up another paper from the pile, "have you seen what the *Evening Journal* wrote about poor Mr. Martin's death?" She handed the paper to me. I scanned the page until I found the article. SHOCKING DEATH OF SILENT PICTURE PATRIARCH, the headline read. I scanned the article but it had no new information. It seemed to regard the whole incident as a chance to make clever witticisms about electricity at Arthur's expense. No suggestion was made that the death was anything but an accident. I wondered who in the cast or crew had been talking to the press.

I stood up to leave but Sid jumped up and put a hand on my arm. "Don't go yet, Molly," she said. "That just reminded me, I haven't shown you the results of your darling children's work last week."

"You have a film of them?" I glanced around, wondering how we were going to watch it. Did Sid have a way to display her moving pictures yet? I had to confess I did not understand how the whole process worked.

"Not yet. I haven't developed the roll. However, I was working on an idea that Alice had and it is utterly brilliant." She pulled open an oak box with a crank handle on it and I recognized an Edison phonograph. I sat back down to listen while she fitted a hard wax cylinder onto the spool and began to turn the crank.

"On, every mountaineer, strangers to fight and fear," sung Liam's sweet, high voice from the box. "Rush to the standard of don't listen Hugh." Tears sprang to my eyes, but I also smiled at his mangling of the words. I sang this song to him often and, having no idea who dauntless Red Hugh was, he had turned him into "don't listen Hugh."

Ryan gave a laugh and caught my eye. He knew the song as well as I. "Poor naughty Gallock lass, thrown from each mountain pass. Onward for Erin, O'Donnell Abu!" was how Liam's voice finished the old Irish song. Ryan was now shaking with laughter. Sid looked at him, frowning.

"What on earth is so funny?" she asked.

"Bonnaught and Gallowglass," Ryan said. "And young Mr. Liam has rendered them 'Poor little Gallock lass.' Where is Gallock, might I ask?" he tuned to me.

"An invention of Liam's," I said. "As well as 'don't listen Hugh.' It is funny how children make sense of old songs." I turned to Sid. "Sid, that's marvelous!" I said, worrying she would feel slighted by our laughter. "What other mother in New York has the gift of her little one's voice being recorded?"

"If I can just match the song to the film," she said, blushing slightly at my praise, "we can watch him marching in the little soldier hat I bought him and singing at the same time."

"He was just darling," Gus put in. "And that sweet little voice."

"I'm sure that I gave you the idea, didn't I?" Ryan asked. "I told you Alice has been recording some of my speeches on her phonograph at the studio."

"Yes, you did mention that," Sid said. "And I had a conversation with Mrs. Prince at the studio about it as well. She has been very supportive of my desire to be a filmmaker. Why should only men be able to make films?" As Ryan was the only man present, she asked her question of him with some heat.

"I completely agree," he said quickly. "Up the fairer sex. Votes for women." This appeared to mollify her.

"Do you think I might bring Daniel over to hear this sometime?" I asked.

"Of course," she said immediately. "And if you decide to purchase a phonograph, I'll give you the cylinder." I thought it was unlikely we would be able to afford a phonograph any time soon but didn't say so.

"What an amazing world we live in," I said. "Little Liam's voice will be on that cylinder even when he is grown. And, if you develop that film, his boyhood will forever be captured. It's almost like a machine for going back in time."

As I said my goodbyes and went back across the street a fanciful thought occurred to me. Our life was like a series of scenes on film, some too dull to watch, some exciting or scary. Now if I could only play back the scene of Arthur's murder, I would be able to see who had emerged from the shadows to push him into the tank to his death.

❧ Twenty-Four ❧

I was waiting eagerly by the door for Daniel when he arrived that night. I had been out to the market, trusting that his prohibition on traipsing across the city did not extend to going out to buy some nice chops, fresh beans, and spring potatoes for his supper. It was all ready and I didn't mention a thing about the murder investigation until the whole family had eaten, Daniel had spent time with both Liam and Mary Kate, and Aileen had taken the little ones up to bed. I tried to send Bridie up to do her homework, but she declared she had none and wanted to spend some time with her papa. So, the three of us were together in the parlor sitting in front of a fire. A cold front had swept in again and the temperature dropped into the fifties that evening.

"So," I began, "tell me everything. What did Edward Shepherd have to say? Were you able to interview him?" Before Daniel could answer, Bridie chimed in.

"Edward the cameraman? From the studio?"

I realized I could not keep Arthur's death from her any longer. If both Daniel and I were going to be investigating it, we would be discussing it frequently around the house.

"There was an accident at the studio," I said, continuing hurriedly

225

in case she feared for her friends. "I am afraid that Arthur Martin is dead."

"The grumpy man who dresses just like his twin brother?" She sounded relieved. "What sort of accident?"

"An electric lamp fell into the water tank while Mr. Martin was in it," I said. "Electricity is deadly in water."

"Everyone knows that," she said, "but why is Papa investigating if it is an accident?"

"Your mother seems to think that there was foul play involved and I am inclined to believe her after today," Daniel said.

"You are?" I turned to him eagerly. "What did you find out? What did Edward say?"

"He was very nervous," Daniel said. "He said that Arthur and Harry were upset at him because he was leaving the studio to take a job at Edison's."

"I knew it," I said.

"But," Daniel cautioned, "he didn't admit to any sabotage. He said he was afraid he was going to be attacked so he hurried downstairs and outside."

"Did anyone see him go?" I asked.

"We will need to verify his story," Daniel said. "He's got to come to the coroner's court as a person of interest in the inquest on Tuesday." He looked at me. "There's no sign that Arthur was hurt before he fell into the tank."

"Is that what the coroner says?" I asked. "Did he find anything else?"

"Well, to begin with, we found a note in the dead . . ." He stopped and looked at Bridie. "Mr. Martin's pocket."

"I'm not squeamish, Papa," Bridie said. "Treat me like a detective, like Mama." Daniel gave her a look that was half amused, half surprised. "After all, I have grown up with a police captain for a father."

"Yes, I suppose you have at that," he said.

"And I want to be a policewoman when I am done with school," she said confidently. "So you had better start teaching me now." I almost broke in and reminded her that last week she had been desperate to be an actress, but I held my tongue. By next week she would have moved on to something else.

"Very well, then." He looked at her seriously. "You know that we take a dead body to the coroner."

"Yes, they have to tell how he died," she said.

He nodded. "Correct. It was from electricity going through his body. They also give the police anything that might be a clue. In this case a note signed by a woman named Lily."

"I know her," Bridie said immediately. "Her family attacked me."

"What?" Daniel was instantly alert. "When? Why haven't I heard about this?"

"I told you how Bridie got the part in the picture," I said, a bit defensively. "Lily was the girl who was fired."

"And her family attacked you?" Daniel said, agitated.

"Well, yelled at me, really," Bridie said, sorry she had caused her father to get upset. "No one laid a hand on me. But the whole family came down to the studio to yell at Harry and DW and they yelled at me a bit too."

"Because she lost a part in the picture?" Daniel looked at me, not sure how much of a threat this was to Bridie. I could tell he was thinking—were they upset enough to kill? And was Bridie in any danger?

"I'm not sure that was the whole reason, Daniel," I said, carefully not looking at Bridie. "Perhaps we could talk about it later."

"You mean because Lily had been Harry's lady friend?" Bridie asked brightly. "You don't have to hide that from me, everyone at the studio was talking about it. She and Harry were special friends and she thought it would protect her from being fired. But someone told me that Harry had so many lady friends that he would rather lose one than argue with DW."

Daniel looked at me and then at Bridie. "I don't think this is an appropriate topic of conversation, Bridie. I wish you hadn't been exposed to that kind of talk at all."

Bridie was unfazed. "It is 1909, Papa. I don't understand why men and women can't be friends. After all, it's not like in your day when women needed a chaperone to go anywhere."

"It's still not appropriate for a girl to be alone with a man, Bridie," I said sternly. "Some of their behavior is not always very friendly."

"Like what?" She was curious and, blessedly, innocent. Then suddenly she blushed. "Do you mean kissing?" She looked down at the floor, embarrassed. "Is that why her parents were upset with Harry? But I thought he was going to marry Mrs. Prince." And then, of course, I had to explain to Daniel who Mrs. Prince was.

"But the note, Daniel?" I got back to the main point. "What did it say?"

"I don't remember the exact wording," he said. "And some of the words were smudged or smeared because of the water. It was asking him to meet her at the studio at two P.M. That much I remember."

"I wonder what Lily wanted with Arthur," I mused. "And if the doorman would have even let her in. He should know if she was in the studio that day or not."

"Mama, if this was a murder," Bridie said pensively, "it had to be one of the people inside the studio."

"Yes, of course," Daniel said with a little laugh. "A murderer is usually on the scene, unless you believe in spirits, of course." He did not understand what she meant, but I did.

"You're right," I said, looking at her, and then explained. "The studio has two entrances, Daniel. One for the cast and crew on Fourteenth Street and a fancy one for people coming to the director's offices on Fifth Avenue."

He nodded, now serious and following along.

"The Martins' receptionist, Trevor, sits at a desk in the foyer of the Fifth Avenue entrance and a doorman—I believe his name is Ted—sits right inside the Fourteenth Street entrance and only admits people on his list. That's what you meant, wasn't it?" I turned to Bridie.

She nodded. "Only the cast and crew were at the studio that day, so the murderer had to be someone who was one of the studio family. It couldn't be an outsider."

"Ah." Daniel was thoughtful. "So the clerk and the doorman would have a record of everyone who entered the building?"

I nodded.

"Unless they had stepped away from their post for a while?" He made this a question.

"They didn't the whole time I was there," I said. "The receptionist even chased me up the stairs once for not having permission to pass him."

Daniel looked at me quizzically. "You know my meetings in Washington were about the Black Hand and other gang activity. Could the Martin brothers have made enemies with one of the gangs? Could this be sending a message to the studio?"

"It's possible," I said. "But the person who did it would still be posing as a crew member, I suppose. I gave your lieutenant a list of names to investigate."

"Yes," he said with a withering look, "he thought that he was investigating for me, Molly."

I refused to be withered. "I thought I would give him a job after I caught him following me one day," I retorted. "Under your orders, I understand."

"It is my right to keep you safe." Daniel flared up.

"And scare me half to death?" I matched his temper. "Did you think I wouldn't be able to tell someone was following me? I thought it was the Black Hand."

He relented immediately.

"I didn't mean to scare you," he said, "just keep an eye on you while I was gone. You weren't supposed to notice them."

"Well, I did," I suddenly felt guilty, "but don't say anything to Corelli about it. I told him I wouldn't tell. What did you find?" I said, changing the subject. Daniel took a deep breath and seemed to accept that I had called a truce.

"Just one lead. One of the young men, Antonio, has a cousin who is on our list of known gang members. I can have my men question him to see if he has anything to do with the sabotage you have told me about, or the murder." We sat in silence for a few minutes. It was rather overwhelming. With such a large number of actors and crew, many people could have murdered Arthur. Daniel must have been thinking along the same lines.

"Molly, this is all very complicated," he finally said. "You know I would prefer that you stay out of this completely, so I hate to say this," he paused, and I looked up expectantly, "but could you come down to my office tomorrow? I want you to take a look at that note."

I beamed at him. Perhaps Daniel was going to start regarding me as a partner after all. "Yes, Daniel," I said, "I will."

"I could come too, Papa," Bridie said. "I know all of the picture people."

"The police station is no place for a young girl," he said firmly. "It's bad enough that I'm bringing your mother down there."

"But I'm a good detective," she protested. "I'm the one who figured out it has to be a member of the cast or crew."

"Who else was there who could have been involved, Molly?" Daniel said, changing the subject.

"Well, Harry, that's the twin brother, was downstairs with Arthur. He could have set up the lamp," I said. "It seems suspicious to me that he wanted so badly for the police to regard this as an accident. And you know that Edward was downstairs with him. As far as I know everyone else was on the roof." I tried to picture the scene when I left the roof. "Alice was up and down the stairs getting the pay packets—she's DW's assistant—and Mrs. Prince was up and down arranging the food. And crew members were helping her."

"Did either of them have a reason to kill Arthur Martin?"

I thought about it. "I did overhear an argument between Arthur and Harry. But brothers argue."

"Alice wouldn't kill anyone," Bridie put in. "She's amazing."

"Alice would definitely be capable of planning a murder," I said, "but I didn't see any animosity between her and Arthur."

"He was so mean." Bridie made a face. "I bet lots of people hated him."

"That's true," I said. "He didn't seem very happy about Fanny and Harry's engagement. That could have made Fanny upset, but it's hardly a reason for murder."

Daniel looked interested. "It could be if he was going to interfere with a match that was important to them. Did either of them need money?"

"I'm not sure," I said. "I believe Fanny was an investor in the picture. But what about Lily?" I asked. "Surely, given that note, she is a suspect. We know that she asked to meet with him at the exact time of the murder."

"I haven't forgotten that," he said. "I've already sent someone out to interview her, but her parents wouldn't let her come to the door. They insisted that they bring her down the station tomorrow."

"How did you find her so quickly?" I asked. "I can't even remember her last name."

"Lily La Rosa," Bridie said triumphantly. "She's been in other pictures I've seen with my friends, so I made sure to remember her name when she told me." She added, "They were ever so impressed that I met her."

"We police captains have our ways," Daniel said grandly, then added with a grin, "Her address was on the envelope the note came in."

"I've forgotten someone!" I suddenly said. "DW Griffith, the director. I have no idea why he would want to murder Arthur, but I think I saw him walk downstairs with Arthur and Edward."

"What baffles me," Daniel said, "is how many people were roaming about this studio and yet no one saw the murder. The murderer must have been very clever or very lucky."

"Or both," I said. "Perhaps it was just an attempt. If it had failed the person could have invented a reason to be moving the lamp or wandering around the stage."

"I confess, I'm quite confused by how many people were there," Daniel said, running his fingers through his hair. "When you come to the station tomorrow, I'll take your statement officially and have you write down for me all the people who were there."

"Wouldn't you rather meet them?" I asked. He looked at me quizzically.

"Gus showed me the obituary today," I said. "The funeral service is on West Twenty-Third Street at four P.M. I was planning to attend."

"You were?" His eyebrows shot up.

"It seems like the Christian thing to do," I said with a smile.

"And a good way to interview everyone about the murder," Daniel said. "I don't want you investigating, Molly."

"But I wouldn't be investigating," I lied, "I would be bringing you there to investigate."

"I could go on my own," he pointed out.

"Yes, but I know all these people. If you go on your own you will be a police captain," I said. "If you go with me you may hear something they wouldn't tell a police captain."

"I want to come too," Bridie put in, and before we could argue she went on, "It is perfectly respectable to attend a prayer service. And Mary and Daisy will be there, I'm sure." She turned to Daniel. "They're my friends."

"Very well." Daniel gave in. "The Sullivan family will attend the service for Mr. Martin tomorrow afternoon."

"Minus the little ones," I put in quickly; I would not be able to have any conversations at all if I had Mary Kate and Liam with me.

"Minus the little ones," he agreed.

"So, in the morning I shall spend time with my darling babies and clean our sweet little house," I said. "You see, Daniel, I won't neglect my duties as wife and mother." I gave him an innocent smile. "But after that," I added, "I shall go to your office to look at that note and help the great Captain Sullivan solve this case."

The bells were ringing, summoning the faithful to ten o'clock Mass as I left the house on Sunday morning. Families were hurrying children, dressed in their Sunday best, toward various churches. A group of Irish women, their heads modestly covered in shawls, walked by and I tensed, half expecting them to say, "Molly Murphy, where are you going on the Lord's Day?" A silly thought, since I had been Molly Sullivan for years now and I like to think that the Good Lord would approve of my errand. According to religious people, He was big on justice and that was what I was trying to do.

It was a short walk to the police station at Jefferson Market. As I came up to the entrance a large and noisy group was just exiting, speaking in highly excited Italian. Half a dozen men came out, followed by a woman all in black and wearing a black scarf on her head. Beside her I caught a glimpse of a pretty young woman in a modern blue suit, her hair down around her shoulders in dark curls. It was Lily. Our eyes met briefly, but she showed no recognition.

I approached the front desk and the officer smiled when he saw me. "Captain Sullivan is waiting for you, Mrs. Sullivan." He accompanied me up to Daniel's office where he gave me a little salute and a grin before walking back downstairs. Daniel rose as I entered.

"I see you have interviewed Lily," I said. "I just saw her leaving."

"Yes," he grimaced, "that was a bit of a nightmare. She brought her parents and brothers. They all told me I should arrest Harry Martin for messing with an innocent girl."

"I'm afraid to say, she didn't look all that innocent to me at the studio," I said. "I saw her wink at Harry. She was at least flirting with him."

"Well, she did the innocent young girl routine in front of her parents." He sighed. "They swore that she was home all day yesterday and could have had nothing to do with a murder."

"Is that the note?" I nodded at a piece of writing paper set apart on the desk.

"Yes." Daniel picked it up gingerly and handed it to me. "Obviously we couldn't get any fingerprints since it was soaking wet. It was found in Mr. Martin's inside suit pocket."

I examined it closely. The left side was almost unreadable; the water had smudged and lifted the ink from the page. As much as I could make out the note read: *I must see you. I will be at the studio at* 2:00 P.M. *Leave word with the doorman to let me in or I will go to the papers. You have a responsibility you have to take care of.* The note was signed with a looping signature, *Lily La Rosa.*

"I wonder what the responsibility that Arthur had was?" I mused. "I don't think I ever saw the two of them speak to one another."

I looked at the envelope. There was a return address on Mott Street. It was addressed to Mr. Martin at Biograph Studios on West Fourteenth Street but something in the top right caught my eye.

"Daniel," I said, "there is no postmark. This didn't come by mail." I looked up and he was smiling at me.

"I'm impressed," he said. "I wondered if you would catch that."

"So, you had seen it already?" I was absurdly disappointed that I hadn't found it first. "It seems to me that you need to question the doorman. He will know who could have put this in with the mail and if Lily was actually let in that day."

Daniel nodded. "He's been called for the inquest on Tuesday and we're sending an officer to get the list you mentioned and the guest book from the Fifth Avenue entrance." I put the envelope back on the desk. "That was helpful information, Molly."

"You should send someone out to the Bronx to get Edison's record-of-entrance book as well," I said before I realized that there was something else I had not chosen to tell Daniel yet. Oh well, I thought, now is as good a time as any.

"That might be more difficult," he said. "He rarely gives anything up without a court order. What will it show?"

"It will show that Edward Shepherd visited Edison's studio on multiple occasions," I said. "It's why I think he was the saboteur."

"And how did you happen to find out this information?" he asked, suspicious.

"Mrs. Prince needed someone to go with her to sign some papers at Edison's studio," I said. "I was curious."

"Yes, and you happened to see the logbooks for the studio?" He raised an eyebrow.

"Well, the doorkeeper was gone on an errand," I said. "And it was something I wanted to know." Another thought struck me. "And I saw the Martins' names in the book as well. Mr. H. and Mr. A. Martin. I couldn't tell how long ago they had visited."

"Was that suspicious?" Daniel's curiosity had gotten the better of his need to scold me. I looked at him fondly. We shared a love for solving mysteries and seeing justice done. "That owners of two studios would meet to talk?"

"It is if you listen to the Biograph Studios staff. According to them Edison has been trying to ruin Biograph since its beginnings. He even sent thugs to tear down each day's construction when they were trying to build the place. Not to mention the ongoing lawsuits." I thought of all the stories I had heard. "They have recently formed some sort of an alliance, but I saw their names toward the front of the book. It could have been from years ago."

"So, there was no love lost between Edison and the Martin brothers," Daniel said thoughtfully. "But I'm not sure we can get this book before the inquest."

"I could testify to having seen the names," I said.

"No," he said firmly. "Not only do I not want my wife involved in something dangerous, but if my family is seen to be mixed up in this affair, how can I be seen as impartial?" We looked at each other. Daniel had been accused of corruption in the past and it was an all-too-real possibility.

"You're right." But I was a little distracted, for I had just thought of something else. *H* Martin and *A* Martin looked very alike. I looked at the envelope again. The letters on the front had bled, the blue ink smudged and swollen from the water. But wasn't that an *H* rather than an *A*? I picked up the letter and took it to the window to take advantage of the beam of light shining through. As I held it up, I could better see the first two words of the letter: *Dear Harry.*

I turned to Daniel. "This letter wasn't written to Arthur at all."

"What do you mean?"

"This letter was written to Harry Martin. Which means he may have been the target all along."

"What do you mean, 'the target'?"

"If this letter was used to lure someone to their death, then perhaps the wrong brother was murdered."

❧ Twenty-Five ❧

L et me see that." Daniel joined me at the window and peered at the letter. "Yes, I see the *y* at the end of the name. I think you're right."

If Harry was the target, then I had been looking at everything upside down. Was it possible that someone had mistaken the brothers for each other? Yes, of course. I myself had never been able to tell them apart until Arthur had spoken and revealed his sour personality. In the gloom of the studio, if someone had been waiting for Harry, they would have no reason to think it was Arthur walking toward the tank. But why did Arthur have this letter addressed to Harry?

"We need to go to that funeral this afternoon," I said aloud, "and ask Harry about this letter. Did he know about it and if so, why was Arthur the one to handle it?" An explanation occurred to me as I said those words. It seemed that Arthur had been the brother who handled all the messes that Harry made. And another thought followed immediately: I needed to talk to Lily. This note was the key to solving this murder. And if Lily had sent it, she was most likely the murderer. I took note of the address on the letter one more time, determined to seek her out that day.

I left the precinct having extracted a promise from Daniel to be home in time to accompany me to the funeral.

It was not until I was heading into the Italian section that I wondered if this were a good idea. I had never been afraid to walk down Bleecker Street before, but now all the talk of the Black Hand and gangs made me feel somewhat apprehensive. I cheered myself up with the thought that I would buy some cannolis on the way home. That would also be a convenient excuse if Daniel happened to ask me what I had been doing in this part of town. But the shop I was thinking of was closed. Of course, it was Sunday. All good Catholics were at Mass!

But as I turned down Mott Street, it seemed that the whole of Italy was out doing their Sunday shopping. The shops here were open. Their signs were all in Italian. Pushcarts filled the streets and children lined up in front of a candy shop with a red-and-white-striped awning. Banners and elaborate lights in the shapes of crowns and stars were strung across the street, perhaps left over from the Easter celebrations. Everything seemed more vibrant and alive than the streets I had just left. I was now used to seeing automobiles mixed with horse-drawn carriages on the streets around Washington Park, but there was not one to be seen. Instead, horse-drawn wagons clopped down the cobbled street. Tall buildings, some of brick and some of brownstone, lined the road. Each window had a metal balcony or grate and fire escape and women sat on them chatting and yelling down to friends in the street. Everyone I passed was speaking Italian and I drew some stares as I looked for the 200 block. When I came to the address on the letter, it turned out to be a large building with so many windows that I guessed fifty families lived there at least.

I hesitated outside, feeling conspicuous. A young woman came out with two little children. I smiled at her, and she smiled back in a friendly fashion.

"Excuse me," I asked, "do you know if Lily La Rosa lives here?"

"Lily?" She thought for a moment. "No, I don't know Lily. No La Rosas in this building."

I started to walk around the building wondering if I had the address correct. I knew I was at the address on the letter. Had Lily put the wrong address? Then I realized that the police had found her. Perhaps she was known to the local patrolman. I stopped at the corner of the building wondering what to do next. It had been an impulse to talk to Lily, feeling that she might tell me something she wouldn't tell the police, but now I hesitated to go into the building. I knew what it would be like inside, much like the tenements where I had lived with Bridie's aunt when I first came to New York: crowded and dark.

"Hey, lady." The voice came from a little boy with dark curls and the face of an angel. The rough accent he spoke with didn't match his innocent looks. "Whatcha doing here? You lookin' for someone?" Two other boys, who, by their looks and their short pants, were about twelve, came and stood beside him, blocking my way.

"Yes, I am," I said, trying to sound confident. He was only a little boy, but I wondered if bigger boys were just around the corner. "I'm looking for Lily La Rosa, do you know her?"

"Lily La Rosa?" The boy sounded doubtful. "That sounds like a name outta Diamond Dick or some picture story."

"That sounds made up," another boy put in. "Never hearda no Lily La Rosa."

It suddenly occurred to me that they might be right.

"She's an actress," I said. "That might be her stage name. Do you know any actresses, someone who is in the pictures? Someone the police spoke to yesterday?"

"Around here?" The angelic boy looked wary at the mention of the police.

But his friend said, "She might mean Lola. Ain't she done a picture or two? And I saw a cop at that building yesterday."

"Does she live in this building?" I gestured to the one behind me.

A glint came into the first boy's eyes. "Who wants to know? Information ain't free."

"I'll give you a dime for her address and another for her last name," I said.

"Two bits," he said with a smirk at his companions. "Not a penny less."

"Done."

"It's Lola Rosetti and she lives round the back of this building," the boy said as I put the quarter into his rather grubby hand.

"Do you know what apartment?" I asked but the three boys had already taken off, running across the street to the candy store. I felt quite pleased with myself. I remembered from my time working as a detective that children were the best people to ask if you wanted information. They knew everything that went on in a neighborhood and were normally happy to tell you for the price of some candy. It also struck me that Daniel must have known about the stage name and not told me. So, he was not sharing every part of his investigation.

I went down the side of the building until I came to a narrow alley at the back. It smelled of garbage and, indeed, I could see a rat scuttling away with what looked like the end of an onion in its mouth. There was a strong smell of cigarette smoke. I followed the alley down. The fire escapes here were hung with clothing. Two men leaned out a third-floor window, chatting. They eyed me curiously but didn't say anything. Then I saw a woman sitting on a metal grate just above the second floor. She was leaning back against the building and taking long puffs from a cigarette.

"Lola?" I called up.

"Yeah?" She looked down. It was Lily.

She didn't recognize me. She had only seen me once and probably hadn't paid much attention to Bridie's mother.

"Lily?" I asked this time. She stood up quickly.

240

"Who are you? Are you with the police?" She sounded nervous. I thought fast. I really should have thought out what I was going to tell her.

"No," I said, "I know you from the studio. I'm the mother of one of the actresses."

A young boy poked his head out of the window beside the ledge and gawked down at me.

"Who's that, Lola?" he asked. A little girl stuck her face out of the window beside him.

"No one, go inside, both of you," Lily said angrily. The two children disappeared to be replaced by an older woman. *"Chi è questa? Altri problemi?"* she said to Lily.

Lily quickly moved her cigarette to the hand away from the woman. *"No, Mamma, va tutto bene.* Go back inside." The two women said more in a fast Italian that I didn't understand. Finally, Lily's mother pulled her head back inside the building.

"I'll come down," Lily said. "I don't want to get my mother involved. She's upset enough as it is. Can you wait for me on the Mott Street side?"

"Sure," I said, wondering if she would really come or disappear inside the building. How would I find her then? But five minutes later she came out the front entrance.

"Well." We both stood there awkwardly in the entrance. "What do you want?" Then she added hopefully, "Does DW want me back?"

"I can ask him," I said. "I'm going to see him this afternoon." A wave of relief swept over her face making me feel guilty. If she imagined I had any pull with DW Griffith, she was wrong, but it was my best chance to get her to answer some questions. I held out my hand. "Molly Sullivan."

She shook it. "Nice to meet you. Around here I'm Lola but all the theater and picture people know me as Lily."

The street was busy, and pedestrians kept giving us annoyed

looks as they moved to one side to pass us. "Is there somewhere we could go to talk?" I asked. She nodded.

"I know a café." She led us down the street to a little shop with a few tables outside and ordered two coffees. Luckily, I had been trained by my friends to drink Turkish coffee, because the small cups that came were strong and black. We both sipped them in silence for a moment.

"So, you know DW?" she asked.

"Yes, I worked on makeup for the last picture," I said. "You know that after you left someone sabotaged the picture. There was a fire in the studio and an accident in which a girl almost was killed."

"No, I hadn't heard," she said gloomily. "I don't got any friends left at Biograph."

"I guess Harry was your friend there," I ventured, and she stared down at her coffee.

"He seemed real sweet to start with. You know how those guys are." She kept talking but didn't look at me. "They tell you all sorts of stories about how they're going to make you a star." Her face hardened. "But he didn't lift a finger to save me when DW fired me. I was counting on that picture money. I was going to make it out of here. Now my mother's on at me every day to come to work with her at the shirtwaist factory." She stopped and stared out of the window.

"I heard your family was pretty upset you got fired," I said. "They came down to the studio and threatened Harry. Do you think they . . ." I hesitated.

"Do I think they could what? Do something to hurt the picture?" She laughed. "No, my family doesn't have any connections like that. Is that what all you Irish people think? Every Italian is the Black Hand." Her voice rose. "Well, most of us are just working in factories or selling stuff." Her cuff was frayed and she picked at it. "Or trying to make it in the pictures."

"I'm sorry," I said, "I didn't mean to suggest anything bad about your family, but I know the police will be suspicious. You are fired and the picture is sabotaged. Your family threatens the Martins and one of them is killed. And there is a letter in your handwriting asking Harry to meet you."

"What?" She looked up. The expression on her face told me Daniel hadn't shared that bit of news with her. "A letter? From me?"

"Yes." I nodded. "That's how the police got your address."

"What does it say, this letter?" she asked cautiously. I could tell she had information and was debating whether she should tell me or not.

"It asks Harry to meet you at the time of the murder," I said. "And says you will go to the press if he doesn't. I am sure the police will want to compare it to your handwriting to see if you wrote it."

"My handwriting," she said, and looked at me scornfully. "What handwriting? The police won't find a scrap of it." I looked at her quizzically and she went on. "I can't read or write. Just enough to sign 'Lily La Rosa.' A girlfriend taught me that, but that's all."

"You can't read?" I asked, too surprised to be tactful. How could someone get to Lily's age without learning to read? I had been lucky enough to be educated with the young ladies of the big house in Ballykillin, but even the poorest farmers' children had gone to school long enough to learn their letters.

Lily must have read my thoughts. "I have five brothers and sisters younger than me," she said, "and we needed the money from my mother's job. So, I had to stay home until they could all go to school. By the time the baby turned six, I was sixteen and it was too late."

"But you still managed to work as an actress," I said. I had thought Lily was arrogant and had deserved her fate when Bridie took her role. I realized with a prickle of guilt that we might have misjudged her. "That's impressive."

"It's hard in the theater," she acknowledged. "They like me on

account of my looks so I've done some good parts if I can get someone to run my lines with me. But pictures are great. DW just yells at
you what to do and say and it's no problem."

"Until Ryan wrote a script," I guessed, "and wanted you all to
learn your lines."

"That guy," she said angrily, "some bigshot playwright. If he'd
only given me a little longer to learn them, I coulda done it. But he
kept changing them at the last minute and handing me a script to
read."

"I'm sure he had no idea," I said, wanting to be loyal to Ryan. Self-
absorbed as he was, I was confident he would be shocked to have
been the cause of Lily's losing her job.

"Well, whether he knew or not, that's what happened." Lily
sighed. "And it's hard to pick up new work right now. I've been out
on a million auditions, but my parents are after me to make some
money. I was planning on moving in with some actress friends this
summer and now I'm back where I started. Nowhere."

"I really am going to see DW this afternoon," I said. "I'm going
to Arthur's funeral, and I imagine DW and all the cast members will
be there. He doesn't know me very well, but I'll try to put in a good
word for you."

"That would be really nice of you, Mrs. Sullivan," she said. "I'm
sorry that Arthur is dead. That was a little rude of me not to start
with that, but it was confusing having the police drag me downtown
and embarrassing for my brothers and parents to get all upset."

"But you didn't have anything to do with the letter?" I asked. "You
didn't get someone to write it for you?"

"I didn't know anything about it until you told me," she said solemnly, "I swear to God." And I believed her.

I have to admit I was quite sad as I went home. From the stories I
had heard of Lily La Rosa, I had had a picture in my head of a flirta-
tious, perhaps even immoral, actress who lost her job through arro-

gance. Now I was seeing her in an entirely different light. We women were sometimes the hardest on our sex, even though we knew well the pitfalls of men such as Harry Martin and the tightrope all of us walked between success and ruin. I reflected as I turned into Patchin Place that the experience had been a sermon on compassion better than any I would have heard at church that morning.

And Lily's story had caught my attention in another way as well. Men like Harry rarely stopped at only one woman. Had someone else been put in a compromising position by Harry Martin? And was she angry enough about it to kill?

❧ Twenty-Six ❧

Daniel wore his dark suit and I put on my blue wool coat and skirt with a black hat. I hoped it was appropriate because I did not own an all-black suit or dress.

"I can't believe it's almost May and still so chilly in the afternoon," I remarked as we walked toward the Sixth Avenue El station. Daniel laughed.

"You say that every April," he said. "Just wait until July when you would sell your soul for a cool breeze."

"It's a shame I can't bottle one up to open in July," I said with a smile. We took the El north and then turned east on Twenty-Third Street. I was a little curious to see a funeral parlor. All the families that I knew would have a wake at home and a funeral mass. It seemed a bit strange to view the family member and have a religious service at a private business. Would it look more like a house or a church?

It turned out to look like a shop, complete with a sign out front that read STEPHEN MERRITT. Once we entered, however, there was a large parlor for the mourners with some coffee and biscuits set out and a chapel-type room behind it with the body displayed in an open coffin. Harry Martin had chosen to match his outfit to his brother's one last time, giving the disconcerting impression that the same man was dead in the coffin and walking around the funeral parlor. There was no one giving formal introductions, just a rather subdued crowd of people speaking in hushed voices. Harry was surrounded with condolers, but I saw Alice across the room and went to her.

"Miss Mann," I said, "can I introduce you to my husband, Captain Sullivan? Daniel, this is Miss Mann."

"Call me Alice," she said, shaking hands. "I don't stand on ceremony."

"It's a sad day," Daniel said. "I'm sorry for your loss."

"It is indeed, Captain Sullivan," Alice said. "Arthur was not an easy person to work with, not meaning to speak ill of the dead, but he believed in pictures and wanted us to make the best pictures ever made. That counted a lot with me."

"Will the studio be able to keep going?" I asked. "Wasn't he one of the owners?"

"As far as I know, Harry was his only living relative," Alice said, lowering her voice. "I imagine that Harry is the sole owner now. DW said we are dark for the next few days, so I guess they're sorting it out."

That reminded me of Lily and my promise to ask DW if he had a job for her. Alice would be the perfect person to talk to, but I was not willing to reveal my trip to Mott Street to Daniel just yet so I merely nodded.

"Molly," Alice said, her face anxious, "I heard there is going to be an inquest. Is it really true that this wasn't an accident?"

"I'm afraid so." I looked at Daniel, wondering how much I could say.

"You might be called, Miss Mann, if the coroner has any questions about what you told the police. But for now, I've only been asked to have Edward Shepherd and your doorman . . ."

"Ted Johnson."

"Yes . . . Johnson . . . give testimony and to get copies of your logs and guest books."

"So, you must think it was someone in our studio family." Alice was certainly one of the brightest people I knew and she got the point instantly. "Someone who was officially let into the studio."

"That is what it looks like," Daniel said. "But today, I'm just here to pay my condolences, not as a police captain."

"Molly!" I heard my name and looked up to see Ryan coming toward me, Cecil at his side. "You came!" He grabbed both my shoulders and gave me dramatic air kisses, which I noticed made Daniel extremely annoyed.

"O'Hare," he said, nodding curtly at Ryan.

"Captain Sullivan." Ryan nodded back. "Who's been deserting our poor Molly and leaving her to her own devices for weeks at a time." I saw the color rise in Daniel's face. "Daniel the Deserter" had been my friends' nickname for him many years ago when he had broken off our romance because of a previous engagement. But poor Daniel did not deserve to be teased.

"He has been off serving his president and fighting crime, as I'm sure I told you, Ryan O'Hare." I pushed his shoulder playfully. "Do you think we'll defeat the Black Hand by writing plays about them, then? You need my brave husband for that kind of work." I patted Daniel's arm proudly.

"The Black Hand?" Cecil spoke up. "Do the police think they are behind the sabotage and murder at the studio?" He glanced in the direction of the chapel. Through the open door we could see back to the coffin placed just before the altar.

"We are investigating," Daniel said, but his eyebrows went up. "How did you know that it is a murder, Mr. . . . ."

"Armitage," Ryan put in. "A brilliant actor." His gaze rested on Cecil for a moment and then turned back to Daniel. "I told him."

Before Daniel could ask the obvious question, he added, "Molly told me, and she is usually right about such things."

"As I said," Daniel said, pointedly not looking at me, "we are investigating. There is an inquest on Tuesday."

"Well, I hope you call Edward Shepherd," Alice said darkly. "He has a lot to answer for."

"We will be calling him," Daniel said. "Is there any particular reason you suspect him?"

"You know that Molly found his name in the logbook at Edison's studio?" she asked. Daniel nodded. "We had petty sabotage going on for months while he was part of the crew. Key props were broken or missing, costumes came apart at the seams. Then he turns in his notice in the middle of a picture, which is unheard of. And the day he comes back to the studio Arthur Martin is murdered."

"You make a compelling case." Daniel looked impressed. "I promise I will let the coroner know all that information and he can question Mr. Shepherd about it."

"I've never been to a coroner's court," Ryan said. "Is anyone allowed to come?"

"I believe they are open." Daniel's face showed what he thought of Ryan attending the coroner's court like it was a play at the theater, but that only seemed to make Ryan more eager to go.

"Cecil, dear, you'll come with me to coroner's court, won't you?" Ryan laid a hand on Cecil's arm. Cecil didn't look excited about the prospect.

"I don't understand why we are not starting filming tomorrow," he said, looking at Alice. "On the new picture."

"Not this week," she said. "The police want to search the studio tomorrow and the inquest is on Tuesday. Surely Harry must be there."

"We don't need Harry to shoot a picture," Cecil said, not wanting to give up the argument.

"Has it occurred to you that Arthur was a large investor in the pictures and the co-owner of the studio? We need to wait to see if there is even a budget for the next picture," Alice said. From Cecil's shocked face it was evident that thought had not crossed his mind. "And I think some of us should be there in case the coroner wants to call witnesses."

"I, for one," Ryan said dramatically, "will do my civic duty."

"You know it will probably start at a god-awful hour of the morning," Cecil put in grumpily. "And you said you were getting out of the moving picture business because of the hours."

"Eight A.M.," Daniel said.

"Very well." Ryan took Cecil's arm. "We can always stay up all night tomorrow and go to bed after the inquest." He confided, "You must know I am thinking of doing a drama. There has never been a play set in a coroner's court. Imagine the possibilities. A death every day." His face lit up. "What a wonderful title: *A Death Every Day.*"

"I'm just teasing," Daniel murmured to me. "It really starts at ten." I made a mental note to tell Ryan.

Just then the Reverend Merritt guided Harry and Fanny into the chapel, leading us all to take our seats. He had the full beard and mustache that King Edward had made popular in England and lacked the mournful disposition I expected of an undertaker. He looked more like a cheerful sailor than a reverend. However, he had obviously taken some time to get to know the man whose life he was memorializing.

"Mr. Arthur Martin was lucky enough to have a passion in his life," he said, to begin his sermon. "He and his brother, left orphaned at a young age, were able to turn their scientific knowledge into a new invention that is bringing innocent joy to people across the country." I noticed Fanny stir slightly at the mention of the brothers' invention. Harry looked at her and she put her hand on his arm gently.

"From their humble beginnings as workers in a photographic shop, the two brothers helped to pioneer this new field of . . . kinematography." Reverend Merritt stumbled over the word. He did not strike me as the sort of man who had ever set foot in a moving picture storefront. "Although tragedy stuck Arthur down too soon, still we must trust in the timing of the Lord." His voice warmed to the theme. "The Lord takes his servants in his own time. And how blessed it is for them to enter the kingdom of heaven."

I privately had my doubts as to Arthur Martin having been any sort of servant of the Lord or having given the kingdom of heaven a second thought during his time on earth. But what was the poor reverend to say? It seemed obvious to me, as the service ended and we once again stood in the parlor, awkwardly exchanging small talk, that no one truly mourned Arthur, except perhaps his brother. He and Fanny were, for the first time, alone in the room and I decided it was time Daniel and I expressed our condolences.

"I am terribly sorry for your brother's death," I said, holding my hand out to Harry. He took it with a grateful look.

"Thank you so much, Mrs. Sullivan. The apartment is so quiet without him just down the hall. I've never been completely without family before." He shook his head sadly. "And this must be Mr. Sullivan?"

"Captain Sullivan," Daniel said, and gave a firm handshake.

"Oh, yes, the police captain." Was that a flicker of alarm in his eyes? "And my fiancée, Mrs. Prince," Harry said, introducing Fanny. "I believe she and Mrs. Sullivan already know each other."

"Yes, Mrs. Sullivan posed as my secretary in a little scheme," Fanny said. I smiled at her. She was impeccably dressed in black silk with a lace collar and matching black hat. Of course, she must have had many such garments made as she mourned her husband for a year.

"I hope we can put this whole accident behind us and get on with mourning the death of my brother," Harry said to Daniel in the tones of one man speaking to another. "It was bad enough that his body had to be examined by the coroner, but now there is to be an inquest." He let the words hang. "I wonder if you could put a stop to it. After all, your talented daughter might be acting for us again in the summer."

"She might?" Daniel turned to look at me. My eyes told him to just go along with it and he turned back. "Yes, of course, it is a pity the film she acted in was destroyed."

"Exactly," Harry nodded, "but now this accident is shutting down the studio, which my brother would have hated."

"And I'm afraid electricity is very dangerous, and the coroner might not understand the risks involved in a studio," Fanny put in.

"And naturally my fiancée is not happy about being mixed up with the police in any way." Harry hesitated. "No offense meant, of course. But there may be publicity."

"I'm just a police captain," Daniel said solemnly. "I assure you that I have no power over the coroner. I don't think that Mrs. Prince will be called at all."

"But I'm going to go and support Harry," Fanny said immediately. Harry beckoned Daniel to one side and asked him a question in a low voice. Fanny must have been waiting for an opportunity. She turned to me and said softly, "Mrs. Sullivan, won't you come too, and support me?"

"Of course, if you want me there," I said, surprised. "I don't know what I can do." Daniel returned to my side and Fanny shook her head slightly, warning me not to say anything further.

"Excuse me, I think the reverend needs me," she said and headed off across the room.

"When can we get back into the studio?" Harry said to Daniel, watching Fanny walk away. "We've got pictures to make."

"Not until after the inquest, I'm afraid." Daniel was watching Harry carefully. "It's a crime scene and my men and I will need to go through it."

Harry's knuckles tightened on the glass of whiskey he was holding. He adopted a confidential tone. "I don't want to worry my fiancée but between us I think you may be right that my brother's death was a murder. And . . ." He looked around and spoke softly. "I have some information you may need."

"About Miss La Rosa?" Daniel guessed.

"You know about that?" Harry jerked and spilled a little whiskey out of his glass. "Damn," he said, "excuse my language, Mrs. Sullivan. My nerves are all to pieces." He took a swig of the whiskey and grew still. "Let me guess, Arthur still had the letter in his pocket?"

"A letter intimating that Miss La Rosa had to discuss something of an indiscreet nature." Daniel's voice was low. "And that letter was addressed to you."

"Have you talked to Lily about it?" Harry asked. "I don't think she would be capable of murder, but it looks like . . ." He trailed off.

"It looks like she tried to get you alone so she could murder you," I said, "and then she killed Arthur instead."

"I can't believe that Lily would do this. She's a sweet girl, really," Harry said. "That letter didn't sound like her at all."

"In point of fact, Lily has an alibi for the time of the murder," Daniel said. "Is there someone else who might use what they know of your relationship to get you alone?"

"Her parents were quite upset and accused me of a number of things of which, of course, I am quite innocent," Harry said, speaking so low that I could barely hear him. "But they don't speak English very well. I doubt they would have thought of a letter as a way to get me alone. They might have had thugs wait for me around a corner."

"I see what you mean," Daniel put in. "Did anyone else know of your *relationship*," he emphasized the word, "with Lily?"

"Don't make it sound sordid, Captain Sullivan." Harry was on the defensive now. "There is a lot of gossip in a picture studio. People may have made certain assumptions. Practically anyone at the studio could have written that letter, including Lily."

"Lily didn't write it, Harry," I said.

"I want to believe that," he said, "but why are you so sure?"

"Because she never learned to read or write," I said. "So, there is someone else at the studio who put in place a plan for murder. And that person's target was most likely you."

❧ Twenty-Seven ❧

hat do you mean, Lily can't read or write?" Daniel began as we started for home. "You saw the letter yourself."

"She says that she can't, and I believe her," I said. "That letter was a forgery."

"When could she possibly have said this to you?"

"This morning when we had coffee." I refused to let any guilt creep into my voice. "After I found her apartment in Little Italy. I thought she might be more truthful with a woman, and I was right."

"Are you sure you found the right person?" Daniel asked. "Because Lily La Rosa is—"

"Her stage name, yes, I know. Her real name is Lola Rosetti."

"Molly, you said you were going straight home." Daniel's voice had an edge to it.

"And you failed to mention that Lily La Rosa was a stage name, after agreeing to share your investigation with me." My voice held the same sharpness.

"I did not promise to give you every detail of my investigation," Daniel said.

"And I did not promise which route I would take to get home," I retorted. "I chose one that went down Bleecker Street. I was hoping to buy some cannolis for your dinner, but the shop was closed."

"What are cannolis?" Daniel asked.

I smiled triumphantly. I was done being bullied for my investigation. I described the cannoli I had eaten at Sid and Gus's and promised to return to Bleecker Street to buy him some the next week. Speaking of the ladies made me recall the recording of little Liam and I described it to him as we walked.

"His voice preserved for posterity," Daniel said, impressed. "I hope they will let me hear it."

"I'm sure you are welcome at their house at any time," I said. "They are my very best friends." We went on in silence for a few moments until Daniel asked about Lily and I described the whole of my conversation with her.

"It was broad daylight on a Sunday." I raised my hands to forestall his possible criticism. "So, I was in no danger."

"I was actually going to say it was a neat bit of detective work," Daniel said with a smile, "and quite useful." I was stunned into silence. Wonders would never cease. That statement gave me the opening I had been looking for.

"You're going to search the studio tomorrow?" I asked casually.

Daniel nodded.

"It is a shame you weren't on the scene to start with. That old constable wanted to believe it when Harry kept telling him that Arthur's death was an accident." I made a face. "I don't think he did a very thorough investigation."

"Now that there is going to be an inquest, I want to handle it myself," Daniel said.

"I agree. You want to see if anything is out of place. That's why you need me to come too."

"Molly, you know how I feel about you getting involved in my investigations. It's bad enough that you were there when a murder occurred."

"I would be perfectly safe if you came with me." He shook his head, but I went on. "You see, I was there, in Harry's office, just before the party. I will know if anything is out of place."

"Well . . ."

"I don't have to be there as an investigator." I pressed my advantage. "You can bring Alice in as well, and Harry's secretaries. There was a girl named Sarah and that awful man who chased me downstairs. They can open the safe for you and answer any questions about the papers in the room."

"They can do all of that without you being present," he pointed out.

"Yes, but I have been around that studio for weeks now. I know what the people are like when they aren't being questioned by the police. And," I played my trump card, "you promised you would include me in your investigations if I didn't run off and investigate on my own."

"And you think you have kept your part of that bargain, do you?" He raised an eyebrow at me.

"I think there are many dangerous and foolish things that I restrained myself from doing," I retorted, "and you don't want me breaking into the studio to investigate on my own."

"Good luck with that," he snorted. "There are doormen on duty at both the doors to make sure no one enters."

"Yes, well, I got into Mr. Edison's studio," I said.

"And a policeman just down the street, a telephone call away," Daniel went on, "as you will see when we go tomorrow."

"But—" I took a breath to argue before I fully took in what he had said. Then I stopped in my tracks and gave him a beaming smile. "You won't regret it."

"I'm sure I will," Daniel said, offering me his arm. "I just find it hard to say no to you, Molly."

"I wish I could come to the studio with you both," Bridie said the next morning at breakfast. "I'm sure I would help find all the clues and solve the murder."

"Jesus, Mary, and Joseph, you're not solving cases as well now, are you?" Daniel exclaimed. I laughed at his use of an expletive. I was clearly rubbing off on him after years of marriage.

"Yes, I want to be a female police detective," Bridie said between bites of her porridge. "I've wanted to for ages now."

"How can you be a film star and a policeman? I mean woman?" I corrected myself.

"Well, I'll be a film star first," she said seriously, "but when I'm grown up I want to join the police force, like you, Papa." She gave Daniel a big smile. I could tell he was both flattered and appalled at the idea.

"Well, for now it is off to school with you," I said, leaving that dilemma for another day.

"Molly, what are we teaching her to be?" Daniel said as we heard the front door close behind Bridie.

"Perhaps whatever she wants," I said. "I never thought I'd be anything other than a peasant girl, even though I was as good at my studies as those English girls in the big house. And Bridie should have been happy to be a pig farmer's daughter. But here we both are, living lives we could never have expected. Who knows what the future will bring for her." Daniel didn't answer but looked thoughtful.

"Anyway, Bridie has a different idea every week of what she wants to be when she grows up. The best thing is to smile and say, 'Grand, my love,' and she'll forget all about it in a few days."

"If you say so," Daniel said.

"I do." I put my hat on and pinned it onto my swept-up hair. Really, I was looking very respectable these days. I wonder what the girls I had grown up with would say if they could see me now. "And we had better get going if we want to have time to poke around before anyone else gets there."

"I've asked one of my men to gather them at ten, so we should have at least an hour to ourselves."

We set off toward the studio. Daniel had offered to have a patrol car drive us, but I preferred my own two legs on a day like today. The sun was out and, it may have been my imagination, it seemed that everyone we passed smiled at us. There were pink and white blossoms on the crabapple trees and a warm breeze filled the air with a sweet scent. We might have been going for a walk in the park rather than heading to a crime scene.

The doorman at the Fourteenth Street entrance let us in immediately, touching his cap to Daniel.

"Is it true about Mr. Martin, sir?" he asked. "Was it really murder?"

"That's what I'm here to find out," Daniel said. "You might be able to help me."

"How could I help?" Ted shook his head. "I was out here the whole time, wasn't I?"

"I bet you know a lot about the studio," Daniel said, trying to put the doorman at his ease. "Had they had problems with the electricity before?"

"I don't hold with that electric stuff," Ted said. "I'm just as glad there's none of it out here." His motion took in the small room. "Just an accident waiting to happen if you ask me. That's what I told Mr. Griffith when he came to give me my instructions this morning, but he never listens to me." Ted's voice was sour. "He just said we were closed for the investigation, to guard the door, and to not let anyone but the police in unless he said so." He looked hard at me, as if I were trying to break into the studio.

"Mrs. Sullivan is helping with the investigation," Daniel said, "and my men will be bringing some other people who work here by to help us. Please come and get us when they arrive. Have any of the crew been in the building that you know of?"

"Not since I've been here. Of course, it's been locked up since the accident until this morning. DW—uh, Mr. Griffith—was here when I arrived so he may have let someone in." He picked up his visitor list. "I don't show anyone has signed in, but Trevor at the other entrance may have let someone in; he's here today as well." The sight of the list made me think of a question.

"Is Mr. Griffith still here?" Daniel asked, before I could.

"No, he just came out, gave me those instructions, and left."

"Came out? So, he was in the studio this morning? Not just in this room?" I asked, giving Daniel a look. I thought the police had wanted the studio left untouched.

"Well, yeah, he's got his own key. He goes in and out whenever he wants." The doorman shrugged. So, DW had been in the building earlier this morning. I wondered what he had been doing here.

Daniel said nothing, just nodded, and we stepped into the large stage area. As he motioned for me to follow, I tried to remember what I had been about to ask the doorman. But it escaped me entirely. Inside, the electric lights were on and the stage area looked just as we had left it on the day Arthur died. Was that only Friday? It seemed weeks ago.

"This is the tank?" Daniel went over to the water. The mannequin was still lying beside the water, the lamp with its broken bulb standing beside it. I described to Daniel what I had seen when I first found the body, shuddering as I thought of Arthur's cold, dead face floating in the water.

"So, in order for this to have been an accident, Mr. Martin would have had to grab the lamp and fallen in with it." Daniel walked around the tank and traced the electric wire to the edge of the room. "That might be a natural thing, to clutch at something if he felt he was falling."

"The thing is," I said, "it wasn't there when we went upstairs. I'm sure the lamp was not beside the tank. And then there is the mannequin. Who put it in the tank?"

"Could someone have been playing a joke?" Daniel mused. "One of the crewmen said that they frequently played jokes on one another."

I considered that. "The dummy alone could have been a joke, but all of it together." I shook my head. "I don't think so."

"I tend to agree with you." Daniel nodded. We were both speaking softly, almost whispering. "Then who could have come down here to set it up? Who was trying to lure Harry or Arthur to this spot?"

"The party was going on up on the roof," I said. "But I've thought about it, and almost anyone could have gotten down here." I motioned at the large scenery pieces. "Anyone could have been hiding behind those sets and just come out when the rest of the cast and crew arrived." I tried to think of the voices that I had heard calling out as I moved through the shadows to the tank. Alice had been there quickly; she had helped with the lamp. Harry had come from a different direction, and Fanny had been there too. She had fainted when she realized that Harry was still alive. I wracked my brain to think who else had been there. Had I seen Edward Shepherd? I didn't think so. That was what I had meant to ask the doorman. When had Edward Shepherd left?

Daniel disappeared behind the sets. "You're right." His voice echoed in the big chamber. "But where would they have come from?"

I opened the door to the stairs. "From here. In fact, this is the stairway that most people came down. There's another across the building that I used but I think I would have heard anyone who came past me that way." We climbed the narrow wooden staircase.

There was an eerie silence as we stepped into the hall. The first office on the right was Arthur's. I had never been in this office before. It was much smaller than Harry's and much neater, almost barren. There was only room for a desk, chair, and a small file cabinet; a phonograph machine like the one Sid had shown me sat on the desk along with a leather book. I hesitated with my hand hovering over the book.

"Will you be checking for fingerprints?" I asked.

Daniel shook his head. "Not much point; almost anyone could have a legitimate reason for handling most things in a studio this size."

I opened the book and saw neat rows of figures. A bankbook of deposits and withdrawals. "It's strange that this is lying here on the desk," I said. "Almost as if someone has placed it here to be found."

Daniel took the book and rifled through it, examining the later pages more carefully. "I'll have to go over this in detail, but one thing that strikes me right away is the amount of recent withdrawals marked 'cash' to Harry."

"Wouldn't that be natural if they were working on a picture together?" I asked. "I understand that Arthur handled most of the financing."

"It's possible." Daniel opened each of the desk drawers in turn. There was not much more than pen and ink, stamps, and a pile of typed letters.

"I wonder where the typewriter is?" I said.

"What?"

"Those letters are typed but there is no machine in here. The secretary must have one somewhere else, but I doubt she carries a great thing in and out of the office. So where is it?"

"Excuse me, sir?" Ted Johnson poked his head into the room. "One of your men is here with Alice and Sarah."

"Perfect timing," Daniel said. "Could you send them up?" At a dead end in Arthur's office, we moved on to Harry's. It was just as messy as I had seen it on Friday afternoon. I looked around carefully, trying to notice anything that was out of place.

"It's quite a mess, isn't it?" Alice said as she entered the room, the young secretary, Sarah, behind her looking nervous. I smiled at her.

"You remember my husband, Captain Sullivan." They shook hands.

"Molly suggested that you would be the best two people to know if anything is out of the ordinary in the rooms on this floor."

"So, you really think it is murder, then?" Alice's voice was soft but resolute.

"We are looking into all the possibilities." Daniel was noncommittal. "I will have my men look through all the papers in the offices for evidence," he added, "but before we go through them, I wanted to see if anything was out of place."

"This office always looks like a crime scene," Alice said with a small smile. "Nothing is ever in place." She looked around. I picked up a wooden basket filled with some black cylinders from the desk.

"I don't remember seeing these."

"They were here all right." Alice examined them. "Although I thought they were over on that back shelf."

"What on earth are they?" I thought I had seen something like them recently, but I couldn't place what they were.

"They're recordings." Sarah spoke up for the first time. She shrank back when we turned to look at her but went on, "The Mr. Martins used to dictate their correspondence and then I typed it for them."

"That's one mystery solved," I said. "I suppose that is why there is a phonograph on Arthur's desk?"

"There is?" She looked genuinely surprised and looked at Alice. "I thought it was down in the studio with you?"

"Yes, that's right," Alice said. "I was using it to get some audio of the actors' voices." She turned to Daniel. "I can open the safe if you like. I know the combination." She moved behind the desk.

Daniel nodded.

"Can you show me how the phonograph works?" I asked Sarah. I remembered Liam's voice coming out of the phonograph at Sid's office. Could there be something on this recording that we should hear?

"Sure. You say it's on Mr. Arthur's desk?" I followed Sarah into the office. "How strange. I could have sworn it was down in the studio." She made a face. "I hate it when Alice and Mrs. Prince take that machine to experiment with," she said confidentially, winding the crank at the side of the machine. "Then I have to take shorthand and Harry always asks me to sit so close to him and then 'accidentally' brushes up against me." She flushed. "He's very handsy and him being engaged to Mrs. Prince doesn't seem to make a difference."

"Was Arthur that way as well?" I asked.

"Him?" She laughed. "I don't think he knew I existed. I was just a part of the furniture for him. I'm not sure which was worse."

"I've had to duck some unwanted advances in my day," I said, and shared what I hoped was a sisterly smile. "I find it useful to carry a hatpin." I pulled one from my hair and mimed stabbing an unwanted suitor. She giggled.

"Does Harry have a lot of women around him, then?" I asked.

She nodded. "He promises the pretty ones a job in the moving pictures and invites them up to his apartment from what I've heard." She flipped a switch on the side of the machine and the cylinder began to turn.

Arthur's voice came from the bell. "You have some damn nerve! I swear one day I'll kill you." We both jumped. How was a dead man swearing at us from beyond the grave?

"I'll kill you," the disembodied voice repeated. Daniel rushed in, followed by Alice.

"That was Arthur's voice." Alice's face was white.

"Sarah thought it was strange that this phonograph was in Arthur's office," I said, "so I wanted to play the recording."

"Let's hear the whole thing." Daniel was as fascinated as I. Arthur's voice had been slightly distorted as it came out of the machine, but completely recognizable. Sarah obediently cranked the handle on the side again.

"Thank you, I can take it from here," Harry's voice said. "Please accept my apologies that the payment has been delayed. You will be receiving it by Thursday next at—"

"What the hell is this?" Arthur's voice broke in. "Not another girl, Harry. You're going to bankrupt us."

"What is the point of having money if you can't have women?" Harry's voice was light, untroubled.

"The point is—you have gone through all your own money and now you are going through mine." Arthur's voice was furious but low. "I don't know why I put up with it."

"You do know," Harry said. "You would be in big trouble if I decided to spill the beans."

"You can only hold that over me for so long," Arthur spat, and then he lost control and his voice boomed out the words I had already heard. "You have some damn nerve! I swear one day I'll kill you. I'll kill you." The words distorted strangely as the machine slowed and stopped. Sarah cranked the handle again but there was no more to the recording. We looked at each other in silence. I didn't want to say anything in front of Alice or Sarah, but the picture had become clear to me. Why had the phonograph and the bankbook been left on Arthur's desk? They both implicated Arthur in the murder, which made no sense unless a mistake had been made. It was Harry who should have been lured downstairs by the supposed letter from Lily La Rosa. It was Harry who should have died by electrocution. And if Harry had been the one to be killed, I had very little doubt that Daniel would right now be arresting Arthur for his death.

❧ Twenty-Eight ❧

I explained my theory to Daniel as we crossed the stage floor. Uniformed policemen were coming up and down the stairs with boxes of papers from the offices.

"So, we are looking for someone who wanted Harry dead and Arthur in prison?" Daniel stopped and gave some instructions to a young patrolman, then took my arm. We stepped out onto Fourteenth Street.

"I don't suppose there is a long-lost relative who inherits a big estate if they are both out of the way?" I asked hopefully.

"We certainly will go through all the documents we can find, and I can look into their estates, but from what I understand they were self-made men with no other family," Daniel said as we stepped into the street.

"I know it sounds crazy, but have we considered Thomas Edison?" I hurried as a horse-drawn carriage came toward us without slowing.

"Thomas Edison, the world-famous inventor? Why on earth?" He turned to me as we reached the safety of the pavement and looked at me as if I had lost my mind.

"I believe that Edison was behind the sabotage at the studio," I

269

said, "and they held a patent that he wants. You have to admit it is a possibility."

"I'm not sure how to even look into that without being a laughing-stock," Daniel said. "After all, the moving picture business wouldn't exist without him. Why, our city would have no lights without him."

"Perhaps," I said darkly, thinking of the stories that Fanny had told me. "Or perhaps he is very good at getting his hands on other people's inventions by any means necessary."

The next morning I waited until Daniel had left for the coroner's court to set out myself. I didn't want to give him a chance to forbid me from coming, and I had promised Fanny I would be there for support. In truth, I also wanted to hear the evidence for myself. Who had been missing from the roof? Had anyone noticed Edward Shepherd leave the building or Lily La Rosa enter? I was almost completely convinced that she was innocent, but I had been taken in by sympathetic young women before.

After getting Bridie off to school and sending Aileen to the park with the children, I made my way by streetcars down to the Lower East Side and the big criminal court building. I shivered as I went under the bridge over Franklin Street that connected the court building to the Tombs. I had visited Daniel in the Tombs when he had been wrongfully accused. That memory made me thoughtful as I climbed the interior marble steps to the coroner's court on the second floor. The most important role of justice, I reflected, was to free the innocent.

Coroner's court looked like any other court, except with no box for the accused. The marble and wood made the room echo and I closed the door carefully behind me, mindful that a slamming door would cause everyone in the room to look up. Daniel was on the stand, to the right of the judge's bench. He saw me come in and his eyebrows raised, but it didn't interrupt the smooth flow of his testimony as he shared with the coroner the police findings.

"We are not convinced this was an accident, Coroner Nutt," he said. "And we recommend that you call the people on the list I have given you. They have all been summoned by my officers to be in court today." I saw Fanny sitting in the second bench on the right and slid in beside her. She gave my hand a grateful squeeze.

"Thank you, Captain Sullivan, you may step down," the coroner said, reading down a list he held. "We will begin with the doorman at Biograph Studios. Is Theodore Johnson here?"

"Yes, sir." The doorman from the studio stood up. "It's Ted, sir."

"Very well, Ted, come on up and be seated."

Ted sat in the chair to the right of the judge's bench. A clerk of the court swore him in on a big leather Bible.

"Now, Ted, this isn't a criminal court," the coroner said kindly. "We aren't trying to determine guilt or innocence. What we want to find out is if this was an accident or a purposeful death. And who we might hold to blame for it."

"Yes, sir," Ted said nervously.

"If we suspect a person has done this on purpose, then Captain Sullivan here," he waved his hand to indicate Daniel, "will arrest that person and he or she will be tried by a jury."

"Yes, sir," Ted said again.

"So, this is the list that you keep of people going in and out of the studio?" the coroner asked, holding up the ledger book that I had seen the doorman check when he let people in or out of the studio.

"Yes, sir," Ted said, drawing a little chuckle from the audience. He glared at the room. "Well, it is."

"And I understand that the studio is a closed environment, so that everyone who was on the premises had to be admitted by you, is that correct?"

"Yes, sir," Ted began and then said, "except the ones who came in the other entrance. Trevor—that's Trevor Cauley—would write them down in the guest book."

"Thank you, that's very clear," the coroner said. "And are you fairly certain there was no other way in or out of the studio?"

"Not unless you could climb up to the roof or in a window," Ted said.

"And is it an easy roof to get up onto?"

"No sir, I would say impossible unless you had a rope hooked up there," Ted said. "Besides which, there was a party going on up there, so a person would have been seen."

This caused the coroner to raise his eyebrows in surprise. "A party, on the roof," he said, making a note.

"Now, I have the names of all the people who have admitted they were in the studio that day," the coroner said, "but there are a few more I want to ask you about. Did a Miss Lily La Rosa enter that day?"

"No, sir," the doorman said. "She . . ." he started and then stopped, unsure if he should speak any further.

"Go on," the coroner urged.

"Mr. Martin told me to put her name on the list," the doorman said. "You can see it is written there. But she never showed up, so there's no checkmark by it."

"Mr. Arthur or Mr. Harry Martin?" the coroner asked.

"Mr. Harry," the doorman said.

I looked at Fanny to see how she would take this. I was not sure if Harry had told her about the letter from Lily at all. Her lips pursed slightly but she made no other movement. Where was Harry? I suddenly wondered. I craned my neck to look around the courtroom but didn't see him anywhere.

"And what about Mr. Edward Shepherd?" the coroner went on.

"He went in all right," the doorman said. "I have a check mark right there."

"And did he seem distressed when he came out?" the coroner asked.

"Yes, he was practically running. He didn't say a thing, just took off out of the front door and down the street."

I heard a stir from the other side of the courtroom, looked over, and saw Edward half rising. "I was being chased," he said.

"We'll get to you soon, Mr. Shepherd," the coroner said mildly. "You'll have your chance." He questioned the doorman for several more minutes and then called Trevor, who affirmed that no one had entered or left from the Fifth Avenue side after the party had started.

There was a murmur of excitement as Edward took the stand.

"Traitor!"

I looked quickly in the direction of the shout but couldn't tell who had spoken. In the back of the left-hand benches were Alice, DW, and Mary Pickford, with Ryan, Daisy, and Johnny seated right behind them. I wondered if any of them would be called as witnesses. We all had given our statements to the police. Ryan had a notebook out and appeared to be sketching. Edward flushed. He was asked by the clerk if he swore to tell the truth and mumbled, "I do."

"Mr. Shepherd, Captain Sullivan has some information about your activities in the weeks leading up to the incident. He is going to ask you some questions. Remember that you have sworn to tell the truth," the coroner said in his firm but pleasant voice.

Daniel rose. "Mr. Shepherd, why did you run out of the studio during the party last Friday?" he began.

"I was being chased," Edward said. "Both of the Martin brothers were after me."

"And why were they chasing you?" Daniel asked.

"They were mad that I had chosen to work at Thomas Edison's studio," Edward said. "I just came by to get my last pay packet and I didn't want to stick around and get beaten up."

"They wanted to assault you because you had changed studios?" Daniel clarified.

"Yes," Edward said, nodding.

"And it had nothing to do with the fact that you were behind incidents of sabotage at Biograph Studios that had almost killed a young girl?"

"No," Edward said but his voice broke as he said it.

"If I were to show you the records of everyone who entered Edison's studio in the Bronx, would you be able to explain why your name is there multiple times?" Daniel's voice rose.

"To apply for a job," Edward shot back.

"And does that explain why your bank records show you deposited large sums of money in February, March, and April?"

"I . . . I . . ." Edward's face crumpled.

"Were those payments from Thomas Edison to help sabotage Biograph Studios?" Daniel thundered. "Remember that you swore to tell the truth."

"They were from Edison," Edward said in a defeated voice. "But not to do anything harmful. Just to slow down the picture so he could get his out first."

"You broke things, props and sets?" Daniel asked.

Edward nodded.

"You set a fire to burn the studio down."

"No, just the film. I didn't intend any damage to the studio. I waited to make sure someone was around. I would have put it out if Arthur hadn't discovered it. I swear," Edward said. He was sweating and a look of terror began to creep into his eyes. "I wouldn't hurt anyone. That's why I quit. That girl almost got hurt and I quit."

"And you practiced knocking over lamps, seeing how close you could get the electricity to the water," Daniel said.

"No!" Edward leaned forward. "You have to believe me. I had nothing to do with that."

"And when Arthur Martin discovered your scheme, you killed him." Daniel's voice was low, but Edward's came out like a shriek.

274

"No, I would never kill anyone." He rubbed his eyes as if that would wake him from a bad dream. "I admit I did the sabotage, but I had no reason to hurt anyone after that. I just ran so that Harry and Arthur couldn't have the crew beat me up."

"That's all the questions that I have, Coroner Nutt," Daniel said, looking up at the bench.

"I assume you will arrest Mr. Shepherd for arson, at the very least," the coroner said in his mild tones, but with a look of disgust on his face.

"If I may?" Daniel indicated that he wanted to approach the bench and the coroner waved him forward. They had a conversation in low tones. Finally, Daniel stepped back.

"I have statements from Mr. Martin's colleagues"—Coroner Nutt nodded toward the group of actors watching the proceedings with interest—"but we need to hear from the deceased's brother before I can make a ruling on this case," he said. "Is Mr. Harry Martin here?" There was a general stirring in the courtroom as people craned their heads looking for Harry, but he was not there.

"Captain Sullivan, was Mr. Martin summoned for today?" the coroner asked sternly.

"Yes, Coroner," Daniel answered.

"Then please send a patrolman to bring him to this court," the coroner said. "We will recess for one hour to give them time to fetch him." The coroner consulted a sheet in front of him.

"Then we will hear from," he examined his notes, "Mr. Martin, followed by Mr. Griffith and Miss Mann." He rapped his gavel on the desk, rose, and went into a back room. The noise level in the courtroom increased as those present began to converse.

Fanny turned to me. "Where can Harry be?" she asked, lines of worry around her eyes.

"I was going to ask you the same thing," I said. "I thought he would accompany you here."

"Well, he didn't want me to come," Fanny said. "He told me to stay home and he would see me this evening."

I could well imagine that Harry did not want Fanny learning about Lily's letter. Was it possible he had been in the room and left when he saw her here? "Somehow I just couldn't stay away," she went on, turning to face me full on. "I feel under a curse, Mrs. Sullivan. I want to understand what caused this death and if it was related to . . ." She broke off, looking around the room as if afraid. I thought I understood her though. Was Arthur's death also related to the film camera patent? Was everyone who held it doomed to die?

A thought kept nagging at me as I went over Edward's testimony in my mind. Surely his whole guilt or innocence in the matter hinged on one vital question—a question no one had asked, the one I had forgotten to ask the doorman at the studio. I had to let Daniel know. He was standing at the back of the courtroom, talking with Lieutenant Corelli and another policeman.

"Excuse me," I said with a smile, "can I borrow my husband to ask about dinner tonight?"

"Mrs. Sullivan, what are you doing here?" Corelli asked with a quick look at Daniel. Daniel's face began to redden. I knew that any suspicion that his wife was involved in investigations would make him a laughingstock.

"I am a friend of the deceased," I said, stretching the truth. "Here to support the family. Daniel," I tried to convey my urgency in the look I gave him, "could we talk about what I should buy for dinner tonight?"

"Lucky captain," Corelli said with a grin. "Your wife takes good care of you."

"She does indeed," Daniel said with an answering smile that faded as soon as we were out of earshot of the officers.

"What is it, Molly? You're surely not that interested in my dinner tonight," he said.

"No one has asked the most important question," I began without preamble. "The doorman saw Edward Shepherd leave the building, but when?"

Daniel caught my meaning immediately. "The lights," was all he had to say. "Thank you." Then he raised his voice. "Don't put the roast in so early, my dear. It was quite dry before I got home. Perhaps I should ask my mother to come over and teach you the way I like it cooked." He winked at me before he turned back to his men.

I resisted the temptation to stick my tongue out at him. Really! And after I gave him such valuable information. The doorman was no longer in the courtroom and Daniel dispatched Corelli to locate him.

It was actually closer to an hour and fifteen minutes before the coroner returned to begin again. I took my seat beside Fanny, who kept glancing back at the door to the courtroom with concern. Daniel once again went to the front to confer with Coroner Nutt, and Ted Johnson was recalled to the stand.

"Mr. Johnson, there is no need to be nervous." The coroner looked down at the doorman from his bench. "You are not being accused of doing anything wrong. But there is one piece of information that we neglected to ask you."

"Yes, sir?"

"Please answer as truthfully as possible. A man's life and liberty may depend on it." The coroner spoke solemnly. "When Mr. Edward Shepherd left the building, was the electricity still functioning?"

"The electricity?" Mr. Johnson looked confused.

"The electric lightbulbs in the building," the coroner went on. "Were they on?"

"I'm afraid I wouldn't know," said the doorman, shaking his head. "There is no electric light in the doorway where I sit." The coroner looked at Daniel, who shrugged his shoulders slightly. I ground my teeth with frustration, willing the coroner not to give up.

"Was there anything different that you noticed before Mr. Shepherd left, perhaps a loud sound?"

Mr. Johnson's face cleared. He sat up straighter. "Yes," he said excitedly. "Was that sound the electricity going out? Because I did notice that. Mr. Shepherd ran past, through the room, and out of the door. Then there was a banging noise. I thought at first he had slammed the door behind him but it was still open. I forgot all about it when I learned Mr. Arthur was dead."

Edward jumped up. "I told you I had left the building," he said triumphantly.

"Sit down, Mr. Shepherd," the coroner said sternly. "You have only this man to thank for the fact that I am not binding you over for murder."

"But I'm not a murderer," Edward said, then sat down quickly as he saw the coroner's face.

"I'm sure the police will still be looking into the facts of the arson and destruction of property." Coroner Nutt looked down from the bench with distaste. "We have just one more witness, I believe?" he said, looking to Daniel.

"Yes, sir." Daniel rose and looked around the room. Corelli was just entering, but no one was with him.

"You can step down with the thanks of the court, Mr. Johnson," the coroner said. As Ted Johnson stepped down, Lieutenant Corelli hurried forward.

"No one answered the door at Mr. Martin's apartment," he said, his voice oddly strained, "so I had the cleaning lady open it for me." He was speaking to Daniel and the coroner, but his manner had attracted the attention of everyone in the court. He took a breath.

"Will Mr. Martin be joining us?" the coroner asked.

Corelli shook his head. "Harry Martin is dead."

❧ Twenty-Nine ❧

There was an uproar in the courtroom. "No!" I heard Fanny's voice above the others. I turned to support her. She buried her head in my shoulder.

"How?" the coroner barked, not bothering to call Corelli up to the stand.

"Unclear, sir," Corelli said. "He was still in bed, but clearly beyond medical help. There is no sign of foul play."

"Come closer." The coroner beckoned him to the front.

"Could he have taken his own life?" he asked in a very low voice that I could nonetheless still hear. I was sure that Fanny could hear it as well. She shook in my arms.

"There was no note immediately evident," Corelli said. "I looked around only briefly and then left a man guarding the entrance while I came to get the captain."

"Good man." The coroner nodded with approval. "Captain Sullivan," he said in a voice designed to carry to the whole room, "I am declaring this inquiry suspended until you gather evidence about Mr. Harry Martin's death. I think we all must suspect that the deaths are connected. Of course, I'll be ready to receive the body"—Fanny shuddered again—"and provide the medical details to the police."

"Thank you, Coroner, I'll head over there immediately," Daniel said. He came over to me.

"Molly, can you make sure that Mrs. Prince gets home safely?" he asked.

She looked up, her face tearstained.

"Can I come with you, Captain?" she said. "I want to see him."

"I don't think that is a good idea, Mrs. Prince," Daniel said gently. "It will be a distressing sight." She pulled a lace-trimmed handkerchief out of a small purse and dabbed the corners of her eyes.

"Yes, but I have been a frequent visitor to his apartment." She flushed, realizing how her statement could be taken. "Nothing inappropriate, of course, but I am his fiancée. I know how things should look. I would be able to tell you if anything is out of place."

Daniel considered this and she went on, "Of course, Arthur would have been the best person to ask, but since he is no longer with us, I am the person who knew Harry best in the world." She was no longer crying; the hollow look in her eyes was more haunting than the tears.

"Very well." Daniel nodded. "I can ask for a man to take you over in a patrol wagon."

"No need," she said. "I have my runabout here."

"I'm not sure you are in a fit state to drive right now," Daniel said, beckoning one of the uniformed police officers over.

"Perhaps if Mrs. Sullivan accompanies me," she suggested.

"I'm afraid I can't drive," I said hastily. Then it occurred to me that this would be an excellent opportunity to see what I suspected was a crime scene. I would see the evidence firsthand rather than relying on Daniel for information. "But I would be happy to give you moral support."

Daniel gave me a look. He knew exactly what I was doing. But Fanny had made up her mind. "Sisterly support is what I need right now. I would appreciate it very much." She put her handkerchief away and said in a more steady voice, "I have myself under control and can do my duty with your wife's help, Captain Sullivan."

And what could he say to that. He nodded at me.

"Take Edward Shepherd into custody," he said to the uniformed police officer, a man I didn't recognize. "Charge him with arson and destruction of property."

"Shall we?" Fanny took my arm for support. I looked around the courtroom, wanting to see who was there. If Harry had been killed this morning then no one in the courtroom could be a suspect. Ryan was close to the front, a look of fascination on his face and a sketchbook in his hand. I suspected that if he put this scene in a play, he would be accused of making it too theatrical. Cecil was not by his side, however. Perhaps that fascination was dying. Ryan's flings did not tend to last too long. It struck me that all of the other principal actors had come to the inquest. Why had Cecil stayed away?

Alice, Mary, Daisy, and Johnny were seated on a bench together. Daisy and Johnny had their heads together in conversation. Alice had swiveled around, watching Edward be marched out of the courtroom, his hands behind his back. She had a look of grim satisfaction on her face. Mary was staring out into space, a faraway look in her eyes. DW was leaning against a wall, his head in his hands. No one tried to approach Fanny or speak to her. Perhaps no one knew what to say. I certainly didn't. We exited the building in silence.

Her runabout was parked just across the street from the courthouse. At first, I was concerned that driving would be too much of an effort given the turmoil that must be going on within her, but she maneuvered the little car expertly onto Canal Street in the direction of Sixth Avenue. What could I say to comfort her? Just a few days ago she had been engaged to be married and a part of a thriving, creative business enterprise. Now two people were dead and possibly the enterprise in ruins. It seemed impossible. The scenery added to my feeling of unreality. So many new buildings were under construction along our path that dust filled the air, and the almost-finished Manhattan Bridge loomed behind us like a giant dragon.

"Thank you for coming with me," she finally said.

"I'm glad to be of some help," I said, thinking to myself that it was strange that this posh English woman would want to receive help from me. What support could I really be?

"I'm sure you think it strange that I have no closer friend to help me in this dreadful time," she said, as if she had read my thoughts. "And I'm afraid I don't." She made a right turn onto Sixth Avenue, stopping first for some pedestrians to pass. "I had women friends and family in England, of course. But since moving to New York, I had my husband, the studio, and then Harry." She drove around a horse-drawn van, causing the horse to shy away skittishly and the driver to pull on the reins and fling a curse in her direction. "I didn't have time for much else." She ignored the curse with the air of a polished New York driver.

We arrived at the Osborne apartments on Fifty-Seventh Street before the rest of the police and crossed the marble-floored foyer and into a gigantic lobby. The walls were silver and little alcoves held colorful glass mosaics. Chandeliers hung from a twenty-foot-high ceiling. At the far end of the lobby, two marble staircases led up. "Holy Mother of God," I said, "it looks like a palace." I looked around, wondering which of the four elevators went up to the apartment. A doorman came hurrying from behind his desk.

"Mrs. Prince," he said, touching his cap, "we haven't seen you for a few days."

"Yes," she said noncommittally.

"I'm so sorry about Mr. Arthur," he said, shaking his head. "That electricity is dangerous to play with."

"Yes," she said again. He looked at her curiously but when it was clear he would get no more information from her he touched his cap again.

"Give my regards to Mr. Harry," he said, opening the doors to one of the elevators and ushering us in. I thought it better to let the police inform him of Harry's death. Daniel might want to question him before he knew.

"Mr. Harry has been so upset by the death of his brother," I improvised, pulling a quarter out of my pocket. "Some of our friends from the studio were going to call last night to try to cheer him up. Do you know if they came?"

"Not a one," he said, clearly not finding it strange that I would ask for information. It was part of a doorman's job to learn all of the information he could and pass it on when a tip was a possibility. "But then, I get off at ten P.M. If they came after that, they would call up," he gestured at a telephone sitting in a small alcove, "and the resident would have to come and get them or send the service elevator down."

"Thank you." I put the quarter into his hand. He reached into the elevator and pushed the button for the sixth floor, then stepped back with a salute as the doors closed.

Fanny looked at me questioningly. "Your friends from the studio?" she asked.

"It occurred to me that we should know if anyone visited Harry last night," I said. "And that seemed to be the most tactful way to ask."

"I see," she said, a little frostily, as the doors opened and we stepped out. "And you have decided to investigate. I thought you were here as my friend."

"I am," I said seriously. I stopped and she turned to face me. "Fanny, I'm afraid there are only two possibilities here. Either Harry took his own life, which would indicate guilt at somehow causing his brother's death—"

"That's ridiculous," she interrupted, but I held up a hand to stop her.

"Or," I went on, "someone has murdered both Arthur and Harry, in which case, everyone is in danger until we catch whoever did it."

"Oh," she said, going white. And put a hand to her mouth. "That hadn't occurred to me." We made our way to Harry's apartment door where a uniformed police officer barred the way. Luckily, I knew him from Daniel's precinct.

"Constable Callahan," I said. "Captain Sullivan asked me to allow Mr. Martin's fiancée to see him."

A pained look crossed his face.

"Ever so sorry but I can't let anyone in, Mrs. Sullivan," he said. "Not until Captain Sullivan gets here." I took a breath to argue.

"Captain Sullivan is here," I heard behind me and turned to see Daniel walking down the hallway, Lieutenant Corelli beside him. "I'm glad to see that someone can resist my wife's entreaties, Callahan." Daniel clapped the man on the shoulder and motioned for him to open the door. "We'll keep an eye on them now."

We entered the apartment. It had its own foyer with high ceilings that opened into a parlor full of tasteful dark furniture and mahogany walls. It was a very masculine room. Nothing looked out of place. The fire in the grate was out, but the room was not cold. I surmised that the building must have central heating.

Beyond the parlor was a hallway leading to the bedrooms. Corelli opened it and Daniel motioned for me to follow him. Like the parlor, this room was full of dark wood furniture. A clean, medicinal scent lingered in the air. The windows had heavy drapes across them, making the room dark. Lieutenant Corelli pulled them back. Light flooded the room and fell on the large four-poster bed. Harry was lying on his back, his silk sheets pulled up around him, but his eyes were open and staring. I put an arm around Fanny as Daniel stepped between her and the corpse. He bent down to examine Harry's face and then gently closed the eyes. But before he did, I saw what had made him hesitate: red spots in the eyes, a clear sign of cyanide poisoning. Fanny stepped tentatively toward the bed.

"I'll let you say your goodbyes," Daniel said gently. "Please don't touch anything."

"Let me just hold his hand," she said, picking it up as she spoke and then gasping and letting it go. "It's cold."

I looked around the room. There was no sign of a struggle, nothing out of place. With his eyes closed Harry might have been asleep. Fanny began to cry, and I led her out of the room and back into the parlor. She sank onto the settee.

"I'll be myself in a minute," she said in a faint voice. "That was more upsetting than I thought."

Daniel came and sat across from her. "Can you tell me when you saw your fiancé last?"

"Yes," Fanny said. "Sunday night at the service for Arthur. We said goodbye at the funeral parlor. He didn't want me to come to the inquest this morning, but I felt I had to be there to support him. I didn't understand why he wasn't there. Now it makes sense."

"I'm sorry to ask you, but could you look around and tell me if anything is out of place?" Daniel said.

Fanny rose obediently and began looking around the room. A door was open to the room on the left. I glanced in. It was a library. From the door I could tell that it had a more lived-in look than the formal parlor. If Harry had been entertaining, I bet he would have done it here. I slipped inside.

This room had a large window with a view of the street below. Round water stains on a sideboard showed me that Harry did his drinking in this room. Sure enough, a glass was left on a side table; the remains of what smelled like whiskey were in the bottom. A faint line of white powder dripped down the inside. My pulse quickened. This must be what caused his death. So it could be suicide, then, I thought. I was careful not to touch the glass. On a shelf, not far away, was a clear glass jar filled with a white powder. It had a white, handwritten label but the ink was too smeared to make out the words. The jar of powder was right in the open. I tried to picture Harry mixing it into his own glass and drinking it down, setting the glass down here, and then going into his bedroom, getting into bed, and never waking. That was plausible. But why? Could he not face life without his brother? I thought of Fanny in the next room, who had been planning their marriage. Harry had a lot to live for. Would he really have taken his own life? But surely, he would not have sat here watching someone put poison in his drink, drunk it, and meekly gone to bed without calling for help or struggling.

If he had killed himself, he would likely have left some sort of explanation in a note or letter. I scanned the room, and even crouched down to look under the furniture, but I saw no sign of one. A low wooden cabinet held an assortment of bottles with spirits in them. I opened the doors using my handkerchief. There were more bottles jumbled on the shelves and four glasses identical to the glass on the sideboard. A dusty space was large enough to fit two glasses. I looked around the room for the sixth glass. Had Harry been drinking with someone else? There was no other glass evident. Of course, it was possible that the glass had been broken years ago.

"Do you mind looking in here as well, Mrs. Prince?" Daniel ushered Fanny in behind him.

"We shouldn't touch anything in the room, Daniel." I spoke quickly in a low voice. "I think you will need to take that to check for fingerprints." I pointed to the glass on the sideboard. "I think there may have been poison in that glass." I didn't mention my suspicion that another glass was missing. I wanted to be more certain before I said anything.

"I'll take it back to police headquarters," he said, opening the cabinet filled with bottles with a handkerchief just as I had done. "Do you know how many glasses Mr. Martin had in here, Mrs. Prince?" Daniel was just as quick to wonder if Harry was drinking alone or with someone.

"I, what?" Fanny looked at Daniel blankly. "No, this room was more for the men, I think. I mean, Harry entertained me in the parlor. I don't drink whiskey."

I pointed to the jar. "Did Harry have this here last time you visited?"

"This jar?" She came toward it and Daniel held up his hand warning her not to touch. "I don't know what he would be doing with that. He never took the chemicals home, that I knew."

"Chemicals?" Daniel queried.

"Yes, that's a developing powder." We both looked at her. "For film. It is used in the darkroom. They have a shelf full of identical jars at the studio."

❄❅ Thirty ❆❇

Fanny was so unnerved at the sight of Harry that a policeman accompanied both of us to her apartment. I stayed with
her long enough to leave her in the hands of her maid, who
promised to give her sleeping powders and put her to bed. Then I
gratefully accepted a ride home. One would expect that the events
of the morning would make me content to walk into my peaceful
home and never have to think about murder or the studio again.
But in reality, my brain was spinning with possibilities. Was Harry's
death truly a suicide? If someone had killed him, then who? I knew
he entertained women up in his apartment—had one of them killed
him? And why?

It was an agonizingly long afternoon. I was impatient for Daniel's
return with information about the case. I fed my little girl and listened to Liam chatter, but my focus was elsewhere. I started on my
chore for the day, which was giving the kitchen floor a good scrub.
The house had been neglected while I had been focused on my investigation. The rhythm of the scrubbing and the sheer hard work
of it helped to focus my thoughts. Two brothers dead. Was the first
one a mistake? Was Harry the target all along? Or was he a murderer

who had killed himself out of guilt? The studio was shut down. Who wanted to harm it? Who wanted no more pictures made?

At the end of an hour my floor was clean and my hands red and chapped from the carbolic soap. I looked at the floor with pride. I loved it when my house looked and smelled clean. Then it occurred to me. Carbolic. That was what I had smelled in Harry's bedroom. I pictured the curtains being drawn back and the light falling on the floor. The floor there had also looked clean and shiny.

I was no closer to solving the mystery, but I felt more focused and calm. There was a murderer out there and I was determined to find him. Or her, I amended, a picture of Alice swimming into my mind. I felt a bond with Alice and a sense of trust, but I had to admit she would be the most capable of pulling off a murder and getting away with it. Who would have the timing to lure Arthur to the tank and push in the lamp at the right moment? Who would know that developing powder might be fatal? But was it one murder or two? Was Harry's death murder or suicide? *Murder or suicide?* I thought over and over again as I scrubbed.

"Did you want something?" Aileen came in, the baby on her hip, and looked at me with a strange expression on her face, standing carefully at the edge of the wet floor so as not to track dirty footprints. Had I been chanting out loud? I was afraid I had.

"Nothing," I said hastily, "almost done." I realize that most people would give their maids the dirty chores like the scrubbing, but I have never been afraid of hard work. I preferred to let her keep the children out of my hair. It gave me a strange pleasure to see my floor gleam and the rhythm of the scrubbing helped me think.

There was something, I couldn't quite put my finger on what, about Harry's death that felt staged. Of course, the doorman had not seen a woman going into Harry's apartment, but he had said that he left the building at ten o'clock. Could anyone have come up to the apartment at night? Or, the thought occurred to me, were the doormen paid to turn a blind eye to the comings and goings of women to Harry's apartment?

When Daniel came home, long after dark, I restrained myself from jumping in with a thousand questions. The children were already fed and put to bed. I served Daniel a big bowl of chicken soup with fresh bread to dip in it and sat at the table with him.

"What, no roast?" he said with a smile. I was momentarily confused, then remembered the conversation we'd had at the courthouse.

"Well, you said my roast was too dry," I smiled back, "and hell will freeze over before I ask your mother to teach me to cook."

"Your roast is delicious, as you well know." He tasted the soup and gave a groan of pleasure. "But I think I like your chicken soup even better." He carefully buttered his bread and dipped it in the soup. "And you were very helpful this morning. You know I don't like involving you in an investigation, but Mrs. Prince needed a womanly touch."

I noticed he didn't mention the information I had given him about the doorman. But I thought he had had long enough to relax with his dinner.

"Well," I said, "were there fingerprints on the jar? What was in it? And what was Harry's cause of death? It was cyanide, wasn't it?"

He held up his hands to stop the flow of questions. "So you saw the red dots?"

"Yes, was it cyanide?"

"It was, and before you ask, the powder in the jar was potassium cyanide. I sent a man back to the studio and it certainly came from there. They have enough potassium cyanide in that place to kill half of New York."

"Harry must have been very familiar with that powder," I said. "Do you think he used it to commit suicide? I remember reading a newspaper article about a woman who killed herself that way."

"He could have," Daniel said slowly, "but if he did, he was extremely lucky."

"Lucky?"

"Well, obviously not lucky in light of the fact that he is dead," Daniel said, rising to fill his bowl with more soup.

"I'll do that." I jumped up and took the ladle from him. "You've had a long day."

"Death from cyanide is normally very messy," Daniel said. "The victim vomits," he made a face, "excuse me for giving you the gory details, and thrashes about. What he doesn't do is tuck himself into bed and peacefully doze off."

"I see what you mean," I said. "Could the whiskey have somehow masked the symptoms? Made him so tired he passed out in the bed before the cyanide could take full effect?"

"It's possible," Daniel said, eating the bowl of soup I put in front of him with as much gusto as the first. "I'll ask the coroner, but I highly doubt it."

"That recording made it sound like Arthur and Harry were arguing violently." It felt good to be discussing theories with Daniel. "Harry was in the right place to kill his brother. Perhaps he felt remorse or was worried that the police would find out, and killed himself."

"If it were suicide, I would expect to find him collapsed in the library," he took a long drink of water, "and not a pretty sight."

"Daniel, what if he actually drank the cyanide in the bedroom and collapsed on the bed?" I rose as the idea came to me.

"That means that someone else took the glass away to the library," he said. "Which means . . ."

"Murder." I paced, full of restless energy. "Did you notice how clean the floor was in the apartment? I smelled carbolic soap."

"You smelled what?"

"It's what I wash the floor with," I explained. "The floors were just washed in both the library and the bedroom." I gestured at the floor. "I just washed ours today. Can you smell it?"

"I do." Daniel gave a big sniff. "The apartment did smell like this. But I imagine he has maid service at his apartment. Perhaps they had just cleaned the floors that day."

"Perhaps," I said. How long did the smell of carbolic linger in the air? Would it stay fresh from the day before? "Let's imagine that someone was there, drank with Harry until he was too drunk to notice, and then slipped the cyanide into his drink. They could clean up any mess after he was dead."

"They watched him die, cleaned up the room, and tucked him into bed?" Daniel raised his eyebrows. "Quite cold-hearted. It must have been a strong man to have lifted Harry from the library into the bed. He must weigh at least two hundred pounds."

"Or, it could have been a woman who lured him into the bed," I suggested. "Everyone suggests that Harry was a womanizer."

"But why?" Daniel said. I looked at him.

"Why?"

"Let's assume that the killer did clean up after themselves. What did they gain? Wouldn't it make more sense to leave Harry where he fell? Doesn't this just point to murder?"

He had a good point. "Perhaps to wipe away their fingerprints?" I made it a question.

"They certainly did that," he said. "There were no fingerprints on the jar or the glass."

"How strange," I said. "It is as if someone wants the police to know that this is murder, the same way that someone wanted us to find Arthur's bankbook and listen to the recording. It is almost as if this is a play or a picture and someone is directing it."

"Or misdirecting us." Daniel rose and put his bowl in the sink. "There is another possibility. Criminals are not always thinking clearly. Perhaps they are trying to be too clever and have just gotten lucky so far."

"Like murdering a man by dropping a lamp in a pool," I put in. "There were so many ways that could have gone wrong, but it worked."

"One thing is for sure," Daniel said. "That potassium cyanide came from the studio. This murder was committed by someone in the moving picture business."

Something Daniel had just said struck me. "So far," I repeated. "So you think this may not be the last murder?"

Daniel raked his hands though his hair. "Honestly I don't know what to think." He looked worried. "Some reporters have picked up the story. It is rather sensational, the death of two brothers in such a short time frame. I don't want it to get out yet that we think this death may be murder, too, or it will be on the front page."

"No one will hear it from me," I said. "Where will your investigation go next?"

❧ Thirty-One ☙

As I put on my dark blue suit for the funeral, I had a powerful feeling of repetition. Here I was dressing for a funeral, taking the same route to the same funeral parlor. The only difference was that Bridie was with me. Daniel had agreed that it was only right that I should come and bring Bridie. He had only made me promise not to discuss Harry's death. The police had not mentioned any theories about murder and Daniel wanted to keep it that way.

Bridie ran right over to Daisy and Mary as soon as we entered, happy to see them again, but mindful that she should appear appropriately sad at the occasion.

"Isn't it tragic, Mrs. Sullivan?" Daisy's eyes were red, and she wiped them with a handkerchief. "I can't believe he's gone."

"And right after his brother." Mary's eyes were clear, but her expression was solemn. "Mrs. Sullivan, do you know what happened? The obituary just said 'passed away' but Harry was a healthy man."

"I don't know for sure," I said, aware that I had promised Daniel that I wouldn't talk about the case. Looking around I guessed that many groups of people were having the same conversation. The room was more full than the previous funeral with many faces I didn't recognize. Perhaps many people had come out of sheer curiosity.

"What will happen to the picture that you made?" Bridie asked. "Weren't you getting ready to shoot another one?"

"I don't know." Mary frowned unhappily. "I'm not even sure who is in charge right now. It's a disaster."

It was a disaster to the studio, I thought. The people in the room would all suffer from the loss of the Martin brothers. It made no sense that one of them was a murderer. I looked around at the men in the room. Who would have been strong enough to carry Harry into his bedroom? Johnny was strong and fit. Ryan and Cecil were speaking animatedly with DW Griffith. I couldn't suspect Ryan, but what did I really know of Cecil? Edward Shepherd was under arrest and not here, but he was strong enough to have done it.

Or could a mysterious woman have visited Harry in the middle of the night? There were several women I recognized here: Fanny, of course, Alice, Daisy, Mary Pickford, and several women I didn't know. With Harry's reputation as a womanizer, they could be ex-girlfriends who had come to pay their respects, or a killer come to gloat over a job well done. I searched the room for Lily La Rosa but didn't see her. She had been very convincing in person. I couldn't help thinking that Harry had partly been the result of her downfall, and that she was someone who could have arranged a rendezvous with him in the middle of the night.

"You look like you are investigating," Alice said, making me jump.

"Do I?" I smiled at her.

"You are staring around most intently."

"I'm afraid my thoughts are rather dark," I said honestly.

"You're wondering who murdered the Martin brothers." As usual Alice got right to the point.

"The police haven't said that Harry was murdered," I kept my voice low, "and they won't thank you for spreading that rumor."

"I'm sure they won't," she said in an equally quiet voice. "I'm not sure if you are aware but there are quite a few reporters in the room, anxious to see if anyone talks about Harry's cause of death. Did you see the piece in *The New York Times* this morning? BORN TOGETHER AND DIED TOGETHER: MYSTERIOUS DEATH OF TWINS IN SAME WEEK."

"Alice, do you have any idea who might have wanted both Harry and Arthur dead?" I looked around the room as I spoke. The Reverend Merritt had just arrived in the doorway to call the assembly into the chapel.

She shook her head. "No one in this room. It's a disaster for all of us." I realized her words had mirrored my thoughts exactly.

One of those unnatural silences came over the chapel. All those who had been softly speaking were waiting for the service to begin and we sat in silence as the reverend prepared for the service. Several people were still gathered around the coffin, saying their final goodbyes. A man in a tailor-made black morning coat entered, took off his top hat, and joined them. A gasp and a whisper went around the room. I looked more carefully at the man. It was Thomas Edison. He held out his hand to Fanny Prince, who was standing by the coffin. She shook it and he leaned down and began to speak with her in a low, confidential tone.

"That shows some class," I heard Alice say behind me. "They were rivals in life, but he must have really respected Harry."

"Don't you believe it." DW's voice was so low I had to strain to hear it. "I think he has just seen a studio that is ripe for the picking."

The funeral itself seemed an eerie repetition of the one I had just attended for Arthur. Reverend Merritt saw no need to vary his sermon about the blessed future for the chosen of God. As far as I could recall, it was word-for-word the same. With many of the same people in attendance and even, by appearance, the same man in the coffin, it felt like I was living a nightmare. Sometimes truth is stranger than fiction. Those that I knew from the studio looked stunned. Harry and Arthur had no one in the world but each other. There were no children, cousins, aunts, or uncles at the service. It was a testament to the Martin brothers that, as far as I could tell, every actor and crew member from the studio was there. The studio was a family as well as a place of business. I thought of all the loss I had seen in the last few weeks: Petrosino's funeral, Arthur's, and now Harry's. I had my arm through Bridie's, and I squeezed her closer, thinking how lucky I was to have my children and my Daniel.

Fanny Prince was the one sitting up front in the place of honor. I supposed she must have arranged for the service. For the widow to have lost her new fiancé was tragic to me. She was dressed again in black silk, but her face, which had been sad but composed during Arthur's funeral, was now covered with a black veil that hung from her hat. Every few minutes she held a delicate lace handkerchief up to dab her eyes. When the service ended, she pushed the veil back to reveal eyes red with weeping. But she moved into the parlor and politely began to offer refreshments to the guests and accept condolences.

After the service I just wanted to get home. Bridie and I came out of the funeral parlor, blinking a bit in the light. In the distance a group of the attendees was walking off together. DW and Alice were standing on the sidewalk in conversation. We went up to them.

"Mr. Griffith," I said, "how sad that we see each other again at this memorial so soon after the other."

"It is overwhelming, I confess," he said. "Does your husband have any idea how this happened? Mrs. Prince was too distressed to discuss it."

"I'm afraid he is not certain," I said, not willing to share any theories of murder yet. "It looks like Harry may have taken his own life. Did he seem very despondent after his brother's death?"

"Harry, take his own life?" he scoffed. "Impossible." He gave a derisive snort. "He was full of plans for the studio and new pictures."

Alice chimed in, "If it weren't impolite to speak ill of the dead, I would almost say that he had a new energy. I think the money he knew he would inherit from his brother relieved some financial difficulties he was having."

"Surely he couldn't have been relieved at his brother's death?" I asked.

"Of course not." DW frowned at Alice. "He was devastated. They were so close they were almost like one person."

"A person can be sad and relieved at the same time, DW," Alice said.

"What would you know about Harry's financial situation, girl?" DW was not going to let it go.

"There is not much that goes on around the studio that Alice doesn't know," Bridie said, instantly coming to Alice's defense. Alice could do no wrong in Bridie's eyes.

"And Harry and Arthur's arguments were loud enough that everyone in the studio overheard them at some time," Alice retorted. "I am sure that Harry was pleased to be the sole owner of Biograph." Was it Alice who had left that phonograph recording to be found? Had she wanted the police to find evidence that the brothers were at each other's throats?

I turned to DW. "How will you keep the studio open?" He looked affronted. I suppose three women arguing and talking about finances was just too much for him. "I don't understand how these financial things work." I opened my eyes and fluttered my eyelashes. DW's expression softened.

"It is very complicated, Mrs. Sullivan," he said, his voice now more patient as he explained. "It depends on who inherits his assets." I took a breath to ask if he knew who that was, but he misunderstood. "That means the person named in his will."

I smiled with what I hoped was a grateful female smile and he went on. "That person may want to keep the studio open or sell it."

"I think she'll want to keep the studio open," said a voice behind us. Daisy was coming down the steps and had joined us just in time to hear the last of DW's words.

"Who do you mean?" I asked.

"Well, Fanny, of course," she said as if it were obvious.

"If they had been married, she would have been," Alice said. "But she never had the chance, poor thing."

"They made wills naming each other right after they got engaged," Daisy said. "Harry told me. It was ever so romantic. It's just tragic how it has all ended."

I thought of Fanny, who had already lost one husband, now losing her fiancé. It *was* tragic. If I were her, I would feel cursed. "Where is Fanny?" I asked, looking back at the funeral home. I had not seen her when I left.

"She left a while ago, with Mr. Edison," Alice said.

"I can't believe he was here!" Daisy said. "After all I've heard I would have expected him to be the devil himself, but he was nice enough, very polite."

"With Edison?" I asked, starting to feel uneasy. "Where?"

"I don't know where they were going," Alice said, "but she was asking him to look over some papers. I saw her get into his automobile." A thought staggered me. Fanny Prince was now the only person between Edison and that patent, and she had just gone off alone with him.

My heart started racing. What on earth could have induced Fanny to go off alone with Edison? It was common knowledge that he had used his bully boys to rough up rivals in the past. He had paid Edward to slow down the shooting of Biograph pictures. But murder? That was a different kettle of fish, wasn't it?

I paused, oblivious to the street noises around me. There were too many suspicious deaths, weren't there? The elder Mr. Prince who got on a train and never got off. Fanny Prince's husband who went duck hunting and was shot by mistake. Arthur Martin who just happened to fall into a pool and drag an electric lamp with him, and now Harry Martin who drank a glass of whiskey laced with cyanide in his library and then calmly put himself to bed. Could all of these be linked to the same person? And what person would benefit most from the death of all those rivals? Why, Thomas Edison, of course. And now he had lured Fanny Prince, the one who would inherit Biograph Studios, away with him on some pretext.

Bridie tugged at my arm. "Mama, come on. Everyone else has left."

I looked down at her. "Oh, so sorry, darling. I was deep in thought."

"About the murders?" she asked, her innocent little face looking up at me.

I stared at her, shocked. "We don't know they were murders," I said.

"Of course they were. Someone wanted the Martin brothers out of the way," she said. "That's obvious."

"And why would that be, do you think?"

"Well, to stop them from making moving pictures, I expect." She stated this as if it was obvious.

Thomas Edison, then. My instincts were right. And Fanny had gone off with him.

"We must get you home," I said. "Let's take a hansom cab for once."

I spotted one and hailed it. We set off up Broadway.

"You know something, don't you, Mama?" Bridie asked as the horse set off at a lively trot. "Or you suspect something."

"I'm afraid I do," I said. "I think Mrs. Prince might be in danger. I just wish I knew where she was going."

"That man who was with her said something about the papers at the studio," Bridie said.

"You're a smart girl, do you know that?" I patted her hand. I looked up to the driver. "Stop here, please." I turned to Bridie. "You can find your own way home from here, can't you? I need to go on."

She paused, then nodded. "All right," she said. "Are you going to do something dangerous?"

"I hope not," I said. "But do you know how to use the telephone?"

She stared at me, wide-eyed. "I'm not sure. I never did."

"You've seen us do it, haven't you? Just pick up the receiver and ask the operator to connect you to police headquarters. Ask for Papa and tell him that I've gone to the studio. Can you do that?"

She still looked scared, but she nodded. "I'll do it, Mama." She broke into a run and disappeared into the crowd.

I looked up at the driver again. "Fourteenth Street, corner of Fifth," I said.

There was no doorman waiting to admit me at the studio. In fact, when I saw the heavy doors standing shut and no doorman, I thought I had got it wrong. Fanny must have gone with Edison to his studio, not ours. There was no way I could follow them there. But I tried the door and it swung open with an ominous creak. I stepped inside a dark foyer. I didn't know where the switch was for the electric light and stood there, all my senses fine-tuned, listening in the half darkness. Silence greeted me. Had the doorman been told he wasn't needed if the studio was supposed to be shut? I was tempted to call out to see if anyone was here but I didn't want to alert a murderer to my presence. I hesitated to go any farther if I was all alone. But if Fanny was here and in danger, someone had to help her.

I crossed the foyer and hesitated again on the threshold of the large stage room. Someone must be here, or who had opened the door? Who had the authority to open the studio and send the door-man home? Harry and Arthur would have. DW would, but surely he had gone off in the other direction. The only other person I could think of was Fanny. Was she not afraid of bringing Edison here alone?

I crossed the stage floor, trying to walk silently, all too aware that someone had been murdered here. I told myself I'd be wise to go outside and find the nearest constable. I was about to do this when I froze, hearing voices on the stairs. They came closer. I drew back into the shadows of the scenery.

"Please talk to your lawyer and rethink your position." The voice belonged to Edison. "Your patent and this studio will be safer in my hands." He sounded annoyed. "Contact me when you have had a chance to think it over." Then his tone changed. "Of course, this is a difficult time for you. Take time to grieve your fiancé." The footsteps stopped. They came into view, standing together. Edison turned to face Fanny and she took a step back.

"You have had a tragic life, my dear." His voice was soft. "Wouldn't you like to give up the responsibility?"

"What responsibility?" Fanny's voice was trembling.

"Your husband's legacy, my dear," he said. "It's a heavy burden for his wife to bear. His father was a great inventor. But you don't have to live your whole life for his memory. His invention seems to have led to tragedy rather than triumph." He took another step toward her, and she stepped back again. I tensed, wondering if I should show myself. I couldn't believe that Thomas Edison would attack Fanny. Of course, I knew that Fanny's father-in-law had disappeared, her husband had been shot, Arthur and Harry were dead. But surely a man as wealthy as Edison would send someone to do his dirty work, not publicly threaten a woman himself. Then I shivered. We weren't in public. If he tried to hurt her, could I intervene? Could the two of us overcome him together? But then Fanny spoke again.

"I can't think about it today, Mr. Edison," she said, her voice steadier. "As you said, I am mourning my fiancé. He is not even buried yet." Edison stood silently looking at her; then he nodded and turned to go. He had only taken two of his large strides when Fanny spoke again. "Did you work together with them to have him killed?"

I peered out between the scenery flats. Holy Mother, she had a gun pointed at him. True to his character, Edison was quickly in control of himself. He stared at her calmly.

"I'm not going to hurt you, my dear," he said. "There is no need for that. I didn't get you here to do you harm."

"You didn't get me here at all." Her laugh was brittle. "I got *you* here. I knew you would come if I said I wanted to go over paperwork. You thought you could trick me while I was weak and mourning, get full control of the patent."

"Not at all," he said, his voice calm, like a man talking down a growling dog. "I came to offer my assistance."

I was frozen in the shadows. If I spoke and she was startled, would she shoot?

"I lured you here," Fanny said. "I set the stage, to put it in language you will understand. I planned for you to die right where you are standing." Now it was she who stepped closer, and he who took a step away. "I meant to do it while your back was turned, but damn it, I have to know. Did you help Harry and Arthur kill my husband?"

"You're unhinged." His voice rose. He took a breath in to steady himself. "My dear, you are hysterical. Think. Harry was your fiancé, Arthur your partner. Are you accusing them of being murderers?"

"They accused themselves," she spat at him. "I overheard them just months after his death. And they mentioned your name too. The great Edison would never stop bankrupting them until they made a deal, and my husband would never make the deal. So, they had to get him out of the way."

"I'm sure you were mistaken," Edison said. "And even if you weren't, I had nothing to do with it." Now he took a step toward Fanny, who raised the gun. Her hand shook. "Why don't you let me walk out that door and we will forget this ever happened."

"I don't want to live in fear anymore!" Fanny's voice was harsh and shrill. "I'm not safe until you are all dead." I couldn't wait any longer. Any moment she would pull the trigger. I took a deep breath.

"Fanny, stop!" I shouted as I stepped out of the shadows. She gave a cry of surprise and turned to look at me. In that second Edison leaped forward and grabbed the gun.

"No!" she screamed as they struggled. "I want you to die." As he wrenched the gun out of her hand, it fell to the floor and went off. The sound was deafening in that great echoing space and the bullet whizzed past me, too close for comfort. I rushed at the gun and snatched it up. Fanny lunged for me, but Edison was there first and grabbed her by the arms.

"No!" Fanny screamed again. "Let me go."

The gun lay heavy in my hands. I wasn't sure what to do with it, other than to make sure neither of them got their hands on it.

"You're her secretary, aren't you?" Edison looked at me. "I believe there is a telephone in the hallway upstairs. Go upstairs and call the police. I will restrain Mrs. Prince."

"No." Fanny struggled against his grip. "Don't leave me alone with him. He'll kill me."

"You are the one who was pointing a gun at me," Edison pointed out calmly. My mind was spinning. Had all the tragedy been too much for Fanny? Had she lost her reason?

"Please, Molly. Please, Mr. Edison." Now Fanny began to cry. "Please just let me go. You would have done the same thing. They killed my husband for that patent."

"The police called your husband's death an accident," Edison said.

"I tell you, I heard them." Fanny's voice rose. "Arthur and Harry. They arranged it. I don't know how but they needed him dead and then he was dead. And then they never left me alone. Arranging for the funeral, acting as if they were my only friends in the world. And then Harry proposing marriage to me. He wanted the legal ownership of that patent, and he was willing to marry me or kill me to get it."

"People don't murder each other over patents," Edison scoffed. Fanny was no longer struggling.

"Molly, I'm not insane. It was self-defense. I tried to tell myself that I was mistaken, but they were always plotting together. You saw the accidents that kept happening at the studio. I kept expecting something to fall on me. That lamp almost fell into the tank and that gave me the idea. I would turn the tables on Harry and he would have an accident."

"Edward arranged the accidents," I said. "He's confessed."

"You said he was doing it for Edison." She tried to wrench herself free from his grip again. "They were all three out to get me."

"Preposterous," Edison snapped, tightening his grip on her arms. "Calm yourself, madam."

"But you killed Arthur," I said, to keep Fanny talking. She was confessing to a murder, and I had a witness.

"Stupid Harry, couldn't even give his mistress the dignity of a meeting," she muttered. "He sent Arthur to meet with Lily."

"But Lily didn't know anything about that note." I wanted her to confirm my suspicion.

"No, I wrote the note and handed it to Harry with the mail." An edge of madness had crept into her voice as she crowed about her triumph. "I set the whole scene, and no one doubted me for a second. Just like Harry never suspected the drink I handed him contained poison. I would have been a great filmmaker if they hadn't murdered my husband." At the last word she suddenly wrenched herself away from Edison. He was taken by surprise and tried to grab her. She ran for the open door, both of us behind her, and straight into the arms of Captain Daniel Sullivan.

"Hold that lady," Edison yelled. Daniel looked at him calmly. His body was blocking Fanny's exit, but he made no move to take hold of her until I shouted, "Daniel, hold her. Don't let her escape." Instantly he held her in a grip of steel.

I gave a sigh of relief. "You'll need to take Mr. Edison's statement," I said. "Fanny pulled a gun on him, and we both heard her confess to murder." I showed him the gun that I was holding carefully by the handle.

"Mr. Edison?" His eyebrows rose in surprise. "Mr. Thomas Edison?" He looked over at where Edison stood, then back at me and shook his head in disbelief.

❧ Thirty-Two ☙

Yes, I'm Edison," he said quickly. "We must summon the police."

"I am the police," Daniel said, holding Fanny as she struggled to get away. "But I could use some assistance. I believe there is a patrolman on the corner. Could you run and get him?" Edison looked affronted at being asked to run anywhere.

"Send this woman, Sergeant," Edison said. "She is Mrs. Prince's secretary."

"It's Captain," Daniel said as Fanny fought to free herself. "And that woman is my wife." He pushed Fanny back into the room and turned her around, grabbing her arms firmly but not roughly. "Mrs. Prince, I'm a policeman and I need you to come to the precinct with me to answer some questions." She continued to struggle. It was clear we would need more help.

"I'll go, Daniel," I offered.

"No, you stay here where I can see you," he said. "Mr. Edison, I'm instructing you to go for help." And, surprisingly, Edison went, closing the door behind him.

I set the gun down on the desk and went over to Fanny, putting my hand on her shoulder. "Mrs. Prince, no one will hurt you. This is my husband, Captain Sullivan."

Amazingly Fanny stopped struggling.

"Am I going to be arrested?" she asked, looking from one of us to another. "It was self-defense."

"Fanny, I saw you pull a gun on Mr. Edison while his back was turned," I said, "and you almost shot me."

"What?" Daniel's expression hardened.

"She dropped the gun and it went off." I saw his face. "I'm okay. Don't worry."

Just then the door opened again. I looked up hoping to see a uniformed policeman coming through the door. Instead, it was Harry's receptionist, Trevor, his arms full of flowers. He looked as startled as we did as he took in the situation.

"Police," Daniel called out. "This woman is being detained. Please stay where you are."

"Mrs. Prince, is that true?" I could see the confusion on the clerk's face.

"It's true," I said. Trevor's face changed as he recognized me. "Mrs. Prince just tried to shoot someone." I nodded to the gun on the desk. I didn't mention Edison's name. It was hard enough for me to believe that he was her target. "More police are on their way."

Then it struck me as strange that the receptionist would be here at all. Wasn't the entire studio closed? And with Harry gone, who could have asked him to come in?

"Mr. Cauley, why are you here?" I asked. I looked from one to the other. Fanny, no longer struggling but standing with her arms locked in Daniel's iron grip. Trevor with flowers in his arms.

"She asked me to come at this time," he said, pointing to Fanny.

Fanny suddenly came to life. "I did no such thing." She glared at him.

"I have this note right here." Trevor carefully put the flowers down on the desk, giving a wide berth to the gun lying across the guest book, and pulled a piece of paper out of his pocket. "Asking me to open the studio after the funeral, go to buy flowers, and meet her here."

"You would have walked in to find Thomas Edison dead on the floor," I said grimly, "and Mrs. Prince would have been long gone." I looked at Fanny, who still was the picture of the grieving widow, dressed in her black silk with a black bonnet and long black gloves. Trevor stared at me, his mouth open. "I wouldn't doubt if there is some evidence against you planted somewhere in the studio." I turned to Daniel.

"She asked me how police find out who shot a gun," I said. "I imagine that is why she wore gloves."

"Thomas Edison?" Trevor looked incredulous. "And she was going to frame me for his murder? That sounds like something in a penny dreadful."

I nodded. "First Arthur, then Harry. I'm afraid she is developing a habit of murder."

The door opened and two policemen entered at that moment, flanked by Thomas Edison.

"Captain Sullivan," the first man said, then saluted and took out a pair of handcuffs. "We heard you needed assistance?"

I sighed with relief. "Well, saints preserve us, thank God for that!"

It was late at night when Daniel finally came home from work. He had taken my statement himself, glowering at me when I described entering the deserted studio in search of someone I believed to be a killer.

"Molly, what on earth possessed you? Do you never stop to think? You could have been killed," he had growled.

"It was not my finest hour," I admitted. "Next time I promise to wait for you."

"Next time!" His eyebrows rose. "Next time I expect you to be home watching the children."

"Yes, Daniel," I said meekly, adding, "although I think this time that you should be glad that Edison was not murdered."

"That is not the point," he said sternly. I thought it was precisely the point, but not wanting to push him too far, I had let it go. And then I had gone home to my children and my peaceful life and Daniel had gone to the station for many more hours.

He was tired but grimly satisfied as he sat down to a late supper. I had fed the children hours ago but waited to eat with him.

"She confessed to it all," he said as I served him a bowl of tomato soup and toasted bread. With no time to shop today I had nothing else in the house. "Two murders and one attempted murder. Her only surprise was that she was caught."

"Well, she almost got away with all of it," I said. "The police would have called Arthur's death an accident if you hadn't gotten involved."

"If you hadn't gotten me involved, you mean." He smiled at me fondly. "She has come to believe herself a criminal mastermind, but it was purely luck that she was able to murder Arthur at all. It just happened that everyone else was suitably far away and she was able to push both Arthur and the lamp in the water."

"She was the one who decided to have the party on the roof, put the mannequin in the water, and wrote the note luring Harry downstairs," I said. "That seems like intricate planning to me. Like setting a scene in a picture."

"She thought she would get them both at once by murdering Harry and framing Arthur for his murder." Daniel looked at me thoughtfully. "But she made a mistake and killed the wrong twin."

"That makes sense," I said. "That's why there was so much evidence against Arthur at the studio: the papers and the wax cylinder recording of the argument. And why she was so distressed that she fainted when she realized Harry was still alive."

"And that she still had to kill Harry or marry him," Daniel said, "if she wanted to be rid of both brothers."

"Not a pleasant choice." I made a face. "But how did she kill Harry? She almost got away with that as well."

"She used the cyanide just as we thought," Daniel said. "She disguised the bitter taste in his fourth shot of whiskey. Apparently, she had offered to . . ." He looked embarrassed and stopped. "I don't want to expose you to the seamier part of these investigations, Molly."

I laughed, understanding what he meant. My husband was fearless in the face of criminals but could be a little prudish. "Don't worry, I won't make you say it. We'll just say she was going to anticipate the wedding night. She must have kept him drinking until he was so drunk she could slip the drug into his drink. We only found the one whiskey glass." I looked at him inquisitively, wondering if she had told him more.

"She washed up her glass and cleaned up the mess," Daniel said. "Just as you thought."

I'm afraid my active imagination ran away with me at that point. I pictured Fanny handing Harry the drink and watching him toss it down. Her false concern as he became ill, telling him to lie down while she fetched a doctor, and waiting while the life drained out of him. Then coming into the room and making sure all signs of her presence were gone, even the glass she had drunk from, washing all traces of her crime away. I shivered.

"Will you need evidence against her if she has confessed?" I said, wondering.

"My guess is that she will plead not guilty because of insanity," Daniel said, "and maybe she *is* insane, who knows."

"The courts are more inclined to believe that women who kill are insane," I agreed. "I thought she might plead self-defense. She kept telling me that she had no choice."

"However," Daniel went on thoughtfully, "Harry did make a will leaving everything to her. If she encouraged him to do that, she doesn't sound insane or frightened."

"That makes it look more like a murder for gain," I said.

"Either way, it is not my job to judge one way or another," Daniel concluded. "I need to make sure I gather all the evidence. I will need to find out where she obtained that gun as well."

"I would have your men check the prop room and ask Alice if a gun is missing," I said, rising and refilling Daniel's empty bowl without being asked. I knew how hungry he got when he worked into the night like this. "There were various guns in the room when I last was there."

"Those are guns that they use in the moving pictures?" Daniel asked and I nodded. "I'm surprised anyone survives in a studio." He gave a wry smile as he dipped the last of the toast into his soup. "It seems to be able to supply enough guns, poison, and electricity to kill half of New York."

"Would you like me to pour you a whiskey?" I asked as I cleaned up the plates after dinner. "You could take it through to the parlor and relax. I think you have been working too hard."

That statement earned me a snort. "Whose fault is that?" He leaned on the doorframe, smiling at me as I dumped the plates into a sink of soapy water. "I will pour my own whiskey, thank you. And check it to make sure it is not bitter before I drink it down."

"If I wanted you dead, Daniel Sullivan," I said, returning his smile, "you would never see it coming." I went over and hugged him, soapy hands and all, laying my head on his shoulder. "But I most definitely do not. May you live a thousand years, my love, and be in heaven a half hour before the devil knows you're dead." Daniel put his finger under my chin, lifted my face to his. I looked deeply into those green eyes, drinking in the love I saw in them. Then he kissed me.

✂ Epilogue ✂

May 1909

"You're in the paper again, Molly," Gus said, peering at a page of *The New York Times*.

"Hopefully for the last time," I said. "The jury is deliberating on the case now so hopefully my testimony will be of no more interest to the citizens of New York."

"You are quite a hero, according to the *Times*," Gus continued. "Listen to this—*The pretty young wife of the gallant Captain Sullivan refused to be bullied by the lawyer for the defense. In response to his asking if she might have been mistaken when hearing the defendant's confession, she replied, 'Well, I was standing as far away from her as you are from me. Can you hear what I am saying when I confess that I have been telling the truth?' This remark drew general laughter in the courtroom. Captain Sullivan is credited with saving the life of no less than Thomas Edison in the incident at Biograph Studios.*"

"They don't have that exactly correct, do they, Molly," Sid said with a smile. "You had already disarmed Mrs. Prince, hadn't you?"

"If you consider picking up a gun that has already been fired as disarming, then yes I had," I said, not smiling back. I still couldn't feel quite easy about that scene. If Fanny had pulled the trigger as she swung to look at me, I could have been killed. But Sid and Gus regarded all the events as intriguing and exciting, much like everything in their lives. "If Daniel hadn't arrived, we could not have detained her," I said loyally. "And then it would have been her word against mine."

"And Mr. Edison's," Sid added; we had been over this story multiple times. As I said, they were thrilled that I had solved such a public case, even if Daniel was getting the credit for solving it.

"And Mr. Edison's," I agreed. "He has said some very nice things about Daniel." I picked up the last bite of a cannoli and popped it in my mouth, savoring the cream that squirted out. Morning coffee at Sid and Gus's house was my idea of heaven.

"There was only one thing still bothering me about Harry's death," I said once my mouth was no longer full, "and Daniel was able to find new evidence just before the case went to the jury."

"What was that?" Gus looked intrigued.

"Fanny could easily have made Harry's death look like a suicide," I said. "If she had forged a note, we might never have suspected murder."

"Why didn't she?" Sid's eyes sparkled with the mystery.

"A life insurance policy," I said. "In her name. It was taken out with a small firm. It took Daniel weeks to track it down, but he found it."

"Harry took out a life insurance policy with Fanny as the beneficiary?" Gus asked.

"Yes, and of course it wouldn't pay off if he committed suicide."

"So, she had to make it look like murder," Sid said with satisfaction. "The mystery is solved. Well done, Molly."

"It was Daniel who solved this one," I said proudly. "And, speaking of that, I have something to share with you." I hesitated, wondering what their reaction would be to my news.

"You're pregnant again?" Gus looked up from her newspaper.

"Saints preserve us, no!" I said so emphatically that they both laughed. "I am still trying to survive my daughter's first year."

"She has your personality, Molly," Sid said, looking fondly at Mary Kate, who was miraculously asleep in my arms.

"For my sins," I said, and they laughed again.

"Tell us the news, then." Sid refilled my cup of coffee, and I happily took another cannoli with my free hand. The May sun was streaming in and bathing the kitchen in a warm light. I felt warm myself, and happy to be with my friends.

"Daniel is leaving the police department." Their faces registered surprise. "He will still be an officer of the law," I went on. "In a new bureau that the Justice Department has formed to fight national crime."

"The federal Justice Department?" Gus asked. "That doesn't mean you will be moving to Washington, does it?"

"No," I hastened to reassure her. "They are opening offices in a few big cities, including New York. Daniel was already being considered when he took his trip to Washington, DC, but I think it was Edison's recommendation to Mr. Wickersham, the new attorney general, that put Daniel in line to lead the department."

"He will be leading it?" Sid asked.

"Yes." I nodded. "He will be the special agent in charge of the New York office of the federal Bureau of Investigation."

𝕾 Historical Note 𝕾

In April of 1909 Mary Pickford made her first moving picture with Biograph Studios directed by DW Griffith. Billy Bitzer was the innovative cameraman for those early feature films, including exciting and dangerous footage from train yards. Griffith, one of the early pioneers of many of the techniques of movie-making, was a controversial figure even in his own time for his pro–Ku Klux Klan movie, *The Birth of a Nation*.

Biograph and Edison Studios formed the Motion Picture Patents Company, also known as the Edison Trust, in December 1908. The Edison Trust was so strong and litigious that all other moviemakers in the US eventually decided to move as far away from the New York–based trust as one could in the continental United States, thus creating Hollywood.

While we have tried to be true to every aspect of the early movie-making business, we have fictionalized most of the characters in the novel.

Alice Mann is based on the French secretary **Alice Guy-Blaché**, who, though her name was removed from much of the film record, was one of the first directors and pioneered many film techniques in French cinema.

Harry and Arthur Marvin were brothers, but not twins. They were a cofounder and cinematographer for Biograph Studios, respectively, and involved in patent disputes with **Thomas Edison**. We have fictionalized them as Harry and Arthur Martin.

Louis Le Prince, his mysterious disappearance during a court battle with Thomas Edison, and his son's unsolved death while duck hunting were the inspiration for our fictional Lewis Prince and his daughter-in-law, Fanny Prince.

On Easter Sunday, 1909, the body of Lieutenant **Joseph Petrosino** really did lie in state on Lafayette Street. The next day the streets were lined with over 200,000 grateful citizens as his coffin passed from St. Patrick's church on Mott Street to the cemetery. Fear of the Black Hand and other gangs gaining hold nationwide, as well as congressional fear of a powerful Secret Service, were a spur to the creation of a new federal law enforcement agency, the Bureau of Investigation, which later became the FBI.

❧ Acknowledgments ❧

As always, many thanks to our brilliant agents, Meg Ruley and Christina Hogrebe, as well as Kelley Ragland and the whole team at Minotaur. Finally a thank-you to our patient husbands, who are forced to endure hours of our chatting on the phone or in person as we plot the next scene and then have to read the manuscript as our beta readers.

❧ About the Authors ❧

Duke Morse Photography

Timothy Broyles

Rhys Bowen is the *New York Times* bestselling author of the Anthony Award– and Agatha Award–winning Molly Murphy mysteries, the Edgar Award–nominated Evan Evans series, the Royal Spyness series, and several stand-alone novels, including *In Farleigh Field*. Born in England, she lives in San Rafael, California.

Clare Broyles, who is Rhys Bowen's daughter, is a teacher and a musician. She began collaborating with her mother on the Molly Murphy mystery series with *Wild Irish Rose*. She has worked as a composer and arranger in the theater for both the Arizona Theatre Company and Childsplay and was nominated for an ariZoni Theatre Award. Clare is married to a teacher, and they have three children.